PRAISE FOR

The Lockhart Women

"O.J.'s famous white Bronco flight and his trial for murder is the perfect backdrop for this story of a mother and her two daughters watching their lives implode. Great writing, compelling, and fast-paced, *The Lockhart Women* is impossible to put down."

—DIANA WAGMAN, award-winning author of
Extraordinary October and *Spontaneous*

"Touching on themes of motherhood, fidelity, and responsibility, this is a coming-of-age tale for both Brenda and her daughters, teaching us that the indelible bonds of love can steer families through the roughest of passages."

—JULIE ZUCKERMAN, award-winning author of
The Book of Jeremiah

"Like Mona Simpson's *Anywhere but Here*, *The Lockhart Women* sensitively illustrates what happens to children coming of age under the influence of childish parents and provides hope that everyone—parents and children—can grow and develop. An authentically hopeful and realistic novel."

—SHELLEY BLANTON-STROUD, award-winning author of
Copy Boy

"Brenda Lockhart and her two daughters are complicated and not always admirable characters but they are relentlessly human. Camarillo laces her debut novel with concise prose, dry humor, and flinty realism, allowing love, resilience, hope, and eventual forgiveness to shine through."

—SAMANTHA DUNN, best-selling author of *Not By Accident: Reconstructing a Careless Life*

THE

LOCKHART

WOMEN

THE

LOCKHART

WOMEN

a novel

MARY CAMARILLO

Published 2021
Printed in the United States of America
Print ISBN: 978-1-64742-100-7
E-ISBN: 978-1-64742-101-4
Library of Congress Control Number: 2020921641

For information, address:
She Writes Press
1569 Solano Ave #546
Berkeley, CA 94707

She Writes Press is a division of SparkPoint Studio, LLC.

Book design by Stacey Aaronson

This is a work of fiction. Names, characters, places, and incidents either are the product of the author's imagination or are used fictitiously. Any resemblance to actual persons, living or dead, is entirely coincidental.

A version of Chapter Two was previously published as a short story titled "Promises" in Volume 22 of *The Ear* (Irvine Valley College 2018).

For Alma Parker

And the days that I keep my gratitude
higher than my expectations
Well, I have really good days

MOTHER BLUES
BY RAY WYLIE HUBBARD

CHAPTER ONE

June 17, 1994

BRENDA CAN'T DECIDE WHAT IS WORSE, WATCHING HER HUSBAND DRIVE LIKE a maniac or worrying about some idiot on the San Diego Freeway crashing into his brand-new truck. Everyone is driving too fast, following too closely, and changing lanes without signaling. *At least the traffic is moving,* she tells herself, somewhat of a miracle on a getaway Friday. And then for no apparent reason, all the brake lights go red and every vehicle in all eight lanes across the freeway comes to a dead stop. She braces her hand on the dashboard as her foot instinctively reaches for the nonexistent brake pedal.

"Will you stop that?" Frank says.

"You should have taken surface streets."

"Surface streets would have been worse." Frank drums his fingertips on the steering wheel. "Jesus Christ. What the hell is going on?"

"It's Friday night. What did you expect?" Brenda wonders again why he's so intent on going to a housewarming party in Torrance just because some woman he works with at the post office bought herself a condo. It doesn't seem much to celebrate, but Frank changed into his best Hawaiian shirt and a new pair of shorts as soon as he came home from work.

"I could have at least made my seven-layer dip. I wish you'd given me a little more notice." She never goes to parties empty-handed. She's famous for her dip, her guacamole, and her double fudge Bundt cake. "Why would you take the girls and not me?"

"I told you, you didn't have to come. There must be an accident ahead."

She flips down the visor to check her hair. The new style is very blond and very short, with loose spiral curls gelled away from her face. Her hairdresser copied it from a magazine photo of Drew Barrymore, which her daughters find ridiculous, their ancient mother imitating an actress their age. Frank either hasn't noticed or has chosen not to comment. His red hair is flecked with gray and there are tiny lines etched around his green eyes, but (luckily or unfortunately, lately she can't decide which is more accurate) he's still the best-looking man she knows.

Peggy and Allison laugh together in the back seat about something. She glances at them as she touches up her lipstick. Her daughters are barely ten months apart in age but could not be more different in temperament or appearance. Peggy's a pretty girl, a somewhat sturdier version of herself. They are both brown-eyed blonds, although Peggy's hair is more of a dishwater color and her eyes are always too serious. If only she'd wear something more flattering than that flannel shirt and those overalls. Allison's especially adorable today in her slip dress over a plain white T-shirt. Her youngest is suddenly breathtakingly beautiful, tall, redheaded, green-eyed, impatient, and easily irritated with her all the time, just like Frank is.

"Who is this woman again?" Brenda asks.

"You've met Linda before at Bill's barbeque on Memorial Day. She transferred here from Denver."

She vaguely remembers Linda now. Single, older, with big horsey teeth. "I don't understand a woman buying a place on her own."

"Me either," Allison says. "Has she just given up on ever getting married?"

"God," Peggy says. "Women can buy houses on their own, you know. You are aware it's almost a new century."

"That's my girl," Frank says.

"I know women can do whatever they want," Brenda says, noting Peggy's satisfied grin at Frank's praise. "But I don't understand why anyone would buy a condo in Torrance."

"Don't even think about it, asshole," Frank says as a green Corolla tries to cut in in front of them. "Linda wanted to live closer to her mother."

"Condos don't appreciate like houses do. Especially in Torrance. She'll never get her investment back."

Now the Corolla is blocking both lanes and Frank blasts his horn.

"Let's just get off at the next exit and go out to dinner," Brenda says. "I saw a Cheesecake Factory a few miles back."

"I can't get off the freeway right now," Frank says. "I'm locked in."

"Why are all those people standing on the overpass?" Allison asks.

Brenda looks up and indeed, there are dozens of people on the overpass, staring intently through the chain-link fence at the freeway below. A few of them hold signs. HONK IF YOU LOVE THE JUICE! RUN O. J. RUN! The man driving the green Corolla shuts off his engine and gets out of his car.

Frank rolls down his window. "What are you doing?"

"O. J.'s making a run for it," the man says. "He's behind us now, in a white Bronco, heading this way."

"Who's O. J.?" Allison asks.

"Some guy whose wife was murdered," Peggy says.

"He's not just some guy," Frank says. "He's the greatest athlete of our time."

"Remember those commercials," Brenda says, "where he jumped over suitcases at the airport?"

"The Juice is loose," a woman getting out of a car behind them yells. The crowd is giddy with the exhilaration of standing on the normally forbidden freeway. On the southbound side, cars are parked in the carpool lane, and their passengers lean over the center divider as if they are joining a neighborhood barbecue.

"This is crazy," Brenda says.

"Let's get out." Frank turns off the engine and jumps out of the truck, both girls right behind him.

"Be careful!" she says as he reaches for Allison's hand and glances over his shoulder, waiting for Peggy. She smiles. He may not be a faithful husband or a forgiving man, but he's always been a good father. She gets out too and leans against the hood of Frank's truck. It's a beautiful metallic blue color, a nice contrast to her white midriff top.

The circus atmosphere around her, however, is unsettling. This morning's newspaper said O. J.'s two young children slept through the attack on their mother and that the entranceway to Nicole's pink stucco house was slick with blood. Brenda hasn't been able to get the images out of her head.

She feels a rumbling sound overhead as a swarm of helicopters hovers above the freeway. The blades stir the warm mid-June evening air into a dusty cloud of cigarette butts, drink straws, and fast-food wrappers. Lights flash from the tops of at least twenty police cars and half a dozen motorcycle cops. The noise from the crowd intensifies as people cheer. "Go, O. J., go!" Frank pumps his fist in the air and Allison waves her hands overhead. Even the hard-to-impress Peggy is smiling, her face flushed with excitement.

Brenda's heart beats faster as a white Bronco with dark-tinted windows approaches, barely going twenty miles an hour. She doesn't recognize the man hunched over the steering wheel, but she's seen the larger man in the back seat before. He came into the steak house where she worked years ago, before she was married. O. J. Simpson, staring right at her, right now with big brown eyes. He doesn't look like a murderer. He looks like a grieving man with a dead wife and two motherless children. She raises her right hand and waves. He nods slightly as the Bronco passes, followed by more police cars and motorcycles.

They all climb back in the truck.

"That was pretty exciting," Allison says.

"We'll probably be on the news," Peggy says.

"O. J. looked right at me," Brenda says. "I think he recognized me."

Frank snorts. "From where?"

"He came into the steak house once. I told you that."

"You actually met him?" Allison asks.

"Well, he sat in a different section. But I must have made an impression."

"It's been twenty years since you worked there," Frank says. "There's no way he'd remember you. Although you are his type."

"What's that supposed to mean?" She knows from the newspapers Nicole Simpson was also tall, tanned, and Orange County raised, but Nicole had a huge chin, which took away from her prettiness. Brenda's chin is nowhere near that large.

"Blond and beautiful, of course." It doesn't sound like a compliment and Frank's smile is cold as he turns to the back seat. "Aren't you guys glad you decided to come with me tonight?"

"They're going to be bored to death," Brenda says. "No one brings their kids to work parties anymore."

"Linda's place isn't far," he says. "We can still make the party."

"Lucky us," Brenda says.

"DID you think any more about Orchard Hills?" she asks once traffic is moving again. She'd left a flyer next to his side of the bed about a new housing development going up near one of the best high schools in one of Orange County's nicest neighborhoods. Frank doesn't like to discuss money in front of the girls, but now she's in the mood for a fight.

They'd made a huge mistake buying into their housing tract, not realizing the school districts would be remapped. Instead of attending Huntington Beach High School like they'd planned, the girls were stuck at Ocean View. The name itself is ridiculous. There's no view of the ocean, just a strong scent of garbage from the city dump down the street. Peggy's apparently happy about attending Cal State Long Beach this fall, but Brenda had hoped for a college with more prestige, especially considering Peggy's almost all As. She doubts Allison's barely C average will get her into a decent art school. If she's serious about being an interior designer, Allison's going to need connections, which means meeting a better class of people.

"How much could we get for our place?" There's not much more they can do to their two-story Colonial. They've replaced the aluminum windows with double-paned vinyl, scraped off the cottage cheese ceilings, added crown moldings, remodeled both bathrooms and the kitchen, and relandscaped the front and back yards. It's primed to sell.

"I don't want to talk about this right now." Frank nods his head toward the back seat. "And we can't afford Orchard Hills anyway."

"Am I still going to be able to live in the dorm?" Peggy asks.

"I'm not changing schools my senior year," Allison says.

"Of course, you're going to live in the dorm. Your father's overreacting as usual." She turns to Frank. "You're the one who just spent all that money on your boat."

"I just put money in *our* boat so *we* can sell it."

"This is so typical of you. You have no vision."

"I make decent money. Which you don't seem to have any trouble spending."

"I just want a better life for our girls. And it would be nice to live someplace with a view. I'm sick of all the cinderblock walls."

"It's called suburbia. You don't think people should have walls around their property?"

"It's ugly. I'd like some open space around me. And some trees."

Frank's lips tighten, and he turns up the radio. Classic rock, as usual. She'd give anything to hear something with a little soul, something from this decade at least.

"If Bill's at this party, I'm asking him about New Orleans."

This is something else Frank won't want to discuss right now. He'd announced over breakfast he was going to Louisiana in July to look at some new kind of mail-sorting machine, which sounded like another boondoggle, and she expected to tag along, as she'd done before on his trips to Washington, DC, and San Francisco. It's the only way she ever gets to go anywhere.

"I already told you, the district manager specifically said, no spouses."

"New Orleans is the one place in the world I've always wanted to visit. You know that."

"There's nothing I can do. Bill says they're concerned about how it might look to the auditors."

She glances over at the woman alone behind the wheel in the car next to them and tries to imagine being on her own. What a relief not to have to argue about everything, to make her own decisions about where to live and travel and what to listen to on the radio. They might as well sell the boat and make some room in the driveway. They haven't gone to the river in years. Frank is always working or traveling for work.

Back in the day, before he'd started finagling his way

through the maze of post office politics, they'd caravanned with friends out to the Colorado River for long weekends. They both had more stamina then, fueled by youth, alcohol, and occasional lines of cocaine. Frank had the biggest boat, and she was the only woman who could drink as much as the men did. She was fun. At night, they'd leave their girls asleep in the tent and take the boat across the river to the bars on the Arizona side. They'd dance on a deck under the stars until it was almost dawn, cruise back across the river, nap for a few hours, and then drive back to Huntington Beach in time for Frank to make it to work. She misses those days. She can still be fun.

WHEN Frank parks in front of what must be Linda's building, Brenda half wonders if he's been there before since he doesn't seem to have any written directions, but she can't imagine how or why he would know this neighborhood. The building is a beige concrete box on a street lined with identical concrete boxes, one right after another. It's the kind of place where people who don't have any choices would live.

Frank dangles the keys in her face. "You're driving home. It's my turn to drink."

"I can drive," Peggy says. "I need the practice."

"You drive like an old lady," Allison says. "It'll take forever to get home."

"So what?" Peggy says. "It took us forever to get here."

Frank is already heading across the brown grass toward what must be Linda's building. Brenda puts the keys in her purse. "Peggy can drive us home as long as we leave before it gets too dark."

Inside the condo, the usual crowd is huddled around the television set, the other postal couples they've known forever: Julie and Rick, Bill and Sue. It's an incestuous job. Julie sells stamps, Rick supervises custodians, Sue is a mail carrier, and Bill (much to everyone's surprise and Frank's obvious jealousy) has just been promoted to plant manager, which technically makes him Frank's boss. A half dozen other familiar faces sit or stand around Linda's tiny living room. Brenda recognizes Phyllis, from accounting, and her husband, both heavy-set, both wearing not-exactly-clean cowboy boots. They live out in Riverside and raise chickens. Ginny, Frank's secretary with the big fake boobs, and her latest husband, whose name Brenda can never remember, sit on the love seat next to the couch. They all stare at the screen, watching police cars follow O. J.'s white Bronco. No one else has brought their kids.

"We just saw O. J. on the freeway! He looked right at me." Everyone seems suitably impressed, so she goes on. "He came into my restaurant once, a long time ago."

"Your restaurant?" Franks laughs.

Linda gets up from one of the couches. "They say he's heading to his mother's house to turn himself in."

Linda could not possibly have chosen a less attractive outfit. The elastic waist on her skirt bunches across her stomach. The paisley-printed tunic doesn't go with the turquoise earrings or the clunky brown sandals. Her eyes are a nondescript color and her lashes and eyebrows are almost invisible. She doesn't color her hair and she should. The woman needs a makeover.

"Let me get you a beer," Linda says.

"Nothing for me," Brenda says as Frank follows Linda out of the living room past the dining room table loaded with gift bags and cards. She could have easily put a housewarming gift together. Gift bags are her strong point. "I didn't realize there was a party tonight. Frank didn't give me enough time to change." She knows it doesn't matter what she wears to these things since no one gets dressed up. Sue and Julie still have on their uniforms.

Still, she believes in making an effort. She glances down at her wide-legged jeans and midriff top, which suddenly feels a little too slinky, the way it gapes open above her cleavage. She adjusts the neckline and tries to ignore her daughters' expressions across the room. They don't think she should wear midriffs anymore. They'd rather she dressed like a nun.

Bill raises the glass of scotch in his hand in salute from where he's leaning against the wall of the dining room, untucked shirt, loosened tie, face slightly flushed. He's a softer and slouchier version of Frank with the same Irish coloring, nearly handsome with a tendency to be obnoxiously extroverted. "You always look glamorous, Brenda."

"You're definitely our fashion plate." Sue's tone borders on sarcasm, but Brenda lets it slide.

"We missed you at step class last night," Brenda says. "We learned a new routine."

Sue says she couldn't talk herself into going. "It was Penny-Saver day. I was beat when I got home."

The postal uniform doesn't do Sue any favors. She's slim and trim above her waist with narrow shoulders and small breasts but look out below. Her hips, ass, and thighs are enormous. Penny-Saver or not, Sue needs the exercise.

"You should have seen Brenda," Julie says. "Up in front of the class with all the twenty-year-olds."

"You were working hard too," Brenda says.

Julie is skinny with ridiculously sized double-D-cup breasts, a hawklike nose, and thin hair that she wears in an unattractive bun. Last night she was in the back of the class, talking more than moving, but everyone needs a little encouragement.

"You know what I just realized, Brenda?" Bill says. "You look a lot like Nicole Simpson. No wonder O. J. was staring at you. He probably thought he was seeing a ghost."

"Do you think so?" Brenda smiles. "We're the same age, but Nicole's chin is different than mine."

"You're not the same age," Sue says. "Nicole Simpson was only thirty-five. You'll be thirty-eight this year, won't you?"

"Thanks for reminding me." Sue will be forty next year, Brenda is about to say when Linda comes back with Frank and says, "There's food in the kitchen if you girls are hungry and some Cokes in the fridge." Linda turns toward Brenda. "Would the girls like to watch a movie upstairs?"

"We can't stay long." She tries not to stare at Linda's big horsey teeth and crinkled neck and wonders how old she is and why she's so anxious and awkward. The woman can barely maintain eye contact.

"What movies do you have?" Allison asks.

"I just bought *When Harry Met Sally*. I know it's kind of corny."

"They've seen it before," Brenda says, but both girls nod and follow Linda up the stairs as if she's the Pied Piper. Brenda trails behind them, taking in the framed diplomas and certificates. What single, career women hang on their walls, she supposes, instead of pictures of their families. Impressive, but sad.

"I might as well give you guys the nickel tour," Linda tells Allison and Peggy, still ignoring Brenda. She laughs nervously. "My bedroom's to the right."

A beautifully embroidered Mexican peasant dress lies across the foot of the bed next to a ratty pair of slippers. Brenda walks closer to examine the dress. "This is pretty," she says, fingering the hem. The colors are vivid, the design intricate. It looks like an expensive work of art.

"I spent my senior year of college in Mexico City. Let me pop in the movie. The VCR's in there." Linda hurries to the second bedroom.

I've made her uncomfortable, Brenda realizes, which isn't unusual. Women can be jealous of her sometimes, especially women who do absolutely nothing to make themselves more attractive, don't exercise, eat whatever they want, and barely run a comb through their hair. She glances around the room at the framed album covers on the walls and recognizes most of the classic rock bands Frank likes so much. Crosby, Stills, and Nash. The Eagles. Fleetwood Mac.

Linda crouches down on the floor and puts the video tape in the player. It spits out immediately. "I had it in backward." She tries once more, but when the video starts, the picture jumps back and forth in a frenetic loop. "I always have trouble with this stupid player. Should I adjust the tracking?"

"Give it a minute," Peggy says. "Ours does the same thing." The movie starts, and Linda sits back on her heels, laughing with the girls at just about everything Billy Crystal says. Brenda leans in the doorway, watching. This is actually nice of Linda. Even a sappy comedy is a better choice than letting them watch O. J.'s Bronco coast toward Brentwood and certain death by police. She remembers the video of the Rodney King beating playing over and over again on the news not so long ago and shivers. She doesn't want the girls to see something like that on live TV. Linda might be the kind of woman who would make a good friend.

"You want something to drink?" Linda asks, standing.

"White wine if you've got it." Brenda follows her back down the stairs.

"You can use this." Linda takes a glass out of one of the gift bags. "I'm really more of a beer drinker."

That explains the belly. She used to like beer too, but it's too fattening. Red wine gives her a headache, hard liquor doesn't seem sociable, and mixed drinks go down too fast. She started sipping white wine because she doesn't like the taste.

"Just a splash." The remains of a six-foot-long sandwich sit on a board on the counter in the kitchen, next to a bowl of chips and some onion dip. None of it looks remotely appetizing. Linda grabs a handful of chips. "It's nice to finally meet the girls. Frank talks about them all the time."

Linda's eyes sparkle when she says Frank's name, which is normal. Women adore Frank and he loves the attention. It's a full-time job making sure his eyes eventually refocus on her and it gets harder every year. Time and gravity are powerful foes. At least she doesn't have to worry about this woman.

"Frank says you transferred here from Denver. How do you like California?"

"I grew up in Torrance and went to school in Berkeley. I've been waiting a long time for a job to come up closer to my mom. She's not in the best health."

"What is it you do at the post office?"

"I'm a mail processing analyst. My background's in engineering. I've always loved math."

"Our Peggy wants to be a CPA and do taxes if you can believe that. It sounds so boring."

"You can make good money with a tax practice."

"Well, I'm terrible at math. And Frank isn't much better."

"I'd be happy to help Allison if she needs tutoring. Frank says she's struggling a little. Did you talk her into going to summer school?"

Where in the world did that idea come from? "Allison's enjoying her friends this summer," Brenda says and takes a sip of wine. The taste is smoother than she expected.

Enjoying her friends is one way to put it. Just before school let out for the summer, Allison announced she needed birth control pills because she was going to start having sex with her boyfriend. Although Kevin Nelson is definitely not the right boy for Allison,

Brenda made appointments with her gynecologist for both girls and bought a jumbo-sized box of condoms, insisting they keep a few in their purses. She watches the news. Sex isn't like it was when she was young and everyone was jumping into bed with each other, pregnancy their only worry. Sex can kill you these days if you're not careful.

She and Linda go back to the living room and watch what seems more of a police escort than a car chase since the Bronco is still barely going twenty miles an hour. There's no place to sit once Linda takes the spot next to Frank on the couch, so Brenda glances around the room at Linda's eclectic collections of Indian pottery, Japanese fans, African woven masks. Linda's either quite the world traveler or she's a frequent Cost-Plus shopper. It seems a little show-offy and way too much to dust.

Frank isn't paying attention, so she tops off her glass in the kitchen and slides the screen door open to a small patio. There isn't much to see. A barbecue, a table with two chairs, a couple of trash cans. Linda could use a few potted plants and a fountain to cheer the place up. She goes back in the kitchen and down the hallway to the bathroom and stares in the mirror over the sink, wondering if it's time to get her eyes lifted. At least her neck is still good.

"We saw O. J. at the airport once," Julie is saying in the living room. "He's very good-looking."

"He's the real deal," Bill says. "Heisman Trophy winner, NFL most valuable player, Pro Football Hall of Fame."

"He left a suicide note," Rick says. "That makes him sound guilty."

"They wouldn't have charged him with two counts of murder if they didn't have evidence," Frank says.

"What happened to innocent until proven guilty?" Brenda asks the mirror. At least there's something different to talk about tonight instead of the usual topics: the post office and the people who work at the post office. She goes to the kitchen, opens the fridge, and pours the rest of the bottle into her glass, making a note of the label. The wine is tastier than what she usually drinks. Peggy will need to drive home.

Linda's refrigerator is too large. It sticks out almost a foot in front of the stove. She'd move it across the room, rip out these tile counters and put in granite, and do a nice laminate floor. She's got an eye for this sort of thing. She'd wanted to be a designer once upon a time before she met Frank.

A huge real estate magnet holds an SPCA calendar in the center of the fridge. The month of June features an extremely ugly cat with a long, thin face, spectral, like something from an Egyptian tomb. The appointments on the calendar (doctor next Thursday, haircut in two weeks, dinner with Mom every Sunday) show that poor Linda with all her degrees and fancy trips isn't exactly living a wild, single life. She walks back through the living room, heads up the stairs, and sits down on the floor to watch the movie with her girls. The screen is split, showing Harry and Sally talking on the telephone while watching their respective television sets in their respective bedrooms.

"I don't know why Meg Ryan is so freaked about not being married," Peggy says. "She's only thirty-two."

"Thirty-two's old," Allison says. "Especially if you want to have kids."

"Thirty two's not old," Brenda says. "I wish I'd waited longer to start my family."

"I know," Allison says. "Peggy was an accident and I'm the surprise. Story of our lives."

It's the story she's always told them, but she's alarmed at the bitterness in Allison's voice. "Don't be silly. You two are the best things that ever happened to me."

"That's kind of depressing, Mom," Peggy says. "Since not much has happened to you."

"That's not true," Brenda says, although it is.

"Harry's right," Allison says. "Men and women can't just be friends. Men are always going to want to have sex."

Brenda sighs. Both girls seem intent on pushing her buttons tonight.

"You're the sex expert," Peggy says.

"You're jealous. At least I have a boyfriend."

"Kevin's nothing to be jealous of."

"If you two are going to argue, we should go home." Brenda agrees with Peggy, though—she's never been impressed with Kevin Nelson either. In elementary school he was a spoiled kid whose two fat parents held him back a year, so he'd be more competitive in sports. He's all grown up now, another blond, blue-eyed golden California surfer boy, tanned, muscular, and way too full of himself. According to the newspapers, he's Ocean View's big hope for this year's football season, as if that means anything. He'll end up doing construction just like his father. Somehow, she's going to convince Allison she can do better.

"We should go home anyway. You still want to drive, Peggy?"

"The movie barely started. And we're not arguing."

"I want to stay," Allison says.

"Fine. We're leaving as soon as it finishes."

She heads down the stairs. Frank isn't sitting on the couch in the living room and neither is Linda, which seems weird. Brenda retrieves another bottle from the fridge, but she can't find a corkscrew. *Where's our hostess?* she wonders as she hears voices outside.

"I wanted to meet the girls," Linda says, "but I really don't understand why you brought *her*. This is awkward for everyone."

"She invited herself. I couldn't exactly kick her out of the truck."

Brenda's heart pounds as she slides the screen door open. The way Frank and Linda sit together feels overly familiar and makes absolutely no sense. A wet drop from the wine bottle lands on her toe and she shivers despite the warm evening air. They look up at the same moment. Frank drops his hand into his lap.

Linda stands immediately. "Are the girls okay with the movie? I have others they might like better."

"The girls are fine. I was looking for a corkscrew."

"You're drinking?" Frank asks.

"Peggy can drive us home. This is a cute place, Linda. I bet you could fix it up and flip it. We're thinking about selling and buying something nicer ourselves. Upgrading to a new development in Orchard Hills. It's in a much better school district."

Frank shakes his head. "That is absolutely *not* what we're doing."

"The thing about Frank is he has no imagination."

"Oh, I don't know about that." Even in the dark, Brenda can see Linda's blushing. "I'll find the corkscrew," she says, taking the bottle.

"Can we go?" Brenda asks after Linda scurries inside.

"We just got here. At least let the girls finish their movie."

"What are you doing out here alone with her in the dark?"

"Talking."

"About what? What could you possibly have to say to her? She's a strange one."

"Please don't drink anymore." He stands and goes inside.

She takes a few deep breaths before she follows him. She's misread the situation. The wine has gone to her head.

JUST before 8:00 p.m., O. J. pulls into the driveway of his Brent-wood home. For a long time, it seems like the police are going to shoot him, or that he may shoot himself, but in the end, no guns are fired, and he's arrested. Brenda's relieved but confused about what happens next. She'd like to hear more, but Frank changes the channel back to the basketball game. No one else seems to mind. They all start talking about the new flat-sorting machine and she nearly groans out loud.

What did she expect, marrying someone who only wanted a steady check and ten paid holidays? Frank started as a mail handler as soon as he came home from Vietnam, and it's admirable how he's worked his way up from unloading trucks on the dock to supervising the clerks who sort the mail, and most recently to managing distribution operations. But it's still the post office, mindless blue-collar work. No skills required. Although Frank is finally wearing a suit and tie to work, he's making less money since he doesn't get paid for overtime anymore, even though he puts in more hours. And judging from the happy hour receipts she finds in his pockets, he's spending a lot of money lately trying to impress someone.

"I'm not sure the Santa Ana plant has enough room for a flat-sorter," Rick says.

"There'll be plenty of room once we junk the letter sorter," Bill says. "They'll have more information when they come back from New Orleans."

"Frank gets to go to all the cool cities," Rick says. "The only place I've ever gone for work is Kansas City."

"Good strip clubs in Kansas City," Bill says.

Sue punches his arm. "How would you know that?"

Bill grins. "Just something I heard."

Brenda goes to the kitchen and refills her wineglass. Bill said "they" as in plural and it doesn't sound like he or Rick are going to New Orleans with Frank. She stares at the ugly cat on the calendar and lifts the page to July. There's a photograph of a pit bull puppy and the letters "NOLA" written across the third week. This can't be right. She puts the glass down carefully on the counter and goes back to the living room.

"You're taking Linda to New Orleans?" Her voice is too loud, and all the conversations immediately cease.

Frank turns and looks at her, his eyes steady. "She's the analyst on the project."

His tone is infuriatingly condescending, and she feels her blood pressure rise. "How convenient. You must think I'm an idiot."

"I think you're drunk."

"What's wrong?" Linda asks as she comes out of the bathroom, acting all innocent. To think she imagined this woman as a possible friend.

"What wrong? Frank's an asshole. And you're just another one of his cunts."

Someone gasps.

"Whoa," Rick says. "Take it easy, Brenda."

"We should go." Frank walks closer. "Get your purse."

"She's not even pretty. You're just trying to humiliate me."

"That's enough. I'm sorry, Linda."

"Why are you apologizing to her?" Brenda slaps Frank hard across the face. She's never hit him before and it frightens her how good it feels, but it scares her too, how much he wants to hit her back. She can see it in his eyes.

"What's going on?" Allison's voice. Dear God. Both girls are standing at the top of the staircase with their mouths wide open.

They've heard everything. And of course, Frank makes this all her fault.

"Your mother's had a little too much to drink."

"Your father's had a little too much to fuck," she says and then immediately regrets. Her hand stings. She spots her purse under a chair, lunges for it, slings it over her shoulder, and opens the front door. "I'll wait for you in the car, Frank."

"You know what? I wasn't going to do this tonight, but it's time. I'm moving in with Linda."

"No, you're not." Brenda turns. Frank has his arm around Linda's waist.

"Dad," Peggy says, her voice starting to break. "What are you doing?"

"Can you drive your mother and Allison home tonight, Peggy? I'll call you guys tomorrow and explain everything."

"I guess." Peggy starts down the stairs, her face so pale Brenda's afraid she might faint.

"Why do you have to always ruin everything?" Allison rushes past Peggy and flies out the front door, heading toward the truck.

Brenda glances around the room. No one makes eye contact. No one comes to her defense. She follows Peggy down the sidewalk and hands her the keys. "I'm sorry," she says, but neither girl answers. Allison climbs in the back seat. Peggy adjusts the mirrors and turns the key. Brenda rolls down the passenger window and lets the night air flood in.

"Roll up the window," Allison says. Brenda thinks about turning on the radio, but Peggy looks so nervous, the way her hands clinch the steering wheel. When Brenda glances over her shoulder at Allison, she's staring straight ahead, an equally grim expression on her face.

"I know you're both upset, but there's a lot you don't understand."

Allison makes a spitting noise in the back seat. Peggy tightens her death grip on the steering wheel. She'll find a way to make this up to them. There's no way Frank is serious about that woman. She shouldn't have called her a cunt and she shouldn't have slapped him either, but it isn't the first time they've fought in public. Their friends have known them a long time. They'll understand and forgive her. She might even call Linda later and apologize. Offer to take her out to lunch. Maybe they can be friends.

There's no traffic, but the drive home feels endless, the silence, relentless. When they finally pull in the driveway and the garage door opens, she admires her beautiful black BMW. The lease is up next month, and she'll have a new model soon. Silver or white, she hasn't decided. Frank spoils her. He'll get someone at the party to give him a ride home. They'll make love, and she'll cook a good breakfast tomorrow morning and not complain about him watching basketball all afternoon.

She thinks about eggs and bacon and wobbles a little when her feet hit the ground. She leans against the hood for a moment, trying to steady herself. The girls file straight past her into the house and slam the door. Her head spins, her stomach lurches, and she barely makes it to the utility sink. She wipes her mouth and is sick again. There's no one to hold her hair out of her face, to wipe her tears, to get her a drink of water, to help her into the house. She's alone.

CHAPTER TWO

PEGGY AND ALLISON ARE ON THEIR BIKES, FOLLOWING THE LAST FLOAT OF the Fourth of July parade down Main Street, red, white, and blue bunting strung on the eave of every house, residents sitting on their curbs in patriotic finery. Peggy rides behind her sister, dizzy from the fumes of alcohol rising from the red plastic cups in every hand. Everyone's looking at Allison of course. Her red hair is loose and wild, her white eyelet top drops slightly off one shoulder, and her blue jean shorts are cut off at the exact curve of her hips. She's the perfect American Girl.

Normally Allison is shy and reserved to the extent people assume she's stuck up, but today she's holding her head high, smiling and waving, actually making eye contact, as if she is in the parade too, as if she's the one they all came to see. Some people call her by name even though this isn't their part of town, although Peggy doesn't really have a part of town, not one she feels comfortable in anyway.

This is Huntington Beach High School territory, not Ocean View, where she just graduated. No one knows her here at all, thank god, but a lot of people seem to know Allison, due to the boyfriend, Kevin, who surfs the pier and gets written up in the *Orange County Register* because he plays football, baseball, and basketball.

Peggy wishes she'd worn a pair of shorts that fit better and didn't stick in her crotch. It's too hot for the plaid flannel shirt she's wearing over her bathing suit, but it hides the roll of fat above her waist. She keeps her head down, steering her bike around the steaming piles of horse shit left by the Budweiser

Clydesdales ahead of them. The Huntington Beach parade is the biggest west of the Mississippi, their dad has told them every Fourth of July since she can remember. He always staked out a square on the Main Street sidewalk before midnight on July 3rd, writing their name in chalk in block letters, as if they were celebrities. Today, they can't find any place to park their bikes and sit down.

They turn around at Pacific Coast Highway where the parade ends and ride three miles inland on Goldenwest Street. When they get to their house, there's an outline of rust in the driveway where the boat was parked. They put their bikes in the garage and go inside. Brenda's in the living room pulling Frank's dress shirts off hangers and throwing them in a pile on the floor on top of winter jackets, swim trunks, CDs, golf magazines, socks, T-shirts, and underwear. The fact that she's dressed in something other than her nightgown and has possibly combed her hair might be encouraging if it wasn't for the manic gleam in her eye.

"Your father sold the boat," she says, struggling to open a black plastic garbage bag. "Pick out what you want. The rest of his things are going in the trash."

"He was here?" Peggy asks.

"With that woman. Selling the boat was probably her idea."

"You can't just throw his stuff away," Allison says.

"What did he say about the check for my dorm room?"

"You'll have to ask him."

"I don't understand why you want to live in a dorm with a bunch of girls anyway," Allison says. "You should move into your own place. That's what Kevin and I are going to do as soon as we graduate. One more year and we're out of here."

"Isn't Kevin supposed to get some football scholarship? He'll be out of here without you."

Allison's cheeks flush. "Shut up. Just because you have to be perfect all the time doesn't mean you know anything."

"I wish you two wouldn't argue all the time," Brenda says. "You used to be best friends. Decide what you want to keep. I'm tossing the rest."

The television is on, of course. The television has been on since the day after the party when Linda dropped Frank off at the house, so he could pick up his truck and some clothes. He took her and Allison to Denny's for breakfast, apologized for the way he and their mother had acted, promised he still loved them, and insisted nothing would change. That part was hard to believe as they stood together in the driveway and watched him pull away without them.

Since then, Brenda spends her day switching back and forth from the local news to Court TV, from Hard Copy to the Entertainment Channel. The reporter on the screen now is interviewing a dealer at a sports-memorabilia show at the Anaheim Convention Center. He holds up the latest O. J. trading card, the mug shot from the night of his arrest. The dealer says he might as well make money while he can.

"Who would buy something that sleazy?" Peggy asks.

"Your father used to collect baseball cards. Do you guys know what happened to them? I could sell them and make some money."

"They aren't yours to sell." Allison slips Frank's Swiss Army knife into the back pocket of her shorts and stomps up the stairs to take a shower. Peggy finds an old Springsteen T-shirt in the stack of clothes, which all smell like Brut cologne and cigarettes. She pulls it over her head, goes in the kitchen, calls her father again, and leaves another message on Linda's answering machine.

AFTER Brenda fills twenty trash bags and hauls them out to the street, she pours a glass of white wine. Peggy and Allison exchange glances. "You never drink wine during the day," Peggy says.

"It's a holiday." Brenda turns up the volume on the television. Geraldo Rivera explains that the grand jury is trying to decide if Simpson should stand trial or not.

"Obviously, he should stand trial," Peggy says. "Can we watch something else?"

"There's nothing else on," Brenda says. "And I think this is fascinating. Do you think O. J. killed them?"

"Who cares?" Allison says. "Are you just going to turn into a wino now? Isn't that why Dad left? Because you got drunk and called Linda a cunt?"

"You should apologize, Mom," Peggy says.

"That's an ugly word and I should never have said it. And I *have* apologized."

"What are we having for dinner?" Peggy asks.

"We'll barbeque hamburgers, like we always do on the Fourth."

"Do you even know how to light the barbeque?" Allison asks. "Isn't that Dad's job?"

"Of course, I do," Brenda says. "I'm not helpless and neither are the two of you."

When they find her passed out on the couch before dark, Allison slips a twenty out of her purse. Peggy takes the car keys. They drive through McDonald's and bring home hamburgers and fries. After they eat, they climb up on the roof to watch the neighbors light fireworks. Every house around them is outlined in six-foot-high cinderblocks, and some of the walls have been built up even higher, with wooden trellises and creeping fig.

"Remember the first time Dad brought us up here?" Allison says. "I thought Mom was going to have a heart attack."

"We were pretty little. It was a crazy thing to do." Peggy smiles, remembering how equally terrified and excited she'd been that night, holding her dad's strong arm as tight as she could. The explosions sizzle, pop, and strobe-light the palm trees up and down the street, illuminating the mountain of the twenty black trash bags on the curb in front of their house. In between cherry bombs, a fruit rat slinks across the aerial highway of electric, telephone, and cable lines.

"Dad had other women before Linda," Allison says.

"You don't know that for sure."

"You always defend him."

The garage door lifts, and Brenda wanders out like a sleepwalker. She grabs a plastic bag in each hand and drags them up the driveway and into the garage.

"What are you doing?" Peggy calls down from the roof.

Brenda stares up as if she can't make out who they are. "This was a mistake."

"We should go help her," Allison says.

They drag the last bag into the garage and go inside. Closing the door, Brenda asks if they've had dinner.

"We bought you a hamburger." Peggy gets out a plate and puts the burger in the microwave to warm.

"Don't worry, Mom. Dad's not serious about Linda." Allison stands in front of the mirror in the hallway, putting on lipstick. "She's not remotely pretty. He'll be home soon."

"You're going out?" Brenda asks as a horn beeps in the driveway.

"There's a party."

"Let's have a girls' night. Mani-pedis and facials. Make popcorn and watch a movie."

The horn taps again, longer and louder.

"I promised Kevin I'd go."

"Take a sweater," Brenda says, but Allison's already out the front door and halfway down the driveway.

"He could at least come inside the house." Brenda stands in front of the mirror now, examining her neck from different angles.

"I don't like Kevin," Peggy says.

"You know how your sister is. If I tell her to stop seeing him, she'll just sneak around behind my back and see him anyway."

"You're not going to do anything?"

"I'm sick of you criticizing me all the time."

"I'm on your side, Mom." She takes the burger out of the microwave. "You want ketchup?"

"I'm not hungry. You can have the burger. Although you certainly don't need the calories."

"I can't wait until school starts."

"Why? So you can pig out alone in your dorm room?"

"I'm going to bed."

As Peggy goes up the stairs, she whispers, "You're a horrible person. It's no wonder Dad left you."

SHE can't sleep, so she turns on the light and picks up the Cal State Long Beach catalog of classes. She's got every semester plotted out for the next three years, highlighted in three different colors. She'll get the units she needs to sit for the CPA exam, graduate early, go to work for an accounting firm for two or three years, and then start her own tax practice. She can see her future, laid out like a balance sheet. It was the woman who spoke at Career Day her junior year who'd convinced Peggy to major in accounting. Megan Barnes, in her conservative suit, discreet pearl earrings, and sensible pumps, had positively glowed with poise and confidence.

"There is always a place in our field for meticulous, detail-minded professionals," Megan said, looking right at Peggy. "Everyone says accountants are boring, but what's wrong with being boring?" All the other kids had laughed except Peggy. "What's wrong with being cautious and conservative," Megan went on, "and keeping track of where the money is? What's wrong with stability and with being involved in all major business decisions of a corporation? What's wrong with making money?"

"Nothing," Peggy said, ignoring the other kids' faces. She'd decided right then she wanted to be Megan. Her counselor at Ocean View helped her make a list of business schools. Peggy knew private schools were out of the question. "There are loans," the counselor said, but Peggy didn't like the idea of owing so much money. "Berkeley's a great school," the counselor told her. "Your grades are good enough and your SAT scores are decent." She'd hated being so timid, but Berkeley was a long way from home. She'd never even been on a plane before. "UCLA, then," the counselor said, "or UCI. You could go home on the weekends." By then she'd done more research. A state school would cost less, in the long run. Fullerton or Long Beach were closer to home.

"At least live on campus," the counselor argued. When he raved about the experiences she would have, making lifelong friends and connections that would serve her career, Peggy had agreed on Cal State Long Beach. The closer it gets to September, though, the more she finds to worry about. She's never made friends easily. She won't be able to study while living with strange people. She'll end up spending all her time in the library like some hermit. A dorm room seems like a big waste of money. She hears the electrical hum of her mother's vibrator down the hall and throws the catalog on the floor, pulling a pillow over her head. Megan Barnes never had to worry about any of this.

"I shouldn't have said that last night," Brenda says the next morning. "You know I'm proud of you."

"Whatever." Her mother never apologizes, so she obviously wants something. Peggy pours herself a cup of coffee, studies the calorie count on the carton of cream, and puts it back in the fridge, deciding to drink her coffee black from now on.

"What should I do about this?" Brenda slides an envelope across the table, stamped with a pale pink rose Love Stamp. Peggy collected stamps for a while when she was a kid. It was one thing to share with her dad. The invitation inside the envelope is printed on scalloped-edged linen with embossed pale pink roses. "Amber's wedding. You think your father will go?"

"I have no idea." She vaguely remembers camping next to Amber's family at the Colorado River—the campground was asphalt, there was no shade, the boat engines revved up at dawn, and the adults kept the music turned up full blast.

"Pink roses are such a common design," Brenda says. "The wedding probably won't be all that special either."

"Don't go then."

"I already bought a wedding gift. People will talk if I don't show up."

"Who cares if they talk? Or are you worried Dad will be there with Linda?" When her mother's eyes immediately fill with tears, she feels bad. "Good grief, Mom. Just call and ask him if he's going. You have Linda's number."

"I'm not calling that woman's house to talk to my own husband. And he's at work now anyway. Would you call him? I don't want to talk to his secretary either."

"I thought you liked Ginny."

"She's such a gossip."

Peggy looks closer at the date on the invitation. "This is the same week Dad's going to New Orleans."

Brenda puts her head in her hands and sobs. She's always loved any excuse to dress up and has probably bought a new outfit to wear. Peggy can't stand weddings, doesn't have anything in her closet that fits, and is sure Amber won't remember her. She hates herself for being such a doormat. "I'll go with you if you want."

"Would you really?" Brenda wipes her face with both hands and beams. "That would be wonderful. Who knows? Maybe you'll meet someone nice."

"THERE must be a mistake," Brenda says when they find their place cards on the table farthest away from the wedding party and closest to the door. "I'm sure we're supposed to be up front."

"Just sit down." Peggy glances around the room. There are pink roses on every table, pinned in the bridesmaids' hair, embossed on the napkins and tablecloths. Amber's mother, in an unflattering dress printed with large red roses, is taking pictures with the bride and groom.

Brenda makes a stunning contrast in her turquoise blue suit. "St. John Knits," she'd said that morning as she ripped up the price tag before Peggy could see what it cost. A lot, she's sure, especially when you add in the matching shoes, but it fits her perfectly and her freshly highlighted hair catches the light, offsetting the sadness in her dark eyes, behind the liner, mascara, and expertly contoured shadows. An older couple, already seated at their table with two other women, introduces themselves as neighbors of Amber's grandparents. The women are Amber's mother's middle-school friends. Brenda takes a glass of champagne from a waiter.

"We should go talk to them." She points to the table in the

front of the room where Bill, Sue, Rick, and Julie are sitting. "Otherwise they'll think I'm avoiding them."

"You *should* avoid them."

"Come with me. Please?"

"This is a bad idea."

When they get to the table, whatever conversation Bill, Sue, Rick, and Julie were having abruptly ends. Brenda admires Sue's red sling-back heels. Sue turns to Peggy and asks if she's excited about starting college.

"Of course, she's excited," Brenda says. "Going off to live in a dorm and leaving her poor old mother behind."

She hates how her mother says things like this and expects someone to disagree. And of course, someone always does. "There's nothing old about you, Brenda," Bill says. "You haven't changed since the day we met."

She's never liked how Bill acts around her mother, all lecherous and creepy, when he's supposed to be her father's friend.

"Are you guys following the Simpson case?" Brenda asks. "Peggy and I drove up to Brentwood yesterday to see the condo."

Peggy sighs. A normal person would be embarrassed to admit spending the day standing in the hot sun trying to look over a fence at a dead woman's condo. Her mother insisted she go with her. Nicole's neighbors yelled at them to get a life.

"Why on earth would you drive all the way up there to see that?" Sue asks.

"Nicole's place is much smaller than I expected," Brenda says. "Not nearly as nice as O. J.'s estate, at least from the pictures I've seen. We couldn't get close to his house at all."

"That man's a murderer," Sue says.

"Always two sides to every story. What kind of woman stays with a man who beats her? If Frank hit me, I'd be out of there so fast he wouldn't know what happened."

Everyone at the table studies their charger plates. Brenda takes a swallow of champagne. "Let's talk about something else. Anyone have vacation plans? I'm going to Mardi Gras next year."

Rick coughs softly.

"I've always wanted to go to New Orleans. I'm not going to change my mind just because Frank and that woman are there on their little business trip."

"I bet you'd get lots of beads," Bill says.

"We should go sit down," Peggy says. "They're starting to serve."

"We're over there in a different zip code." Brenda points to their table. "See you later."

People stare as they walk back to their table, but it's impressive, how her mother manages to hold her head high as if she's just won the lottery. Peggy straightens her spine, sucks in her stomach, and follows behind, wishing she were prettier and taller. They should have brought Allison.

AFTER the last drunken bridesmaid finally finishes her toast, Peggy heads straight to the ladies' room, hurries in a stall, closes and locks the door, and sits down on the toilet, sighing in relief. What a total waste of time and money. Amber could have put a deposit down on a house for the price of what this probably cost. She's never going to another wedding. As she flushes the toilet, she hears the bathroom door open.

"I love your lipstick," Sue says.

"Avon," Julie says. "One of the window clerks brought in a catalog. You want to try it?"

"Can you believe she came?" Sue asks.

Peggy adjusts her skirt, debating if she should wait them out, but they probably heard the toilet flush. As Peggy opens the stall door, Sue says, "Can you believe that remark about wife beaters?" Peggy freezes. They still don't see her.

"More like husband beating," Julie says.

"Isn't that what O. J. called himself in that interview? A battered husband?" Sue's eyes widen when she sees Peggy in the mirror. "Oh dear. We didn't know you were in here, honey."

"You poor thing." Julie pats her hand on Peggy's arm. "Dealing with this must be so difficult."

"I'm not sure what you mean," Peggy says, but her head nods yes, as if it's not connected to her brain.

"That performance your mother put on about New Orleans," Sue says. "You looked like you wanted to crawl under the carpet."

"She always talks about New Orleans."

Julie has a firm grip on her hand now. "We feel awful for you and your sister."

"Your dad's such a sweetheart," Sue says. "He deserves someone nice."

Like my mom, Peggy knows she should say, but she can't get the words out and her head is still nodding. "Nice" isn't the right word for her mother anyway. Beautiful, athletic, strong, selfish, careless, overly opinionated—especially when she doesn't know what she's talking about—vivacious always, magnetic constantly, and completely overwhelming.

"Your parents were never a good match," Sue says.

"Opposites attract," Julie says, "but that doesn't mean they belong together."

"She loves him," Peggy manages, trying to figure out if what they really mean is, she shouldn't exist either. "He loves her too."

"His priorities have changed," Sue says. "He doesn't need a trophy wife anymore."

Why not? Peggy wonders as she stands between the two of

them, breathing in their nauseating perfume and alcohol breath (Opium and Cucumber Melon is not a good combination with red wine and tequila) and nodding like the stupid bobblehead dog in the back of her uncle Tim's Volkswagen. She should tell them they're wrong, but there's no point in arguing with two drunk old women.

"You can talk to us anytime you need to." Julie finally releases her hand.

"We're here for you," Sue says.

Peggy nods, backs toward the door, pushes it open with her hip, and flees to the reception hall.

"There you are." Brenda sits alone at the table. "I don't like this hotel. We'll find something nicer for your wedding."

Peggy looks away, sure guilt is engraved on her face. "I'm never getting married."

"I imagine your father will want to invite a lot of these people."

"These people aren't your friends, Mom." She should say more, but she can't think of where to start.

"They're just having a tough time picking sides. Couples' splitting up makes friendships awkward."

"Can we go?"

Brenda glances around the room. No one is looking. Peggy follows her out the door. Brenda says goodbye to anyone who makes eye contact. The waiter. The man behind the front desk. The valet in the parking lot. She hands him twenty dollars as she slides into her car. Normally Peggy would complain. She's never understood why people expect a tip for doing their jobs and twenty dollars is a lot, even for her mother, but today she decides to let it go.

"That was fun." Brenda puts on her sunglasses. "I really appreciate you going with me." Her voice cracks imperceptibly.

Peggy nods. She doesn't trust her own voice not to break. She puts on her sunglasses too.

A few days later Peggy's in the passenger seat as Brenda peels out onto Pacific Coast Highway in a brand-new silver BMW. The young and very nervous lease manager at Crevier BMW didn't have a chance once Brenda made a quick and subtle adjustment to her blouse, revealing more cleavage, dropped her voice to a seductive purr, lowered her gaze slightly, raised her eyebrows a millimeter, and magically looked twenty years younger. It was impressive and embarrassing, and it worked. Unbelievably the man let Brenda drive the BMW home so "your husband can finish signing the paperwork. Frank's one of our best customers." Brenda didn't bother mentioning Frank wasn't living at home anymore.

"It's important to keep up appearances," Brenda says as she turns right onto Pacific Coast Highway. "Money attracts money and my plan is to look like a million bucks. Don't you love the way this leather smells?"

"My plan is to *earn* a million bucks." Her mother's the only adult she knows who doesn't have a job. She's almost forty and she's never worked except for a half a minute waitressing at some steak house.

"Your father never wanted me to work," Brenda says, as if she's reading her mind. "He promised to take care of us."

"I'm going to make a lot of money and take care of myself." And when she does, she'll *buy* her own car. Something economical that gets good mileage. *Money* magazine just ran an article about how leasing a car is a big mistake.

"You're certainly smart enough. I'm really proud of you, Peggy. Can we just enjoy this moment? Look at that blue sky. Think about how lucky we are to live here."

She exhales. It is a nice car. "These seats are really comfortable, Mom."

"This is so much fun! It reminds me of playing hooky from school. Let's go have an adventure."

Peggy laughs. "I never ditched school once."

Brenda's face falls momentarily. "Oh, Peggy. Promise me you will in college, then. I want you to have fun and enjoy yourself. Be reckless! Make lots of friends."

"I'm kind of worried about that part."

"You'll do fine. You'll meet a different sort of people in college."

"I hope so."

"How about we go to South Coast Plaza? We need to buy things for your dorm, and I need some new workout shoes. Tomorrow I'm going back to the gym. I've missed my step classes. Sue and Julie will have to teach me the new moves."

"They called you a trophy wife."

Brenda raises her eyebrows over her sunglasses. "It was Sue, wasn't it? She's always been jealous of me. She's wrong though. Trophy wives have better wardrobes and jewelry. Trophy wives are married to rich and powerful men."

"Who wants to be a trophy wife anyway? Look what happened to Nicole Simpson."

Brenda grimaces. "Good point."

And then she proceeds to recap everything she's heard on the news and read in the paper about how the LAPD is obviously trying to frame O. J. and isn't even looking for the real killer. Peggy nods at the appropriate pauses and pretends she's interested, because it is a beautiful day and it's fun to fly up the California coast past all the car dealerships and swanky restaurants in an expensive car with her vibrant mother. Maybe this is the start of new lives for both of them.

"WHAT did you guys do for the Fourth, Peg-a-Leg?" Frank asks when he finally calls. His using her nickname is a good sign. She's his Peg-a-Leg and Allison's the Alley Cat and he loves them and keeps his promises. "We had hamburgers and saw fireworks." She doesn't mention the fireworks were the neighbors' illegal ones or the hamburgers were from McDonald's because it seems disloyal to her mother. She doesn't mention the new BMW either. Instead, she asks if he's sent the check for her dorm room.

He doesn't answer right away. She hears a screen door slide open and shut. He's probably outside on Linda's patio, lighting a cigarette. Taking a sip from his beer. Her heart moves up into her throat.

"I was thinking maybe you could get a job," he says. "Help pay for some of this. You're going to need a car."

"Not if I live in the dorm." He's quiet again and she swallows the sick taste in her mouth. "You promised me, Dad."

"I'm sorry, honey. There are a lot of expenses I didn't see coming. And you don't seem all that excited about the dorm anyway."

"We already bought sheets and towels and everything."

"I can get you on at the post office. You could still take classes at Long Beach."

"You always said you didn't want us working there."

"Or maybe you could think about community college. They're a lot more flexible. Golden West for example." He's talking faster now as if community college was his plan the whole time. "You could get your basic units out of the way without spending that much money. We're going to have to sell the house. Your mother will need help with rent."

"Mom needs to get a job, not me."

"Just think about it, will you? Pick up a schedule from Golden West and see what classes you could get into. Will you do that for me?"

"I guess." It's irrational, this feeling she's lost something important when she really didn't want to live in the dorm anyway.

"I knew you'd be reasonable. We'll figure this out. Come by this weekend."

"WHAT if I dent it or something?" Peggy asks when Brenda hands her the keys to the BMW Saturday morning. "Maybe you should take me."

"You're a good driver. You'll be fine. I just can't stomach seeing your father right now. He had no business telling you he's selling the house. I'm not moving anywhere."

He had no business promising she could go to Long Beach and live in the dorm either. She'll never use those extra-long twin sheets and matching comforter that her mother spent too much on and can't take back now because she's washed them three times and written her name on the tags.

The waste of it all makes her angrier than anything, how her parents are so reckless with money. It's not only the new sheets and towels, it's the new cars they lease every two years, the clothes her mother wears once and puts away. The matching shoes and purses and jewelry. Her father's ever-expanding collection of golf hats and rock concert T-shirts. Lights left on in every room, food spoiling in the refrigerator, unfinished cans of soda losing their carbonation. Her father's packs of cigarettes cost more every year.

She's nothing like them. She prefers vegetarian pizza; they'll only eat pepperoni. She hates the situation comedies they love. They can recite the weeknight TV schedule without consulting

TV Guide. Which they subscribe to and never even look at. The fact that they thought they had to get married is a prime example of their carelessness. Even back in the old days, there were other options.

If her mother's willing to risk her wrecking the new car her father doesn't even know about, she shouldn't care either, but she's still nervous as she heads north on the San Diego Freeway, expecting every mile of the way to slam into something or something to slam into her. When she finally gets to Torrance, it takes her a while to figure out which condo is Linda's since the buildings all look the same and there's no one outside to ask. She parks around the corner, so she won't have to explain the new car. It's hot and smoggy and the air smells like petroleum. Frank opens the door and holds out his arms, and she's so glad to see him that she hugs him, even though she'd already decided she wasn't going to.

"I appreciate how you've been so mature about all of this," he says.

"I have to pee."

His robe is hanging on a hook behind the door in the downstairs bathroom as if it belongs there. The toilet needs scrubbing and the sink is speckled with hair. He must hate living here. He's used to freshly mopped floors, clean towels, polished surfaces. She opens the medicine cabinet. His cologne, razor, and deodorant are lined up next to his toothbrush. She slams the door shut and stares in the mirror, which is streaked with what is probably his toothpaste. She looks awful.

"Pretty exciting," he says, looking up from the sports page when she goes back to the kitchen. "What they're saying here about Kevin." He's wearing his usual day-off clothes, cargo shorts and a faded Tom Petty T-shirt, but something's different about his face. His hair is longer, but that's not it. He looks calm, she realizes, even happy, relaxed. Like he used to look when they went camping at the river.

"I can't stand Kevin. Allison just does whatever he says."

"She could do all right with someone like him. Your sister's never been college material like you are."

And look at me, Golden West bound, she wants to say, but there's no point. She's already agreed to enroll there because he needs her help right now.

"Here you go." He holds up a credit card. "For your classes and books."

"This has Linda's name on it."

"I cut up all my cards. Linda wants to help. Golden West isn't going to be that bad. And your mother says you can use her car until you can afford one of your own."

He's right of course. Golden West has the classes she needs. She's already done a cost-benefit analysis in Excel, her usual decision-making method. The units will transfer. She wasn't planning on having a job though. He got her a position on the 2:30 to 11:00 p.m. shift at the post office, with Tuesdays and Wednesdays off.

"There's a party crew on that shift," he says. "They're all hard workers but they aren't the kind of people you should be friends with."

"I won't have time to make friends."

"I wish you were happier about this, Peggy. I pulled strings to get you this job. There's a waiting list of people who want to work there. The pay's better than anything else you're going to find."

It's too much, to be expected to act happy too. She picks up the keys.

"Maybe this is for the best. Linda paid for her education herself. She got a scholarship and she took out a loan."

"This isn't Linda's business." She should have applied for a scholarship or taken out a loan and gone somewhere far away instead of being so timid and practical and accommodating. He holds out the credit card. She puts it in her purse. "I'll pay her back."

The heat slams into her when she opens the front door and heads down the sidewalk.

"Hey, Peggy? It's probably better not to mention Linda's credit card to your mother."

"Okay." She doesn't turn around.

"How about if I take you and Allison out for dinner sometime soon?"

She doesn't answer.

"I'll call you guys?"

A yellow cat slinks out from under the shade of the back tire and gives her a bitter look. She gets in the car and cranks up the air-conditioning until her hands are almost too cold to hold the steering wheel. When they'd camped at the Colorado River, she'd dug deep into the ice in the cooler, retrieving endless cans of Budweiser for him as they watched her mother dry her hair by the water, catching all the light in her white bikini, blond and suntanned. "Isn't she gorgeous?" he'd say. "You'll look just like her when you grow up."

Another promise he couldn't keep.

He stares at the silver BMW as she passes, a bewildered look on his face. She gives him a parade wave, laughing at his confusion, until she glances in the rearview mirror. His hair has more gray now than red, and he's growing a watermelon-belly over those stupid cargo shorts. He looks his age and she's already starting to forgive him. It's what she does.

CHAPTER THREE

ALLISON TASTES SALT ON THE OCEAN BREEZE WHEN SHE GETS OUT OF HER mother's new car. She hears a muffled lawn mower somewhere on the distant golf course. The Pelican Hill Athletic Club sits on top of a bluff overlooking red tile roofs, swaying palm trees, and a winding road down to the Pacific Ocean. She has a headache. She sniffs hard and feels a tiny gram of cocaine left over from last night dislodge from her right sinus passage and dissolve. Her head clears briefly and her heart drums a little faster. *There. That's more like it.*

The valet offers his hand, and she reminds herself to pretend she's beautiful and confident and belongs anywhere she chooses to be because that's what Kevin keeps telling her. Seriously legit animal magnetism is what he calls it. She smiles back at the valet and feels her mother's glare, unhappy about being ignored, but when the valet glances over at Brenda and says, "You two look like sisters," she gives him a big smile and hands him the keys. Another clean-cut young man opens the door for them, and Brenda flashes her teeth again.

"Do you have to do that all the time?"

"Do what?" Brenda says.

"Never mind. Why are we here?"

"Bill's daughter Jenny was in their program last year. It got her a scholarship."

"What does that have to do with me?"

"You have swim trophies."

"They're 'good sport' trophies, Mom. Everyone gets them."

"Give yourself some credit. You've been swimming all your life. And keep your voice down. This is all so beautiful," Brenda says, as they near the reception desk. "It reminds me of Italy."

"Don't you love Tuscany?" the platinum blond behind the desk says.

"Tuscany is one of our favorite places in the world," Brenda says.

Such bullshit, Allison thinks. They've never been out of the country, not even to Mexico, less than a two-hour drive away.

"The main buildings were inspired by the work of a sixteenth-century Italian architect, Pietro Paolo Agabito," the woman says, exaggerating all the syllables. "The landscaping as well—the olive trees, the lavender, the cypress, all imported from Italy."

"Lovely," Brenda says.

"The pool is this way." The blond woman turns to Allison and gives her arms and torso a discreet appraisal. "Are you a swimmer?"

"I swim."

Brenda shoots her a warning look. "She's got a room full of trophies."

"Our teams are quite competitive. The program starts at the end of August."

"Isn't this exquisite?" Brenda says.

The pool is enormous, the water crystal blue, but "exquisite" isn't a word her mother ever uses. "Simply divine, Mother dearest."

Brenda grabs her bicep and squeezes hard as the blond turns and says, "Let me show you the ladies' lounge." Her platinum hair is dazzling in the sun. The lounge is elegant. The locker room is expansive. A few girls with impressive shoulders and biceps put on bathing caps in front of a large mirror. Allison's head throbs.

"See?" Brenda says as they walk back toward the lobby. "You'll make new friends."

"Those girls are way out of my league. They'd plow right over me."

The woman turns around and raises her perfectly arched eyebrows.

"She's just being modest," Brenda says. "She's beautiful in the water."

"She's a beautiful girl," the woman says.

Brenda circles her arm around Allison's waist and squeezes her closer. "She's really come into her own lately."

Allison pulls away, expecting her mother to add, as she usually does, that Allison takes after her father, making it sound like a curse. It feels that way sometimes. She's always been the only redhead in class, the tallest girl in school since first grade, five eleven now and still growing.

"Don't talk about me like I'm not here, Mother."

The woman pats Brenda on the arm, sympathetically. "Teenagers. Now if you'll just follow me into the office. Would you like a mineral water?"

"Perfect," Brenda says, and they are alone for a millisecond. Allison stares at a wall-sized photo behind the desk of a swimmer captured at the crest of a perfect butterfly stroke, muscled arms raised above the water, resolute face, goggled eyes.

The blond is back with two bottles of water. "She was a gold medalist in Seoul *and* Barcelona. She used to train here."

"That could be you one day," Brenda tells Allison as a man with an expensive-looking silk shirt and heavily gelled hair joins them.

"Mark Mitchell, club representative." He obviously thinks he's important as he explains the variety of membership plans. "Gold, platinum, and silver."

"Gold's always been my favorite color," Brenda says.

"The annual fee is five thousand dollars. We'd need a ten percent deposit today to start your application."

Allison kicks Brenda's ankle under the table.

She doesn't even blink. "Can I give you a credit card?"

"Mom!" Allison says when the man leaves the room with her Visa. "We can't afford this."

"This is a wonderful opportunity. It's a way for you to stand out on your college applications, maybe get a scholarship."

"No one's giving me a scholarship to swim. Does Dad know about this?"

"Your father wants what's best for you."

The man returns. "I'm so sorry," he says in a not-sorry-at-all voice. "Your credit card didn't go through."

"Try running it again," Brenda says.

"Let's go." Allison stands.

"They've asked me to confiscate the card. You'll need to call your bank."

"I have another card." Her mother's voice is crisp and cool as she pulls a Discover card out of her wallet.

"I'm afraid we don't take that one."

"THERE'S no reason to get so upset," Brenda says when they are at the bottom of the hill, waiting for the light to change.

"You were seriously going to spend five thousand dollars so I could swim in a pool?"

"I'm trying to make a better life for you."

Someone behind them honks. "I guess it's easy to throw Dad's money away."

"Your father and I had an agreement. I ran the house and raised you two and he worked."

"We're raised. The light's green, Mom. Drive the car."

The horn honks again. "Give me a fucking break." Brenda stomps on the gas and screeches out on the highway.

"He cheated on you before Linda." The color drains from

her mother's face. She's struck a nerve. "Was that part of your agreement?"

Brenda lifts her chin and exhales. "Maybe I'm better off without him."

"You'd better find a new husband before you get too old."

"That's a mean thing to say."

She wants to be even meaner. "You'll be forty soon. You don't have much time left."

"You're grounded for the rest of the summer. You never used to be this cruel."

"You can't ground me for telling the truth."

"I blame Surfer Boy for your lousy attitude. You're not allowed to see him anymore."

"Don't call him that. You can't stop me from seeing him anyway."

"I'M sure you're mistaken," Brenda is saying on the phone when Allison comes downstairs looking for something to eat. She opens the fridge and stares at the empty shelves in disbelief. There has always been too much food in their kitchen, meals planned a month in advance, menus seldom repeated.

Brenda's voice is louder. "I never saw the last bill. It went to the post office box." She slams down the phone. "I'm sick and tired of people telling me they have to talk to your father about everything."

"There's nothing to eat."

Brenda brushes past her and pulls out a package of turkey bologna.

"There's no bread."

Brenda opens the cabinet and takes out a box of Ritz crackers.

"That's not lunch. That's just weird."

"I haven't had a chance to go shopping."

"I'm hungry."

"Then learn to cook. You need to start taking some responsibility for yourself."

"I'd cook if there were groceries."

"What am I supposed to do without a credit card?"

"Call Dad."

"*Call Dad*," Brenda mimics her in a horrible singsong voice. "Your hero. Fine, I will call him."

Brenda's hand trembles as she punches numbers into the phone. Frank's voice blasts through the receiver. "What the hell were you thinking, leasing a new car? We agreed we'd cut down on expenses."

"I've always had a new car every other year. I'm not taking it back."

"It's too late to take it back now. The penalties will kill me. They knew exactly what they were doing letting you drive it off the lot. I'm stuck with it now."

"Why didn't you tell me you canceled the Visa? I tried to use it today and they took it away from me. Your daughter was mortified."

Allison's mouth goes dry. He's going to think this is her fault. "Don't tell him that! I don't even want to swim at that club."

"Hush," Brenda hisses.

"What club?" Frank says.

"Let me talk to him." Allison reaches for the phone, but Brenda waves her away. "I'm trying to give our daughter an opportunity."

"I'm trying to avoid bankruptcy. You still have the Discover card."

"No one takes Discover."

"Can you please just stop throwing money away until I get things sorted out?"

"You're the one who moved out and ruined everything."

"Things were ruined between us a long time ago."

Allison hears the dial tone. Her mother's face is a death mask.

"Don't say one word." She sets the phone carefully back in the cradle.

ALLISON arranges the pillows on her bed so she can pretend she's making love to Kevin—her evening routine since she first realized he might actually be interested in her. Normally she ends up grinding into the edge of her mattress until she climaxes, but these days, she's too angry to fantasize. Angry at her father for leaving, although she understands why. Angry at her sister for going along with whatever he wants her to do. Angry at her mother, snoring down the hall as if nothing is her fault and not even trying to understand how lucky she is.

Kevin loves her. Kevin Nelson, handsome and confident whether running down the field or sliding into second base or skimming over a wave, wants her. He was so gentle the first time they made love; it didn't even hurt as much as she'd heard it would. Now she has friends who never acknowledged her existence before. Danielle, Katy, and McKenzie with their perfectly tanned bodies and long blond hair, girls who used to make fun of her freckles and chalky white legs. Now they invite her everywhere. They think she's one of them.

She throws the pillows on the floor and sits up. The light under the door in Peggy's room is on, so she gets out of bed and crosses the hallway. Peggy is scribbling on a pad of paper, chewing on a pencil, and squinting into what looks like an algebra book spread open on her bed.

"I can't sleep with her snoring either." Allison sits down on the end of Peggy's bed. "She's not going to stop me from seeing Kevin."

"Probably not," Peggy says. "I'm pretty sure she knows that too."

Allison glances around her sister's room at the piles of paper on the desk, Post-it notes around her computer screen, and books stacked everywhere—mysteries, historical novels, textbooks. Peggy carries a book with her everywhere, and even reads while she brushes her teeth.

"What are you doing anyway? Is that algebra?"

"Solving equations helps me relax."

"You're so weird. Why aren't you upset? You don't have to do everything Dad says. You're almost eighteen."

"The post office pays twice as much as any place else that is hiring plus they have health benefits and a Thrift Savings Plan."

She has no idea what Peggy is talking about, but this is what her sister always does. She decides whatever their father wants is really what she'd planned to do all along. It's depressing, although she's actually glad Peggy isn't moving. She couldn't handle living alone with her mother. "Dad's coming back eventually."

"I don't think so. He seems happy. You saw them together. They practically finish each other's sentences. They're always touching each other too, which is disgusting."

"That's just an act for us to see and report back to Mom. He only left because she picks on him all the time. Men don't like to be nagged. Men like it when you listen and try to understand what they're going through."

Peggy shakes her head. "Is that what Kevin likes?"

Here comes the lecture. Peggy's never forgiven Kevin for making fun of her zits in middle school, which wasn't a nice thing to do but it was a long time ago. And her sister's skin was pretty bad then. It's better now, thanks to the birth control pills. "If you'd give Kevin a chance, you'd like him."

"I doubt it. But he's your problem not mine." Peggy sets her books on the floor. "You can sleep in here if you want." She turns off the light next to her bed. "So, other than never nagging your already perfect boyfriend, what *are* you going to do when you graduate?"

Allison fluffs a pillow and stretches out. She hates this question and lately it's all anyone asks. "Be rich and famous, of course. If you're lucky, I might still talk to you."

"Are you still thinking interior design? Because Golden West has a certificate program. I can show you the schedule."

Allison rolls to her side away from Peggy. Interior design has been her standard answer to the career question for years, although she's never demonstrated any artistic talent at all, other than keeping her room tidy and folding dinner napkins into imaginative shapes. Her mother especially loves the idea because that's what she claims she wanted to be. "I'm not going to Golden West. I can't believe you're okay going there. It's like you've given up or something."

"I haven't given up anything. I got the classes I wanted. I can transfer later."

After a few minutes, Peggy's snoring as loudly as their mother. Allison pulls a pillow over her head. She's never admitted to anyone what she really wants to do after graduation. Her friends talk about becoming rock stars or sports heroes or inventing a cure for cancer, but she only dreams of raising children, making a man happy, creating a home. No one would understand, especially not Peggy.

IT'S hot already when she comes downstairs the next morning. Brenda's lying on the couch in front of the television set, listening to the commentator discuss Judge Ito's decision to deny reporters access to photographs of the Nicole Simpson and Ron Goldman crime scene.

"I don't want to see those photos either," Allison says.

"The judge is worried about the potential jury seeing them," Brenda says. There are deep circles under both of her eyes and the spiral curls have un-spiraled. So much for trying to look like Drew Barrymore.

Some legal expert is on the screen now. "It's a near-impossible task to silence public speculation in this case."

"What speculation?" Allison says. "He killed them. He's guilty. The end."

"He deserves a fair trial. He's an American citizen."

She's not prepared for a civics lesson this early in the day, especially from someone who hasn't taken a shower lately. She goes in the kitchen where Peggy's sitting at the table drinking coffee. "I'm hungry."

"There's cereal but no milk."

"I'll just have fruit then."

"There isn't any fruit."

"I'm making a grocery list," Brenda says from the living room. "How about some grilled salmon for dinner and that summer salad you guys like?"

"The one with the corn?" Allison asks. "I'll help you make it."

"And maybe a blackberry cobbler?" Peggy asks.

"It's too hot to turn on the oven. Do you really think Nicole Simpson looks like me?"

"You're prettier," Peggy says. Allison makes a face, and her sister shrugs and says under her breath, "It's what she needs to hear."

"I'm going to the beach today," Allison says in a loud enough voice for Brenda to hear and remind her she's grounded.

"Can I go with you?" Peggy asks.

"You hate the beach. And you don't like my friends."

"It's supposed to be a hundred degrees today. And I can't stand listening to this murder crap anymore."

Her friends think her sister is weird and Peggy will want to leave as soon as they get there, but it's too hot to ride her bike. She takes the keys to the BMW off the hook.

"You can come if you drive."

"We shouldn't take that car to the beach. Something might happen."

"Go ahead," Brenda says from the living room. "If something happens, it's your father's problem, not mine."

Allison smiles. Either she's no longer grounded, or her mother's simply forgotten, but at least she can go see Kevin for a while.

"We'll get groceries on the way back, Mom. Do you have any cash?"

"Take my ATM card. Your father promised to put money in the checking account."

"Why don't you turn off the TV and go take a shower?" Peggy says.

Brenda turns up the volume. "Have you guys heard this?" There is static at first and then the operator's flat voice. "911. What is your emergency?" Then Nicole Simpson's voice, on the edge of mania, "He's O. J. Simpson. You've been here before."

"She sounds terrified," Peggy says.

"She sounds like a good actress," Brenda says. "If he really was beating her, she would have left him."

"I don't get why you are so into this, Mom," Allison says. "Do you wish you'd married O. J. instead of Dad?"

"My life would have been different."

"Because you'd be dead," Allison says.

"Maybe Nicole didn't love him enough. Maybe she provoked him."

"He beat her up and then he killed her," Peggy says. "You can't believe she deserved that."

Her mother's eyes remain fixed on the screen. "I just can't imagine things escalating to that point."

"Let's go," Allison says. "Try not to run off with any murderers while we're gone, Mom."

KEVIN doesn't like it if she's not paying attention when he surfs, so she's learned to visor her hand over her eyes and watch closely when he's out in the water, to wave enthusiastically after he catches a wave, to stand occasionally and make sure he sees her watching. It's not much to ask. She's there for him, one hundred percent. A few of the girls have warned her about Kevin's temper. They say his last girlfriend broke up with him because of it, but he's not that way with her. Everyone agrees they make a great-looking couple.

This morning the surf's flat and Kevin's just sitting out there in the brown sandy water talking to his friends, easy to spot—the tallest and strongest. She lies in a circle on the brown sand with the other girls in their usual spot, a little north of the Huntington Beach pier, down past the volleyball nets. They all have boyfriends out in the water. They wear different versions of the same bikini. Their beach towels are various shades of pink. Their hair is tied on top of their heads in matching scrunchies. Peggy sits a few yards away, crouched under the umbrella she hauled across the sand, wearing her plaid flannel shirt over her bathing suit, reading one of her detective stories and not talking to anyone.

"Why is she wearing that?" Katy asks. "She must be broiling."

"It's just the way she always dresses," Allison says.

"She doesn't look like you," Danielle says.

"My dad has red hair. Peggy looks more like my mom."

"She's not really fat," McKenzie says. "Her boobs are decent, judging from what I can see anyway."

"Isn't she like some kind of a brainiac?" Danielle asks.

"She's the Smart Sister," Katy says. "Allison got the looks."

"You could totally model," McKenzie says, and all the girls nod.

"Thanks," Allison says. She knows it's supposed to be a compliment, but it really means no one expects much else from her.

"YOU'RE getting sunburned," Peggy says an hour later. "And I'm bored. Let's go."

"I just need to tell Kevin we're leaving."

"Why? He'll figure it out."

"It'll only take a minute." She runs down to the water's edge and waves, then wades out into the water. Kevin paddles over and smiles.

"Peggy wants to leave."

"You barely got here."

"I'm sorry. Call me later?"

He whips his board around and paddles out without answering.

"I'm sorry," she says. He doesn't turn around.

Peggy has the umbrella folded and under one arm, her keys in her hand. Allison dries her legs and wraps the towel around her waist, and they walk to the car. Peggy heads the BMW up Goldenwest Street toward home.

"Does Kevin have to know where you are every single minute?"

"He would wonder where I went. I'm just being considerate."

Of course, Peggy doesn't understand relationships. She's never really had any friends. She's always been fine on her own.

"What's the deal with Goldenwest Street?" Peggy asks. "Is it supposed to be one word or two? Every single sign is different."

"Who cares?"

"It's sloppy. They should pick a spelling and stick with it. And Mom was right about the cinderblock walls. Look ahead of us. It's like driving through a concrete tunnel."

"Someone's in a bad mood."

"I'm just being observant. It's all asphalt and concrete."

"I think the walls make the street tidy and clean. Look at all the palm trees."

"It's boring and oppressive and I hate it."

"I like living here."

"I wouldn't mind having a boyfriend one of these days, you know. I just don't have time for one right now. Maybe in a few years, after I start my tax practice."

Allison laughs. "Write that down in your Franklin Planner. August 19, 1998. Obtain boyfriend."

"Ha ha, very funny. I can't help it if I like being organized."

"You can't plan every second of your life, Peggy. Be spontaneous. Go with the flow."

"I *am* going with the flow."

"Because Dad asked you to rearrange your life."

"My life is fine. Mom's who we need to worry about. What she said this morning, about Nicole Simpson getting what she deserved? Don't you think that's disturbing?"

"I pretty much ignore everything she says these days. She's in denial. She's letting herself get sucked up into all this O. J. drama, so she doesn't have to deal with her own big failure."

Peggy looks at her, impressed. "You might be right."

"Don't act so surprised. I'm right sometimes."

WHEN they get home, the television is off, and Brenda has actually showered and put on a sundress. Allison chops veggies as Brenda mixes salad dressing. When she offers to light the barbecue, Brenda grins. "Thanks, dear. Us Lockhart women are resourceful, right? We're doing just fine on our own."

They eat outside on the picnic table. They all drink iced tea. The sunset lasts forever, the sky fading from pink to orange to purple, the air still warm. They play Hearts until the candles aren't enough light to see the cards. The game's not much fun with only three people, and when a fat possum waddles along the top of the cinderblock wall, they decide to go inside.

IT'S totally amazing to be in love in the summertime with the entire day to spend together. She sits in a folding chair in a pair of short shorts, watching Kevin shoot pool in his friend's garage, watching him check out her legs. He cuts the grass at his parents' house with his shirt off; she admires his muscles from the front steps. He drives; she wears a halter dress in his passenger seat. He takes out his wallet; she lets him pay. Their bodies fit together perfectly. He thinks it's cool that she carries condoms in her purse, but he says they don't really need them because he doesn't want anyone but her.

She's learned to not interrupt when he reads to her entire articles from *High Times* magazine over the phone. She passes him a joint while he's driving. He's taught her to hold it at the exact point where he can see it in his peripheral vision and keep his eyes on the road. When he's out with his friends, she waits at home by the telephone. When he doesn't call, and she can't wait any longer, she rides her bike over to his house. "Just wanted to see what you were doing," she practices in a laid-back voice.

He lives three blocks away in a house with an identical floor plan as her parents' house, the staircase on the opposite side of the dining room, cherry cabinets in the kitchen instead of her house's blond wood, burgundy carpet throughout the downstairs instead of the hardwood floors her parents put in last year, a strong scent of lemony air spray instead of the fresh flowers her mother buys every week from Trader Joe's.

"Kevin's not home," his mother says when she opens the door, "but please come inside."

Connie's wearing her usual black business suit. She's a short and wide woman, plain faced, a little nervous. "I'd like for the two of us to be friends," she's said several times, a weird thing for someone else's mother to want but also kind of sweet. Kevin's father, Sal, smiles a lot and doesn't say much. She sits with them drinking Diet Cokes and watching the Discovery channel. Although the lemony smell grows more intense until she can barely breathe through her always-clogged sinuses, it's a relief to get away from the O. J. trial.

When Kevin finally comes home, she follows him upstairs to his bedroom. He goes into his bathroom, fills a glass with water, shakes a few pills out of the bottle, and swallows. Vitamins, he's already told her. The coach has him on a program. He locks the door and lights the glass bong that he keeps on his desk. "We can play Nintendo if you want. I've got *Mortal Kombat.*"

"I don't really like those games."

He smiles. "I'm going to need to change your mind about that."

"Your parents don't mind you smoking weed? Or locking the door?"

"It's my room. They pretend they don't know I smoke. Sal's a huge stoner and Connie doesn't mind if I spray afterward."

He points at a can of Ozium air freshener on the shelf above his desk. She takes a hit and hands the bong back to him. He drags deeply, exhales a cloud of smoke, and then sprays the room. She wrinkles her nose. The smell reminds her of the janitor's bucket at school.

"I know it stinks, but you'll get used to it." He pulls off his T-shirt. His stomach is flat, his muscles are firm. She can't believe she's here with him, doing this.

"Why do you call your parents by their first names?"

"I'm adopted. Can't you tell? I don't look like either one of them. My real parents didn't want me."

Something lonely and desperate flashes across his face, and for a half second she wonders if he's just like her and never believed he fit in either. There's a reason he's come into her life at the moment her own family is splitting apart. They need each other.

"That can't be true. Of course, they wanted you."

He shrugs. "They were speed freaks. They gave me away when I was six months old." He puts a Nirvana CD in the player on the shelf over his bed.

"Maybe that was the right thing to do. If they knew they couldn't take care of you."

"I don't want to talk about them." He slips off his shorts and lies down on the bed.

She loves his crooked smile, the sound of his laughter, his strong arms, his smooth hairless chest, the way he makes love to her. There is something incredibly thrilling about being locked in a room together.

"Is this your parents' wedding picture?" she asks later, picking up a framed photograph on his desk. He lies on his side in bed, his hand propping up his head, watching her walk around his room naked. She feels like a different person, confident in her own skin, not shy about letting him see all of her.

"The Family lived in Hawaii then." He said *the* family not *my* family. Or maybe she's mistaken, still floating from the lovemaking and the weed.

"You're amazing. That noise you make right before you come? Man! That's something else."

Oh my God! His parents are down in the living room, watching television. "Was I too loud?"

"No, babe. You're awesome."

In the photo, Kevin's parents are young, barefoot, and much thinner, standing on either side of a shorter man wearing aviator sunglasses and a huge mustache. "Who's the guy with them?"

"Connie's business partner. David Bledsoe."

"What's with the mustache? He looks like a porn star or something."

He frowns. "Bledsoe's a cool dude. Excellent businessman too."

"Sorry. I didn't mean to make fun of him." She should have known this man was important by the way Kevin said his name. "Is he a relative?"

"Not exactly."

"Your family lived in Hawaii?"

"I was a baby."

"I'd love to go to Hawaii. Which island?"

"Do you know how hot you look right now? Like that Venus chick in the seashell painting. Serious animal magnetism. You're making me hard again."

She puts the picture down and crawls under the sheets next to him. She's louder on purpose this time, but when she puts on her clothes later to go home, she's relieved that Connie and Sal have gone to bed. It'd be embarrassing to have to look them in the eye and say good night.

JUST before sunset the next day, Kevin's at her front door, fresh from a shower, hair slicked off his face, holding a bouquet of flowers—two dyed blue carnations and some baby's breath from the grocery store, Allison can tell, even though he's taken them out of the plastic wrapper. He kisses her hello. "For you, Mrs. L," he says, handing her mother the flowers.

"I'll get a vase," Brenda says.

She goes in the kitchen and Allison turns the volume down on the nightly news. Kevin sits down on the couch next to her and gives her a quick kiss. His eyes are glassy. He's obviously stoned. Allison wishes she was.

"Connie likes it when I give her flowers too."

"Carnations start to stink after a few hours," Brenda says when she returns. "You know I don't like you."

"Mom!"

"It's okay, babe." Kevin leans forward and looks right at Brenda. "I'm hoping to change your mind, Mrs. L. I'm captain of the football team this year. Senior rep on the student council. My grades are decent. I'm hoping to get a scholarship and go into business. I've never been arrested. You know my parents."

"This isn't a job interview."

"I see it more as a life interview. I'm in love with Allison. She's my destiny."

"Destiny!" Brenda laughs. "You're a comedian too?"

"I'll grow on you, Mrs. L."

"I doubt that."

He's quiet for a moment. Allison squeezes his hand. This means so much, him trying like this, even if it doesn't work.

"What's going on with the murder investigations?" he asks, pointing to the muted television set, Nicole Simpson's face on the screen. "O. J.'s wife was so beautiful. She looks a lot like you."

"Ex-wife." Her mother is always too easy to flatter. She smiles of course and then launches into her spiel about the LAPD planting evidence at O. J.'s house, trying to frame him for the murders. She lists all the mistakes the police have made so far. Kevin listens and nods. When she stops talking finally, he stands. "I was hoping you'd let me take Allison out for a walk. It's a really nice night."

"Make sure she's home before ten."

"SHE'S really into O. J., isn't she?" Kevin asks, once they are outside, walking toward the park.

"She's his biggest fan. That was nice of you to put up with her."

"It got you out of the house." He takes a joint out of his pocket, thicker than his usual ones. "This stuff's supposed to be cured in mescaline."

He always has weed. She wonders where he buys it. One of the players on the team, she supposes. They walk to the small open space under the electrical towers and lie down in the damp grass. He lights the joint, and she watches the moon move across the sky and listens to the electricity coursing through the wires. After a while she can feel her blood flow through her veins as Kevin explains the difference between stars and satellites. She listens and feels the earth's gravity. She can't move her legs; she can barely feel her own hand in his as the stars spin above them.

"This might be animal tranquilizer," he says later. "It doesn't feel like mescaline."

"It doesn't matter. I like being tranquilized with you."

"You're the only one who really understands me."

She's his destiny. That's what he told her mom. "You have lots of friends."

"No one really knows me. And if they did, they wouldn't like me."

"Well I like you a lot."

"Oh, babe. I love you so much."

His eyes look wet in the moonlight. She's not sure if he's crying or it's the tranquilizer, and when he wraps his arms and legs around her, it doesn't seem like the right time to ask. Later, when they stumble hand in hand back to his house, laughing and nearly falling and laughing again, his parents have gone to bed. The television's off, the lights are turned down low.

"I should walk you home. It's late."

"Your house is so quiet." She lies down on the couch in his living room. "Just for a minute and then I'll go."

She's floating. It's like being on her dad's boat at the river, rocking back and forth. What sounds like Connie's voice is high above her, somewhere up where the satellites spin in between the constellations.

"I don't like you going into my bag without asking first."

"She's fine, Connie. You said you liked her."

Even though she knows she's dreaming, Allison smiles. She can see the imprint of a streetlight behind her closed eyes, or maybe it's the moon.

The same voice again. "What have you told her?"

"Nothing, yet. Don't worry. Allison's cool."

"I hope you're not making a mistake."

She waits to hear Kevin's response, but there is only silence.

SHE likes how her name sounds on his lips when he tells his friends about the mescaline the next day and says, "Allison's down for pretty much anything." He's the one she's been waiting for. He's how her real life will finally begin.

CHAPTER FOUR

"HOW ABOUT SOME COFFEE?" BRENDA ASKS WHEN FRANK SITS DOWN IN THE chair opposite the couch.

"Maybe a glass of water."

She can't remember him ever sitting in that chair. It's where they pile coats in the winter, where the girls' books and backpacks accumulate, where guests sit who aren't staying long. Frank has put on a few pounds and needs a haircut, but he still tricks her heart into beating faster.

When he'd called and said he wanted to talk, she rehearsed all the ways she could tell him she's sorry about the misunderstanding with the car lease, sorry about the credit cards, sorry about storming out of Linda's house and leaving him behind. She's said all of that already and it didn't work, so she put on a tiny pair of shorts with no underwear, wore her new Wonderbra under a tank top and dabbed some of the Angel perfume he'd bought her for Christmas in between her breasts. Both girls are back in school. They have the house to themselves.

She tells him about the spreadsheet Peggy left on the kitchen table, an assignment, Brenda assumed, titled: "Cost Comparison of Cal State Long Beach vs. Golden West College." Golden West proved to be several thousand dollars cheaper. "That's my girl," Frank says and then points to the television screen. "I see you're still hooked on O. J."

"I'm not hooked," she says, wishing his tone wasn't so dismissive, "but I do think it's fascinating." And better than worrying about what she's supposed to do with the rest of her life.

A criminal law professor from UCLA is on the television screen now, being interviewed about police racism. "One important theme the defense has pushed insistently is that we can't necessarily trust the credibility of police officers."

"Bullshit," Frank says. "If we can't trust the police, who can we trust?"

"Well, I wouldn't trust those cops who beat up Rodney King."

"Oh please, they were highway patrol officers and they were acquitted."

"Which started a riot," she says. This isn't what she wants to talk about at all. Why is Frank distracting her like this? "It just sounds like the police made a lot of stupid mistakes. That's all I'm saying."

"Everyone makes mistakes, Brenda. That doesn't mean they're not credible."

She feels a tiny bit of hope. Frank might be in a forgiving mood. "You're right. Everyone does make mistakes. Especially me." She goes in the kitchen, puts ice in a glass, opens the fridge to get a bottle of sparkling water, slices a lemon, and then takes the glass back to Frank in the living room and arranges herself on the couch. "How are you?"

"I'm okay. Heading up to San Francisco next week for the area presentation. Is my blue suit still in the closet?"

"Your lucky blue suit." She wonders if the girls have told him how she'd crammed all his clothes in plastic bags and hauled them out to the street and then reconsidered and brought everything back in the house and rehung it where it belonged in their closet. "You'll need my help to find it."

He follows behind her as she climbs up the stairs toward their bedroom. She sways her hips back and forth, emphasizing the curve of her waist, and when she glances over her shoulder, he's grinning. He stands behind her as she flips through the hangers in their bedroom closet. "There it is," she says, moving back slightly, pressing into him. He puts his hands on her hips and it's all instinct after that, the way their clothes come off and they're back in their bed, the way they fit together, the way they've always fit together. He misses her, she can tell, and she's missed him too, the way his skin tastes a little like maple syrup, how his ass is so firm in her hands. The sex is urgent, intense, and incredibly satisfying until he rolls off her and stands, then bends over and picks up his boxers from the floor.

"That shouldn't have happened." Frank pulls on his pants.

She sits up suddenly, so light-headed she wonders if her heart has stopped. He's already buttoning his shirt, taking the suit from the closet, heading down the stairs.

"Wait a minute." She grabs her robe and catches up with him downstairs, her heart coming to life in her chest. "Didn't that mean anything to you?"

"You tricked me, wearing that outfit."

She puts her arms around his rigid body, but when he doesn't embrace her, she pulls away. She's not going to beg. She's not going to cry either. "Why did you come here?"

"To talk about what we're going to do next."

"Sit down." She looks at her hands, noticing a ragged edge on her thumbnail.

"I have to go back to work."

After a long minute, Frank perches on the uncomfortable guest chair, still holding his blue suit in its plastic dry cleaner bag. A bleached-blond correspondent is on the television screen, importantly stating: "A pornographic film star claims O. J.'s friend told her the gloves were his."

"Do you want a divorce?" Brenda asks, almost succeeding at keeping her voice steady.

He studies the carpet for so long she stares at it too, trying to figure out if there's a stain. He finally looks up at her with his beautiful green eyes. "I don't see any reason why we'd have to go to court. Not using an attorney would save a lot of money."

She pulls the edge of her thumbnail in between her teeth. She should get a nail file. One of O. J.'s defense attorneys is on camera now, saying the porn star's story is ludicrous.

"Can you turn that garbage off?" Frank says.

Ludicrous is a good word, Brenda thinks as she mutes the sound.

"The girls can stay on my health plan. We can split what we can get from the house down the middle. I'll cover your expenses until you find a job."

"Find a job! Doing what?" He never wanted her to work. He was proud of having a stay-at-home wife. "I'm not splitting anything with you. A judge would give me everything."

"All we have is the house and a shitload of debt. It makes more sense to do this without going to court."

"More sense for you." *What debt?* They refinanced the house last year to pay off the credit cards. She remembers signing the papers.

"More sense for the girls. Why should we waste money on lawyers and court fees if we can file the paperwork ourselves?"

She bites down hard on her thumbnail, severing it to the quick, tasting blood. She's been a fool to trust him and his paperwork. "I need a Band-Aid."

"I've never seen you bite your nails before."

She's afraid he'll leave while she's gone, so she rushes, and, in her haste, she can't get the bandage on straight or the wrapper in the trash can. She leaves the first aid kit open on the counter and hurries back to the living room. He's holding his head in both hands, crying. She hasn't seen him cry since they put their old dog down, fifteen years ago. He stands and puts his arms around her, then burrows his wet face in her neck. She pats his back, heartened.

"I didn't mean to hurt you." His voice breaks. "Or the girls. God, I feel awful."

"We'll go to counseling. Julie and Rick went. She said it really helped them."

Frank pulls away from her and wipes his eyes with his hands. "Counseling won't work."

"Don't be so negative. You can't just say you're sorry and expect everything to go back to the way it was."

"I don't want to go back to the way it was."

He wants things to be different. She does too. "I can change. Tell me what you want me to do."

"You don't need to do anything. I'm not in love with you anymore."

"Oh, you don't mean that. You're certainly not in love with Linda. She's at least forty-five and she's got a face like a horse."

"I think she's pretty." Frank pulls a handkerchief out of his pants pocket. "And actually, she's forty-seven." He blows his nose.

"She's older than you are?" Her abdominal muscles clench as if she's been punched. She stares at the television for a moment, trying to compose herself. Marcia Clark is on the screen now, with her sour, whippet face and unfortunate perm. Everything about the prosecuting attorney is harsh, her pointed chin and sharp browbone, her unflattering suits, her too smart for her own good expression, the snooty way she speaks, but Marcia Clark has divorced two husbands and is raising small boys on her own as well as running what everyone is calling the trial of the century. Marcia Clark wouldn't put up with this kind of treatment.

"Linda hasn't raised your daughters or kept your house or fed and fucked you for almost twenty years." Brenda squares her shoulders and pulls in her stomach. "No one in his right mind would leave me for an old hag like her. You're having some kind of midlife crisis."

Frank's face is red. "She makes me feel good." He stands. "She makes me happy."

"That's just plain selfish. You have a family to take care of. You have responsibilities."

"I'll want to see the girls as much as I can."

"That's up to them."

"I'll come by sometime this week when they aren't home and get the rest of my things." His hand hovers on the doorknob. He's going to apologize now, she's sure of it. He'll suggest they go back upstairs. "Do you by chance know where my Swiss Army knife is?"

"Get your things out of here by the end of this week, or I'll take it all out in the street and set it on fire."

She's too stunned to cry after he leaves. She pulls out the phone book and finds the listings for divorce attorneys, picking out names that sound tough and ruthless, and calls a few of the firms. The hourly rates are stunning. Steele and Associates charge two hundred an hour just to sit down with someone. Preuss and Heller will let her put it on a credit card if she'd like to. She would like to very much. Unfortunately, none of the firms take Discover cards.

"Why don't you move to my dad's place?" her cousin Tim says when she calls to vent. "It's paid for and empty right now. He'll be in assisted living until he dies."

"I thought the county was tearing down those houses to expand the freeway."

"That'll take forever. You'd only have to cover the utilities."

"I don't even know how much we pay for utilities here. I don't have a key to our PO box. Frank's kept me in the dark on everything."

"I'm sure he'd give you a key if you asked."

"He's the one who left. Why do I have to move?"

"Frank can't afford that house plus child support and alimony on one income."

"Why are you defending him? He never liked you."

Tim almost laughs. "So that's why you never invite me over."

She's hurt his feelings, but it's true. Frank's always said Tim only came around when he wanted something. "I like you. And it doesn't matter what Frank thinks now."

"Honestly, Brenda, neither one of you has seemed happy for years. Maybe this is for the best."

"What do you know about relationships?" Brenda feels blood rush to her head. "Picking up guys in bars doesn't make you an expert." She hears Tim breathe in and out. This is mean, she knows, but it's equally cruel of Tim to dismiss Frank's abandonment as inevitable.

"I'm going to forget you said that," he says after a moment, his voice clipped and angry. "I know you're upset right now."

"I'm sorry."

"Your mother never thought Frank was good enough for you. And my parents didn't like him either."

"That's not true. Your mom was happy for us. She gave us a set of four wineglasses from Tiffany's for our wedding." She can see the crystal sparkle in the china hutch across the room. She's afraid she'll break them every time she takes them out to dust. Frank will probably expect her to split up the set. She should start using them now.

"My dad doesn't even recognize me anymore. I'm glad my mom's not around to see him like this."

"He was never nice to you. Our parents weren't happy people. You know you're my favorite cousin. Forgive me?"

"Of course, I'm your favorite. I'm the only cousin who still speaks to you."

"You are careful, aren't you, Tim? With whoever it is you see? I watch the news. I worry."

"I just got tested. And I'm careful."

When she hangs up, she wishes she'd made Frank wear a condom. Who knows what kind of men this Linda person has slept with? She needs to be careful too.

SHE goes to the gym later because working out always helps her think. She can tell from the approving glances as she shows the receptionist her card and walks toward the aerobics room that her new workout clothes are a hit. It's a bold look, black thong over hot pink tights and a matching pink sports bra, but she can carry it off. Sue and Julie are already setting up their risers for the step class.

"Hey, guys!" Brenda says. "Long time no see."

Sue raises her eyebrows. "A thong? You're not twenty anymore."

"That's kind of a younger person's outfit," Julie says.

The music starts and Brenda tells herself she doesn't care what they think. She likes the way she looks in the mirror, strong and beautiful. An hour later she's drenched in sweat and rejuvenated.

"You were on fire today, Brenda," one of the young girls says as they put away their risers.

"It was fun." Brenda watches Julie follow Sue out of the room. She was planning on asking them to go out for coffee afterward, her treat. She wanted to ask Julie about getting a key to Frank's post office box, but the two of them are laughing about something and don't look back or wait for her to catch up.

"How old are you anyway?" the girl is saying. "If you don't mind me asking."

There's no good way to answer this question. "Thirtysome-thing."

"Well, you sure are in great shape."

For your age is what she means, but Brenda decides she'll pretend it's a compliment. "Thank you."

SHE lies in the middle of their king-sized mattress and stretches her arms and legs out to each corner, trying to appreciate how wonderful it is to have all this space. The freshly washed sheets smell like her shampoo and lotion instead of cigarettes and beer. She can sleep all night now undisturbed, without Frank snoring and shaking the bed each time he turns over, or she can turn on the light and read or watch television or use her vibrator.

Instead she can't stop thinking about that young girl Frank was involved with years ago, Mary, who kept calling in the middle of the night, crying on the telephone. "Could I please just talk to Frank for a quick second?" Mary was a fool, but at least she was pretty. She's the bigger fool. She never saw this thing with Linda coming.

Today was another series of embarrassing events. Julie wouldn't give her a key to the mailbox without Frank's signature, and when Brenda insisted on talking to the supervisor, it turned out to be Phyllis, who was also at Linda's horrible party. Phyllis wouldn't do anything for her either even though she'd resisted all impulses and not caused a scene, determined to take the higher road.

She'd slipped ten dollars into the hand of a young woman sitting cross-legged on the sidewalk outside the post office door, hoping to generate some better karma, imagining one of these days it will be her sitting there since Frank obviously doesn't give a rat's ass if she has a roof over her head or sunscreen on her face or tampons in her purse. She knows she wouldn't make it five minutes on the street no matter how big of a shopping cart she managed to fill. The woman thanked her, but when she came home, all Frank's clothes were gone from the closet, his half of the bureau drawers emptied, his golf clubs missing from the garage.

So much for karma.

What would have happened if O. J. had sat in her section that night twenty years ago? She could be living in his Brentwood estate right now, helping him spend his money. Or she might have met O. J.'s handsome friend Robert Kardashian and married him. Her mother would have preferred Kardashian because she didn't like Black people. Her mother could be an unpleasant woman, critical and complaining. She looked down on women who "had to work," and Brenda assumed from the start Frank would support her. She'd have felt like a failure if he'd expected her to get a job. And now she's going to have to find one.

After her father smashed his car into the retaining wall of the Garden Grove Freeway, coming home from a bar, and died, her mother's brother, Charles, started coming for lunch with his family every other Sunday to check up on them. The visits made her mother nervous. She bought too much takeout from the deli, got out the good china and silverware, and changed her dress three times. Brenda put on a dress too. She liked feeling pretty more than anything, and she missed the way her father's eyes lit up when she'd bring him a can of Budweiser to his recliner in the den. When she twirled around on her almost tiptoes, showing off what she'd learned in ballet class, her father would always say, "Do that again."

Uncle Charles said ballet lessons were a waste of money. He

had ramrod posture and barked out orders in a military voice, and no one ever argued with him. After lunch, Aunt Tina took the dishes into the kitchen and washed them silently, somehow preventing the china from clinking against the glasses and the silverware from rattling in the stainless-steel sink because Uncle Charles had to concentrate while he went over their bank account. Her older cousins, Teresa and Todd, went to the den to watch movies with the sound turned way down, but Tim made a beeline to the Barbie dolls in Brenda's bedroom.

Tim had a good imagination and Brenda had all the paraphernalia: the pink Corvette convertible, the travel case full of clothes, the Malibu Dreamhouse, the pink-canopied speedboat. Normally, she was bored by the dolls' blank expressions and rigid plastic bodies, but in her cousin's chubby little hands they seemed more valuable. And then they'd look up and find Uncle Charles standing in the doorway, scowling, one hand on the doorjamb, the other holding a glass of something gold with ice. The drink meant he was finished correcting her mother's math. The scowl meant a variety of things, none of them ever good.

"What are you doing, Tim?"

"He's just sitting here," Brenda said, looking straight into her uncle's eyes as she removed the naked Barbie from Tim's plump hands. "He's just watching me." With her bare toes, she scooted the tiny pink heels and the black-and-white striped bathing suit toward her. She arranged an expression she'd seen in a movie. Eyes down, flutter lashes twice, eyes up, open wide, smile just enough to flash the dimple in her right cheek.

Uncle Charles cleared his throat. "No son of mine plays with dolls." He went back to the living room and told her mother she was spoiling that girl. Tim blinked back tears, and Brenda got up and closed the door. "I bet you'll look like Barbie when you grow up," Tim said after a while.

Her mother thought she was ruining her life when she married Frank. "He's the kind who will cheat on you," she predicted, but by then her cancer was at stage four, her disapproval slightly diminished by chemo. She died before Peggy was born.

Brenda had wanted Frank as much as she'd wanted a baby, enough to pretend she was a silly, clueless woman, astonished to find herself pregnant with back-to-back baby girls, when the truth is, she'd gotten pregnant both times on purpose. Why hasn't she ever told the girls this? Why has she always repeated that same stupid story about Peggy being an accident and Allison a surprise as if both girls weren't desperately wanted, by her from the start, and certainly by Frank, once he'd held them in his arms?

She rolls on her back and checks the clock. Three thirty in the morning. She'll have circles under her eyes and her face will be puffy. Tomorrow's Peggy's eighteenth birthday, she remembers suddenly, sitting straight up in bed, and she hasn't even bought a gift. She'll go shopping in the morning, find a card, make a nice dinner, take Aunt Tina's Tiffany glasses out of the china hutch, and start using them. If that woman in Torrance can wear a hand-embroidered dress like a bathrobe, she certainly deserves to drink out of a nice wineglass.

WHEN she gets up the next morning, the Santa Ana winds are blowing hard and there is zero humidity in the air. She's too tired to think clearly when the doorbell rings, and she opens the front door even though she hasn't taken a shower or had her coffee. The chain on the neighbor's flagpole across the street clangs in the wind. She doesn't recognize the heavy-set woman on her front porch and guesses Jehovah's Witness, except they always travel in pairs. This woman is alone.

"Hi, Brenda. You may not remember me. I'm Connie Nelson, Kevin's mother?"

"Is something wrong?"

"I just thought I'd stop by on my way to work. May I come in?"

It would be rude to say no. Brenda glances over her shoulder at the untidy stack of *National Enquirer*s and *People* magazines on the coffee table. Connie's already aiming herself toward the couch. She wonders if she should offer coffee. There isn't any cream though and Connie looks like the type of woman who would want cream. She'd probably also like a donut or a cookie with her coffee, but she doesn't have those either.

"Let me move those out of your way." She picks up the papers and stacks them on the floor. "I was just getting ready to tidy up in here."

Los Angeles District Attorney Gil Garcetti is on the morning news show, saying he won't seek the death penalty.

"That's outrageous," Connie says. "If Simpson wasn't a celebrity, they'd electrocute him."

"It's actually the smart thing to do. People really like him. A jury might have a hard time sentencing him to death since most Californians don't believe in the death penalty." She can't remember which of the talking heads on television said this, but Connie seems impressed. Brenda notices how well her black suit fits. The pants don't ride up and the jacket hangs properly. Her shoes look expensive too. "That suit is a beautiful fabric. Is it merino wool?"

"I have to have all my clothes tailored. Sal and I are so thrilled Kevin is seeing Allison. She's perfect."

"She is?" Brenda says. It comes out sounding less motherly than it probably should, but the quick change of subject is confusing.

"She's so good for Kevin's concentration. He needs to focus on sports this year so he can get into a good college. Sal and I are happy he's settled down with her."

Brenda doesn't like the sound of *settled down.* "They're both so young. I'm sure it's not serious."

"Sal and I met when we were their age. We just celebrated our twentieth wedding anniversary in New Orleans."

"I've always wanted to go to New Orleans."

"It was fun. We took a cooking class. I have the recipes if you'd like to borrow them."

"Frank travels so often for business. We haven't had a real vacation in years."

It's a dumb thing to say if Connie knows Frank is no longer living here much less taking her on vacation, but there's no sign of judgment on Connie's round face. "I know it's only September, but I wanted to run something by you. We spend the week between Christmas and New Year's up at our cabin in Big Bear. I'd love it if Allison could join us."

Tailored suits, cooking lessons in New Orleans, and a cabin at Big Bear? This butterball's list of assets is confusing. "Who knows if they'll still be together by Christmas?"

"We feel like Allison's part of our family now. I'm making oyster stuffing and praline pecan pie for Thanksgiving. Maybe you could join us?"

"You certainly like to plan ahead." Allison already has a family to eat Thanksgiving dinner with. Connie's starting to get on her nerves. "It sounds delicious. But we'll have our turkey here, just like always."

"I'd better get to work," Connie says, rising. "Think about the cabin."

"I went by your store last month to get the battery changed in my watch, but you were closed." Connie has owned Nelson's

Jewels, a small store in the strip mall across the street from the high school, for as long as Brenda can remember, but she can't imagine how it makes any money since it's hardly ever open.

"We don't really do that kind of work. You could try Target. Or the swap meet."

"I hate these awful winds," Brenda says when she opens the front door and a gust of warm air sends dry leaves skittering across her lawn. Which she suddenly realizes is dead.

"Kevin could take over your yard."

"We have a service." She can't remember when they came last, and judging from the number of weeds, it's been a while. She probably owes them money. She has no idea how much. "I'd be happy to pay him."

"That's not necessary. He'd love to do it."

The woman means well, Brenda thinks as she watches Connie waddle down the driveway and get into her Buick, but she's going to have to find some other perfect girl for her son to settle down with. Allison won't be going to Ocean View much longer.

When she goes back in the house, she intends to start cleaning, then get dressed and go shopping for dinner, find Peggy a nice birthday gift, and bake a cake. Peggy's been such a good sport about everything lately she really should do something special for her, except Peggy's such a good sport she won't expect much of a fuss. And now she can't remember exactly when Peggy will be home. She works until eleven and has classes in the morning. Allison's never home either. When, exactly, will they celebrate?

There is an entire day ahead with no one to talk to. She watches the palm fronds in the tree next door shudder in the devil winds. Her skin feels as dry as sandpaper. She removes her rings and lotions her hands and arms. She's going to have to stop wearing the wedding band and engagement ring eventually, she supposes. She could use the diamonds for something else. Earrings maybe or a necklace. Connie might give her a fair price to rework them.

She takes one of the Tiffany glasses from the china hutch, pours a glass of chardonnay, and sits down on the couch. *Look at me*, she thinks. *Day drinking and it's not even a holiday.* She'll have a vegetarian pizza delivered later and leave it on the counter for whenever Peggy comes home. She'll write a check too, a big one, from the joint account and hope it doesn't bounce.

The good-looking detective, Mark Fuhrman, is on the screen now, very earnest in his fitted blue suit and bright red tie, but she doesn't believe a word he says. Johnnie Cochran has convinced her he's lying. She prefers O. J.'s devoted and even more handsome friend Robert Kardashian anyway. Thank God she has all of them to distract her.

CHAPTER FIVE

PEGGY STANDS IN FRONT OF A WOODEN CASE SORTING ENVELOPES THAT WON'T go through the post office machinery for all kinds of reasons. Illegible handwriting, odd sizes, pieces too slick or too thin or too chunky.

"Tell your dad Mary says hello," a young woman walking behind her letter case whispers.

"Uh, okay. If I see him." Everyone likes Frank Lockhart, and everyone wants to talk to her.

"Slow down a little," Dolores tells her now. "They'll just expect you to do more." Dolores has worked at the post office for thirty years. She dyes her hair an inky black and twists it up in a bun held by a chopstick, wears too much eyeliner, and looks bored out of her mind except when the men who work on the docks unloading trucks come inside and flirt with her. Peggy's been trying to make a game out of sorting as fast as possible to make the time go faster, but the clock refuses to move. She's been standing for six straight hours. Her right shoulder aches. Her nose is full of black snot from the dust and grime. She had no idea mail was so dirty.

She stretches her arms and looks overhead. "Are those windows?" She wonders if there is some sort of attic above the workroom floor.

"It's the lookout gallery," Dolores says as Russ, John, and Chico come in from the dock for their break. "Postal inspectors are up there watching us all the time, making sure we don't steal anything."

"What is there to steal?" Peggy asks as they follow the men to the lunchroom.

Russ looks over his shoulder and laughs. He's a Black six-foot-four retired Marine, intimidating until he starts talking about his grandchildren. "You'd be surprised, Peggy. People mail all kinds of valuable things. Cash, credit cards, jewelry."

"People mail drugs sometimes too," John says. John always smells like pot and French fries. His acne makes him seem younger than twenty-four.

"We keep hoping some nice bud from Hawaii will fall out of a box," Chico says. Chico's cute in kind of a gangster way with his headband and white T-shirt. He has a three-year-old daughter at home and drives a ridiculously oversized red truck so high off the ground he needs a step to climb in.

They're all nice and Peggy likes them, much to her surprise, how they tease each other constantly and have opinions on everyone that make her laugh. She watches and listens, happy to be different from all of them and glad she won't be working with them much longer (and definitely not for thirty years like Dolores). But in the meantime, she's lost ten pounds without even trying and everyone thinks she's smart and funny. They're glad to see her when she clocks in. They ask about school. They tell her to be careful driving home. "See you tomorrow," they say as if they're looking forward to it—as opposed to the people in her classes at Golden West College who don't seem remotely interested in her at all.

Most of her classmates are half-asleep, and some of them even come to school in their pajamas and don't appear to have combed their hair. She'd assumed students in business classes would be practical types like her, focused and driven, but these people seem so much younger. A couple of them asked if she wanted to join their study group, but when she explained she had to be at work at two thirty in the afternoon and that she worked weekends too, they seemed confused, as if she was deliberately being unfriendly.

"GLORIA and I bowl before work Monday mornings," a young blond named Tessa tells her in the bathroom when she washes up one night before their shift ends. Tessa drives a car with a ski rack and has her own apartment. "You should come."

"What's your handicap?" Gloria asks, redoing her lip liner. Gloria has serious brown eyes and never smiles.

"I have class Monday mornings."

"You've got to have fun sometimes," Tessa says. "Otherwise, what's the point?"

"I'm a terrible bowler anyway," Peggy says as they walk toward the time clock.

"Chico and I are going up to Big Bear this weekend for Oktoberfest," a man she hasn't seen before tells Tessa as they wait in line to clock out. He has a thick head of sandy brown hair and his eyes are blue, the color of faded denim, framed by brows that arch sympathetically when he talks. "You and Gloria should come." He looks at her and she realizes she's staring. He grins.

"I'll get a letter of warning if I call in sick again," Tessa says.

"So, we'll see you at Big Bear?" he says, and everyone laughs.

Peggy watches him walk away. There's something about the way his worn jeans hang on his slim hips that makes her eyes linger.

"He's trouble," Dolores says.

"What?" She's forgotten Dolores was standing behind her.

"Glenn." They both watch him make his way to the door. "Half the women here think he's in love with them."

"I should go home," Peggy says. "I still have a paper to write."

THE next day Glenn takes the flats case next to hers. When he grins, she can't help but grin back and hope she doesn't smell. She hasn't washed her face or brushed her teeth since she laced up her Doc Martens at six this morning. She sorts a stack of *People* magazines into the city holdouts. This week's issue is the "Complete Guide to the O. J. Simpson Trial." She has the locations of the cubbyholes memorized. Garden Grove, Yorba Linda, Laguna Beach, Anaheim. She can sort with her eyes closed, and she definitely does not need a guide to the O. J. trial. She has her mother at home who can remember every minute detail of the murder investigations but somehow managed to forget her birthday. Not that she really cares. At least there was pizza and a ridiculously generous check that Peggy knows better than to try and cash.

"What I don't get," Russ is telling Chico, "is why would a brother who had it all throw it away over a woman? O. J. could have any chick he wanted."

"You got a point," Chico says.

"You know they're trying to frame him," Russ says. "LAPD's full of lying-ass crackers."

"Always has been," Chico says. "Nothing new about police telling lies."

Peggy starts to say that her mother would agree when a dark-haired woman runs her fingers down Glenn's back, takes the case on his other side, and gives Peggy a proprietary look. "I left my sandals in your truck," she says. Peggy's still trying to figure out what the look means when Tessa stops behind Glenn's case. "We still on for tonight?"

"Not if there's overtime. I need the money."

Tessa shrugs. The thin, dark-haired woman's lips tighten. Peggy smiles and shakes her head. She puts a *People* magazine into the Silverado cubbyhole.

Glenn lifts his eyebrows. "What's so funny?"

"Nothing," she says. "Nothing at all."

"WHAT happened to the beamer?" Glenn asks in the parking lot a few weeks later. She's got the keys in her hand for the used Ford Escort Frank and Linda brought over last night. "A late birthday present," he'd said. It's an ugly metallic blue but has low mileage and didn't cost her anything except the hug Frank insisted on. She hated how good it felt to be enveloped in his arms, breathing in his cologne and his last cigarette, not wanting him to let her go, feeling her mother's eyes watching them through the living room window. She'd invited him in for leftover pizza, but he wouldn't stay.

"The BMW's my mom's car. My dad gave me this. It was his girlfriend's mother's. She's too old to drive anymore, I guess. It's complicated." It's not a complete coincidence she's taking her lunch break the same time as Glenn. She saw him clock out. She just got a haircut this morning from the place Tessa recommended and she's caught up on her homework.

"Take me for a ride." Glenn's already in the car, sliding the seat back. His legs are long. His thighs are lean, much leaner than her own. His grin shoots straight down her spine.

"Where do you want to go?"

"Why?" Glenn's eyelids never seem to fully raise over his thickly lashed eyes. "Where were you thinking?"

She blushes.

"How about Del Taco?" he says.

She checks the rearview mirror three times and backs up

slowly, sure he's judging her driving skills, and hits the brakes a little too hard. The car jerks forward. "Sorry."

He rolls down the window on his side. "Okay if I smoke a joint?"

She's already decided to never eat or drink in her car. It still has an old lady smell and now it will stink of pot, but she can change her own rules. "Sure," she says as she turns on the radio, the same station her father has always listened to, and Neil Young is in the middle of singing about shooting his baby down by the river. Glenn nods his head to the music and lights up as casually as if he were lighting a Marlboro cigarette. He even looks a little like the Marlboro man, and she can imagine him on a horse in a ten-gallon hat, a bandanna around his neck.

"No thanks," she says when he holds the joint toward her. "Pot gives me a headache. And I have class in the morning." She sounds like what she is, a dork.

"That's right, you're a college girl."

"It's just community college. Golden West."

"Nothing wrong with that." He takes another hit and flicks the ash out the window. "Smart actually. Get your requirements out of the way without spending a bunch of money. I should go back to school. What are you studying?"

"Accounting. I want to do taxes. Eventually." He grins, so she goes on. "I'm taking this class right now, Taxation Principles. The teacher is amazing. He says taxes are the price we pay for civilization."

The eyebrows arch. "Huh. I'm not so sure about that."

"It makes sense when you think about it. I mean taxes pay for stuff everyone needs. Roads and bridges and schools. I'm sorry. I'm probably boring you."

"You sound excited."

"Figuring out how much tax someone owes is like solving a

puzzle. Plus, it helps people make sure they don't pay too much."
God. Why can't she shut up?

"I like your ambition, Peggy Sue. You can do my taxes."

"I'm just Peggy," she says, but she sits up a little taller as she
pulls into the drive-through line, concentrating so hard on not
hitting the curb that she nearly overshoots the speaker box.
"What do you want?"

He grins and the eyebrows arch up again. She wonders if his
face ever gets tired. "A bean and cheese burrito and a Diet Coke."
He hands her a twenty.

She orders the same thing and pulls the car forward. "My
purse is in the back seat."

"My treat this time."

This time. She manages to hand him the change, drive back
to the post office, park her car, and eat her burrito without
spilling it down the front of her shirt.

ACCORDING to the man on the local news, the hottest-selling Halloween costume is an O. J. Simpson mask. Peggy wonders who in
their right mind would let their kids go trick-or-treating as
Simpson and if someone at work might have a Halloween party
and what she would wear if she was invited and if Glenn might
be there. She doesn't like how her brain starts to spin out of control whenever she thinks about him because she has other things
to focus on. One of her teachers is encouraging her to take part
one of the test to qualify to become an IRS enrolled agent. She
has homework to do for her classes. She needs to update her
Franklin Planner. She has things to discuss with her mother, like
the open house tomorrow. There's a FOR SALE sign planted in
their front yard.

She pulled some empty boxes out of the dumpster behind

the post office last night and brought them home to start packing. Clear out the photos first, she's already decided, not liking the idea of complete strangers comparing her tragic school pictures with her beautiful sister's photos. Brenda's on the phone when she goes in the kitchen to find tape and something to mark the boxes with. "Oh, Bill, you know I can't."

Peggy digs through the junk drawer. The only Bill she can think of is her father's pervy friend, and it's obvious her mom wants to do whatever it is he's asking. She finds a Sharpie and masking tape and goes back to the living room, noting the groove in the seat cushion of the couch, the crumbs in the carpet, the empty wineglass on the coffee table. The good crystal one, she realizes. Her mom used to save those glasses for Christmas dinner.

"There's an open house tomorrow, remember?" Peggy says when Brenda returns to her couch-nest.

"Your father's handling all that." Her eyes dart to the television screen. "What do you think about this friend of Nicole Simpson's?"

"I don't know who that is. Shouldn't we run the vacuum or something?"

"Jeez, Peggy. How do you not know this? Faye Resnick wrote a book about Nicole, how she broke into a new neighbor's house while he was sleeping, got in bed with him, and gave him a blow job. She even has a name for it. The 'Brentwood Hello.' I told you there was more to this story. Nicole was a slut."

"This Faye person doesn't sound like much of a friend."

Brenda sighs. "Most women can't be trusted. I've learned that the hard way. At least O. J. had a friend in Robert Kardashian. Don't you think he's handsome? And loyal too."

"We should at least clean the bathrooms."

"Look how my old friends treat me."

"There's some 409 under the sink in the kitchen. Have you thought more about where we're going to move?"

"You girls are just as bad. You like Linda, don't you? You *admire* her."

"I never said that. I only said Dad seems to be happy. We need to start looking for a place. Dad says the house should sell quickly."

"He's priced it too low. He can't wait for us to be out on the street."

"That's not true, Mom." She takes the framed family photos off the table in the hallway and puts them in a box. Christmas in Laguna Beach, she and Brenda in red sweaters, Allison and Frank wearing green. Standing in front of a waterfall at Yosemite, ten years ago. Even in T-shirts and shorts her mother and sister look stylish. The Colorado River, all of them on the boat. Her sister is dead center in each photo, wedged between their parents, while she's either in the background or off to the side, gazing off in space, looking like a slob.

"I'm hoping to get your sister into a better school district. I've been checking out apartments in South County."

"Have you found anything?" Peggy stacks the frames in a box and rips off a piece of masking tape. Brenda hasn't left the house in weeks.

"Your father says he can't afford anything I like." Brenda's eyes are back on the television screen now. "Johnnie Cochran claims the prosecution isn't asking Black jurors the same questions they ask white jurors."

"Will you stop changing the subject?"

"Marcia Clark even made one of the jurors cry the other day. That isn't the right way to treat people who are simply trying to do their civic duty."

"Earth to Mom. We need to figure out where we are going to live."

"You need to buy some clothes that fit you now that you've lost all that weight. Those baggy jeans don't do anything for your figure. Let's go shopping."

"I need to get ready for work," she says even though it's much too early to leave.

WHEN she gets out of her car, she notices John up ahead of her, walking slowly through the employee parking lot, half turning around now and then, glancing over his shoulder at her. She doesn't really want to be seen walking into the building with him. Tessa says that out of all the employees, he's the most likely to go postal. Tessa might be right, but today, Peggy finds his hesitation kind of flattering. She's hung back like that a few times, wanting to walk in with Glenn when she's noticed him behind her, but she's never worked up the nerve to actually stop and wait for him.

"Hey, John! You're here early."

He turns around slowly, keeping his eyes on the ground. "The gym didn't take as long today." His voice is low, as if he's prepared to pretend he's only talking to himself.

"I should join a gym."

"You have school."

"Taxation Principles and Auditing this semester."

"I could never do math." He keeps his head turned away from her, staring at the empty handcarts and dirty canvas sacks on the back dock.

"What are you reading?" she asks.

He looks at her for a millisecond, bewildered, until she points to the paperback book tucked in his back pocket. "Oh." He licks his lips. "*Get Shorty.*"

"Seriously? I love Elmore Leonard."

"You do? I read in the paper they're making a movie of it next year. Probably screw it up. Books are always better."

"That's so true." Their eyes meet for a second. He looks as surprised as she is that they have something in common.

"Have you read *A Scanner Darkly*? It's about a bunch of druggies in Orange County."

"Sounds interesting."

He licks his lips again. "How's your dad?"

"Uh, fine, I guess."

"Do you think maybe you could tell him about me?"

"Tell him what?"

"I'd be a good supervisor. I keep applying, but I never get interviews. I think if he knew you thought I was okay, I might have a chance."

"I don't see him much, working nights." *Seriously? The only reason he wants to talk to me is because of my father?*

"Anyway, I could bring it in for you. The book, I mean."

"I don't have much time to read these days. Too much homework."

"It's okay. You can keep it as long as you like."

When he brings the book the next day, she pretends surprise and then disinterest and carelessly sets the paperback on the shelf next to the time clock. She takes it home with her that night because it seems too cruel to leave it behind, but she's certainly not telling her dad to give John a promotion.

SUNDAY morning, she pays for toilet paper, tampons, and cleaning supplies at Target with her mother's Discover card and tries not to blush when she signs Brenda's name. She expects the pimply-faced clerk to ask for an ID, but he's too busy staring openmouthed at Allison and can barely manage to stammer that he hopes they have a nice day.

"I should have time to mop the floors and clean the bathrooms before I go to work," Peggy says when they get in her car. "Maybe you can talk Mom into going to a movie this afternoon, so she won't be there for the open house."

"Can't. I have plans with Kevin."

"It would be better if she wasn't home."

"I really don't care. I don't want Dad to sell the house. I don't know why you're killing yourself trying to help him."

Because he asked me to. "The more money they get, the better for everyone."

"Kevin's mother says I can live with them if Mom can't find an apartment in Huntington."

"Mom will never let you do that."

"Dad will." Allison pulls a flowered tank top (the same one Peggy had admired and immediately put back when she saw it wasn't on sale) out from underneath her shirt and hands it to her, a triumphant look in her eye. "Happy late birthday."

"You're going to get caught one of these days."

"I'm careful. And it's not really stealing if it's for someone else."

"That's ridiculous," she says, but it's impossible to be mad at Allison when she looks so pleased with herself. "I didn't get you anything for your birthday."

"It's okay. You're still my favorite sister."

The top looks good on her, especially with the new pair of jeans Tessa had talked her into buying last week when they met before work. "Glenn likes you," Tessa had said, out of nowhere, as they waited in line at the Broadway. "He talks about you all the time."

"Are you guys a thing?" Peggy asked.

"Me and Glenn?" Tessa laughed. "Hell no. I mean, we were. A long time ago. Glenn's too old for me and he's living with some woman named Martha anyway. She works at a bank or something."

"How old is he?"

"Thirty last year. He had a huge party."

"Thirty," Peggy said, swallowing hard. "He's worked at the post office a long time then."

"Glenn's not going anywhere. He's fun but no one to get serious about. I'm sure you already know that."

"Of course."

HALFWAY through her shift on Monday, the parcel sorter goes down. Both maintenance technicians are out sick, so Mr. Acosta has the crew set up the old manual racks in the back of the building. The conveyor belt hasn't been used for a while and needs oil; there's a creaky frog sound way down in the mechanism. Glenn and Chico work farther down the belt from Peggy, talking how they might get some tickets for a Lakers game.

Tessa sings along to the radio on the PA system as a five-ton truck pulls up outside. Air brakes squeal, exhaust bellows, metal ramps clank down on the concrete loading dock. "Don't stop, believing," Tessa screeches.

"Did you hear Ray Martinez got promoted?" John says as he comes back from his break. "White guys don't stand a chance around here anymore with that fucking Mexican for a fucking district manager." The acne scars glow red on his pasty white face, and Peggy hopes no one heard what he said or, even worse, assumes she agrees with him. Too late. Peggy sees Gloria's dark eyes flash.

John takes his spot across the belt and ties a green canvas

work apron over his T-shirt. "Fucking Ray Martinez." He picks a cardboard box containing Bank of America checks out of the stack, looks at the address label, and hurls it across the conveyor belt into the outgoing sack marked Anaheim.

"You need to work on your vocabulary," Russ says, from the end of the belt where he is dumping more parcels out of canvas sacks.

"What do you even know about fucking, John?" Gloria asks. Tessa stops singing. They all look at each other and laugh. The rumor is John's a virgin.

"Good one, Gloria," Glenn says.

Peggy feels bad when she sees John's face but still wishes she'd thought of something clever to say, wishes Glenn was grinning at her like that.

"Cut the chatter. You've got airport dispatch at ten fifteen," Mr. Acosta says, as if they don't know what time the mail needs to leave for LAX. Gloria starts to replace a full sack and Glenn steps in to help her. Peggy lifts her arms and twists her hair up on top of her head, watching him buckle the latch. *Ask me if I want to go to the Laker game. Ask me anything.*

"Who are the Lakers playing?" she asks as a box of checks projectiles in a perfect arc off John's cocked wrist, straight past her face, ricocheting off the side of Gloria's head.

"God damn it, John!" Gloria yells. "You could have put my eye out."

Everyone freezes. John stares straight at Peggy, his eyes flat and angry, and she wonders for a half second if he really meant to hit her. Mr. Acosta scurries over in full supervisory glory, barking out orders. "Gloria, go see the nurse. Walk with her, Peggy. John, you come with me. The rest of you finish the dispatch. It's almost ten fifteen." He and John head off in the direction of the supervisor's office. Gloria makes a beeline to the women's locker room, and Peggy has to walk fast to keep up with her.

"Aren't we supposed to go to the nurse's office?"

"What's the nurse going to do? I'll be here all night filling out forms."

In the locker room, Gloria pulls wads of brown paper towels out of the dispenser and wets them in the sink, then goes to the couch in the back behind the lockers, lies down, and puts the towels on her face.

"I hope this doesn't leave a scar."

"Let me see."

Gloria lifts the wad of towels off her face. There's a bluish-black mark next to her right eye and a red broken vein the same shape as a box corner.

"It might. Do you want an Advil? I have some in my locker."

"I want a beer. You know Glenn is with someone already."

"What?"

"John's jealous."

"Of who?"

"Of you, flirting with Glenn."

"I wasn't flirting with anyone."

"Whatever. I'm going to lie here until it's time to clock out."

"You sure you're okay?"

"Go. Glenn's probably wondering where you are."

"I'm sure he isn't." *This feels like some grade-school drama*, she thinks as she hurries back to the parcel racks, *except I was never part of any dramas. I was always the observer.*

"Gloria okay?" Russ asks. He and Tessa are hanging empty sacks.

"Pissed. But all right."

"The union rep is in Acosta's office with John. He'll most likely get a letter of warning."

"So much for him supervising," Tessa says.

"He's too hot-headed," Russ says. "He lets this place get to him."

"Why would anyone want to supervise?" Tessa says. "We make more money."

"You've got a point," Russ says. "At least we get paid for our overtime."

"Chico and Glenn are going to the Hunt Room after work," Tessa says. She blows a blond strand out of her eye as she hangs the last sack on its hook. "We're invited."

"I'm going home," Russ says. "If you girls had any sense, you would too."

"If we had any sense, we wouldn't be working here." Tessa takes off her gloves.

"It's a paycheck. With benefits." Russ heads toward the men's locker room.

"If I ever get that old," Tessa says, "will you please shoot me?"

"I'm going home too. I have school tomorrow."

"Okay. Do me a favor and put my gloves away, will you? I'm going to catch up with Glenn and Chico."

"Do you guys ever go out on Friday nights? I don't have class on Saturday."

"We go out every night."

SHE'S never been in a bar before and expects something a little more glamorous than a dark, smelly room off to the side of a bowling alley with some guy vomiting his guts out right outside the door. Once inside, she orders a Diet Coke and goes over to the jukebox to study the titles.

"Anything good?" Glenn stands close and she smells juniper

and spices, and imagines him taking off his shirt in the locker room, rolling on deodorant, and splashing on aftershave. Her face reddens.

"I've got quarters," she says. "What would you like to hear?"

His eyes trace down her tank top toward her Doc Martens and then slowly back up to her face. "I know a place with better music. Want to follow me?"

Tessa and Gloria are watching from the bar. She sees John glance over his shoulder and turn away. She remembers Martha, who works in the bank.

"I should go home. I have a test Monday."

"Suit yourself." He turns and walks over to the pool table. "Who's buying the next round?"

What is wrong with you? she asks herself on the drive home. It would just be sex. It doesn't have to mean anything. She knows how to compartmentalize. She isn't one of those girls, like her sister, who believes she has to be in love to go to bed with someone. And she isn't going to be working with these people forever anyway. She has bigger plans.

THE following Friday night, she and Glenn work the parcel sorter together alone, in the back of the building. She likes working with him, keeping time with the machine's steady output, pulling down full sacks and replacing hampers. It's almost like a dance. He tells her he owns a house in Norco and was married once, no kids. She notes his emphasis on 'no kids.' He plays softball and likes skeet shooting and four-wheeling in his truck. She asks if he's ever wanted to work somewhere else and he shrugs. "Sure. But the pay's good. And I get five weeks' vacation now."

She can lift more than when she'd started, but the last pouch is too heavy. He takes it from her, and she hates how her hands look. Her nails never come clean and her cuticles are ripped and dry. She jumps when Chico whistles from across the floor.

"Wash up time! Let's go!"

"I'm in the black four-wheel drive with paper plates," Glenn says. "First row of the lot." He turns and walks toward Chico.

"Should I follow you?" She's not even sure if she's said the words out loud, but when he's about thirty feet away, he raises his right hand and gives her a thumbs-up.

EVEN with no traffic, Norco is a long drive and she has too much time to worry that she's misunderstood. Is Chico going to be there too? And Martha? And if they aren't? She's on the pill and she has condoms in her purse. She's not a virgin, not since she was sixteen and followed a friend of a friend up to a hotel room at her cousin Teresa's wedding. It was surprising, how quickly it happened, how soon she was back at the reception, watching the man dance with his wife. She never told anyone, not even Allison, and she never saw the man again. It was exactly the way she'd planned it. But this is different. She will see Glenn again, every day until she finally can quit this job. It would be a mistake to sleep with him, so she won't.

Chico isn't at Glenn's house, and there's no evidence of a Martha either. The kitchen is a mess and the bathroom worse. Glenn says he wants to show her something, so she follows him back to his bedroom. She won't stay much longer; she'll make an excuse and go home soon.

He pulls out a skeet gun, and she sits down on the corner of the unmade bed. He shows her how to load and unload it, and explains how he cleans it after every use. It gets later. She yawns.

"I should go," she says.

"Stay," he says. "I mean, if you want to." He grins. He's nervous, she realizes, which is surprisingly charming. *He wants to make sure I'm okay with this. He wants it to be my idea.* She moves closer. He puts the gun away, sits down next to her, and kisses her. His lips are warm, his hands are suddenly everywhere. She doesn't know what to do with her arms or legs or mouth or tongue, but he does. He knows exactly what to do with all of her.

"You're something else," he says.

She can't sleep and gets up before sunrise to avoid any awkwardness about breakfast or showers or the fact that he has the day off and she doesn't. She lifts the sheet silently before she leaves and takes a quick look at his body. His legs are long and tanned, his stomach is flat, and the hairs on his groin are brown and gray. He is breathtaking, and she feels wonderful.

Her mother's up when she gets home, sitting at the kitchen table going through the classifieds, circling items with a red pen. "Where have you been?"

Peggy opens the refrigerator door, trying to avoid eye contact. "I spent the night at Tessa's house. We got to talking, and I didn't call because I figured I'd wake you."

"I was worried. This isn't like you."

She takes out a carton of yogurt and glances over at her mother, who has stopped studying the newspaper and is staring right at her as if she knows she's lying. "Are you looking for a job, Mom?"

"There's nothing but telephone sales, and I'm not even qualified for that. Next time call me, Peggy. I don't care how late it is."

ALL through her Saturday shift, she thinks about how Glenn might be waiting in the parking lot after work. This time she will definitely insist on a condom. She takes her time in the locker room, puts on lipstick, and combs out her ponytail. He's not there, which is fine. He probably went to some Halloween party and she has stuff to do. He's not there Sunday night after work either and he calls in sick on Monday. She's off Tuesday and Wednesday. She doesn't have his phone number. She didn't give him hers. On Thursday, he grins when he walks in the lunchroom and sees her open book on the table, her yellow highlighter, her peanut butter sandwich. He tells Chico to "quiet down, Peggy Sue's studying." She keeps her eyes on the chapter and tells herself this is working out exactly the way she wants it to.

Later, when everyone is working flats, Mr. Acosta says he needs someone to run the canceling machine and she volunteers. She takes her timecard from the rack and has a moment of regret when she sees the new girl, Jill, move into her empty spot, but then she feels Glenn's eyes on her ass as she walks away. She's glad she's worn the new jeans. She's strong and independent, a woman with her own mind, who will have a degree eventually and a much better-paying job. A woman who can take care of herself.

After work, Glenn is waiting by her car.

When they get to his house, she waits until he goes into the bathroom, and then she uses the phone in his kitchen to call home. She leaves a message that she's staying with Tessa tonight, takes a couple of condoms out of her purse, sets them on Glenn's nightstand, and undresses. The sex is even better this time, and when he kisses her goodbye in the morning, he circles her wrists with his fingers and grins his Glenn grin. His eyebrows arch. "I always knew I should be with someone smarter than me."

She tells her heart to stop beating so fast. "You're only after me for my brains?"

"I never met anyone like you before."

As she drives home on the Riverside Freeway, she takes in the panorama of mountains: the San Gabriels to the north, Saddleback to the east, and way out in the distance, San Jacinto. She thinks of early settlers following a dusty trail through this pass in their covered wagons, the optimism they must have felt, yearning for a glimpse of the Pacific Ocean. Bob Dylan croons on the car speakers, telling some lady to lay with him. She turns it up and sings along. She'll buy a brass bed and a silky robe once she gets her own place.

It would be foolish to quit the post office now and miss out on all the Christmas overtime money. Dylan begs the lady to stay as the freeway curves south into the suburban sprawl of Orange County and—despite the huge inflated Santa Claus towering over a car dealership, the yellow haze of smog outlining the horizon, no sight of the Pacific Ocean at all—Peggy feels as optimistic as those early pioneers, as if she can finally breathe.

CHAPTER SIX

DAD'S DEFINITELY SETTLED IN, ALLISON THINKS AS SHE GLANCES AROUND Linda's condo at his magazines piled on the coffee table, his tie draped over the staircase, his shoes by the couch, suit jacket on the chair. He and Linda wear matching sweatpants and are barefoot. Linda doesn't even have a pedicure. Her mother would have made him put his clothes away as soon as he came home from work and would never go barefoot without painting her toenails.

They are celebrating Frank's birthday by eating pizza off paper plates and passing around a bowl of ripped-up lettuce and tomatoes that Linda apparently thinks constitutes a salad. Frank keeps saying how much he's missed them until Allison finally asks, "Then why did you leave?" That shuts him up for a minute, but Peggy hasn't stopped talking since they got here. She's told him every single thing that's happened at work and all about her classes, how much she loves learning about taxes. How much she appreciates the car. It's a major suck-up and it's disgusting.

Linda has a stereo system that plays six CDs at a time. Tonight, it's all Tom Petty, and Linda and Frank keep singing along and smiling at each other. They know the lyrics to every song. Tom Petty's nasal voice makes her skin crawl. She picks up a *Rolling Stone* magazine. The cover is the creepy, old lead singer from Aerosmith next to his daughter Liv Tyler, who is beautiful and talented and didn't even know who her real father was until she was eight years old. How cool would that be—finding out your real father is a rich and famous rock star?

"Are you buying me a car too?" she asks once Peggy takes a breath from her monologue.

"You don't even know how to drive," Peggy says.

"Kevin's teaching me." Which isn't true, although he keeps promising.

Frank's eyes light up when she mentions Kevin, her one accomplishment. "Has he picked out a college yet? I'm sure a lot of schools are interested."

"Didn't you see that photo of him in the newspaper?" Peggy says. "Where he's sitting on the bench crying after the last game?"

"He wasn't crying," Allison says. Which also isn't true. Kevin's been in a horrible mood since that photo.

"It wasn't his fault they lost," Frank says.

"You're right, it wasn't." According to Kevin, everything is her fault. She distracts him with too many questions. She's too demanding. She's never satisfied. "Kevin hasn't made up his mind about college yet. He's not sure he's going."

Frank laughs. "Don't be silly. Of course, he's going to college."

People are always telling her not to be silly. She should be used to it. The truth is no schools have made any offers. "We're going to look for an apartment near Santa Cruz after we graduate." Kevin's never mentioned Santa Cruz, but she likes the sound of it.

Frank looks nervous. Peggy rolls her eyes. "How are you going to afford that?"

"We'll get jobs."

"Doing what? Working in a diner?" Peggy turns to their father. "That's her big dream."

"She doesn't have to decide right now. She has plenty of time."

People are always talking about her as if she isn't there. She should be used to that too.

SOME mornings her mother's like she used to be. Dressed in gym clothes, breakfast on the table, making a list of ingredients for dinner, excited about some new outfit or eyeliner or celebrity gossip. Nagging them to put their dishes in the dishwasher, hoping they've remembered to squeegee the shower. Wanting to know what their friends are up to and what's going on in school.

This is not one of those mornings. Brenda stares blankly at the television with uncombed hair, wearing a dirty nightgown. Allison hates to leave her alone, but she can't wait to get away. Kevin honks the horn and she runs down the driveway to his little white Datsun truck. He kisses her hello and lights a joint. She loves how time slows and the colors of the trees vibrate and the song on the radio is always her favorite. He kisses her again before they get out. She keeps her head down in class, so the teacher won't call on her, closes her eyes, and feels the room pulse around her, grasping at individual words from the lecture, stringing them together, trying not to laugh at how nothing makes sense and everything's funny and beautiful and sad at the same time.

Kevin has really nice weed these days, mellow bud from Hawaii, regular strength, not dipped in anything psychedelic. He's sorry he's been so grouchy. He doesn't mean to take things out on her. At break time, she stands with him and his friends near the amphitheater, watching the seagulls fly overhead and then swoop down to the trash on the ground as the dramas play out. Danielle's in a terrible mood because she didn't get the part she wanted in the school play. Katy's in tears because McKenzie is flirting with her boyfriend. McKenzie's trying to make her boyfriend jealous, but he's not paying attention because he flunked his English test and might get cut from the team.

No one seems to realize how insignificant all of it is, how

Ocean View is just a tiny speck on the spinning globe, how high school represents such a tiny percentage of life. What matters is Kevin loves her and only wants her to be happy. She doesn't have to say anything. She has nothing to prove. She just needs to look nice and stand next to him. He puts his hand in the back pocket of her shorts and she knows her place in the world.

"Let's get out of here at lunch," Kevin whispers. "Let's go get stoned and fuck."

AFTERWARD, Kevin has practice, so they drive back to Ocean View and she sits in the bleachers with Katy, McKenzie, and Danielle. They're discussing this Saturday's party at McKenzie's house. Parties are their main conversational topic. What will they wear? Will they invite new blood or the same crowd? Who will hook up for the first time? Who might hook up with more than one guy? Not any of them of course because they are not skanks. They all wear today's uniform: short plaid skirts and tight white T-shirts. McKenzie called everyone last night to let them know. It would be expensive, being friends with these girls, if she had to pay for every outfit. Luckily, she has her own resources.

Katy says it's too bad Kevin never has parties.

"His parents have always been really strict," McKenzie says. "They don't even drink."

Everyone nods. Everyone knows there's no alcohol at the Nelson house, which her friends think is sad, but Allison finds a relief. She fingers the Swiss Army knife in her pocket, wondering why her father hasn't looked for it. It's the classic model with sixteen functions, and as long as she can remember, her dad's had it with him, part of his charm arsenal, at the ready in case anyone needs a bottle opener or a nail file or a pair of tweezers.

"Kevin always has the best weed," Danielle says.

"And coke," Katy says. "Can he get more?"

"Probably," Allison says. "I'm not doing lines right now. My sinuses are ruined."

"That's the kind of problem I'd like to have," Danielle says. "A boyfriend with enough coke to ruin my sinuses. You're really lucky."

"What's Kevin's house like?" McKenzie asks. "I don't know anyone who's ever been there except you."

"His mother's kind of a clean freak."

"What about your house?" Katy asks. "Can we party there?"

"My mom's always home."

"She doesn't work?" Danielle says.

"She's looking for a job, I guess."

"When my parents got divorced," Danielle says, "my dad took me to Hawaii because he felt so guilty."

"I have my own room at my dad's house," McKenzie says. "I have two sets of everything. Two entire wardrobes. Two Nintendos. Their divorce was the best thing to happen to me."

"My parents are just separated." She should give her dad the knife back. He must miss it by now.

SATURDAY morning, she flips the bacon in the frying pan, pours batter into the waffle iron, and tries not to worry. Last night she'd asked too many questions about Kevin's dealer, wondering if he could get weed instead of cocaine all the time.

"Did you read this article about DNA?" Peggy points to the front page of the *Orange County Register* spread out on the kitchen table. "They're testing dog hairs to figure out who was at Nicole's condo. Isn't it amazing what they can find out now from body fluids?"

"Gross. I don't understand that stuff."

Of course, Peggy knows all about it and thinks she has to explain it in excruciating detail. Allison wishes she could invite Kevin for breakfast, but her mother would freak out and he's probably still angry.

"So, there's more to it than just blood types," Peggy says. "Are you even listening?"

Kevin loves her. She just needs to stop being so nosy. "I'm listening. DNA is amazing. You want another waffle?"

"Sure," Peggy says. "These are delicious."

"I'm glad you like them." Waffles don't take much, flour, eggs, and milk, water if there's no milk. A splash of vanilla is the secret ingredient. It turns out she's good at putting together whatever she can find in the refrigerator, and it's even more fun to cook for someone who enjoys eating. Peggy isn't counting calories anymore. Her skin is clear and she's lost weight. Even her posture is better. She actually seems happy and Allison has an idea why.

"So," she says casually. "Why are you coming home at five thirty in the morning?"

Peggy flushes. "I already told Mom I spent the night at Tessa's house."

"I can tell when you're lying. What's his name?"

Peggy hesitates. "Glenn. Don't say anything to Mom though. Or Dad either."

"Why? They'd be happy for you. You've never had a boyfriend. When do I get to meet him?"

"It's not like that. We've decided not to tell anyone we're seeing each other. This just kind of happened."

"That's very . . . modern of you." Nothing ever "just kind of happens" to Peggy. "Are you sure you know what you're doing?" she asks as the phone rings.

"Go ahead, answer it," Peggy says.

"I don't want you to get hurt."

"It's just sex. I'm too young to be serious about anyone and so are you."

"Fine. Forget I said anything."

It's Kevin on the phone, saying his parents are gone for the weekend up to their cabin in Big Bear. "Come hang out. We'll have the place to ourselves." She almost skips to the sink after she hangs up.

"Salivate like a Pavlov dog," Peggy sings in a horrible off-key voice.

"What's that supposed to mean?" She takes her hooded sweatshirt from the back of her chair and slips her arms through the sleeves.

"Is that a bruise?" Peggy says.

"No." She zips up the hoodie quickly. The mark above her right elbow is the exact shape of Kevin's thumb and index finger gripping hard, pressing into the skin. It shocked her how angry he got, so quickly, but he was right, what he buys and where he gets it is his business, not hers.

"Let me see," Peggy says, in her big-sister voice, as if she can fix everything wrong in the world.

"You know how clumsy I can be. I'm always bashing into something." She takes her house key from the hook.

"Since when are you clumsy?"

"I have to go." Peggy would never understand. Peggy's too busy trying to fool herself into thinking she doesn't need anyone.

KEVIN'S in the living room, tapping out two lines of cocaine with a razor blade. She sits down next to him and looks around the meticulous room, trying to figure out why his house makes her so nervous. Normally she admires a lack of clutter. Peggy's piles of papers and stacks of books drive her crazy. Linda's messy condo is irritating. Even her immaculate mother has suddenly turned into a slob. But Kevin's house feels like no one really lives here.

"First, I want to say that I'm sorry about last night." He holds out a cutoff drinking straw.

She wasn't going to do any cocaine today, but his apologizing is a good start. "It's okay." She takes the straw and snorts the line. "I shouldn't ask so many questions. I'm sorry." The bruise doesn't hurt much right now, especially compared to the blood vessels throbbing in her nose.

He takes the straw and snorts his line. "I have to be able to trust you."

"Of course."

"My connection is Bledsoe. My mom's partner?"

"That guy in the picture in your room?" She closes her eyes for a moment, wondering if Advil might help. "Is he part of The Family?"

"It's complicated. Connie gets Sal's weed from him and she knows I buy weed from him too. But the coke's a different story. And you really can't tell Connie or Sal. Sal's convinced cocaine's evil and Connie promised him she'd stay away from it."

"I won't say anything." Something metallic tasting drips down the back of her throat. "I need some water." She goes in the kitchen and fills a glass at the sink, staring out the back window. The only colors are green and gray. The grass is clipped, the creeping fig on the cinderblock wall has been recently trimmed, and the patio furniture is covered with plastic tarps. There's no sound, no movement, no bird, no butterfly. Even the sky is gray. She goes back to the living room.

"The cool thing is," Kevin says, "Bledsoe can get more coke if we can move it. And you know all the kids at school are interested. I told him we'd stop by. He's looking to expand. It's a huge opportunity, babe." He smiles. "I know you like weed better, but the real money's in coke." He stands. "Let's stop by your house first so you can change."

She looks down at her jeans and Nirvana T-shirt. "What's wrong with this?"

"Just show a little skin, babe. And remember, Sal and Connie can't know anything about this."

A damp fog has settled over the coast and she feels ridiculous in the thin sundress and sandals. Her sinuses throb. Another infection. Kevin waves up at the security camera in front of Nelson's Jewels. After a buzzing noise, he pushes the door open and she follows him past glass cases, glancing quickly at the jewelry. Nothing she'd ever want: gaudy pieces old women would wear and children's silver rings in animal and fish shapes.

A man sits in the back office behind a large metal desk stacked with envelopes and a digital scale. There's an impressive steel safe behind him, a black leather briefcase on the floor next to the desk. A video monitor on the wall shows the sidewalk out in front of the store. The man stands, shakes Kevin's hand, and takes hers. He still has the same bushy mustache from the picture in Kevin's room, but now his hair is slicked back off his low, sloping forehead and his glasses are black Ray-Bans. He wears an untucked long-sleeved dress shirt over a pair of cuffed dark-washed jeans.

"Mr. Bledsoe," she says. "Nice to meet you."

"Just call him Bledsoe." Kevin sounds nervous. "Everyone does."

"I'm going to call you Red." Bledsoe's lips are thin under his mustache, and he has no chin.

"My name is Allison."

"Feisty." Bledsoe smiles.

"Red's a good nickname," Kevin says immediately.

"No worries. I like feisty. No offense meant, Red. I had a major crush on a redheaded girl once, but she was way out of my league."

I'm out of your league too, old man, she thinks, and then she feels bad. She wasn't in anyone's league either before Kevin.

"You like cocaine, Red?" Bledsoe asks. It's unnerving how he keeps staring at her when she can't see his eyes behind the dark glasses.

"Not really."

"She has sinus problems," Kevin says.

Bledsoe laughs. "Perfect. I mean, sorry about the sinuses, but the idea is to sell it, not snort it. A lot of people don't understand that part."

"Absolutely," Kevin says. "Not a problem with us."

"The problem is your parents. You know we have an agreement."

"They'll never know."

"Can you keep secrets, Red?"

"Sure."

"I'm assuming you'll need me to front you the money. These days, kilos start around seventeen K."

Allison's eyes open wide. "Seventeen thousand dollars?"

"You okay, Red?"

"That's a lot of money."

"A lot of responsibility too. I'm taking a big risk with you two."

"We're good for it," Kevin says.

"Let's start with a quarter kilo and see how it goes." Bledsoe opens a desk drawer and takes out a package the size of a brick, triple-wrapped in plastic. "You bring anything to put it in?"

Kevin looks at her and she shrugs. "My backpack's in the car. Will that be big enough?"

"Go get it," Bledsoe tells Kevin. "I'll wait here with Red."

"Back in a flash."

She hears the front door open, close, and then lock.

"You're a senior this year too?"

"Yes, sir."

He shakes his head. "Don't make me feel old. What are you going to do when you graduate?"

"Get a place somewhere. We're trying to save money. We really appreciate this opportunity, Mr. Bledsoe."

"Please call me David."

She hears a buzzer and looks over at the monitor. Kevin is at the front door with her backpack slung over his shoulder. David takes off his sunglasses. His eyes are almost colorless.

The buzzer again.

"Kevin's impatient," he says. "Not a good quality in any profession."

"Doesn't Connie know you deal cocaine?"

He smiles. "Let's just say Connie is a practical woman." He pushes a button and the front door unlocks. "You good at math, Red? Ever use a scale?"

"No."

"I bet you're a fast learner."

"YOU made a great impression," Kevin says later when they drive back to his house, her backpack loaded with small envelopes of cocaine. "He really liked you, I could tell."

She has a headache. "I'm not sure I want to go to McKenzie's party tonight. I think I'm getting a sinus infection."

"Are you kidding? We have to go. You look hot and we've got party favors. The holiday season is just getting started, babe."

CONNIE'S Thanksgiving dinner is too rich and unfamiliar: turkey stuffed with oyster dressing, brussels sprouts roasted with feta cheese, sweet potato soufflé topped with rum sauce. Allison isn't hungry. She watched Kevin play *Mortal Kombat* on his Nintendo all morning. The graphics are incredible, but the violence is nauseating. They each did a thick line of coke and then her nose started bleeding. When he went to get ice, she took a quick look in his gym-sock drawer where he hid the stack of small ziplock baggies full of cocaine. There weren't as many bags as before. She hopes he's sold them. He was right, the kids all want to buy some, but they don't always bring enough money. Kevin can be a little too generous, although it's hard to believe now since he barely speaks during the meal except to grunt sarcastically a few times when Sal tries to draw him into conversation. Connie's quiet too. Allison fills the silence by chattering away about school, the little she knows about the O. J. trial, and what her sister says about the post office. She almost wishes she'd gone to dinner at Marie Callender's with her mother and Peggy. Connie won't let her help wash dishes, so she and Kevin follow Sal out to the back patio.

Sal lights the tiki torches against the cinderblock walls and takes a joint from his shirt pocket. "Since Connie's still busy in the kitchen . . ."

"She won't like that," Kevin says, glancing over his shoulder toward the house.

"It's Thanksgiving. I've been saving this. Purple Haze. Definitely something to be thankful for."

"I'd like a hit." Allison sees Kevin's scowl, but she's edgy from the cocaine and this seems like a chance to get to know Sal.

He hands the joint to her, then leans back in his chair and

stretches, looking up at the sky. "Man, I wish we could see more stars here. It just never gets dark enough. We should all take a trip out to Joshua Tree."

"I've never been." Allison holds the smoke in and then exhales deeply, enjoying the deep resin taste and piney scent. "What's it like?"

"Incredible. You can see the entire Milky Way. Totally blows my mind."

"Your mind is already blown," Kevin says. "Sal believes in flying saucers."

"Really? Have you ever seen one?"

"Unidentified flying objects. I sure have. A couple of times. There's no way we're the only intelligent life forms in the universe."

"Shut up, Sal. You're embarrassing yourself."

"This weed is really nice."

"Herb is sacred." Sal gives her a spacey smile, and in the light from the torches, his teeth look slightly yellow and there's dandruff on his shoulders. The kinds of things her mom would notice.

"Cocaine is evil," Sal says.

"Here we go," Kevin says. "Sal's on his soapbox. Cocaine ruined his hippie paradise."

"It's true! People got greedy. I can't wait for Connie to get out of the business, so we can retire and spend more time in the desert."

"The jewelry business?" She's not sure what Sal is talking about anymore.

"Shut the fuck up, Sal," Kevin says. "You talk too much."

"Chill out, son! Allison's practically family. We can trust her. Can't we trust you, sweetheart?" He gives her the spacey smile again. "Man, you sure are one beautiful creature."

"Of course, you can trust me," she says as he blows a perfect smoke ring. "That's so cool! Can you teach me?"

"Don't encourage him," Kevin says.

Sal shakes a warning finger at her, and when he starts laughing again, she can't help but laugh too.

Kevin's angry now. "You'd better put that out."

"I guess I've had enough. Thank you, Sal."

"It's my pleasure, milady." Sal bows with a courtly flourish of his hand as he stubs the joint out in the ashtray next to him.

"Listen to you two," Kevin says. "All best buddies. You want me to leave you alone?"

"Kevin! Don't be rude!"

"Shut up, Allison." Kevin's expression is almost cruel. She blinks hard and swallows.

"Allow me to apologize for my ill-mannered progeny," Sal says. "He can't help it. His birth parents were speed freaks. It's genetic."

"What the hell's that supposed to mean?" Kevin says.

"They had addictive personalities. Compulsive behavior is hereditary. Like how you always say and do things without thinking them through. You come by it naturally."

"What are you, a shrink now?"

"All I'm saying is you can't change until you accept who you are, son."

"I'm not your son, as you've already pointed out. Those tweakers gave me away."

"To us," Connie says, suddenly appearing in the doorway, holding a tray loaded with praline pecan pie and a bowl of freshly whipped cream. "Because we wanted you." She glances at the roach in the ashtray and gives Sal a disapproving look.

As Allison stands to help Connie, she realizes how stoned she is and how tall she must seem, looming over all of them with her freckled skin, like an out-of-place giraffe, her mind tripping over Sal's description of Kevin's parents. Addictive. Compulsive. Genetic. She carefully passes around the forks and napkins, then sits down, twists her hair into a knot on top of her head, and secures it with a pink rubber band that seems to have miraculously materialized on her wrist but was obviously there the entire time.

Connie bends over to kiss Kevin's cheek. "We have a lot to be thankful for."

There are gray roots in the part of her hair. Something else her mother would notice. Kevin scowls and stares at the ground. They eat the pie in silence.

WHEN Allison comes downstairs the next morning, Brenda's standing at the kitchen table next to Peggy's pile of papers and books. "What is this?" She hands her what looks like a worksheet.

"You shouldn't mess with Peggy's stuff, Mom. You know how she gets. It's probably something for school."

"I certainly hope not. Read it."

INCOME STATEMENT	
INCOME	
Recurring Item	Good sex
Non-Recurring Items	Overnight sex
Extraordinary Items	Orgasms
Total Income	*Hard to quantify*
EXPENSES	
Research and Development	Cost of new clothes, hair, and nails
Tax	All the other women he sees
Total Expenses	Unaffordable
NET INCOME	**OBVIOUSLY NEGATIVE**

Allison laughs. "Well, at least she's having orgasms. Extraordinary orgasms, apparently. I don't get the part about other women though. Maybe it's a joke?"

"Your sister doesn't make jokes. Do you know who this person is?"

"No idea." Hopefully, *negative net income* means Peggy's not seeing that Glenn character anymore. "How was Marie Callender's?"

"The turkey was dry, the cranberry sauce was bland, but the pies were good. How was Thanksgiving with the Nelsons?"

"Connie's food was weird. I wish you would have cooked."

This earns her a smile. "You'd better watch out for Connie. She has you married off to her son, already."

"Would that be so horrible?"

It's a real question. She can't decide which was worse, Kevin's rudeness last night or Sal's description of him as genetically flawed. She wonders if her mother has read anything about addictive personalities in any of her magazines. When Brenda actually looks at her and seems concerned, Allison believes for a split second she's rediscovered her mother's intuition and is about to offer some good advice, the way she used to. Or maybe she's finally going to say something about Allison's miserable grades or ask if she's signed up to take the SATs or applied to a college or thought about a job.

"I don't understand why in the world you'd want to be part of Kevin's family. Aren't you afraid he'll end up just as fat as his parents?"

"He's adopted." She stands. "Why do you always have to be so shallow and horrible?"

"You're just like your father. Neither one of you has any imagination or ambition."

"I'm leaving." She slams the door behind her.

There's nothing wrong with being like her father who obviously had enough imagination and ambition to get the hell away from her mother. She can't wait to do the same thing.

THERE'S a black leather briefcase on Connie's kitchen counter, which Allison suddenly realizes is the same kind of case Bledsoe uses and is probably where she keeps the weed she brings home for Sal. If only she had enough nerve to ask if she could borrow a little, just enough for a couple of joints. Sal wouldn't mind. "How much do you know about Kevin's birth parents?" she asks instead, surprising herself. "Were they part of The Family?"

Connie gives her a steely look and sets her keys down next to the briefcase. "Why in the world would you ask about them?"

"Sal said something about them having additive personalities. Were they really speed freaks?"

Connie seems angry. "Sal shouldn't have told you that. They were young and had a lot of problems. Kevin isn't like them at all."

"It's just . . . he can be sort of impulsive. Like, sometimes, he gets really angry."

"That doesn't mean he has an addictive personality. You need to help him learn how to control his impulses. All he wants is for someone to love him."

"I do love him."

"You need to make sure he knows that. I'm a little worried about his acne. Is he still using his medication?"

"I think so. I know he takes those vitamins."

"I thought regular sex might help, but his skin has really flared up lately. Are you two getting along okay in that department?"

"What?" Her face flames red. Is this what she is to Connie—

her son's provider of regular sex? "Why would you ask that? Did he say something to you?"

"Oh, no dear. And I'd appreciate it if you don't mention this conversation to him either. His acne's most likely stress related. He's trying so hard to get his grades up. And he's worried about the SAT scores."

"I guess." She starts backing out of the kitchen.

"You're not going to break up with him, are you?" There's somewhat of a threat in Connie's voice. "Because you can't do that now, when he has so much on the line."

"I'm worried he's going to break up with me."

"You can't let that happen now. This isn't a good time for him to be distracted." Connie picks up the briefcase and keys. "You're his rock, Allison. I don't know what we'd do without you."

"CONNIE barely left for work," she says when she sees the mirror on Kevin's bed. He snorts two lines and holds out the straw.

"No thanks. She's in a weird mood today."

Kevin barks out a laugh. "Connie's weird period. Ignore her." He snorts the other two lines and stretches out on the bed. "Come here."

She's not a Pavlov dog or whatever Peggy said the other day. "Seriously. I don't think she likes me."

"Buy her something nice for Christmas. She'll like that."

She has the twenties she lifted from Linda's purse. Maybe the right gift would help. "What are you getting her?"

Kevin slides behind her. He smells like an old gym towel. "I'll write her a card, tell her I love her."

She turns to look at him, sure he's kidding. "Seriously? That's really sweet, Kevin."

"Don't act so surprised. I'm a nice guy. And Sal buys her those statues she likes and puts my name on it."

Connie's already shown her the statues. "Lladro, from Spain," she'd explained, adding how nice it was to have a girl in the house who admired beautiful things and that she'd always wanted a daughter. *They could have adopted a girl instead of Kevin*, she thinks now, *and then I never would have met him.* Or maybe we would have found each other anyway. I'm supposed to be his destiny. Kevin's fingers are under her T-shirt now, unhooking her bra. He kisses her neck.

He loves her, she knows that. She wishes she was smart enough to think of the right things to say and do to help him. "Let's take a shower together." She slips off her clothes, drops them on the chair next to the bed, and starts the shower. She hands him the shampoo and the soap. He lathers, rinses, and presses against her.

"Let's get out," she says, suddenly claustrophobic. She reaches for a towel and uses it as a cushion against the cold porcelain sink. The mirror is fogged. He grips the sides of her waist, his fingernails cutting into her skin. "Easy," she says. "Easy." He doesn't stay hard long enough for either of them to come, which isn't that unusual these days. He puts one arm around her neck, wiping the fog in the mirror with his other hand. The pupils of his eyes are surrounded by too much white. "Look at how beautiful you are. I love you so much."

She has to look away. Things will get better once they have their own place. She just needs to be patient.

ALLISON ditches her last class and rides her bike to Huntington Center. She studies three different models of Oakleys at the Sunglass Hut and gives the clerk her friendliest smile. "I can't decide. I'll have to come back." She'd already slipped the most expensive pair into her purse when she asked if he knew what time it was, and he glanced away to look at the clock. The sunglasses are a gift for Kevin to cheer him out of his latest bad mood.

She stops by the Gap next and finds the pink turtleneck McKenzie told everyone to wear on Friday. She takes two different sizes into the dressing room, but the salesclerk is swamped and doesn't notice that she only puts one back on the rack. The other one is folded neatly at the bottom of her purse. She makes eye contact with the clerk on her way out and says thank you because it's important to be polite and friendly and to keep an unimpressed expression on her face.

The Lladro pieces at the Broadway are locked up tight in a glass case. The snooty salesclerk claims he doesn't have the key, and she doesn't like the expressions on the figurines' faces anyway, too pastel and bland. She notices tiny crystal bud vases sitting out on a display case on her way out of the store and slips one in her purse for Connie. The lipstick from the makeup counter tucked in the front pocket of her jeans is for Peggy, who needs to brighten up her look.

No one suspects a girl who looks like she doesn't need anything. She can slide a thin gold bracelet over her wrist like she does at J. C. Penney (a gift for her mother) and exchange her worn-out tennis shoes for a nicer pair and wear them right out of the store. The thrill is better than any drug she's ever smoked or swallowed or snorted, and lately it's even better than sex.

"Mom's on the warpath," Peggy says when she walks in the door. "The school called about you ditching last period."

"I don't know what you're talking about." Allison hears a scraping noise coming from the upstairs. "What's she doing now?"

"Stripping the wallpaper in our bathroom."

"That wallpaper is almost brand-new."

"That wallpaper is hideous." Brenda comes down the stairs, wearing her paint-splattered sweats and a scarf tied around her hair. There are dark circles under her eyes. "Do you realize I could get fined every time you ditch a class?"

"I wasn't feeling well so I went out to Kevin's truck and lay down. It's no big deal. Just write me a note."

"I don't want you skipping class. If you aren't feeling well, go to the nurse's office. Don't just leave."

"Do we have wrapping paper? I got a present for Connie."

"What? Something to eat?"

"I got her a vase."

"There might be some wrapping paper in the Christmas box in the garage. I have work to finish." Brenda goes back upstairs.

"She's destroying the house," Peggy says.

"That way Dad can't sell it," Allison says.

"He just won't get as much for it. He's still selling it. I hope you paid for that vase."

"All you think about is money. I saw your orgasm spreadsheet. You shouldn't leave that stuff lying around. Mom totally freaked out." Peggy turns bright pink, which is satisfying for a brief moment. "How many other women is Glenn seeing?"

"I told you it wasn't serious. You're not going to graduate if you don't go to class. And you're going to get arrested if you keep stealing."

"I'm careful. I just hope you know what *you're* doing."

WHEN she puts the present under Connie's tree later, Kevin says he has something for her and hands her a small box. "I've been an asshole lately. I'll do better." The ring is silver and shaped like a dolphin leaping over the waves, one of the kids' rings from Connie's store.

"I love it," she says, although it barely fits her pinky finger. It's the thought that counts and it's almost Christmas, when only good things are allowed to happen.

CHAPTER SEVEN

THE PIANO PLAYER IS INTO A MEDLEY OF CHRISTMAS CAROLS WHEN BRENDA walks into the Alibi just before 10:00 p.m. A few people sing along, but other than Bill in his white dress shirt and Christmas tie, standing and waving from across the room, there's no one she recognizes from the post office. No witnesses to report back to Frank. All that effort of shaving her legs, blowing her hair dry, putting on makeup, polishing her nails, and squeezing into this slinky black dress that she doesn't remember being so tight was a complete waste of time.

So many things are not worth the effort anymore. Making the bed because she's going to get back in it. Talking to either one of her daughters because one of them consistently lies to her and the other ridicules everything she says. Answering the telephone because it's either someone wanting to talk about delinquent payments or it's Bill, wanting her to meet him for a drink. She should have put a stop to his calls months ago, but she needs an occasional adult conversation. She finally suggested the Alibi, a dive bar in a strip mall with cheap drinks, popular with the post office crowd.

"You look terrific." Bill nearly crushes her in a bear hug. "What do you want to drink?"

"Chardonnay." He waves at the waitress and Brenda wiggles out of his embrace. It's invigorating to smell a man's cologne again, but she wishes she had other options besides Bill to make Frank jealous. *If* he finds out. Right now, there's no one to tell him.

"Single life agrees with you," Bill says.

"I'm not exactly single."

"No one ever accused Frank of being the sharpest tool in the shed. He's a fool to let you get away."

This is exactly what she needs to hear. The waitress sets her wine down on the table. Brenda takes a long sip. "Linda seems pretty sharp."

"Linda's a little too ambitious for my taste. I don't get the attraction. She's always seemed like a career girl to me, and Frank won't do her much good in that department."

It almost sounds like he thinks Frank's not good enough for Linda, and she's certainly not going to try and convince him otherwise. "Is Sue working a lot of Christmas overtime?"

He flinches at Sue's name. "Not yet. The mail volume is way down this year. The internet's going to be the death of the post office."

Everyone she knows has claimed the post office is going out of business since she met Frank twenty years ago. First, the fax machine was going to kill it off, then it was the computer, and now, the internet. This promises to be a dull evening. She'll finish this awful glass of wine and get out of here.

The back door of the bar opens, and a group of men and women come through in a blast of cold night air, all talking and laughing at once, wearing T-shirts and jeans, looking depressingly working class. It's the swing shift crowd, she realizes, probably the people Peggy works with. A cute blond says something to a man with long hair. And right behind him is Peggy with a huge smile on her face. Brenda scans the group, trying to figure out which man might be the subject of Peggy's spreadsheet.

"There's your daughter," Bill says. "I'll go buy them a round of drinks."

Before she can stop him, Bill's already making his way to the bar, shaking hands, playing the big wheel. Everyone, including

Peggy, looks over at her, so she waves. Peggy's happy expression immediately turns to one of disgust, and she spins around and heads toward the ladies' room. Brenda sighs, gets up, and follows her. Peggy stands at the sink, washing her hands.

"What are you doing in a bar? You're barely eighteen."

"I don't drink. What are you doing here with *him*?"

"I'm allowed to enjoy myself. I'm a grown woman."

"Then act like one." Peggy stomps out of the bathroom.

"I'm doing the best I can," she tells the mirror. She tries to outline her lips, but her hand trembles and she has to start over.

"You want to go someplace else?" Bill asks when she returns to his table.

She glances over at Peggy drinking a Diet Coke at the bar next to the blond. Peggy's a responsible person who deserves to have a little fun. They both do. It's almost Christmas.

"Let's go ask the piano player if he knows *Silver Bells*."

Bill stands next to Brenda and sings off-key, enthusiastically. The blond and a young man with bad skin join them. After three more carols, the piano player takes a break.

"I'll order another round." Bill heads to the bar.

"That was fun," the blond says. "I'm Tessa, by the way. This is John. We work with Peggy."

"It's nice to finally meet you. Peggy sure spends enough nights at your place. I hope she's a good houseguest."

Tessa gives her a confused smile. John looks confused period.

"Peggy's so great," he says.

"She's pretty great all right." The hope and despair on his ruined face tell her everything—Peggy's been lying about where she goes after work and he's the one from the spreadsheet.

"It's nice to meet you too," Tessa says. "Merry Christmas." She drags John back over to the bar.

If only his skin wasn't so bad or if he worked someplace else. Or was someone else. He doesn't deserve Peggy. None of these people do. Bill comes back with another glass of wine and his Jack and Coke and sits next to her. Brenda watches Peggy laugh at something the blond says and then pick up her purse and walk out the door. She smiles in relief.

"You're so pretty when you smile," Bill says.

"I'm not going to sleep with you."

Bill chokes on his ice. "Where did that come from?"

"It's good to see you, though. I'm glad you called."

Bill raises his glass. "You'll change your mind eventually."

"I might. But not tonight. Tell Sue we miss her in step class."

HER house looks silent and gloomy when she pulls the BMW past Peggy's car and parks in the garage. For the first time in her life, she's not put up any Christmas decorations. If she could have afforded it, she would have made travel plans, bought tickets to New Orleans. She opens Allison's door slightly and checks she's there, in her own bed, alone. She knows better than to open Peggy's door, so she says from the hallway, "I'm home, virtue intact." No answer. Zero sense of humor, that girl. "It was nice to meet your friends. John seems very taken with you."

Peggy groans. "I'm trying to sleep, Mom."

She tiptoes back down the stairs and turns on the television. There's a recap on the news about the jury and alternate jury selection for O. J.'s trial. Fifteen African Americans, six whites, and three Hispanics. Judge Ito has ordered them not to watch any television, read any newspapers or magazines, or set foot in any bookstore. *How lucky they are*, Brenda thinks. *I'd give anything to be one of them.*

A few nights later, she's half-asleep on the couch, trying to watch *It's a Wonderful Life* on television and wishing Allison would put that old pink aluminum tree in the trash where it belongs, when Peggy comes home from work.

"Oh good," she says. "You changed your mind about putting up a tree."

"This is your sister's idea. I should have thrown that ugly thing away a long time ago."

Allison straightens a pink branch. "I think it's cool. I saw the exact same tree at Pottery Barn."

"Don't be such a Scrooge, Mom," Peggy says.

Peggy's skin glows and her eyes shine. She looks happy, healthy, and full of life, remarkable considering she's worked ten hours today and will probably study for a few hours tonight and then work ten hours again tomorrow. *Oh, to be young.* "You're in a good mood."

"I feel good. There were a ton of Christmas cards when I started my shift, but we got every piece of mail out. It felt great to get it all sorted and ready for delivery tomorrow."

Allison laughs. "That's so lame."

Peggy smiles. "I know. I sound ridiculous. I never thought I'd like working there. I even crawled underneath the canceling machine tonight and rescued a handful of Christmas cards."

"Oh, honey. They shouldn't make you do that."

"It was my idea." Peggy laughs. "When my supervisor heard about it, he said I was a handy girl to have around. And then everyone started teasing me and calling me Handy."

"That's terrible," Brenda says. *What a low-class thing to say.*

"It was funny at the time." Peggy glances over at the pink tree. "So, are we going to decorate this thing or what?"

Allison gives her sister a grateful smile. "I'll be right back."

"I hope you're not going to get sucked into that job like your father did." *Frank always claimed he didn't want the girls to work at the post office. I never should have let this happen.*

"I'm going to quit eventually." Peggy is even more animated now. "I really think I can pass the first part of the EA exam by January. Those review manuals are really good."

"I know you told me what EA means, but I've forgotten." *Because it sounds even more boring than working at the post office.*

"Enrolled agent. Someone who can represent clients before the IRS."

"You really want to do taxes?" *God. How did I raise such an unimaginative child?*

"Eventually," Peggy says. "There are three parts to the EA exam, so I have a ways to go. I'm still going to get my BA so I can sit for the CPA exam."

"It sounds like alphabet soup."

They should be at someone's swanky Christmas party tonight, with tiny white lights in all the trees and a jazz band playing Christmas carols. They should be wearing crushed velvet dresses and posing for pictures next to a ten-foot noble fir, looking like sisters, celebrating the season. Instead, they're moping around a house with a SOLD sign out front, surrounded by cardboard boxes she's supposed to be packing, watching some corny movie they've seen a thousand times.

Allison comes back from the garage with a string of white lights, a handful of silver bells, and a few of the old Santa Claus ornaments. "Help us decorate, Mom."

She should enjoy both girls being in a good mood at the same time, but it's hard to get excited about Peggy crawling around the post office floor or Allison decorating that ridiculous tree with lights and bells she's probably stolen from the Pottery

Barn. Her daughter, the kleptomaniac. Brenda sighs. She should do something about that before Allison gets caught.

The girls had dinner at that woman's condo last night, and when Brenda picked them up, she'd made the mistake of glancing in the front window before she'd knocked on the door. Frank was sprawled on the couch with his arm around Linda, both wearing baggy sweatpants, Peggy next to them on the floor eating popcorn, Allison standing by Linda's Christmas tree telling a story, her face luminous, the lights making everything look so goddamned cozy. She was so jealous she could spit, but instead she had to knock on the door, say hello to that woman, grit her teeth so she wouldn't scream at Frank, and then drive her girls home, pretending everything was just fine. She closes her eyes. She should go to bed, but she's too tired to move.

"Is that her second bottle?" Peggy asks after a while.

"It might be her third," Allison says. "She's not that good at hiding the evidence."

Hiding evidence! Brenda keeps her eyes firmly closed and tries to count glasses. Surely, she hasn't opened a third bottle, and how much she drinks is none of their business. They have no idea what she's going through, what it feels like to be abandoned by everyone at Christmas. She has no friends. Tim didn't even send a Christmas card. That woman has stolen her family and hijacked her life. She deserves a few glasses of wine.

"She's getting a lot worse," Peggy says. "We should talk to Dad."

"Dad drinks more than she does," Allison says.

She should sit up and say something. She's cut down. She will cut down, after the holidays.

"You want to go outside and smoke a joint?" Allison asks.

"No thanks," Peggy says. "Pot makes me feel all fuzzy and confused."

"Fuzzy and confused are my favorite feelings," Allison says. "Reality sucks."

This could be one of those teachable moments she read about in the *Ladies Home Journal* except she agrees with Allison. Reality does suck and it feels so much better to blur all the sharp edges. The first glass of white wine goes down too fast, bitter and metallic. The second glass doesn't taste much better, but it's the floating feeling she's after, the lightheartedness, until halfway through her third glass, she starts to calculate how much is left in the open bottle, wondering if she has another in the refrigerator or maybe in the wine rack and if not, is she too loopy to drive to the grocery store? It's not enjoyable, it's anxiety-provoking, and she can quit anytime.

She will quit. Things will change in the New Year.

IT is almost noon the next day when the school calls about Allison ditching class. Again. This time there will be detention. Next time there will be suspension and fines. Brenda turns on the television. The world is falling apart. Russia is bombing Chechnya, a mountain lion has killed a woman in a park in San Diego, and Orange County has filed for bankruptcy. She changes the channel to Court TV and feels instantly better when she sees the familiar faces of O. J., Johnnie, Marcia, and Chris. One of the *Vanity Fair* reporters is explaining that lead defense counsel Robert Shapiro gave him an odd Christmas present, a large bottle of men's cologne—the brand, D.N.A.

"That's not odd," Brenda tells the screen. "That's hilarious."

Next up on Geraldo Rivera's show is a replay of an interview with Nicole's older sister. Denise Brown is everywhere lately, in the tabloids, in the *Register*, with Geraldo now, and on Diane Sawyer Sunday night, insisting O. J. murdered her sister. Denise has an even sturdier jaw and a much harder edge than Nicole. She claims she's a reformed alcoholic. Brenda doubts the jury believes her as she takes a sip of an overly sweet chardonnay from the Tiffany glass and grimaces. She doesn't like wine. She's not an alcoholic. She's simply trying to get through the day.

She hears a lawn mower start around four o'clock and looks out the front window. Surfer Boy has his shirt off, pushing the mower around the SOLD sign in the middle of her dead lawn. There are more weeds than grass to cut. December has turned warm and dry and the mower kicks up patches of dirt. *Good*, she thinks, *I need to talk to him about Allison ditching school.* His idea, she is sure.

When he shuts off the mower, she taps on the window and motions for him to come inside and then realizes too late she's still wearing her nightgown. She'd meant to take a shower and get dressed, but the day got away from her. There's an empty bottle of chardonnay on the counter and her breath probably smells like wine. She wishes she had some gum. She pulls Peggy's flannel shirt over her bare arms and opens the back door.

"Hey, Mrs. L," he says, raking his hair off his face with his fingers. "Allison said to tell you she went Christmas shopping with Katy and Danielle." He smells like cut grass and musk. His arms are muscular, his stomach flat, and she can't help imagining what he's like in bed. *He can probably go more than twice.*

"You're looking good, Mrs. L. Did you need something?"

There's something knowing in his pale blue eyes as if he's reading her mind. *Dear God, what is wrong with me?* "You're lying. Allison's not shopping. She got detention because you talked her into ditching school again." Her tongue feels thick and her words sound slurred. She takes a deep breath and forces herself to talk more slowly. "Stay away from her."

"She won't like that." Kevin glances around the kitchen,

takes in the dishes in the sink, the bottle on the counter, the empty crystal glass next to it. His eyes come back to her chest, and when he smirks, she looks down. Her nipples are visible through the thin fabric. She clutches Peggy's shirt around her. He gives her a lazy grin. "You all right, Mrs. L? You look a little chilly."

She'd like to slap him, but that would mean releasing Peggy's shirt. "I'm fine. You need to leave."

"You're fine all right." He opens the slider, gives her another knowing glance, and goes outside. She locks the door and paces from the dining room to the kitchen until he packs up the lawn mower and puts it back in the garage. He whistles as he walks back to his truck and drives away. She takes a shower, puts on a turtleneck sweater and a pair of jeans, then washes the dishes. In her haste the Tiffany glass slips straight through her fingers after she rinses it and shatters on the floor. She sinks down to her knees and picks up the glass shards, trying not to cry, replaying the conversation with Kevin over and over again until she's convinced herself there's nothing to worry about. He was the one who'd been rude.

WHEN she hears Allison stroll up the walkway an hour later, long legs in short shorts, hair flying loose, young and beautiful and recklessly bent on ruining her life, she quickly hides the broken glass in an empty envelope behind the toaster.

"I know about your detention," she says as soon as Allison comes inside. "They're going to suspend you if it happens again."

"I don't care." Allison opens the refrigerator. "I hate school."

"You're not allowed to see Kevin anymore."

Allison turns and glares at her and then her eyes widen. "You're bleeding!"

Brenda glances down at the blood dripping from her index finger to the floor. "It's nothing. I broke a glass." A wedding gift, she wants to add, but Allison won't care. It isn't like she's having any dinner parties these days anyway. She'll probably never have dinner parties again. She turns on the water in the sink and holds her finger under the cold stream, watching her blood run down the drain. And then she notices Allison staring at the empty wine bottle in the trash. She should have buried it deeper.

"I should call child services. You're drunk all day and there's nothing for dinner."

"I'm making a pot roast." Except she's forgotten to take it out of the freezer.

"I'm going to Kevin's house."

"No, you're not." Brenda turns to stop her, but Allison is too quick. "I'll call your father," she says as the door slams in her face. And tell him what? He'll blame her for everything, but he won't offer a solution. She needs a friend to talk to, but the only person she can think to call is her cousin, Tim, who isn't very sympathetic and reminds her, again, she's welcome to move into his dad's house.

"Allison could go to Savanna High School."

"We're not moving to Baja-Anaheim, Tim. Savanna's even worse than Ocean View."

"The neighborhood was okay when I lived there. I'm just trying to help."

Once again, she's hurt Tim's feelings. "I appreciate that."

"I have to go."

"Don't be mad at me." Tim's already hung up. She puts the envelope in the trash. The broken glass is beyond salvation.

THE Christmas decorations at the Irish Mist look like they've been up for a few years, judging from the dust. She sits at the bar and downs a glass of an awful Chardonnay, vinegary and sour, which turns to acid in her stomach and goes straight to her head because she hasn't had any alcohol since that unfortunate afternoon with Kevin and she hasn't eaten anything since breakfast. She wanted to make sure she fit in the new gold crushed velvet dress from the After-Christmas sale at Mervyns, much too dressy for the Irish Mist, especially with the three-inch stilettos, but perfect if Bill takes her out to dinner.

She orders another glass of the awful wine because she is young and beautiful and out in the world on a Friday night and not sitting home in her nightgown hoping Kevin hasn't told Allison anything.

The bartender pushes over a bowl of pretzels.

"Thank you, but I don't want to spoil my appetite. My friend's taking me out to dinner."

"Lucky friend."

"Might as well have another glass," she says, although she really doesn't want one and she's not sure how lucky the bartender will think she is once he sees Bill. She wishes she had someone else who didn't work at the post office to make Frank jealous. She wishes Peggy had better choices too. She came home on Christmas Eve proudly wearing a cheap gold chain linked around the word "Booty" as if it were some kind of a compliment. Probably a gift from John with the bad skin. "Like treasure, from a pirate ship," Peggy had insisted when Brenda told her she couldn't wear the necklace in public. Even Allison agreed it was vulgar.

When the pretzels are gone, and her glass is empty, she decides Bill isn't coming.

"Want me to call you a taxi?" the bartender asks when she wobbles a little on her stilettos.

"I'm fine." She doesn't have money for a taxi. There's barely enough in her purse to pay for the drinks and leave a tip.

She assumes a left-hand turn out of the parking lot onto Pacific Coast Highway is legal, and she's shocked when she realizes there's a center divider. She scrapes the bottom of her beautiful car going up and over two concrete curbs and swears when she sees the blue lights flash on top of a patrol car. The cop has no sense of humor.

"How much have you had to drink?"

She holds her index finger above her thumb. "Just a teensy glass." She feels her tongue catch on her teeth, and hands him her license and registration. She can't flirt her way out of the breathalyzer test or touch her finger to her nose or say the alphabet backward. She sits in the back of the patrol car and watches a tow truck hitch up her beautiful and now slightly dented car and haul it away.

At the Seal Beach police station, she tries calling Tim, who doesn't answer so she's stuck calling Frank. It's two o'clock in the morning by the time she gets in his truck. She's grateful he didn't bring Linda. She wonders what he told her.

Frank is furious. "You could have killed someone."

"The windows on the BMW are tinted too dark, which is the only reason that idiot pulled me over. I don't understand why public employees can't be more understanding."

"You could have killed yourself."

"You'd prefer that, wouldn't you? Me, lying in the morgue? Except then you'd be responsible for your daughters."

He exhales. He looks exhausted. "What responsibility are you taking? Allison says you drink all day and there's nothing in the house to eat."

She feels like she's been hit in the face with a glass of cold water. "She told you that?"

"I called Kevin's parents. They've agreed to let her live with them and finish high school."

"You can't decide this on your own, Frank."

"Someone needs to make a decision. Peggy told me your uncle's house is available. Why don't you move there?"

"That house is a dump. I don't appreciate you and Peggy plotting against me."

"Find someplace else then. Escrow closes in thirty days."

"When can I pick up my car?"

"They won't release it from impound until morning and they're not going to release it to you. You don't have a driver's license anymore."

"I'm aware, Frank. I said I was sorry." She waits for him to say he's sorry too. When he doesn't, she asks how much he thinks this will cost.

"Ginny's husband got a DUI last month and they're looking at more than ten grand."

"Oh." Jesus Christ. Jesus fucking Christ. "I had no idea."

"I'm not even going to ask what you were doing in Seal Beach."

"I had a date. I got stood up if it makes you feel any better." She could tell him who the date was, but more than likely he already knows and if he doesn't, she can't afford to hurt his feelings now. She can't afford anything.

"I wish you'd find someone else and stop being my problem."

"I'll always be your problem." She tries to smile. "You're the father of our daughters."

"Which is the only reason I bailed you out."

She watches out of the passenger window at the Christmas lights flashing by. The moon is full, the sky is clear, and she can almost pretend the two of them are going home from a party, like they have hundreds of times before.

"Happy New Year," she says when he drops her off, but he doesn't answer, doesn't even wait for her to get the front door open before he speeds away, hurrying home to Linda.

CHAPTER EIGHT

THE NECKLACE	
PROS	CONS
It's jewelry	It's not real gold
It's personal	I can't wear it in public
It means he likes my ass	He only likes me for my ass

PEGGY CURLS HER HAIR, PUTS ON LIPSTICK, AND CHANGES HER SHIRT THREE times, trying to decide if the necklace looks as cheap as her mother says it does. She was thrilled when Glenn held up the tiny gold chain and motioned for her to turn around, his fingers so warm on her skin. And then she spoiled everything and kissed him in front of everyone. She knew better. They've never been affectionate in public. She just got caught up in the moment.

She tucks the chain under the neckline of her shirt so it doesn't show and goes downstairs. "I'm leaving," she says, but Brenda doesn't answer. She's curled up on the couch under a blanket like a kid sick with the flu, drinking coffee and watching television, her eyes swollen from crying. She hasn't stopped crying since Allison moved out.

Her dad worked out the details with Kevin's parents, so Allison could stay with them until she graduates. He carried Allison's duffel bags down the stairs, loaded them in the back of his truck, and drove her the three blocks away while Brenda stood in the driveway and wept.

"Chico's having people over to watch the playoffs."

"You don't even like football. Why do you insist on socializing with those people? You've always been such a loner."

She should move out when the house sells. She can almost

afford her own apartment. Allison's made her escape. She should as well. "They're my friends, Mom."

And they all saw Glenn not kiss her back on Christmas Eve. He kept his expression steady and stuffed her gift in the pocket of his hoodie. Everyone looked at her and then looked away. She'd slunk toward the back door and then down the ramp toward the parking lot. Glenn hasn't talked to her since.

Tessa says there's nothing to worry about. Tessa took her shopping and talked her into getting highlights and a pedicure. "You deserve it. You're fucking the best-looking guy at work." Now she has a closet full of new clothes, hair she barely recognizes in the mirror, and blood-red toenails no one's even seen because it's raining and too cold to wear sandals. She should have saved the money.

"I could skip the party," she tells Brenda now, "if you need me to take you somewhere."

"I'd like to see your sister."

"You could walk there. It's three blocks away."

"It's raining. And Allison won't even return my phone calls. If it's a party, why don't you wear something besides jeans?"

"Because I have to work later. Maybe you could pack some more boxes today. If you're not too *busy*."

"Maybe you can find out from your father when the movers are coming. If *you're* not too busy."

"Those people who bought the furniture are coming by today." There's no room in the tiny house in Anaheim for the china hutch or dining room set and her mother's king-sized bed won't fit in either bedroom; she's already measured. Her dad paid for the ad in the PennySaver, and she negotiated the best deal she could.

"I guess your father expects me to sleep on the floor from now on." She turns up the sound on the television. Gloria Allred is on the screen explaining that "jurors are not idiots. They are mature, capable adults, who in this case passed through not only the usual screening procedures but a lengthy questioning process."

"You can sleep in Allison's bed. Her queen-sized will fit. Do you have to listen to that crap at full blast?"

"I'd give anything to be on that jury. It would be heaven to stay in a hotel and have someone else do my laundry and cook my meals."

"But you couldn't talk to anyone or watch the news or read a paper. It would be like prison."

"Not much different than my life."

"You're not in prison, Mom. I'm leaving."

"Take an umbrella." Brenda turns up the volume.

It's raining hard. Four inches, the weatherman predicts. At least she can keep her car in the garage. Her dad broke the lease and returned the BMW to the dealer, and Brenda pretends not to care since she can't drive it anyway.

Peggy wonders if the rain will make traffic worse and if Glenn will be at the party and if he might have asked her to go with him if she hadn't embarrassed him. She still doesn't know if he liked her gift. It sounded serious when he'd asked before Christmas if she preferred gold or silver, so instead of studying for finals she drove to South Coast Plaza and walked around for an hour, trying to decide what gift would say enough but not too much. She finally settled on a money clip and got it engraved with his initials, which turned out to be a lot more money than she'd planned to spend and took longer than the clerk promised, giving her too much time to worry the gift was a mistake and said the wrong things about her. Too practical and unimaginative, too focused on material things. Nonrefundable as well because of the engraving.

She should think about something else. She just got a letter from the IRS letting her know she's passed part one of the exam.

Part two will be harder. She should stay home and study. Maybe Glenn won't even be at the party. Maybe she shouldn't go. Maybe she should go back in the house, stick her head in the oven, and turn on the gas. She wonders how long it would take for her mother to notice.

GLENN grins when he sees her sitting in Chico's living room. "Hey, Booty," he whispers as he puts his beer can in the chair next to hers. "I'll be right back. Don't go anywhere." She's about to decide to call in sick when she sees him and Jill in the hallway. Jill says, "You promised," and Glenn lifts his eyebrows and grins. Peggy goes out to the garage and watches Chico play darts with John and Tessa. Jill comes outside after a while. Her expression is hard to read. When she leans over the cooler to pull out a beer, the light catches something familiar and scripted in silver around her neck. When Jill stands, Peggy squints to read the word. *Special.* She clutches her throat. Her chain is still hidden.

"You want to play darts, Peggy?" Chico asks. "You and me against John and Tessa?"

"Where's your bathroom?"

"First door on the left."

She's shocked at the amount of vomit pouring out of her into the toilet bowl. Perfect. On top of everything else, she's getting the flu, karma for thinking about calling in sick to work. She rinses her mouth with a handful of sink water and wonders if Glenn got a bulk rate on necklaces. She should throw hers away. She will when she gets home.

When the sick feeling passes, she goes to the living room to retrieve her purse. Glenn is showing Gloria the money clip. He winks at her from across the room.

"Engraved and everything," Gloria says. "Someone likes you."

"You're leaving, Booty?"

She decides to ignore the smirk on Gloria's face. "I wish you wouldn't call me that."

"Come by when you get off work. We can hang out."

"It'll be late."

"I'll be up."

PEGGY waits for Allison in the strip mall across from the school since Ocean View's parking lot is a nightmare. She has a pile of her sister's clothes in the back seat and a stack of her CDs in the trunk. Lots of rap, which she can't remember Allison ever listening to. Obviously, Kevin's influence. She parks in a space in front of a jewelry store and thinks about how Glenn said this morning she should buy a house with all the money she's saving by living at home.

"It'd be a good investment."

"I can't afford a house."

"Get a roommate. I'm looking for one myself."

"Maybe I should move in with you." She expected him to laugh, but he took her seriously.

"You'd be perfect! You'd never be here."

"Wow." All the air was suddenly gone from her lungs. "Is that your only criteria? Someone who's never home?"

He'd laughed and kissed her. "You know what I mean. We have different days off and you have school. We'd be roomies with privileges. But nothing else would have to change."

"You mean we'd still see other people." She's convinced him she's a free and easy spirit just like he is. She plays racquetball with Chico twice a month, went to a reading at a bookstore with John once, and eats lunch with Russ occasionally, which is not at all what he means by "seeing other people."

"Of course," Glenn said. "We wouldn't have any rules or anything."

"I don't know. It's too long a drive to school from your house."

They'd left it at that. She's not moving in with him. There's nothing free or easy about her spirit. She's incapable of being late, for one thing, like right now. Allison won't get out of school for another fifteen minutes, and here she is waiting for her already. She should run inside the jewelry store and try to exchange Glenn's stupid necklace for something else. She's not wearing it anymore, but she can't throw it away either. She keeps it in an envelope in the glove box of her car. The store seems to be closed anyway.

Tessa says *Booty* is much better than *Special*, that it means Glenn is totally into her and that their sex life must be amazing. Tessa's right, the sex is amazing; she'd just like to have it more often. Maybe she should move in with him. She startles now when Allison taps on the passenger window.

"Hey, Booty," Allison says as she gets in the car.

"Don't call me that. I'm not wearing that necklace anymore." She starts the ignition. "He meant it as a joke anyway."

"You have to admit it was a weird gift. Definitely not your style."

"What's that supposed to mean? What kind of style are you?" Allison's wearing a Nirvana T-shirt knotted at the waist, showing off her perfectly flat stomach, and a short plaid kilt and knee-high socks showing her perfectly toned legs. Even her white Keds are perfectly scuffed.

"I'm edgy. You're more of a classic look: pearl earrings, sweater sets, that kind of thing. I like your highlights."

Peggy smooths her hair and remembers the woman from career day, Megan Barnes, a million years ago. Glenn should have bought her pearls. "You're making fun of me."

"No. It looks really good. I bet Glenn likes it. Or are you not seeing him anymore?"

"I see him once in a while. When I'm in the mood."

Allison laughs. "For a booty call?"

"That's not funny."

"Sorry. I appreciate you bringing my stuff. When are you and Mom moving?"

"Next week."

"I feel bad you have to move out of Huntington. I'm always going to live at the beach."

Peggy wishes she could be as clueless and selfish as her sister. "No one's home?" she asks as she pulls up in Kevin's empty driveway.

"He's at basketball practice and his parents are at work."

"I thought he played football."

"Baseball too. It's amazing, how he's good at every sport he tries."

"He's amazing all right."

Allison frowns and Peggy is sorry. She doesn't want an argument. She's missed her sister. "Where do his parents work?" she asks as she gets out of the car.

"His dad does construction and his mother owns that jewelry store across from the school. I'll get the clothes from the back seat."

"His mother owns *that* store? Where I was parked?"

"She has a business partner but yeah, she owns it."

"It didn't look open." Peggy takes the CDs from the trunk.

Allison shrugs. "She's there every day, nine to five. Some people's mothers have jobs. Some people's mothers actually contribute."

Peggy follows Allison up the sidewalk. "Mom's signed up with a temp agency that's going to try and find her a job. *If* she can manage to turn off the television set. She's convinced the world will end if she misses one minute of O. J.'s trial."

"She'd be better off looking for a new husband." Allison balances the load of clothes on her hip and digs through her purse. "My key's in here somewhere."

"There are other options besides relying on a man to take care of you."

"Not for our mother."

"At least she's quit drinking."

"No way." Allison opens the front door. "She's just hiding it better. You want something to eat? There's a ton of food in the fridge."

"I'm on a diet. Wow, what a huge television."

"It's a thirty-five-inch screen. They have all the cable channels too. And we have Super Nintendo in the bedroom." Allison stacks the pile of clothes in a chair in the living room and turns on the TV.

"I thought you hated video games."

Allison shrugs. "Kevin likes them. We can watch MTV if you want to stay for a while. You can set my CDs there on the table."

"When did you start listening to rap?" Peggy asks as she glances around the living room at the leather couch and recliners, the plush carpet, the thick drapes. It's all obviously expensive and very impersonal. No art on the walls. No family pictures. The room feels cold and dark and smells like disinfectant and citrus air freshener.

"Why haven't you started listening to something from this decade? Check out this video." Allison turns up the sound on the television and Peggy sits down. "That's Dr. Dre and Ice Cube."

"This is awful," Peggy says after a few minutes, as images of dangling corpses next to electric chairs and blood-drenched piles of bones and body parts flash across the screen.

"Wait until the end. Tupac's the sniper who shoots Nicole Simpson."

"What's their point? O. J.'s innocent?"

"It's supposed to be funny. Mom thinks he's innocent."

"She also thinks he remembers her from twenty years ago." She stands. "I need to go. You should call her. She really misses you."

"Then why'd she let me move out?"

"It was your idea to live here. Aren't you happy?"

"Why wouldn't I be?" She opens her arms wide. "Look at all this. Plus, I get to sleep with Kevin every night!"

She doesn't look happy, Peggy thinks as she drives home.

FRANK comes from behind his desk and hugs her and then closes the door and sits down. "It's good to see you." He motions for her to take the chair opposite him.

"I have to clock in in fifteen minutes. You wanted to talk to me?"

"I found your mother an attorney. She'll have to go to AA meetings and pay some expensive fines. But if she follows the rules, she'll have her license back by summer."

"She's already quit drinking."

"Really?" He blinks. "That's great, if it's true."

She starts to tell him how Allison doesn't seem happy living with Kevin when the phone on his desk lights up. "Do you need to answer that?"

"Ginny will get it," he says. "I'm renting a truck next Saturday. Ask some of those guys you work with to help. I'll buy beer and pizza."

"I'll ask." Guys from work and a truck isn't what Brenda is expecting at all, but now she has a reason to talk to Glenn.

"I appreciate how responsible you are, Peggy. We've always been able to count on you. I don't say that enough."

He's right. He doesn't say this enough and the only reason he's saying it now is because he wants something.

"There's a place in Anaheim, not far from your uncle's house, that has morning AA meetings. You could take your mother before work."

She spits out the word, "Unbelievable."

"She only needs to log thirty meetings. It'll go by fast."

"This isn't fair, Dad."

"I know." He pulls out his wallet and gives her eight twenty-dollar bills. "For your books and tuition this semester."

There's a knock on his door and then Ginny's voice. "Frank? It's the area office."

He picks up the phone. "Frank Lockhart," he says in the voice he uses to show he's in charge.

THE early morning classes she needs are at the same time as her mother's AA meetings and anything else is too late in the day for her to make it to work by two thirty, so she signs up for night classes on her days off. Tuesday and Wednesday evenings, Economics and Business Law. The line at the bookstore takes forever and she's ten minutes late clocking in. Mr. Acosta frowns and sends her to work letters. Glenn doesn't even look up when she walks past him. Jill's already sitting in between him and Chico, so Peggy takes the case at the far end of the line next to Russ. Tessa waves from the other side of the line.

"Thanks for helping us move, Russ."

"Glad to do it. You and your mother getting settled in?"

"Sort of."

Brenda's too busy complaining about everything to settle in.

Frank should have hired real movers instead of those idiots from the post office. She couldn't bear to be in the same room with Frank, must less speak to him, which means she has no idea where he put anything. John broke a Tiffany wineglass and now she only has two left. At least the house is wired for cable and Brenda can watch all her channels.

Gloria turns around. "My mother lives across the street from you," she says, her expression as unfriendly as always. "In the house with the vegetable garden out front?"

Brenda has already complained about the garden. According to her, normal people grow vegetables in their backyards.

"Your mother lives across the street from Peggy?" Russ says. "If I would have known that, I'd have knocked on her door. Gloria's mom makes the world's best tamales."

"I'll go introduce myself. Do you visit her often?"

"She watches my kids, so yeah, I'm there all the time." Gloria turns back to her case.

"I guess I'll see you then." Gloria doesn't answer. Jill gets up for another tray of mail and the light catches the letters on her silver necklace. *Special.*

"Your necklace is so pretty," Gloria says.

"I love it," Jill says, and goes back to her case, beaming.

Tessa catches Peggy's eye and makes a gagging face. She tries to smile, but she really does feel sick to her stomach. To fight off the nausea, she sorts letters into the mail case as fast as she can, trying not to watch the clock or glance over at Glenn and imagine what he and Jill are talking about. Just before lunch break, Mr. Acosta comes down the aisle with his clipboard. "I'll need you to work next Tuesday," he says, when he gets to Peggy.

"That's my day off."

"I already gave you time off last weekend to move."

"I have class Tuesday night."

"I can't make exceptions."

"I just registered and bought the books."

"Sounds like a personal problem." Mr. Acosta moves down the line with his clipboard.

"I bet if you talk to him later and offer to work part of your day off and then go to class, he'll agree," Russ says after Mr. Acosta is out of earshot. "He knows better than to get on your dad's bad side."

"I'm not getting my dad involved in this."

"Sweetheart, your dad is involved whether you ask him to be or not. He's the boss. Take advantage. I sure would."

She really doesn't want to miss class, so she considers Russ's idea, keeping a close eye on Mr. Acosta, waiting for him to head to the supervisor office so she can go talk to him privately, but he stands idiotically at the end of the aisle, peeling labels off empty trays and staring into space. What a wretched man. She hates everything about this horrible job, the dust and dirt, the musty smell, the constant noise, the mind-numbing boredom. She's even mad at Russ for calling her sweetheart. She's nobody's sweetheart. She can't wait to quit and never see any of these people again. She jumps when Glenn comes up behind her and puts his hands around her waist and breathes hello in her ear. "You startled me," she says as his fingers linger on a tiny roll of fat above her belly.

"You might want to do something about that," he says in a low voice.

Her cheeks burn, and she sucks in her stomach. No wonder he hasn't wanted to see her lately. She feels bloated. Her cycle hasn't been regular ever since she went on the pill. "I'm going to start running. I've been so busy with moving and signing up for school and everything. What's new with you? I haven't talked to you in like forever."

"How'd the move go? Sorry I couldn't make it."

Russ clears his throat.

"You need something?" Glenn asks.

"I want to hear your excuse."

"I had to replace a friend's transmission."

"Peggy's your friend. You promised you'd be there."

"It's okay," Peggy says. "We had plenty of help."

"I don't know what your problem is," Glenn says.

"No problem," Russ says. "Same show, different day. You've never been Mr. Reliable and I'm sure Peggy knows that now. I need a smoke." Russ gets up and walks out to the dock.

"I'm sorry," Peggy says. "I don't know what that was about."

"How's the new place?"

"It's okay." She could ask if he'd like to come by. She has her own bedroom. It would be weird with her mother there but so what? Or maybe he'll invite her out to his house after work. She'll go even though she has a ton of homework. She's already got a change of clothes packed in a duffel bag in the trunk of her car, just in case.

"Take it easy," he says, and he's gone.

A few days later Glenn announces he's buying after work at the Fling, smiling at her in a way that obviously means she's invited. When he walks past her while she's waiting in line to clock out, he rests his right hand for a moment on her back. In the locker room, she asks Rita, the woman who transferred in from the graveyard shift, if she wants to go have a drink at the Fling after work.

"That place is a dump," Rita says. "We used to go there when I got off work at seven thirty in the morning, and I'm sure it's not any better at midnight. I need to get home to my kid. And you're too smart for someone like Glenn."

"What do you mean?" *There isn't anyone else like Glenn.*

"Glenn's famous. He's gone through all the single women on the graveyard shift."

Which women, and how do I compare? She can't ask. Rita will tell her she's making a big mistake, which she already knows. "One drink."

Rita sighs. "The kid's asleep anyway. One drink."

Rita is right. The Fling is a dump behind a gas station, right next to the on-ramp for the Santa Ana Freeway. There's not even a jukebox. Rita downs a martini and says good night. Peggy plans to finish her Diet Coke and follow her out the door when Glenn sits down next to her and says he has the new Eagles CD at home. "It's called *Hell Freezes Over.* I guess the band's back together."

"I've heard that's a good one."

"MAYBE I should drop out of school," she says the next morning as she watches Glenn stir instant coffee into two cups. "I could only sign up for two classes anyway."

His expression hardens. "Why would you do that?"

"Mr. Acosta says I have to work my day off."

"Call in sick. They're not going to fire Frank Lockhart's daughter."

There it is again, the assumption her father will save her. "I might go to Palm Springs the last week in February. Aren't you off then?" She knows he is. She's studied the vacation board.

He scowls. "You shouldn't waste money on a hotel room. And you shouldn't drop out of school either."

She has a sudden image of what he might look like in the future: those thick eyebrows gone gray and wild, his perpetual grin turned to a sneer, his face lined with cynicism and disappointment. Not that it matters. Not that she has any plans of growing old with him.

SHE hears John grumble how it must be nice to be Frank Lockhart's daughter when she takes her timecard from the rack the following Tuesday. She glances over her shoulder when she clocks out and tells herself she doesn't care Glenn is so busy talking to Jill he doesn't notice her leave. That night she tells the Business Law teacher she's passed part one of the enrolled agent exam.

"That's remarkable, Peggy."

"I study a lot." Her eyes well with tears. She studies a lot because she has nothing else to do.

"There's a tax review seminar starting this weekend. We're looking for students to help us out for a few hours. You interested?"

"What time?" Her voice cracks and she feels nauseous again.

Her teacher looks worried. "I didn't mean to upset you. Nine to noon."

She wipes her eyes. She'll have to tighten up her already too tight schedule, but being asked to help run a seminar is a huge compliment. "Nine to noon works fine for me. Thank you for the opportunity."

CHAPTER NINE

KEVIN HAS BASKETBALL PRACTICE AFTER SCHOOL EVERY DAY, WHICH MEANS Allison has the house to herself until his parents get home. She sits on the sofa, polishing her nails blue with gold sparkly highlights in defiance of McKenzie, who's declared pink the color for February. She's tired of McKenzie's rules and she really misses her mother's manicure table, with its attached light, drawers filled with cotton balls and files, and pink spacers for her toes. Connie doesn't do her own nails. She goes to one of those Vietnamese salons in Garden Grove that her mother claims are breeding grounds for fungus.

Connie comes in the house at five thirty carrying two bags of groceries, her black leather case slung over one shoulder. More weed for Sal. Allison wonders if the case is locked and how difficult the combination would be to figure out.

"I see you made a snack." Connie sets the bags of groceries down and glances at the open jar of peanut butter on the counter.

"I was going to put that away."

"We're going to have to set some boundaries. Lids back on jars. Dirty dishes in the dishwasher, not in the sink."

"There were clean ones in the dishwasher." She sounds ridiculous. Her mother would never let her get away with being this sloppy.

"I'd appreciate it if you wouldn't polish your nails on the couch. It's good leather."

"I'm sorry. I really appreciate being able to stay here."

Connie's smile is forced. "I'm guessing your family's more lenient than we are."

"Maybe about some things," Allison says, trying not to stare at

Connie's briefcase. She takes the bottle of nail polish upstairs to Kevin's room and unplugs the Nintendo so she can watch TV. The trial is on and one of Nicole Simpson's neighbors is testifying about finding Nicole's white Akita wandering the streets on the night of the murders, blood on all four of his paws. The man is very precise on that evening's timeline, which apparently is important based on the gleam in the frizzy-haired prosecutor's eyes. The neighbor explains he watches the *Dick Van Dyke Show*, which ends at ten thirty, and then he takes his own dog for a quick walk so he's home in time to watch the *Mary Tyler Moore Show* at eleven. He is absolutely sure of the exact moment he found Nicole Simpson's dog, which makes Frizzy Hair extremely excited.

God, what a boring life. Allison wishes she could call her mother and ask what the big deal is about the timing, but she talked to her last week on her birthday and if she keeps calling, it will seem as if she wants to come home. She still can't believe her parents agreed to let her live here. Her friends say she's lucky they're so open-minded, but she's starting to feel more discarded than lucky. She's never spent so much time alone.

SATURDAY morning, Connie knocks on Kevin's door and says her sister is here. "If you're going to have guests, I wish you'd arrange it with me first."

"I'm sorry. I didn't know she was coming over." She follows Connie down the stairs. The living room smells like air freshener, but she can tell Sal smoked a joint this morning. Connie picks up the ashtray with the evidence and hurries into the kitchen.

Peggy is standing by the front door. There are circles under her eyes and her hair is tied back in a greasy ponytail. "Can you go somewhere with me?"

"I'll get my shoes."

"Kevin's mom isn't very friendly," Peggy says when they are in her car. "Are you not allowed to have people over?"

"No one ever comes over. They aren't social people."

"Where's Kevin anyway?"

"He's taking the SAT tests over again today, trying to raise his scores." She expects Peggy to say that's what she should be doing too, but Peggy is nerve-rackingly silent. "SATs are a waste of time," Allison goes on, sure this will set Peggy off. "We aren't going to college. As soon as school is over, Kevin's buying a VW bus and we're heading up the coast to find the perfect beach town. Cayucos, maybe." None of this is true. Kevin wants to go to Mexico; he thinks VWs are ugly; and she said Cayucos only because she likes the way it sounds.

Peggy stares straight ahead and makes a left on Beach Boulevard, heading north.

"You're not going to lecture me?" Allison asks. "Okay, what's wrong?"

"You can't tell Kevin. Or Mom."

"I'm not exactly talking to her, so that won't be a problem."

"Or Dad. Promise you won't tell Dad either. You can't tell anyone."

"What's going on?"

"You know anything about pregnancy tests?"

"You pee on a stick and if it turns pink, you're having a baby. Why? When was your last period?"

"Christmas, maybe?"

"Peggy!"

"My periods have been irregular ever since I went on the pill."

"Did you take a test?"

"I took three. They were all pink."

"I'M guessing about seven or eight weeks along," the doctor at the Planned Parenthood office says. "You can get dressed now."

"That's impossible." Peggy pulls the flimsy cotton gown down around her hips, and the paper on the exam table crinkles as she sits up. "I'm on the pill."

"The pill isn't one hundred percent effective," the doctor says. "Especially if you don't take it regularly."

"I do take it regularly." Peggy's voice is indignant. "Every single day at six forty-five p.m."

"That's very precise," the doctor says. "Why six forty-five?"

"It's my meal break at work. I go out to my car, eat lunch, and study."

"She's a business major," Allison says. "She's going to do taxes."

"Good for you," the doctor says. "Have you by chance taken antibiotics recently? Sometimes they interfere with birth control pills."

"No. I don't take anything, except the pill."

"What about on your days off?" Allison asks. "When do you take it when you're not working?"

"I still take it at six forty-five," Peggy says, but her already pale face whitens. "Usually. I mean, it's a cumulative effect, anyway, right? It's not a big deal if you miss a day or two as long as you catch up?"

Allison tries to nod encouragingly. She has no experience with Peggy being wrong.

"If you miss a day, you need backup contraception," the doctor says. "Condoms and spermicide are the most effective. Of course, abstinence is the best."

Allison starts to insist that of course Peggy uses condoms, but her sister looks as if she might pass out.

Peggy takes a deep breath and exhales. "Is it too late to get rid of it?"

Allison shivers. The air-conditioning is on full blast and she wishes she'd brought a sweater. Peggy's obviously in shock. The doctor will talk her out of this idea.

The doctor's expression doesn't change, and there is no sound of reproach in her voice. "The longer you wait, the more risk you take. You need to make your decision as soon as possible."

"Seriously, you never used condoms?" Allison asks when they get back to Peggy's car.

"Glenn doesn't like them. Don't look at me like that. I know it was stupid."

"Please don't decide anything until you talk to him."

"This is none of his business."

"It's his baby too." She feels her pulse quicken. She's never been good at arguing with her sister.

"It's my body." Peggy starts the car and backs out of the space. Tom Petty's nasal voice bleats through the Ford's tiny speakers. "I get to decide what to do with it."

"Did you read that in one of Mom's magazines?" Allison fumbles with her seat belt. There's got to be something she can say to keep Peggy from making the mistake of her life. She could use Kevin's real mother as an example of someone who could have had an abortion and didn't, but Peggy would say Kevin shouldn't have been born. "You can't just get rid of someone's kid without letting him know."

"Glenn already told me he doesn't want kids."

"He might change his mind."

Tom Petty's insisting now that no one knows how he feels. Allison turns the volume down, wondering why Peggy still listens to their father's music. "Mom could have decided not to have us, and we wouldn't even be here. Abortion is murder."

"Wow. I didn't realize you felt that way."

"Maybe Glenn wants to marry you."

"He's living with someone else, Allison. Besides, he's too old. He's almost thirty-one."

"Thirty-one! God! This could be his only chance to have kids and you're taking it away from him."

"He's not smart either." Peggy's talking faster now, obviously trying to convince herself she's right. "He drinks, and smokes too much pot. He's not interested in working anyplace else or getting a promotion or even reading a book or seeing a movie. We have absolutely nothing in common. Plus, he lives in Norco. It's too smoggy and far from the beach."

"You don't even like the beach. Maybe he could at least watch the baby while you go to school."

"Why are you trying to talk me into this? You don't even know him."

"I'd like to meet him. You didn't tell me he smoked pot."

"Everyone on my shift does. They all get high on their breaks out in the parking lot. You'd fit right in."

Her tone is so dismissive and so typically Peggy. "You couldn't pay me enough to work at the post office."

"Oh really?" Peggy's dark eyes smolder. "It's okay for me to work there but not you?"

"I don't know why you haven't quit. You keep saying you're going to."

"I should have known better than to confide in you." Peggy's eyes fill with tears. "You don't give a shit about me."

"I do too! You're my only sister." She's crying now too, thinking of Peggy's dreary life with their impossible mother, working at that boring place. And Glenn's already found someone new. How depressing, to be so alone. *Except Peggy isn't alone*, she realizes. *She has me.*

"I could babysit for you. I'll have plenty of time once I graduate."

She can be the kid's favorite person. She'll be the one who saved her.

"I thought you were buying a van and moving to Cayucos. I'm not having a kid right now. He'd probably grow up to be some wacko, anyway, who'd shoot up a school or something."

"No, *she* won't. She'll be beautiful and smart, and she'll love you because you'll be a great mother. You practically raised me."

Peggy almost smiles. "And look how you turned out." She turns up the music. Another Tom Petty song has started.

Allison groans. "This guy really cannot sing."

"I'm starving," Peggy says. "Let's go get pie at Marie Callender's. Now that I know I'm not fat, I can eat."

"That's not funny. Promise me you won't decide anything until you talk to Glenn."

"I'll talk to him first. But it's still my decision."

KEVIN'S so late coming home from practice that Connie and Sal go ahead and eat dinner without him. Allison waits and watches Nicole Simpson's sister, Denise, on the television in his room. "We were all drinking and goofing around and being loud and dancing and having a great time," Denise says. "And then O. J. grabbed Nicole's crotch and said: 'This is where babies come from. This belongs to me.' And Nicole just sort of wrote it off like it was nothing—like, you know, like she was used to that kind of treatment."

Disgusting, Allison thinks, just like Glenn giving Peggy that "booty" necklace—expecting her to walk around, wearing an advertisement that she's his property. Peggy wrote that off too, as if it was some kind of a joke.

The door to the bedroom suddenly opens and Kevin stomps in, dumps his duffel bag on the floor, and changes the channel to a basketball game. She starts to say she was watching something, but she doesn't want to discuss crotch-grabbing with Kevin right now.

"I was hoping you'd be home a lot earlier."

"Danielle's cousin bought a gram," he says, opening the bureau drawer. "No one else had any money. You want a bump?" He pulls the mirror and the cutoff plastic straw from under the bed.

"No one else had any money" means he's treated everyone again. He taps some powder out, snorts two lines, and holds out the straw. She shakes her head. "You're snorting more than you sell."

"Are you keeping inventory?"

"We'll never be able to pay Bledsoe back."

"Jesus! I'm doing the best I can, Allison. I don't need you nagging me."

"I'm not nagging. You know I'm right." She slides down to the end of the bed, thinking she'll put on her shoes and leave. But go where? Her parents are happy to be rid of her. Peggy's at work. Her friends only want to see her when Kevin offers them coke.

She hates the squeaking noise the basketball players' shoes make on television as they chase each other back and forth across the court. The cheerleaders are crouched on the floor right next to the court, bright smiles on their faces. She wonders how many times the players stomp right over them with their gigantic feet.

"Hey," Kevin says when the game goes to commercial. He plugs the Nintendo back in, moves behind her so she's sitting in between his legs, and wraps his arms around her. "I'm sorry I yelled at you. Forgive me?"

She leans back to kiss him, but he turns and reaches for the Nintendo control. "I wish you'd play *Kombat* with me."

"You play. Just turn the sound down. Maybe I'll look for a job in a restaurant or something. Earn some money so we can pay off Bledsoe."

"I don't want you working anywhere, babe. You belong here, with me." He holds out the straw again. "Just a little taste? It'll cheer us up."

She likes how he smiles when she snorts her lines even though her sinuses burn. He only wants her to feel the same high he feels, because he loves her. They'll figure this out. "We just need to find some new customers," she says. "I'll think of something." He's not listening. His eyes are on the screen.

MONDAY night, she chops vegetables in the kitchen for the salad she offered to make for dinner and smells the joint Sal has just lit in the living room.

"I've asked you not to do that when she's here," Connie says.

"Chill out. My back hurts. And she's almost eighteen. Stop being so paranoid."

"We need to be careful."

"I can't wait until they're both graduated and gone."

March, April, May, June. Allison counts as she mixes a salad dressing. School will be over, and she and Kevin can move out. July, August, September, and Peggy's baby will be born, a girl she is sure. She imagines holding the baby in her arms, waving at Peggy as she leaves for work. Kevin taking her to the park, pushing her on the swings, big smiles on all their faces, Kevin saying he can't wait until they have a few kids of their own but for right now this is pretty sweet.

"I thought you were phasing things out with The Family," Sal says in the living room.

"Can we discuss this later?" Connie says.

"You promised you'd quit. I'm ready to retire. I've been ready."

"One more push and we'll have some real money, and then Kevin can go to any school he wants."

Or not, Allison thinks, as she opens a bag of croutons. She wonders what Connie and whoever The Family is consider "real money" and what they'll think when he tells them he's not going to college. They won't need much money—enough for a small upstairs apartment near the beach with fluttering curtains around open windows, a barbecue on the patio next to her bike, Kevin's truck parked out front, his surfboard in the living room. Making love without Connie and Sal listening in the next bedroom. No Nintendo games, no television either. One bedroom or maybe two, enough room for a baby eventually.

When the phone rings, she answers, almost defiantly because Connie and Sal never answer the phone. "It's always a salesman," Sal claims. "They'll call back if it's important," Connie always adds.

"I need to talk," Peggy says.

"I was just thinking about you. Did you tell Glenn?"

"I haven't had a chance. He's always with Jill. They're even having a party Saturday. I'm just going to make the appointment at the clinic and get this over with."

Peggy would have already made the appointment if she really wanted to go through with the abortion, and she wouldn't have called unless she wanted some advice. "Did they invite you to the party?"

"They invited everyone. I'm not going."

"It would give you a chance to tell him."

"At a party? In front of everyone?"

"You could figure out a way to get him alone for a minute. I'll go with you."

"I work Saturdays, remember?"

"Get off early. Wear something sexy. Aren't your boobs getting bigger?"

"I don't feel sexy. I feel fat and pukey. Would you really go with me?"

"Of course. You're my favorite sister."

"Who was on the phone?" Connie asks when Allison joins them in the living room. The evening news is on the television. Sal stubs out his joint on the rim of the Diet Coke can next to his recliner.

"My sister. I might go to a party with her next weekend."

Connie raises her eyebrows slightly. "You should check with Kevin first. He might have plans."

It's a free country, she almost says. She can make her own plans. She could get pregnant too, if she wanted. A cousin for Peggy's child. Their birthdays would be close. They could take them to see Santa Claus next year. She imagines Kevin's crooked smile on a baby's tiny face. That would totally mess up Connie's plans.

"Man, look at Simpson," Sal says as the television screen shows O. J. muttering to himself and shaking his head as he watches footage of a former LAPD officer testifying that, "O. J. kind of jokingly said he dreamed about killing Nicole."

"Whoa!" Sal laughs. "That dude's definitely off the Christmas card list."

"That cop was never Simpson's friend," Connie says. "Not like Robert Kardashian. That cop said it himself, he was just one of the servants. Simpson used him to fix traffic tickets."

"Everyone used O. J.," Sal says. "Nicole's family didn't have any problem spending his bread."

"Are you on his side now?"

"I'm on my own side." Sal relights the joint.

Connie's lips tighten. "Sal."

"I really don't mind." Allison watches Sal take a deep drag and blow a thick smoke ring. He winks at her.

"I mind," Connie says. "I'll go start the potatoes. Kevin should be home soon."

"I'll do it," Allison says.

Connie gives her a small smile that is anything but encouraging. "You don't need to worry about helping around the house. All you need to do is keep Kevin happy and focused."

"I try to."

Do you? Connie's expression seems to ask. It's crazy, how much it bothers her that Connie won't say what she really thinks. Her mother shares how she feels about every single thing floating through her tiny skull in infinite detail, which is annoying as hell but now seems refreshing. "Is everything okay?"

"Of course," Connie says.

"Everything's groovy." Sal raises his joint in salute.

The weed smells wonderful, sticky-sweet, and strong. She'd give anything to reach over, grab the joint from Sal, and watch Connie's head explode.

WHEN Kevin finally comes home, he's angry and frantic, pacing back and forth, complaining that the coach threatened to bench him for the next game just because he expressed his opinion. Connie stands and puts her arms around Kevin. Sal nods and makes sympathetic noises. Allison slips out of the living room and goes upstairs, glancing at Sal and Connie's room as she walks down the hall. Connie's black briefcase is just sitting there on the bed.

Downstairs in the living room, Kevin whines, "He has it in for me."

"I know it's not fair," Connie agrees. "But basketball will be over in a few months and baseball will start. That's your real strength. All kinds of colleges are going to be looking at you."

Allison steps into Connie and Sal's bedroom, tidy and anonymous except for one picture of Kevin in his football uniform on the dresser. The leather briefcase on the bed is locked of course, but when she kneels and tries the numbers of Kevin's birthday, the latch springs open. There is a worn address book on top, and when she lifts it off the tray, she rocks back on her heels in disbelief.

The case is packed with more than a hundred plastic bags of weed. Her heart beats faster as she flips through the address book. There are listings all over Orange and San Bernardino counties. Customers, she guesses, trying to picture Connie in her prim business suit driving up and down the freeways, delivering her goods.

Bledsoe said Connie was a practical woman.

"I should just quit the team," Kevin says in the living room.

"That won't look good on your record," Connie says. "We'll sign you up to take the SAT test again. We'll get you a tutor."

"Can't Allison help him?" Sal asks.

Connie laughs. "School isn't exactly Allison's strong point."

Kevin says something that is muffled by the television set, and all three of them laugh and none of them sound happy. Connie's right of course, school isn't her strong point. According to Connie, she's not good at making Kevin happy or providing the right kind of sex to keep his complexion clear. She slips a small bag of weed into the front pocket of her jeans and re-spreads the other bags, so it doesn't look like anything's missing.

The television set seems suddenly louder, as if someone has turned up the volume. She puts the tray back in the briefcase, but it won't sit flat, the case won't close, and she starts to panic. She can no longer hear them talking. She holds the tray over-head to check if maybe she has it turned backward, wishing she'd closed the bedroom door. Connie can move quietly for a large woman, padding barefoot down the carpeted hallway. She wouldn't even know Kevin was in the room until he was stand-ing right behind her. Sal couldn't sneak up on anyone, but he would be the most disappointed.

Her heart quivers from breast to pubic bone. She tries the tray again. This time it slips into place and the briefcase closes, the sound of the latch too loud and obvious. Her fingers tremble as she re-buckles the clasps and resets the lock. Her calf muscles cramp and then spasm and she has to stand. She flexes and points her toes, trying to remember exactly where the case was positioned on the bed. She adjusts it slightly, then steps back out into the empty hallway, gasping for air, finally able to breathe again.

She goes in Kevin's room, takes the round plastic case out of her purse, and punches out today's birth control pill. Her heart is still pounding. The pill leaves a chemical taste in the back of her throat as it dissolves.

THE next morning, she pauses in the hallway when she hears Kevin on the phone. "She's almost eighteen." His voice sounds tense. "At least think about it."

"Who was that?"

He jumps as she walks into the kitchen and bangs his elbow on the counter. "Jesus Christ, Allison! Don't sneak up on me like that. You scared the shit out of me."

"I'm sorry. Who's almost eighteen besides me?"

"No one. We need to leave. We're late. And you won't be eighteen for months."

They get in his truck and head to school. Maybe he's planning a surprise party, although Connie would never let him invite people over. And then she remembers Glenn's upcoming party and has an idea. The people Peggy works with would buy cocaine from Kevin. They have money.

"Want to go to a party with my sister?"

SHE envisions something like the get-togethers her parents used to host. A big spread of food, margaritas in the blender, white wine in buckets of ice, coolers of beer on the patio. Her mother lit candles. Her dad spent hours selecting music from his CD collection. Her parents' friends never dressed up much (Brenda did of course), but they made an effort. Women wore blouses and nice jeans. Men changed into Hawaiian shirts and Dockers.

She decides on a short plaid dress. Kevin wears a long-sleeved button-down shirt over dark-washed jeans. Peggy drives because Kevin's truck isn't big enough for the three of them. It's after eight when she picks them up, wearing her work clothes, jeans, and a V-necked T-shirt that's a little too tight across her chest. No makeup. Hair in the usual ponytail. She shrugs when Allison looks at her.

"I didn't have time to change. Nothing looks good on me anyway."

They get on the freeway and drive east forever until Peggy finally takes the exit to Norco, winding through a neighborhood of identical small ranch houses, parking in front of one with a huge four-wheel drive black truck in the driveway and another red one in the garage with the hood up, a pair of blue-jeaned legs sticking out underneath it. A small CD player blasts ancient rock and roll, some old guy moaning about how brown sugar makes him feel so good. Two women wearing jeans and T-shirts sit in folding chairs, drinking out of red cups. The party must have been canceled.

The man under the red truck rolls out and gives her a big flirty smile. "I'm Chico," he says, and she feels Kevin bristle. She grabs his hand and squeezes it. "I'm Peggy's sister, Allison. And this is my boyfriend, Kevin."

"Little sister," Chico says. "That's Bobby with the wrench,

John by the cooler, Jill and Gloria playing like they're the supervisors. And that's Glenn."

Glenn says hello, friendly enough but distant. Allison wishes Peggy would have at least put on some lipstick. John has really bad skin and practically drools when he says hello to Peggy. He unfolds two chairs and sets them next to the two women. "Here you go, ladies."

Allison sits down and glances around the garage. Everything is tidy and organized. There are tall metal toolboxes and pegboard-lined walls with tools neatly hung. A plastic trash can is full of crushed beer cans. The calendar on the wall has a picture of a naked woman with gigantic breasts.

"I'm Jill." The smiling hyper-thin woman in one of the folding chairs raises her red cup. "Vodka and Diet Pepsi. Want some?"

"No thanks," Allison says. Jill could stand to drink real Pepsi and eat a Twinkie. She has no boobs at all compared to pregnant Peggy, and she's wearing a necklace exactly like Peggy's, except the word "Special" is written in silver. Allison has to look away. Seriously? Is Glenn an idiot?

"Nothing for me either," Peggy says.

"Such good little girls." The other dark-haired woman pushes her glasses up her long nose and gives Peggy's stomach a bitchy gaze. "The big boss man's little angels."

Kevin opens a beer and tries to make small talk with John and Glenn, but his jokes fall flat. He's nervous; they both are. They hate classic rock and they don't have anything in common with these people. This party's going to be a waste of time if she doesn't change the mood. She takes a joint out of the pocket of her dress, rolled from the weed she took from Connie's briefcase. "You guys smoke pot? This is some nice herb from Hawaii."

"Now you're talking," the woman with glasses says. "I'm Gloria, by the way."

"Little sister's full of surprises," Chico says.

Kevin gives her a measured look from across the garage. She's taking a risk, but she's given this a lot of thought. She'll explain later that Sal gave her the weed. She's never lied to him before, but he hasn't been honest with her either. She still can't believe how much Connie is dealing. They'll have to work that part out later. Right now, a joint will loosen these people up before they start the cocaine conversation. She can use a little loosening up herself. She lights up and everyone seems to relax, everyone except Peggy, of course, who waves off the joint when Gloria offers it to her.

"I also have this," Kevin says after the joint has gone around twice. He takes out a small glass vial from his shirt pocket and holds it up to the light. "And there's plenty more."

"Excellent!" Glenn says as Kevin twists off the attached spoon and dips out a small amount of white powder.

Peggy's immediately angry. "I am so sorry, Glenn. I had no idea." But Glenn's already reaching for the spoon. "I have a mirror inside. You girls want some?"

Jill and Gloria stand. "This is turning into a real party." Gloria smiles at Peggy as she follows Glenn into the house. "You brought the right people."

"What if Dad finds out?" Peggy says when the garage is empty.

"Who's going to tell him? They're all in there, snorting lines."

"Why aren't you in there with them?"

"My sinuses are kind of wrecked. Glenn's a little older than I expected."

"He's handsome though, right?"

"He could be nicer to you."

"We're being discreet."

"There's no such thing as being discreetly pregnant. You need to tell him."

"Or not," Peggy says. "I haven't decided."

"Does Jill know you have one of those necklaces too?"

Peggy shakes her head. "The thing is, she's a nice person."

"This is messed up," Allison says.

"We're both messed up. It's genetic."

Allison sighs. "Can't argue with that."

Everyone's livelier when they return to the garage. Someone turns up the music, and they all have more drinks. Chico says things that are almost funny. Gloria starts talking about her June wedding at the Elks Lodge in Santa Ana. She's registered at Target. She's bought wedding decorations at Michaels. Her fiancé would rather just go to Vegas because it would be cheaper, but she's set on a big wedding and a nice honeymoon, cruising the Mexican Riviera. Jill wants to go on the cruise too, but Glenn isn't interested. Glenn doesn't seem interested in Jill or Peggy. Peggy stares at Glenn. John stares at Peggy. Gloria says she wishes her fiancé wouldn't drink so much. When she isn't watching, he opens another beer. Kevin hands over envelopes of cocaine, folds bills in his wallet, and looks happy.

Allison lights another joint and wonders if these people realize how dismal it is to spend Saturday night in a garage watching someone work on a truck. The singer on the CD player is bragging now about a girl being under his thumb. After a while, Glenn hands Jill a couple of twenties and his keys and asks her to go buy more beer. Gloria says they need vodka too, and her fiancé opens his wallet and gives her a twenty.

As soon as they pull out of the driveway, Glenn nods slightly at Peggy and goes in the house. When her sister follows, Allison glances around the garage. Judging from the smirks on their faces, all the men in the garage have noticed, except for Kevin who has his back turned, talking to Chico and John.

"I'll give you my pager number. You can call me anytime."

"We get paid this Friday," John says.

"Meet me in the parking lot at work," Chico says. "I take lunch break at eight thirty."

"Cool!" Kevin turns around and smiles. "We should get going. Where's your sister?"

"She might be busy," Chico says. "I'd give her a minute."

Everyone laughs except John. Kevin looks confused until he glances around the garage. "I guess Glenn's busy too." Kevin has the same smirk on his face as the other men, which infuriates her suddenly and irrationally since none of them have done anything wrong.

"I'm going to find the bathroom. It's a long drive home."

Surely Peggy and Glenn are simply discussing the baby, although the kitchen is empty and all the doors down the hall are closed. She'll give Peggy a few minutes and then go find her, tell her she needs to come back outside before everyone decides she's a total skank. The door to what she assumes is the bathroom seems to be stuck. When she pushes on it harder with her shoulder, the door opens partway, enough to provide her with a glimpse of a bare ass and Glenn's face in the mirror above the sink where her sister is sitting, her legs circling his waist, his jeans down around his ankles. His eyes are closed as he thrusts forward and groans.

"Sorry," Allison says as Peggy groans too and her eyes open wide. "Sorry," Allison says again as Glenn kicks the door closed in her face. She stands there for a moment, willing herself to unsee the image now permanently engraved in her brain. Plus, she has an immediate worry that the bathroom sink can't possibly handle her sister's extra baby weight and will probably come crashing loose off the wall any second. She imagines the plumbing ripping apart and water gushing through the house, and then she hears a truck pull into the driveway. She knocks, frantically.

"Jill and Gloria are back."

She goes out to the garage, her face flaming red. Gloria gets out with the vodka. Jill has Glenn's keys. Chico takes a case of beer out of the truck bed.

"There'd better be some coke left," Jill says as she and Gloria go in the house. John and Gloria's fiancé are pretending to study something under the hood, nudging each other, trying not to laugh. She hears Glenn's voice now in the kitchen. Peggy comes out to the garage. Her ponytail has come loose in soft tendrils that frame her glowing face.

"Close call, Peggy Sue," Chico whispers as he walks by to put the beer in the fridge.

"Kevin's ready to leave," Allison says.

"If you're finished," Kevin says. He's still smirking.

"Let's stay a while," Peggy says.

Glenn comes out of the kitchen. "It's late," he tells Peggy, "and we have a lot of work to do on Chico's truck."

Peggy's smile tightens and the pretty flush on her face fades. "You're right. I should take them home."

"I'm ready," Kevin says. As he heads down the driveway in front of them, he starts laughing.

"I thought he'd locked the door," Peggy whispers as they follow him.

"Did you at least tell him about the baby?"

"It wasn't the right time."

"I don't think he's the right guy, Peggy. Maybe you should call the clinic."

"Wow," Peggy says. She stops under a streetlight. There are dark shadows under her eyes. "That's harsh."

Kevin is still laughing as he waits for Peggy to unlock the door. He climbs in the back seat. Peggy starts the car. "I never should have brought you. You're just using me to sell drugs to my friends."

"Some friend you are," Kevin says. "Fucking that guy in his bathroom."

"Everyone knew, Peggy. This isn't like you."

"Maybe you don't know what I'm like." Peggy makes a U-turn and heads out of Glenn's tract.

"I know," Kevin says. "You're both sex maniacs, just like your mother."

"Kevin, stop."

"I'm not complaining, babe. You can get pretty wild. Too wild for me sometimes."

"Peggy doesn't need to hear this."

"Peggy's got no room to judge."

"Maybe it's hereditary." She tries to laugh. "Mom does like her vibrator."

"She came on to me, babe. It was pretty obvious, she wanted to fuck me."

"No, she didn't."

"She doesn't even like you," Peggy says.

"I turned her down of course."

"When was this? And why didn't you tell me?"

"Before Christmas."

"He's lying," Peggy says, as she accelerates up the ramp of the Riverside Freeway.

He's not serious, she decides. The little car shivers as it speeds up, barely enough to merge in front of a giant tractor trailer. Thank goodness the traffic's light. Peggy's such a nervous driver. "Let's don't talk about this while we're on the freeway."

"We don't have to talk about your mother at all," Kevin says. "Ever. I'm glad you're not living with her anymore. You can't trust her."

"The party was a good idea, though, wasn't it? I mean, those people will buy more coke, won't they?"

"We'll see," Kevin says, and he's quiet for the rest of the trip home.

"I'M taking a shower," Allison says when they are finally back in his bedroom. "Unless you want to go first."

"Go ahead," he says, so she pulls her dress over her head.

He locks the door as she takes off her bra. "Where did you get that weed?"

His voice is petrifyingly calm. She crosses her arms over her breasts, suddenly cold. "Sal gave it to me a while ago. I've been saving it."

"Nice little fairy tale." He steps in front of her. His blue eyes have hardened to gunmetal. "You took it out of Connie's briefcase, didn't you?"

"You should have told me the truth."

"What truth? What do you think you know?" He pins her arms to her sides. "How much did you take?"

"Just one bag of weed. She'll never notice. There was so much." His grip tightens. "You're hurting me. Let go."

She jerks away from him as his left hand flies up and catches the side of her nose. When she touches her face, her hand comes away with blood. She's more astonished than hurt.

"Did you just punch me?"

"It was an accident. Let me get a towel." He hurries into the bathroom.

"How was that an accident?"

"Sit down and lean your head back," he says when he comes back with a towel.

"Let me put something on first. I'm freezing."

He picks up a T-shirt from the end of the bed and gives it to her. His favorite Public Enemy shirt.

"I'll ruin it."

"I don't care. I'm sorry."

His eyes are worried. She mops at her nose with the towel. It's a new one, pale yellow and now streaked with bloodstains that probably won't come out. Connie will be pissed.

"Sit down," he says again. She perches on the end of the bed as he presses his fingers over the bridge of her nose. "Hold your head back." His touch is gentle, his voice softer. "Connie used to do this when I got nosebleeds."

She can't relax with her head tilted back. She's still trembling. "It feels like it's stopped bleeding. Can you get me some ice?"

"This is what we use in football practice," he says when he comes back holding a bag of frozen peas. "I didn't mean to get angry. I just can't believe you'd steal from me."

"Well, technically I stole from Connie, not you."

His eyes narrow. "This is my deal, Allison. My house. My rules. And Bledsoe won't trust me if he finds out you're stealing from Connie."

"I thought we were a team. How would he find out?"

"He's dangerous, Allison. They all are."

"You mean The Family? Are they even real?"

"We have to be careful." He sits down next to her, and she tries not to flinch. This is paranoia talking. This is what snorting too much coke does.

"You said Bledsoe liked me."

"Let's try and keep it that way."

"Peggy's friends seemed excited."

"Let's just go to bed. I'm tired."

They both lie on their backs, holding hands. She's glad he doesn't want to make love. She's tired too, but too tired to sleep. Her mom was drinking way too much just before Christmas and she's been jealous of her and Kevin from the start, but it's impossible to imagine her wanting to have sex with Kevin. But why would he lie? She stares at the ceiling, counting the months until summer, when they can start over again someplace new.

CHAPTER TEN

"WHY AREN'T YOU IN DC WITH FRANK AND THE REST OF THEM?" BRENDA asks as she unlocks the screen door. "Aren't you missing out on the cherry blossoms or something?"

"Too early for cherry blossoms." Bill holds up his usual bottle of champagne, which he's brought every time he's come over, as a peace offering for standing her up that awful night in December. "I'm not missing anything. It's not my project. But they left me in charge, so I can stay as long as I want today."

As usual, she tells him she's not drinking and as always, he says champagne doesn't count. He takes the two remaining Tiffany glasses out of the kitchen cabinet, fills them to the brim, finishes his in one gulp, and sets it down next to her still-full glass on the coffee table. She tries to relax as he puts his arms around her, but she can barely breathe. Too quickly his hands find the zipper in the back of her dress and he pulls it off her shoulders. He loosens the hook of her bra, moaning that she has the best tits, mouthing her right nipple. She hopes he's thinking about Sue's flat chest.

"Not here," she says since there are still no curtains in the living room. He follows her into the bedroom. She sits down on the bed, her dress still down around her waist, and watches him step out of his dress slacks. He folds them carefully, places them on the back of the chair, and hangs his shirt over the pants. Sue's trained him well. His chest is fleshy, and she tries not to think about the curly red hairs on Frank's muscled chest. Bill kicks off his white briefs, leaves on his socks, and walks toward her, grinning, holding his oddly shaped penis in both hands. She hasn't been able to get past the crooked shape, how it angles off to the right. He stuffs it into her mouth, grabs her ears, and pushes deeper until she almost gags and pulls away.

This will get better, she tells herself, as she crabwalks backward on her hands toward the bed pillows. *We just need to find a rhythm.* He fumbles with a condom, then lumbers over her, pawing between her legs, pulling her panties, down and then off. He pushes the skirt of her dress up. She opens her legs and he mumbles something, his whiskered cheek in her neck. His breath smells of Tic Tac and onions. He thrusts inside her. *It's satisfying,* she tells herself, trying to ignore the rolls of fat on his back. *It's just different.* Live And Let Live, like Karla, the AA group leader, constantly says in the meetings. Poor Karla has to live with an overly large Adam's apple and a too enthusiastic voice.

"Okay if I take a shower?" Bill asks exactly two minutes later. He doesn't wait for an answer. He pulls off his socks and struts off entirely pleased with himself. There's a scratch on his back. She does her best to leave marks because how else will anyone know, and if no one knows, what is the point? The first time she had sex with him, she even gave him a hickey, to pay him back for standing her up. She likes thinking about how he explained that to Sue. He's in and out of the shower quickly, and dresses efficiently. Briefs, undershirt, dress shirt, slacks, belt, socks, shoes.

"Your tie's in the living room," she says.

"You're the best, Bren. Keep the rest of the champagne. I'll call you."

Once she hears him whistling down her driveway, she adjusts her dress, goes to the kitchen, and pours the champagne down the sink. It's an expensive bottle too. She enjoys wasting his money.

Not being sober might make the sex less disgusting, but

she's determined not to drink anymore. Keep it raw and real, she told herself at first. Atone for her sins and repent. It didn't take long to realize she didn't miss drinking. She likes not having a hangover every morning. She's lost weight, her skin glows, she's sleeping longer and more deeply. The downside is now she remembers her dreams. Last night she and Frank were tying a Christmas tree to the back of his truck, working together in sync like they'd done for so many years. It was so real she woke up crying.

She never thought she was an alcoholic anyway, and the AA meetings have proven her right. She can't get behind all the God business, and she doesn't need any of the twelve steps to realize she drank because Frank did. He opened a beer when he came home from work, so she had a glass or two of wine to keep him company. He liked Bloody Marys on the weekends, so she found the best ingredients. Her recipe made her more popular at brunches and Super Bowl parties.

Karla with the Adam's apple has offered more than once to be her sponsor, but she's turned her down. She's only there to get her paperwork signed off so she can get her driver's license back.

"Back on the record in the Simpson matter," Judge Ito says on the television screen. "Mr. Simpson is again present before the court with his counsel." The trial has finally begun, and this is her favorite part of the day. She loves how the judge says the same thing each morning in the same matter-of-fact, no-nonsense tone. It makes her sit up straight and pay attention. This is real and on the record. Lives are at stake. Two people are dead, and she has witness to bear.

Mark Fuhrman is explaining how he supposedly "found" the glove at O. J.'s estate, but Brenda can barely make out his face because of the afternoon sunlight glaring right into the screen. It's even worse at night when car lights strobe back and forth across the living room, making her feel like she's part of a crime scene. She probably will be if she stays in this horrible house much longer. There are cars pulling in and out of the driveway across the street day and night. She's sure those people are selling drugs. She'd told Peggy that this morning.

"They're just picking up their kids," Peggy said.

"You don't know that."

Peggy had moaned like a martyr, exasperated once again with her clueless mother. "I already told you, the woman who lives there is Gloria's mother."

"Who?"

"The Gloria I work with. Her mother babysits for her and her sisters."

"I can't believe you know people in this awful neighborhood. The only place I feel safe is in my bedroom with the blinds drawn."

"There are two deadbolts on the front door. And you can lock the screen. You're perfectly safe."

"I miss Allison. She doesn't bite my head off every time I ask a question like you do."

"Then make her come home."

"Tell your father. Living with Kevin was his idea."

Peggy won't say anything to Frank. Peggy thinks Frank walks on water. Allison thinks Kevin is the man of her dreams. Mark Fuhrman has a small dimple in his chin when he smiles, although she can't see his face because of the glare. Brenda wonders how many women fantasize about him.

She stands, unplugs the television, and disconnects the cable. The set is heavier than she expected, but once she has her arms under it and starts shuffling toward her bedroom, she has no choice but to keep going. She concentrates on not tripping on the electrical cord and scrapes her knuckles on the doorjamb.

Easy does it, like Karla from AA would say, she tells herself as she reaches the chest of drawers opposite her bed. There is a close-enough cable hookup, but the electrical socket is too far away to reach the plug. *Think, think, think.* Another Karla saying. Hopefully, there's an extension cord in the garage.

The Mexican woman across the street is out front watering her vegetables. Red leaf lettuce, it looks like, and maybe bell peppers. The woman waves so she waves back. Gloria's mother, she remembers. *Why can't she grow all that in her backyard like a normal person?* The garage door is heavy, but she gets it open, although it might have been a good idea to put on her bra and a pair of shoes. She still isn't used to the detached garage or the lack of an automatic garage door opener, and she doesn't intend to get used to either.

It takes a half hour to find an extension cord. She returns to the bedroom and plugs in the television. Success! Johnnie Cochran sports a new tie, one of the African patterns recently favored by the Dream Team. She props cushions behind her head and leans back, cradling the heart-shaped pillow Allison gave her years ago for Mother's Day.

She used to wonder what she was missing by being faithful to Frank and now she knows. *First things first.* She changes the bed, puts fresh towels in the bathroom, and starts the shower. Bill left hairs on her soap, so she throws the bar in the trash can and gets out a new one.

As soon as she lathers up, she hears someone knocking on the front door. She'd like to ignore it, but the window in her bathroom is open and whoever is out there can hear the water running. Another irrational feature of this house, putting a bathroom window next to the front door. Whoever it is knocks again. Hopefully, not Bill.

"Hello?" a woman's voice calls.

For God's sake. Brenda turns off the water, pats herself dry, and pulls on her wrinkled dress. She wraps the towel around her head and unlocks the deadbolts on the front door, keeping the security screen locked.

"I'm Laura. From across the street? Our daughters work together?"

Brenda peers out between the mesh of the security door. The woman is barely five feet tall and fine-boned, wearing a sweater over a coral flowered blouse and skirt. "I brought you some bell peppers." Laura holds up a basket. The peppers are fragrant and plump, glossy green. "That's nice of you. But I can't eat all those."

"They're good in salads or stews. Or stuffed with chorizo." The woman's English is understandable, which is a surprise. Laura smiles. Her expression is elegant, her nose, aristocratic, her eyebrows perfectly arched. "I was wondering if you'd mind if I picked some lemons from your tree?"

So that's what this is about, a ploy to scope out her house. "I don't know." She squints over Laura's shoulder at the street behind her. There doesn't seem to be anyone lurking out there now, but as soon as Laura goes home and makes her report that Brenda is home all alone, they'll be climbing the walls, jimmying all the locks.

"Your tree is the best in the neighborhood," Laura says. "Meyer lemons. No seeds and plenty of juice. The old man didn't tell you?"

"My uncle? He barely remembers my name."

"Such a sweet man. He loves my pies. I'm going to make you one."

Sweet and Uncle Charles don't belong in the same sentence. "You don't have to do that. I'm on a diet."

Laura stares at her and Brenda wonders if she's sizing her up, deciding how much weight she should lose. Or maybe Laura's English isn't that good. When she snaps her fingers, Brenda steps backward.

"You look just like Nicole Simpson."

"You're watching the trial?"

"Of course! It's better than the telenovelas. I like Marcia Clark. She's a smart lady. Maybe too smart."

"I know what you mean." It's silly to hide behind a locked screen door from this tiny woman. *Keep An Open Mind*, as they say in the meetings. She unlocks the door and takes the peppers from Laura. "Go ahead and pick all the lemons you want." She watches through the window as Laura goes through the side gate and walks toward the lemon tree. She can only reach the low-hanging branches, but she's able to fill both arms.

THE next day, Kato Kaelin, O. J.'s roommate/caretaker/friend, is being quizzed by an obviously irritated Marcia Clark when Laura knocks on the front door. Brenda unlocks both deadbolts and opens the screen door. Today Laura's wearing a green flowered blouse, skirt, and cardigan and holding a pie. She gazes toward the sound of the television in her bedroom.

"My husband's asleep. I can only watch with the sound down."

"Kato Kaelin is so goofy. I don't understand why O. J. would let him live with him. This pie smells delicious."

"Keep it in the fridge or the meringue will fall. Kato lived with Nicole too. She even named her dog after him. He's not as young as he looks, you know. He's almost forty and he's got a kid he doesn't support."

"Really?" Brenda says, impressed. She hadn't heard that. Laura might be fun to watch the trial with. It seems safe enough to invite her inside. "Why don't you watch with me? We can have some pie."

"I can't eat that. I have diabetes. Smart, putting the TV in your bedroom so you don't bother anyone." Laura sits down in the bedroom chair. "I was a fan of O. J.'s when he played football. But now, I don't know."

Brenda sits cross-legged at the end of her bed. "I don't understand why Nicole kept seeing O. J. after they divorced."

"Because of their kids, I guess. My oldest daughter, Bertha, is divorced, and she still sees her ex, although she lives with us now, her and her two kids. Two of my grandchildren. I have four altogether. Three daughters. And one son. Alejandro." The syllables roll off Laura's tongue and Brenda tries to figure out how his name would be spelled.

"That's a full house."

"My Alejandro lives in New Orleans."

"Really? I've always wanted to go there."

"He's a chef at Commander's Palace. Have you heard of it?"

"Of course! That place is famous." Laura's obviously mistaken. "What's his name again?"

"Alejandro Hernandez. He went to culinary school in New York. First in his class, too. I sold a hell of a lot of tamales to get him there."

There's no way someone from this neighborhood is a chef at Commander's Palace. The son, Ally-whatever, is probably a busboy. Laura's face is so full of joy, though. She won't spoil her fantasy. "Kato should have at least cut his hair," she says instead. "He reminds me too much of Allison's boyfriend."

Laura looks confused.

"My youngest. She's living with her boyfriend's family until she finishes high school. It was my husband's idea," she adds when she sees Laura's eyebrows raise. "My soon-to-be ex-husband, I mean. I don't like it at all." She's never called Frank her soon-to-be ex before.

"I wouldn't like that either," Laura says. "Daughters should be close."

They watch the testimony the rest of the afternoon, laughing together when Kato says he spent nearly an hour in O. J.'s jacuzzi on the night of the murders.

"That's why he doesn't remember. His brain is pickled." Laura stands.

"You don't have to go." Brenda looks at the clock next to her bed, surprised at how quickly the time has passed.

"The grandkids will be home from school soon, and I have to make dinner. I'll pray for you and your daughters."

"Oh, you don't need to do that." She sounds ungrateful. "But thank you," she adds. "That would be nice."

"THIS pie is absolutely delicious," Peggy says. "Where did it come from?"

Brenda looks up from the eleven o'clock news. "Laura from across the street. She says we have the best lemon tree in the neighborhood."

"You let Gloria's mother pick lemons from our tree?"

"She asked first. She's very nice. She sat here for a long time this afternoon, watching the trial with me."

"You let her in the house?"

"Why wouldn't I? It's nice to watch the trial with someone who is interested."

Peggy laughs.

"What? Am I not allowed to make friends?"

"You thought they were dealing drugs."

"Do you know five people live in that house? I can't imagine how they all fit. And Laura cooks for all of them and babysits four grandchildren. She has a lot of energy."

Peggy sits down on the end of her bed and points at the TV. "What are they talking about?"

"Something called a Columbian necktie. It's when drug dealers slice open someone's neck with a knife and pull their tongue through the slit."

"God, Mom. Doesn't this stuff give you nightmares?"

"Columbian drug dealers might have killed Nicole Simpson. She was into cocaine big time."

"O. J. killed Nicole."

"Why are you so sure of that? He's a victim of the system, just like I am. It's a white man's world."

"That's ridiculous, Mom. Simpson is wealthy and famous and not a victim of anything. And neither are you."

"Your father has controlled my life since I met him. He never wanted me to work and then he abandoned me. That makes me a victim. And the police framed O. J. because he's Black. You don't understand because you haven't followed everything like I have."

"You're right, I haven't. Because I have a life." Peggy licks her fork and stands. "Your new friend makes a great pie. Maybe I'll have another piece."

"You need to be careful. You're starting to gain back all the weight you lost."

SHE needs to be careful too, Brenda decides the next morning as she stands naked in front of the mirror on the bathroom door, slathering on lotion and examining her body from different angles. Her stomach is flatter now since she's stopped drinking, but the bottom curve of her ass is starting to sag a little. She squeezes into a pair of jeans and finds a green sweater in the back of her closet. She has corned beef in the Crock-Pot. It's almost St. Patrick's Day, not that she's Irish, but it's Sunday and her cousin Tim said he'd stop by this afternoon. She's planning on asking for a small loan. She's tired of begging Frank for money.

Tim looks different when he gets out of his Volkswagen bug. She's never seen him with his shirt tucked in and he actually has a jawline. "Have you lost weight?"

He takes a cardboard box stamped with pink letters from the back seat. "Vidavita," he says. "It's a miracle. You drink it instead of having a meal. Shake it up with some milk and voilà! The weight just falls off. It's loaded with vitamins and nutrients. I can get it for you wholesale. I'm a distributor."

Inside, Peggy's spread her books, ledger sheets, and calculator all over the kitchen table. She's already heard about Vidavita, of course; she knows all about it from her business class. It's a pyramid scheme, she says decisively, adding that she hopes Tim hasn't quit his job. It's impressive how Tim knows exactly how to answer her. He explains that Vidavita is not a pyramid scheme, it's something called network marketing, and it's all about living life. He adds that he'll probably clear two thousand dollars this month from working at home. He'll put in his notice eventually, but right now J.C. Penney gives him the opportunity to grow his business. Peggy tells him he sounds like he's brainwashed, but after he mixes up a batch of chocolate and vanilla, they all agree, the shakes are delicious.

"You'd be good at this, Brenda," Tim says. "By summer, you'd be driving around in the Vidavita car you'll win after you become my number one salesperson."

"You're both delusional," Peggy says. "Mom lost her license, remember?"

"I'll have it back by summer. What kind of car?"

"Pink," Tim says. "Everything Vidavita is pink."

"I don't have any money."

"I can front you."

"Peggy and I could both stand to lose a little weight. She can be my first customer."

"I don't know any women who don't think they need to lose weight. How about the people you work with, Peggy? Maybe you could reach out to your circle of influence."

"I don't have a circle of influence and I'm not talking to anyone about this."

"I'll call Kevin's mother," Brenda says. "She's a chunky one."

"Chunky ones are perfect," Tim says.

After dinner he hammers a pink and white sign in the front lawn. VIDAVITA'S THE WAY TO LOSE WEIGHT TODAY.

"People will see that," Peggy says.

"That's the idea," Tim says.

"WHY don't you stop by this afternoon?" Brenda tells Bill when he calls. "I have a business opportunity I'd like to talk to you about. Have you heard of network marketing?" She's practiced the spiel from the handbook Tim left her and she's sure she sounds convincing, but Bill's not listening.

"I can't get away this afternoon. Jack Bowen's in town."

She's heard of Jack Bowen from the Pacific Area office in San Francisco. Frank was always worried about impressing him.

"How about after the Laker game tonight?" Bill says. "Maybe you could invite a friend for Jack to hang out with while we're, you know, busy. You have any girlfriends who like to party?"

"Is that what we're doing? Partying?"

"I thought we were having fun. He'll be with me. I can't get away otherwise."

"Another time, then."

"Oh, come on, Bren. Leave your front door unlocked. I'll have him wait in the living room. You won't even know he's there."

Brenda pulls the phone away from her ear and stares at it. Does he seriously expect her to have sex with him while Jack Bowen waits in the living room? Does he think she's a whore? She doesn't deserve this kind of treatment. She's a free and independent woman with a new business to focus on.

"Bren? You still there?"

She puts the phone back in her ear. "Don't call me anymore. This party is over."

He hangs up on her. "Good riddance," she tells herself. At least no one found out about their affair. If that's even what it was.

PEGGY carries the small cooler inside the building to Brenda's AA meeting. While Brenda sits in the circle listening to the other alkies make their confessions, Peggy mixes shakes in the small kitchen and sets them on the counter next to the coffeepot. She's not particularly happy about being involved, but Peggy's not particularly happy about anything these days. It's obvious from the deep circles under her eyes that her nonstop schedule is taking a toll. She's tired and cranky all the time.

Karla finishes the meeting with a long speech in her perky little voice about the benefits of daily meditation. "Just sit and observe your thoughts."

Brenda wonders who in the world has time to sit around observing thin air as she hurries back to the counter to help Peggy. The shakes are delicious, everyone agrees.

"Let me explain how it works," she says, but Karla cuts her off. "I'm so sorry. AA doesn't allow sales pitches."

"It's not a sales pitch. It's network marketing."

"I should have spiked those shakes with Kahlúa," she tells Peggy later as they load everything back in the car. "I can't wait to be done with those drunks. Hopefully, things will go better at Laura's house next weekend."

"I thought you liked Laura. Why are you dragging her into this?"

"I do like Laura. She's always saying her daughters need to lose weight. I'm offering her family an opportunity to make extra money."

"I can tell you really want this," Peggy says, and the next weekend she offers to carry the cooler across the street. Laura's dark-haired daughters are lined up on her couch waiting, all double-chinned, round-bellied, and thick-thighed, one with a curly-haired baby on her lap.

Laura comes out of the kitchen with her arm looped around the waist of a handsome young man in a linen shirt, pressed slacks, and leather loafers. "This is my Alejandro. Home from New Orleans for some very important meetings." She leans forward and whispers loudly, "I'm not supposed to tell anyone, but he's talking to investors about an executive chef position at a new restaurant."

Alejandro laughs in a deeper and more melodious voice than Brenda expected and holds out his hand. "Nice to meet you. My mom talks about you all the time." His dark eyes are kind and he has a dimple in his chin.

"And this is Peggy," Laura says. "She works with Gloria."

Alejandro shakes Peggy's hand. "Sorry about my sister. Gloria's always been a pain in the ass."

"Shut up, Alejandro," Gloria says, but she's smiling. They're all smiling. The son is obviously beloved.

"We're barbecuing tonight," he says. "You and Peggy are welcome."

"Thanks," Peggy says. "But I have to work tonight."

"That's nice of you," Brenda says. She almost asks what happened to working at Commander's Palace, but she doesn't want to embarrass him. He's obviously overstated his position to impress his mother, absolutely understandable, considering she spent all that money on culinary school.

After he leaves, Brenda passes around a tray of chocolate and strawberry shakes, suddenly nervous about her spiel. "All you need is milk and a shaker cup. Peggy's on the program too. She's trying to drop a few pounds."

She looks over at Peggy for confirmation, but Peggy isn't paying attention. Peggy is staring at the curly-haired baby with a yearning expression Brenda finds very confusing.

"How old is she?" Peggy asks.

"Nine months," the young mother says. "You want to hold her?"

"Be careful with her head." Brenda can't remember Peggy ever wanting to hold a baby. She never even liked dolls.

"How much for a week's supply?" Gloria asks.

"I can get it for you at the wholesale price," Brenda says. "But if you become a distributor, it's even less."

"So that's how this works," Gloria says. "You make money on us."

"Gloria," Laura says. "Don't be rude."

"It's okay." Brenda glances over at Peggy, half-afraid she might agree, but Peggy isn't listening. Peggy is bouncing the baby on her knee and giggling. "It's called network marketing. I tell my friends, they tell their friends, and we build a network. We all save money and we all make money. And we lose weight too."

The heaviest of all the sisters reaches for another glass of the strawberry flavor. "All I have to do is drink this and I'll lose weight?"

"You drink this *instead* of a meal. It's very filling. I have it for breakfast and dinner and then just eat a salad for lunch. I've lost fifteen pounds."

"I don't know if I could do that. It tastes more like dessert."

"You'll probably *gain* weight, Bertha." The young mother laughs and takes the baby back from Peggy. "I'll buy some. I'm still trying to take weight off from this one."

"Me too," Gloria says. "I have a wedding dress to fit into."

"Perfect," Brenda says. "And please tell your friends."

"Thanks for going with me," Brenda says, as they cross the street back to the house. "It was a big help, having you there. You seemed to really enjoy that baby."

"I'm surprised they fell for it," Peggy says. "They all bought something."

"It's a start. Don't mention this to your father though. He's already going to freak out once he sees the Discover card bill."

"I thought Tim fronted you the money."

"Tim says you have to spend money to make money."

LATER that afternoon, Brenda thinks about going over to Laura's for a plate of food, but when she sees all the cars, the aluminum-foiled pans stacked on the folding tables in the front yard, the piñata strung in the tree, and hears the accordion music blaring from inside Laura's house, she realizes she doesn't want to go alone. She won't fit in.

She watches through the window instead, for a long time. There are so many of them, and even though they barely have enough room to sit down in the tiny front yard, they all seem to be having such a good time together. She closes her eyes, thinking she'll try meditation, since her house is so overwhelmingly silent right now, but all she can think about is how she needs to sell more Vidavita.

She turns on the television instead.

THE next morning, she settles in with her coffee. "Back on the record in the Simpson matter," Judge Ito says on the television screen and the phone rings.

"We need to talk," Sue says.

Finally! Sue's noticed the marks on Bill's back. It sure took her long enough.

"Someone should tell you," Sue says. "I'd appreciate it, if it were my Jenny."

What does Sue's mousy daughter have to do with anything? "Tell me what?"

"Tuesday night we stopped by the post office because Bill left his briefcase in his office. I swear to God, that man is getting senile. He left his pajamas at a hotel in Denver. He lost his belt at the gym."

Bill's joined a gym? That doesn't sound like him at all. "I'm confused," she says.

"I'm sorry to rattle on like this. I was nervous about calling you. We haven't talked for a while. Anyway, I waited in the car in the employee parking lot while Bill went inside. I didn't recognize Allison at first. She was wearing a baseball cap over that gorgeous hair."

"Allison? In the post office parking lot? Doing what?"

"I thought she might be waiting for Peggy."

"Peggy has class on Tuesday nights. I think you're mistaken. Allison never wears baseball caps."

"A couple of those guys who work on the dock came down the ramp looking for her."

"How did you know they were looking for her? What exactly did you see?" *This is a weird game for Sue to play.*

"I couldn't really tell, but it looked like she handed them something."

"Handed them what?"

"I don't know. Drugs maybe. Bill says I'm overreacting."

Overreacting or overly crafty. "What time was this?"

"Around eight thirty."

"Allison wouldn't be in Santa Ana that late at night. She has school in the morning. Did Bill see her?"

"She was gone by the time Bill came back. I probably shouldn't have called. I don't mean to worry you."

That's exactly what she meant to do, Brenda decides after they hang up. Worry her. Just to reassure herself, though, she dials Connie's number. Connie can verify that Allison was at her house last night doing her homework, and she can tell her about Vidavita. Connie's phone, however, just rings and rings and never goes to voice mail. *Who doesn't have an answering machine in this day and age?* She'd like to drive down to the school right now and check on Allison, but since she has no car or license, she calls Frank at work. She gets Ginny instead.

"They're all heading back to DC for the national conference."

"Ask him to call me. Tell him it's important."

There aren't many girls who resemble Allison and something about Sue's story is unnerving. This is an odd way for anyone to take revenge.

SHE explains Sue's phone call when Peggy walks in the door just after the eleven o'clock news finishes. "Is there someone at the post office who looks like your sister?"

"I don't know everyone who works there, Mom."

"I was hoping you could take me down to visit her tomorrow."

"I have a tax review seminar in the morning. And then I have to work."

"Can't you skip the seminar?"

"No. I can't."

"You don't have to bite my head off. I'm worried about your sister."

"I can't drop everything just because you've finally decided to pay attention to Allison."

"What's that supposed to mean? It was your father's idea for her to live with Kevin, not mine."

"I'm going to bed."

"I'm sick of you being in such a horrible mood all the time."

After Peggy slams the door to her bedroom, Brenda thinks about calling the police and asking them to knock on Connie's door and make sure they haven't all been murdered, but she's afraid of what else the police might find. What if Allison is selling drugs? Why isn't Peggy interested in helping her and why doesn't Frank call her back?

Because she's overreacting, obviously. Sue's taking revenge, Peggy's stressed out, Connie's phone is simply out of order, and Frank hasn't called because there's a three-hour time difference between here and Washington, DC.

She goes to bed but she's not sleepy, so she turns on the light and studies the Vidavita handbook. There are all kinds of suggestions for growing her business—print and distribute flyers, canvass the neighborhood, reach out to friends and family, go through her address book and the Christmas card list. She's dreaming that she's earned enough money to go to Mardi Gras next year when she hears the phone ring in the kitchen.

"What's so important?" Frank asks. "I have a meeting in ten minutes."

He sounds impatient, so she tries to summarize what Sue said, but it's not even six a.m. and she's groggy. Frank's more interested in talking about the Discover card bill, so she tells him she'd better let him get to his meeting. She puts on a pot of coffee and calls Connie's house again, but there's still no answer. She obviously has the number wrong. She'll call the jewelry store later if she can find it in the yellow pages. *Focus*, she tells herself. Connie's not the only woman with a business to run.

She's loading a small cooler with a quart of milk, protein powder, and the plastic shaker cup when Peggy comes out of her bedroom. She doesn't look like she's slept much either.

"Where are you going with all that?"

"I thought I'd try door-to-door sales."

"That seems kind of dangerous, Mom."

"I'm offering free milkshakes. No one's going to murder me." Peggy looks as if she feels guilty about the way she behaved last night, so Brenda adds, "Come with me, if you want."

"I'll get dressed."

It turns out there was no reason for Peggy to worry since people in their neighborhood either aren't home, don't speak English, or have no interest in a free milkshake. It would be humiliating if she wasn't so distracted.

"This is a waste of time," she says finally. "Let's go home."

"Are you still worried about what Sue said?"

"Sue has her own agenda."

"Allison should not be living with Kevin."

"I agree. There's got to be some way we can convince her to move back in with us."

"The only way she'll stop seeing him is if he's dead or in jail."

Brenda swallows hard, shaken at the resolve in Peggy's voice. It's too nice of a day to be so serious. At least the two of them are together, walking in the sunlight, doing something productive and, for the first time in a long time, not arguing. A red sedan speeds past them and a young man hangs out of the open passenger window. "Hey, baby," he yells. "Want a ride?"

She knows he's making fun of her, but a small amount of flattery is enough to give any woman hope.

"BILL says Sue watches too much *Law and Order*," Frank tells her when he calls later. "He said to tell you he's sorry she bothered you."

I bet he's sorry. He probably just about had a heart attack when he heard Sue called me. "Sue didn't sound like herself."

Frank hesitates for a moment. "They're having problems. Bill's seeing someone else."

Brenda holds her breath and waits. She never wanted to be the one to tell Frank.

"He came home with scratches on his back and Sue confronted him."

Those were her scratches. Bill must have confessed. Her mouth is so dry she can barely swallow.

"Bill's kind of an idiot sometimes," Frank says.

He knows, she's sure, and he's trying to humiliate her by insulting Bill. "He's your best friend." And she fucked him anyway. How Frank must hate her.

Frank laughs. "He's still a damn fool. This new girl is half his age."

Her stomach plummets toward the ground as if she's on that horrible roller coaster at Magic Mountain. "What new girl?"

"The new Delivery Services Management intern. She transferred in from Long Beach before Christmas. She's cute, but I can't imagine what they find to talk about. His daughter Jenny's almost the same age."

Before Christmas! Brenda is so dizzy she has to hold the phone with both hands, so she doesn't drop it. "Poor Sue," she mumbles.

Frank says he doesn't feel sorry for Sue at all because she had an affair last year, and they were already planning on divorcing as soon as Jenny gets her degree.

"Anyway," he goes on. "I talked to Allison yesterday. She wasn't in the parking lot. It's nice of you to take some interest in your daughter. A little late but better than nothing."

She'd like to reach through the phone and strangle him. "I've been worried sick about Allison since you let her move in with Kevin. Why don't they answer the phone at Connie's house? I've called a million times."

"I have no idea."

"Next time you talk to Allison, ask her to call me."

"That's up to her."

He says goodbye, but she sits there with her mouth open, still holding the phone. Bill dumped her for a twenty-year-old? Sue had an affair? How did she not know any of this? Thank goodness she'd made Bill use condoms. Otherwise he might have given her some disease.

PROS OF HAVING A BABY	CONS OF HAVING A BABY
Being a mother	Being a mother
Kid looks like Glenn	Kid looks like Glenn
Not having to wonder what kid would have been like	Knowing exactly what the kid is like: a complete mess

PROS OF ADOPTION	CONS OF ADOPTION
Kid has better life	Kid might be adopted by maniacs
I can get on with my own life	I'll wonder where the kid is the rest of my life

PROS OF ABORTION	CONS OF ABORTION
I have the $500 Glenn gave me	I've waited too long
I won't have to look like a cow for nine months	I'll have to live with the decision the rest of my life
No one will know what I've done	I will know what I've done

PEGGY SHUTS OFF HER COMPUTER AND CONSIDERS THE CALENDAR INSTEAD. It's already April. If she doesn't abort, the baby will be born in September, which will make it a Virgo, like she is. Two perfectionists who'll drive each other crazy. She's eighteen now. When she's twenty-eight, the kid will be ten. When she's thirty-eight, the kid will be twenty and more than likely in jail. Or maybe it'll be a genius, get a scholarship to Harvard, and discover a cure for cancer. It had better get a scholarship. She'll never be able to afford an Ivy League school on a single mother's income. She's the one who should be going to an Ivy League school, not some baby she doesn't even want.

SHE shadows Glenn and Jill out of the post office through the employee parking lot, willing him to turn around. When they get to his truck, he opens the passenger door for Jill and finally notices her. She waits for him to wave, but he ignores her.

"Wait up," she says. "I need a favor." But he doesn't hear her and she's not even sure she's said the words out loud. He gets in the driver's seat and slams the door.

She waits to be nauseous, but the sick to her stomach period of her pregnancy seems to be over. According to the pamphlet from Planned Parenthood that she keeps in the glove box of her car next to Glenn's *Booty* necklace, nausea ends at the beginning of the second trimester. She glances up and realizes she's standing in front of one of the recently installed security cameras, the lens trained directly on her face. Great. Now the Inspection Service will know how pathetic she is too.

The Santa Ana plant is newly fortified. Access badges have been issued to all employees. The parking lot has a fence and a security gate. Cameras have been installed and signs posted. AUTHORIZED EMPLOYEES ONLY. There's been another shooting at another post office, this time in New Jersey, another former employee coming back with a gun, taking revenge on his supervisor and coworkers. Almost two years ago the same thing happened in Dana Point. Before that it was Royal Oak, Citrus Heights, Dearborn, Michigan, and too many others to keep track of. Something obviously needs to be done, and although it's not always former employees who "go postal," the district manager has decided that controlling access to the facility is a good place to start. No one feels any safer. It's easy to follow someone else's car into the lot. Everyone says all the crazies are locked up inside now.

She watches Glenn's truck wait for the security gate to roll open. He and Jill stare straight ahead. "Peggy looked like she wanted something," Jill could be saying. She knows exactly what Glenn is thinking: *I already gave her five hundred dollars.*

She doesn't want to think about what he said when she finally told him: "How do you know it's my kid?"

Waiting this long has reduced her options. It's no longer a medically induced event; cutting and suctioning will now be required and there can be complications. The clinic won't let her drive home after "the procedure" tomorrow, and there's no one she can ask for a ride. Tessa has too big of a mouth, Rita's busy with her kids, and Dolores would be so disappointed. She could never ask her father and her mother can't drive. Allison doesn't have a driver's license either and Peggy wants nothing to do with Kevin. She's heard about him selling drugs in the parking lot. Of course, Allison insists whoever Sue saw wasn't her, that Kevin's the one taking all the risks, but it's impossible to believe anything Allison says.

The security gate creaks open and Glenn's truck accelerates out of the parking lot. She'll have to call him in the morning.

THE next morning, she plans on using the phone in the kitchen to call Glenn, but there's a knock on the front door and she hears Laura's voice, excited about something. "Did you hear?" she says. "The jurors are on strike. Judge Ito canceled testimony for the day and gave them the weekend off."

"They're protesting him changing their deputies," Brenda says.

Peggy hears the television go on. Great. She'll have to call

Glenn from the pay phone at the corner. She stays in her room until the last possible moment, afraid what she's planning is written all over her face. She opens the bedroom door cautiously, carrying her books as if it's a regular work-school day that bleeds over into the night and she's not heading off to be cut apart and suctioned out. Laura is standing in the living room holding the curly-haired baby, who giggles and holds out chubby hands.

"Hey, sleeping beauty," Brenda says. "Want some breakfast?"

"I'll get something on the way." She needs to leave, but the baby is a force field, with her magnetic brown eyes, willing her to move closer. The baby laughs now, fluttering her tiny legs. Peggy takes a tiny foot in both her hands, leans forward, and smells the crown of her head. Sweet milk and powder. The baby takes hold of her little finger.

"She likes you," Laura says. "Look at her smile."

"It's gas," Brenda says. "She's too young to smile."

"You'll make a beautiful baby," Laura says softly.

Her heart nearly stops. She forces herself to release the tiny foot. "I'm late," she says, staggering toward the front door. "I'd better go." She pulls into the liquor store on the corner to use the pay phone and sits in her car for a moment, feeling all the space around her. Her mother was wrong. It wasn't just gas; the baby was smiling because she recognized her. Laura recognized something too.

She looks at her watch. She needs to call Glenn, but there's an old man camped out on the sidewalk next to the pay phone drinking something out of a brown paper bag. One more obstacle to negotiate. She wonders if Glenn will answer the phone or if she'll have to talk to Jill first. She hasn't given this enough thought. She fumbles in her purse for some change and gets out of the car. The man raises whatever he's drinking and salutes her.

"Nice day, isn't it? We're damn lucky to live here."

"We are," she says, and just like that she changes her mind.

The woman on the phone at the clinic has a kind voice. Peggy schedules an appointment for prenatal care and tells herself she's doing the right thing, that she needs this little being inside her right now, someone to talk to who listens. Her sister will be thrilled when she calls her later, not that she cares what Allison thinks. Her mother will freak out and then parrot some ridiculous expression from her AA meetings, but it doesn't matter. She's not keeping it, anyway.

It's a long day at work, trying to not watch Glenn and Jill. The problem with a mindless job is there's too much time to think. The problem with thinking all day is she can't turn off her brain at night when she finally goes to bed. There are too many empty hours in the darkness to fill with remembering all the ways Glenn touched her, all the private, secret things that made her gasp, made his eyes shine. All that can't be over. All that must prove something.

One thing is sure. She'll be huge soon and people will whisper, "What a fool."

PEGGY stands in line with Frank and Linda at Super Mex, wondering what he wants to talk to her about, hoping she isn't going to be sick to her stomach again today. One of the cooks behind the counter slices lemons and limes, and the citrus cuts through the smell of fatty beef cooking in lard. Frank orders two Negra Modelos, a water, and three bean and cheese burritos. The cashier opens the beers, releasing a carbonated burst of yeast. Cigarette smoke wafts in from the window of a car waiting in the drive-through, burning her eyes. The music is loud, chirruping accordions and an earnest tenor voice. Linda whispers something in her father's ear and he laughs.

"Your friend John came by my office," Frank says after they find a table and sit down. "He sure seems to like you."

"He's not really my friend."

"He wanted to know how he could improve his interview skills. I was impressed until he told me he met your sister at a party at Glenn Fielding's house. You want to explain what Allison was doing there?"

"She wanted to go," she says, which is true except Allison only went so Kevin could sell drugs to her friends. She should tell her father this, now, but she wonders what *else* John told him.

"Why would you introduce your sister to Glenn Fielding, of all people?" Frank is asking.

Linda nods, a grave expression on her plain face. "He does have a terrible reputation."

"I don't want your sister getting mixed up with him or his drugged-out friends."

"They're my friends too. And they're all hard workers. You know that, Dad."

"Allison and Kevin are still minors. I'm disappointed, Peggy. I thought you had better sense."

Of course, he's only worried about his precious Allison. She should tell him Allison and Kevin are the druggies, but he won't believe her.

The cashier calls their order number and Frank goes to get their food. Linda leans across the table and squeezes her hand. "He doesn't mean that. He's proud of you."

She blinks back tears and pulls a wad of paper napkins from the dispenser. She's not going to cry in front of this woman. It's the hormones. It's the fact that no one has touched her in a long time.

"I heard you're having trouble getting classes around your schedule."

"Who said that?"

"People talk. There's a job opening in the accounting office. Eight to five, weekends off."

"I didn't know the post office even had an accounting office."

"What's that?" Frank sets down the tray with their food.

"Phyllis needs help in accounting," Linda says. "Peggy would be a good fit."

"That's a great idea. I'll talk to the girls in Personnel."

"You don't have to," Peggy says. "I'm not planning on working much longer anyway. I'm going to school full time as soon as I save some money."

She doesn't sound convincing even to herself.

SHE hears other employees complain how unfair it is for someone who's only been working a few months to get to work days in a cushy office with weekends off, but they are wrong. The accounting office is not cushy. The fluorescent lights hum, the walls are a hideous government-green, her desk is made of heavy steel that she bumps her knee into every time she moves her chair, someone is constantly burning popcorn in the microwave down the hall, and she never sees her friends.

There's not much difference between sorting letters on the workroom floor and filing documents in the horrible green office. It might be 1995, but the post office has yet to enter the twentieth century. The amount of paperwork to complete and the number of file cabinets to fill is staggering. She works with her dad's friend Phyllis, who thankfully never mentions Linda's party last year when everything fell apart. Phyllis is a large woman who owns horses, lives in Riverside on a small ranch, and wears cowboy boots to work every day. They take the elevator down to the first floor and walk past the line of customers waiting to buy stamps and mail packages. On the window line, Peggy recognizes her parents' friend Julie, who closes her station and follows them behind the window section. "We need some money orders," Phyllis tells Julie, handing her a list of the amounts. "Just put the total in suspense for now."

Julie looks at the list. "Four thousand five hundred sixty-eight dollars."

"We'll give you the accounts to charge them to later," Phyllis says. "Peggy will bring you the receipts."

"How's your mom?" Julie asks when she comes back with the money orders. "I feel bad about not calling her. Can you tell her hello for me?"

"Sure." Peggy looks at the money orders. "These are blank."

"Phyllis always fills them out. My handwriting is terrible."

"It's easier to take them back to the office and type them," Phyllis says as they wait for the elevator.

"It's almost five thousand dollars."

"Which might seem like a lot of refunds, but remember these are for all the post offices in Orange County for the last month. Sometimes it's more, especially when LAX gets socked in with fog."

"Shouldn't someone else mail them? We just discussed checks and balances in my business class."

Phyllis looks confused. "It's the way we've always done it. We have supporting documentation for everything in case we get audited. I'll show you."

There's paperwork for everything, of course. Paperwork which would be simple to replicate if anyone wanted to.

THE morning drags. Peggy rests her hands on her stomach and is rewarded with a kick in the middle of her palm. This creature growing inside her suddenly has an opinion on everything. It punches her kidney if she adds chili to her burrito. It doesn't like Johnnie Cochran's voice on the television set. It delivers a tiny sharp elbow to her bladder whenever she thinks about Glenn.

She eats lunch alone, reading a tax manual, then goes back to her desk and her piles of papers to file. At 2:23 p.m., right before her friends are due to start their shift, she stands and stretches. She already has Glenn's $500 tucked in the back pocket of her jeans. She's giving the money back.

"I'll go check the mail case to see if the reconciliation from St. Louis came in."

"Good idea." Phyllis's head is bent over a stack of payroll adjustments.

"Maybe I'll get a Coke from the lunchroom. You want something?"

"You're a sweetheart. How about a pack of those peanut butter cookies? And a Diet Dr. Pepper?"

The lunchroom is full. Someone is reheating fish in the microwave. One of the truck drivers slams his fist against the side of the vending machine, trying to get a bag of chips to fall. Peggy hopes her loose peasant blouse hides her belly as she walks over to the table where Glenn is sitting with Jill, Chico, and Tessa. He's reading the sports page.

"Hey, Peggy," Tessa says. "You look really pretty! How's the day job?"

"Boring."

"Did you just get a facial or something? Your skin is really glowing."

"I'm taking some new vitamins." She feels Glenn's eyes glance up at her for a millisecond and then immediately back to the newspaper.

"How's the traffic?" Chico asks.

"Horrible. It takes twice as long to get here and three times as long to get home."

"We better go clock in," Tessa says. "Call me sometime. We need to catch up."

Glenn doesn't follow them, and when he says, "Sit down," she's relieved. Tessa glances over her shoulder as she heads out the door and gives her a thumbs-up.

"I had an interesting conversation with your father." Glenn's smile is cold, and her heart starts to tap dance against her ribs. "He told me to stay away from you and your sister or he'd make life difficult for me. What did you tell him?"

"Nothing! What does that mean, make life difficult?"

"The usual bullshit. Have Acosta screw around with my schedule or put me on restricted sick leave."

"He wouldn't do that."

His laugh is sarcastic. "He can jack me around all he wants. I'll file a grievance."

"I'll talk to him." *How would that conversation start? Leave Glenn alone, Dad, but don't ask me why?*

"Don't do me any more favors."

"John's the one who told him my sister was at your house, not me."

Glenn lowers his voice. "Did you tell him the baby is mine?"

"Of course not."

"I don't appreciate being manipulated, Peggy."

"How am I manipulating you?" she asks, but he's already standing.

"I have to go clock in." He doesn't look back at her when he walks out of the lunchroom.

She feels everyone staring as she slinks along the wall of the workroom floor, heading upstairs to the office with her full-moon face and ballooning belly. She sits down at her desk empty-handed. She's forgotten Phyllis's drink, the promised cookies, to give Glenn his money back, her self-respect, how to act like she has a brain in her head.

SATURDAY morning, Peggy pauses behind her mother in the parking lot at Anaheim Plaza and admires the pink flyers with the Vidavita slogan, ASK ME THE WAY TO LOSE WEIGHT TODAY, fluttering underneath every windshield wiper on every parked car in front of Wal-Mart. It almost looks pretty. Her mother made the right choice going with pink paper at Kinko's, even though white would have cost less.

"I didn't realize how embarrassing this would be," Brenda says.

The work is grittier than either of them expected. The windshield wipers are grimy, and the parking lot is splotched with oil, gum, and occasional pools of unidentifiable substances Peggy doesn't want to examine too closely. At least she knew enough to wear a baggy T-shirt over a loose pair of sweatpants and old tennis shoes. Her mother's white capris and kitten-heeled sandals were a definite mistake.

"This too shall pass," Brenda says.

"Aren't you sick of those clichés?"

"I like the expressions. They're easy to remember. Not everyone is as smart as you are. Let's go over there." Brenda points toward the Toys "R" Us store across from Wal-Mart. "Tim says new mothers make the best customers. They all want to lose weight and work at home."

There's a steady flow of people streaming in and out of Toys "R" Us. Young couples, grandmother types, mothers, and fathers pushing strollers and carts, kids following along like little ducklings, women in all stages of pregnancy. Peggy keeps her head down as she follows Brenda and watches the crowd. She nearly cries when she sees a young pregnant girl beam up at the boy next to her.

"What's wrong?" Brenda asks, when they finally run out of flyers and walk back to the car. "You look miserable."

"I'm tired. I hope the flyers get you some customers."

"I doubt it. Look."

A man is taking a flyer off his windshield and tossing it to the ground. Half of the pink papers are scattered all over the asphalt. Peggy walks over to pick one up and her back twinges as she stands. She braces her palms on her lower back and stretches. Her stomach feels as if it's suddenly ballooned into a hard and very round melon. Brenda stares at her, assessing her belly under her T-shirt, and gets in the car. Peggy starts the engine and turns on the radio. Led Zeppelin's singer howls about it being a long time.

"You're pregnant, aren't you?"

She backs carefully out of the space, puts the car in drive, and cautiously steps on the gas. "I'm due in September."

"All this time I thought you were just gaining weight. Why didn't you tell me?"

"Because I knew you'd freak out."

Brenda frowns. "September is five months from now."

"You can do math. I'm impressed."

"We'll find an agency. There are plenty of good people look-ing for babies."

"I haven't decided what I want to do. You don't get to just take over."

"How would you manage a child plus work and go to school? I'm not babysitting."

"No one's asking you to."

Brenda sighs when they pull in the driveway. "I never thought this would happen to you."

The singer pleads that he is lonely, lonely, lonely, followed by crashing drums. Peggy cuts the engine. "You thought no one would ever want me."

"I thought you were smarter than this."

"Obviously, you were wrong about that too."

SHE takes a long shower and puts on clean sweats. She's going to need to buy some new clothes soon. Her mom will be happy about an excuse to shop, she supposes.

Brenda is waiting for her when she gets out of the shower. "Come sit down. I need to tell you something."

"There is nothing else to say, Mom."

"I'll support whatever decision you make. Even if you want to marry John."

This is so unexpected that Peggy can't decide if she wants to laugh or cry, but she can tell her mother is about to cry and she's too exhausted for any more drama. "I'm not going to marry someone and have a baby I don't want, like you did."

Brenda exhales slowly. There are tiny lines around her eyes and mouth. "That story was never true," she says after a moment. "You were never an accident and Allison wasn't a surprise. I wanted both of you."

"What are you talking about?"

Brenda swallows and then speaks so softly Peggy can barely hear her. "I got pregnant on purpose both times and lied to your father."

"You never said that before." She sits down slowly on the couch. "Why didn't you just tell him the truth?"

"I was afraid I'd lose him. I was so young. And then he started cheating on me and I felt like a fool."

"I never believed he was cheating."

All these years, I've defended him.

Brenda smiles. "You can be so naïve sometimes, Peggy. I love that about you."

"Why did you stay with him?"

Brenda looks down at her hands. "Because I love him. Because I don't know how to do anything else. Looks like I'm going to have to learn though. He wants a divorce."

"Is that what you want?"

"No. It is not."

"I should call him tonight and tell him about the baby."

"He'll blame me."

"He'll say I'm just like you."

"Don't be. You aren't, anyway. You're way smarter than I am." She wipes her eyes with her hands. "Anyway. I want your sister to come home. We need to be a family right now."

"I want her to come home too, but how will she get to school? I can't drive her to Ocean View every day."

"One day at a time. Now let's talk about prenatal vitamins. You will not believe how good they are for your hair and nails and skin. You are going to be radiant, my dear."

It's so predictable how her mom immediately steers the conversation to the superficial. Peggy's grateful though. The consistency is comforting.

CHAPTER TWELVE

"TRY PAGING HIM AGAIN," ALLISON SAYS. THEY'VE BEEN SITTING OUTSIDE the Jack in the Box for an hour now waiting for Chico.

"I've paged him twice already," Kevin says.

"Are we close to Anaheim? My mom wanted me to come by this afternoon." She has no idea where they are. Kevin drove north on Beach Boulevard for at least half an hour. The street names are unfamiliar, but every intersection looks the same. Gas stations and strip malls with nail salons, dentists' offices, mini-marts, fast food. Hopefully when she learns to drive, she'll have a better sense of direction. "I'm pretty sure my mom has a tent we could borrow for our trip. We used to camp all the time at the river."

"I'm not in the mood for your mother right now."

As soon as school's out, they're heading down to San Diego for a festival and then on to Mexico to surf, eat lobsters, camp on the beach, and hopefully make love every night, something Kevin doesn't seem to want to do these days. Hopefully, she can talk him into never coming back from Mexico, although Cal State Northridge is expecting him to start on the varsity team in August.

"We should at least go look at the tent. I think she also has a camp stove and a cooler."

"I can't leave town until I sell the rest of the coke." He stares at his pager. "Something's up with those post office clowns. None of them are calling me anymore."

She stares out the window, her heart beating faster, trying not to say the wrong thing. "We've been planning this trip for months, Kevin."

"I know, babe. But it might not be in the cards right now."

"Maybe we should start looking at apartments in Northridge then."

"I haven't talked to Connie about that yet."

"It'll be cheaper than living in a dorm. Especially once I get a job."

"I don't want to push her right now."

"Maybe we should get married." She laughs when she says this to make up for how much she wishes he'd said it first.

"Stop acting crazy. You should just keep living with Connie and Sal. I'll be home every weekend."

She'd go crazy, living alone in Kevin's room, waiting for him to come home on the weekends from Northridge. Everything she says lately is wrong. When they start to make love, he can't stay hard. He won't talk about it except to complain that she rushes him, she's greedy and too demanding, she wants more when he's already finished.

"Maybe I should move in with my mom. Peggy says she's stopped drinking. And she's got a job now."

"Selling protein powder is not a job."

"She's answering phones or something. Peggy's pissed because she has to drive her back and forth everywhere."

He looks at his watch. "This is a waste of time. Chico's not going to show." He starts the truck.

She lights a joint, trying not to say the wrong thing again, hoping he'll calm down. When she sees the blue-and-white Wal-Mart sign on the next corner, she knows how to cheer him up. "Wal-Mart has those new Walkmans. I saw an ad in the paper. Which one do you want?"

When Kevin smiles, he looks like an entirely different person. "The D Series with the Mega Bass. It should fit in your backpack easy."

She's never been in a Wal-Mart, never taken anything from a place she's not shopped in before, and never done it stoned either, but Kevin's already putting on his blinker and turning into the parking lot.

"Look for a couple of discs too. Tupac's new one if they have it." He parks in front of the store and watches as she dumps books out of her pack onto the floor of his truck.

"Back in a flash." She takes a deep breath to summon confidence she doesn't feel and slings the empty pack on her shoulder.

"I'll be waiting out here with the engine running."

Wal-Mart is loud, bright, and overly air-conditioned. There is an actual greeter at the front door, which she has never seen in other stores. He asks if he can help her find something, but she's too nervous and overwhelmed to even make eye contact, much less answer his question, which she knows is a mistake. It's important to be friendly. She feels the man's eyes on her back as she heads deeper into the store.

Just act normal, she tells herself. *This is no big deal.*

She follows the signs from BEAUTY to HOME IMPROVEMENT and finds ELECTRONICS. There's a row of television sets all tuned to Oprah Winfrey, who is talking to a hairstylist about Marcia Clark. Allison stops for a moment to watch. The stylist is famous, apparently. He must have done Farrah Fawcett's hair back in the day since her image is on all the screens now. The camera switches back to Marcia, who has given up on the perm and changed to a shag cut. Brenda will be glad.

Focus, she tells herself. Find the CD player and a couple of discs and get out of here. She slinks by the locked-glass cases with cameras and headphones and hovering clerks. Miraculously the disc players are neatly stacked two aisles away, unattended. She looks around to make sure no one is watching and crouches down. The box fits snugly in her backpack. She zips it closed and rises. The CDs are under a sign posted ENTERTAINMENT and arranged by type of music.

It takes her forever to realize there's no rap section. She imagines Kevin, restless in the parking lot. Some other band, she decides, but spends too much time in the Hard Rock section trying to remember if it's Green Day he hates or the Red Hot Chili Peppers. She crams both in her pack and notices, too late, a man wearing a clip-on tie and short-sleeved white shirt watching. She quickly heads toward the door. "Miss," he says, and she starts running. She's never had to run before. Still, she doesn't panic. Kevin's truck is still in front of the store. There are only a few yards to cover and she's outside, in the warm afternoon, almost to the passenger side of Kevin's truck when a huge man in a blue security shirt steps right in front of her and puts a large hand on her shoulder. "I'm going to need you to stop right there."

Clip-on Tie Guy is right behind him. "Park your truck and come inside," he tells Kevin.

"Just go," Allison says.

"What happened?" Kevin asks. "What did you do?"

He looks like he wants to stomp on the gas and get the hell away from her, but when Clip-On Tie writes down his license plate number, he gets out of the truck. The large man is already walking her back inside the store. Kevin follows.

"WE were just about ready to take her down to the station and book her," the police officer says when her mother finally walks into the store manager's office, dressed to impress in a short white skirt, too tight blue sweater, and full makeup, which is probably why it took her so long to get here. Connie came right away but won't even look at her.

"I'm sure this is a misunderstanding." Brenda sits down next to Allison and puts her arm around her shoulder, hugging her close.

"She had all that in her backpack," the store manager says, gesturing to the Walkman and the CDs displayed on his desk next to the Swiss Army knife.

"Is that your father's knife?"

"I'm sorry," Allison chokes out. "I meant to give it back to him." The manager hands her a Kleenex.

Brenda opens her wallet. "How much do I owe you?"

"Wal-Mart has zero tolerance for shoplifters," the manager says. "Plus, she had the knife in her pocket."

"Oh, give me a break! That knife is just a bottle opener and she's a kid, acting out. My husband and I are going through a divorce."

Divorce! Allison wipes her eyes. *So that's why she wanted me to stop by.*

Brenda goes on. "I'm sure she's learned her lesson. This will never happen again."

"It won't happen at Wal-Mart," the manager says. "She's banned from all our stores."

"That won't be a problem. I don't know what she was doing in here in the first place."

The policeman takes Brenda's name, address, and phone number, tears off the top copy, and hands her the form. "The court date is listed on the bottom of the citation."

"What about him?" Brenda asks.

"We're not charging the boy, ma'am," the policeman says. "He wasn't in the store and he didn't know what she was doing."

"That's ridiculous! He put her up to this, I'm sure, and I'd bet anything he's carrying drugs. He's stoned all the time. You should search him."

"You know very well you can't search my son," Connie says calmly.

Allison glances at Kevin, who is studying the linoleum floor. She knows he has coke in his pocket and Connie's black briefcase out in her car is probably stuffed full of weed. If she wanted to, she could get them both in a lot of trouble, but she doesn't want anything except for Kevin to say something that will make everything okay again.

"You'll have to use the back door," the manager says. "We can't let you back inside the store."

"I have no desire to ever set foot in your store again." Brenda grabs the backpack and the Swiss Army knife, glaring at the manager, who swallows hard and doesn't challenge her.

Once they are all outside, Connie turns to Brenda. "Allison is no longer welcome in our home. I can't live with someone I don't trust."

"I never wanted her to live with you people in the first place. Come on, Allison. Peggy's waiting for us out front."

"Sorry, Mrs. L," Kevin says, grabbing Allison's hand. "She's coming with me."

It's going to be okay, she thinks as they start running. Just as they turn the corner of the building, she glances over her shoulder at their two mothers standing side by side, openmouthed. She laughs at their shocked faces.

He laughs too, but when they get in his truck, his expression hardens. "This is bad, Allison. I never thought they'd make me call Connie."

"I'm sorry. I screwed up." He turns right out of the parking lot and heads south on Beach Boulevard. There's a lot of traffic and they hit every single light. "I can't wait until we go to Mexico."

"Yeah. I was just thinking. It's actually not cool what your mother told that cop. He wrote down my license plate."

"No one ever listens to my mother."

"Connie won't ever trust you again." He moves into the left-turn lane and makes a U-turn. "I'll just take you to your mom's house."

"You said you didn't want me living there! Can't you talk to Connie and tell her it was a mistake?"

"Connie doesn't understand mistakes. I'll bring your stuff to school tomorrow."

She's crying again. "How am I going to get there?"

"Can't your sister give you a ride?"

Peggy's probably already pissed about having to miss work to pick her up today. Peggy has school tonight, homework to do later, a job to go to in the morning, Brenda to chauffeur, and a baby due in a few months. "I can ask," she says as he pulls up in front of her mother's house.

"Here." He takes a small bag of weed out of his glove box. "This might help."

She sniffs hard, wishing she had a Kleenex. "That's nice of you."

"I really don't know why you bother going to school anymore. You're not going to graduate anyway."

She picks up her books from the floor of his truck. Algebra, American History, and Modern Literature. He's right. She's behind in everything. "To see you," she says after she closes the door and watches him drive away.

"This place is a dump," Allison says, when Brenda comes out of the kitchen, arms open wide, although really the house is nice. There are flowers on the table, peonies, and baby's breath. She recognizes some of the furniture from their house in Huntington Beach. Whatever's in the oven smells delicious.

"Your father called an attorney. He's coming over tomorrow night after work to discuss the details. He's furious, of course."

"Are you really getting a divorce?"

Brenda swallows. "We've started the paperwork."

"I wasn't stealing. I was going to pay for everything."

"You just never got caught before."

She's not sure she's heard right. "I don't know what you mean."

"I should have done something a long time ago, honey. We'll get you some help. A counselor or something. I don't want us to have any more secrets."

"You're the one with secrets. You're the one who needs a shrink. Kevin told me you tried to seduce him."

"You know that's not true."

"Why should I believe anything you say?"

Brenda puts up her hands. "I want things to be different between us. Starting now."

"I'm not staying here."

"I'm making pineapple upside-down cake. I saved you a couple of cherries."

It's one of her earliest memories, her mother teaching her to tie a knot in a cherry stem with her tongue. What kind of mother teaches a kid something like that? One who's a sex maniac, obviously. "I don't like pineapple upside-down cake anymore." She watches Brenda's smile fade. "What happened to the television?"

"It's in my bedroom. We can move it back to the living room if you want. I'm going to meditate for ten minutes. Why don't you take a shower before dinner? I'll find you some clothes to wear."

"Since when do you meditate?"

"I told you, I want things to be different."

PEGGY insists they leave at six thirty the next morning. "Ocean View is in the opposite direction of everything," she complains. "Mom needs a ride to work too. You're going to have to figure something else out." She has almost two hours to kill before school starts. She calls Kevin from the pay phone, but no one answers. She waits on a bench in the amphitheater. Peggy's borrowed jeans are too short and her mother's blouse too dressy. She lights a joint, takes a few hits, then snubs it out when she hears the janitor rolling his mop bucket into the girls' bathroom.

Katy pulls her aside in the hallway after first period and tells her that McKenzie was at Wal-Mart yesterday and witnessed the manager marching her back to his office.

"It's just a misunderstanding."

"They arrested you. You must have done something."

She sees Kevin come out of class. "I need to talk to him." She hurries down the hallway and slips her arm around his waist. "I've been looking everywhere for you."

He gives her a quick smile and steps away. "I have your stuff in my truck."

"I'll see you at lunch then?"

He shakes his head. "Coach called a meeting. I'm late to class." He leaves her standing there alone, feeling everyone watching.

At lunchtime, there are no empty chairs at the table where she always sits with her friends. She shuffles her books, waiting for one of them to look up, clear some space, ask to hear her side of the story.

"I feel sorry for Kevin's parents," McKenzie says. "They trusted her."

"Seriously," Danielle says. "We trusted her too."

"You guys," Allison says. "It was Kevin's idea." She's never realized how loud the lunchroom can be, everyone talking at once, slamming trays on tables, silverware clattering.

"I always thought there was something off about her," McKenzie says.

Allison flees to the girls' bathroom and takes a few puffs off the joint in her purse. When the end-of-lunch bell rings, she's finally stopped crying enough to go to class, but her eyes burn, her skin is blotchy, her lips swollen. Her algebra teacher gives her a worried glance as he passes out the results of the last quiz. There's a big fat D circled at the top of the paper he sets on her desk. "Come see me after school," he says. She nods, but there is no point in talking to him. She lost the thread of his lectures weeks ago, and now she has no idea how to solve for x or y or why anyone would want to.

She waits by Kevin's truck after school, confused because his truck is empty. *Where are my things?* she wonders. A white mini-van pulls up and some kid she recognizes vaguely from the bas-ketball team rolls down the window.

"You're Allison, right? I have your stuff." The kid says Kevin's really sorry he can't be there and talks nonstop all the way to Anaheim about how Kevin's his hero. He says his mother won't like it when Allison lights a joint. She ignores him and stares out of the window, determined not to cry.

SHE sits on the couch, listening to her family talk about her as if she isn't here. She shouldn't be here. There's no room. All her belongings are piled in a corner of the living room.

"The attorney thinks he can get it dropped from her record," her father says, as he paces back and forth. He still has his tie on, his shirt sleeves rolled up.

"Let's just be glad she's home."

Brenda can't sit still either. She's simultaneously folding a basket of laundry, running into the kitchen to check a roast in the oven, and dashing outside to move the sprinklers around in the postage-stamp backyard.

"It'll be expensive," Frank says. "And she'll have to do community service."

"What kind of community service?" Peggy asks, sitting at the kitchen table staring at her computer screen. "She doesn't know how to do anything."

"This is a chance for us all to start over," Brenda says.

"There's something I need to tell you," Frank says. "If you can sit down for one second."

He looks middle-aged and rumpled. His love affair has transformed him into a genuine slob. Allison wonders if he regrets leaving her mom, who despite all her frantic domestic activity, looks amazing. Her eyes are clear, her skin is glowing, and she's back in full-on Brenda mode—perfect makeup, a new haircut, and freshly polished nails.

Frank says he never should have let her move in with Kevin, and Brenda says she doesn't know why it took him so long to figure that out.

"I'll be eighteen next month," she says, just to test if they can hear her. "We're going to Mexico as soon as school's out."

"Mexico!" Peggy says. "To do what? You don't speak Spanish."

"You're not going anywhere," Brenda says. "Especially not to Mexico with Kevin."

"If you paid more attention to your daughters instead of watching that damn trial all the time . . ."

"I know, Frank. None of this would have happened. You've made your point. All of this is my fault. You are completely blameless."

"Sarcasm isn't helpful, Brenda. The Inspection Service has Kevin on camera getting out of his truck in the parking lot."

"What parking lot?" Brenda asks. "At the post office?"

Both parents turn to stare at Allison now and she wishes she *was* invisible.

"Why would Kevin be at the post office?"

"Selling drugs more than likely," Frank says. "To those losers Peggy works with."

Allison registers the words "more than likely," which means he doesn't have proof of anything.

"Kevin doesn't know Peggy's friends," Brenda says.

"He sure as hell does! She took him and Allison to a party at Glenn Fielding's house."

"I already said I was sorry," Peggy says.

"I don't know what you were thinking," Frank tells Peggy. "Glenn and his friends are always out in the parking lot getting high on their lunch breaks."

"You used to do the same thing," Brenda says.

"That was a long time ago. There's zero tolerance for that stuff now. I can't imagine how Kevin got in. We've locked the gate and issued access badges."

"That security system is a complete joke," Peggy says. "The gate stays open forever. Anyone can get in. Right, Allison?"

Before Peggy goes further and brings up that Sue woman who saw her in the parking lot, Allison says, "Glenn's party was really fun. It was nice to meet Peggy's friends. Glenn has a great bathroom. Right, Booty?"

"Shut up, Allison," Peggy says.

"Booty?" Brenda says. "Who is this Glenn person?"

"He's just a friend." Peggy's eyes are dark stones.

"Oh, Glenn's way more than a friend. He's the father of her baby."

"Glenn Fielding?" Open-jawed, Frank drops down on the couch.

"Don't expect him to marry her either. He's living with someone else."

"Glenn's married?" Brenda asks.

"He's not married." Peggy spits out the words. "I thought I could trust you, Allison."

"Glenn Fielding?" Frank says again. "Good God, Peggy. Glenn Fielding is an asshole. He strings women along until he's done with them and then he finds a new victim."

What a strange expression, Allison thinks, *stringing women along*. She imagines a line of women reaching out for Glenn, wearing cheap necklaces.

"And he's thirty-five," Frank says. "He certainly doesn't deserve you."

"Thirty-five!" Brenda says. "Did he give you that awful necklace?"

"He's thirty," Peggy says. "And it's over between us. He's with someone else now."

"Oh, honey," Brenda says.

Brenda tries to hug Peggy, but Peggy waves her off. Allison starts to say she's sorry, but it's too late to take her words back. Her father's right. Glenn doesn't deserve Peggy. "At least he's decent looking," she says instead. "And hopefully the baby will get Peggy's brains."

"That's enough." Frank wipes his eyes and stands. "You are not allowed to associate with Kevin any longer. No phone calls. No Mexico. You are grounded until you graduate."

"I'm not driving her to Ocean View," Peggy says. "I'm already driving Mom everywhere. It's not fair."

"I don't care. I'm not going to graduate anyway."

"Since when?" Brenda says. "What are you talking about?"

"I won't have enough units."

"Why didn't you tell us?"

"That's not my job. You're supposed to be my parents."

"Connie should have told us," Brenda says.

"Wouldn't the school notify us?" Frank asks. "Did you put in a change of address?"

"I assumed you did. You work at the post office."

"She'll have to go to school in Anaheim then," Frank says.

"It's too late for that," Brenda says. "There's only a month left."

"Summer school then. And she'll get a job in the meantime."

"I'm not chauffeuring her to a job either." Peggy unplugs her computer, takes it back to her bedroom, and slams the door.

"I'm not going to say I told you so," Brenda says, "but I was right about Kevin. My roast is probably done." She hurries to the kitchen.

"I'll call the school tomorrow and figure out what we need to do. I have to go." Frank picks up his keys. "Linda's waiting for me."

And just like that she's invisible again.

SHE pulls the sheet over her head on the couch and pretends to be asleep the next morning when Peggy and her mother get up. Neither one of them makes any attempt to be quiet. "Your father's taking off work to enroll you at Savanna High School today," Brenda says before they leave. "I cleaned out some space in my closet for your clothes."

She calls Kevin as soon as they're gone. Right away he says he's sorry about yesterday.

"Connie made me promise I wouldn't see you anymore."

She expects him to laugh and add how stupid and ridiculous Connie is, but when he doesn't, she feels a chill run down the back of her neck. "Are you breaking up with me?"

"Of course not."

"There's someone else, isn't there? That's why you don't want to have sex with me anymore."

"There isn't anyone else. I'm just trying to go with the flow right now, babe. Until things calm down."

"When will that be? My dad thinks he saw you in some security video of the parking lot."

"Are you fucking kidding me?"

"He saw someone who looks like you. It's no big deal. I shouldn't have told you."

"It is a big deal. I thought someone was following us last week."

"Don't get all paranoid. It'll be fine."

"It's not going to be fine. That's why no one is returning my calls. This is fucked up, Allison."

"Don't yell at me. It's not my fault. My parents are totally freaking out. Can you please come get me? I can't live here."

"Connie's not going to change her mind."

"When will I see you?"

"Soon, babe. I have to go. I have shit to figure out."

"We're a team. We're supposed to figure things out together."

He's already hung up.

SHE walks around in circles the rest of the day, searching all the closets and drawers, looking for anything of value, something she can sell to help Kevin, something to make him realize how much he needs her. She finds her mother's jewelry box in the back of the closet and dumps it all out in a ziplock bag and hides it in her purse. Her dad comes by in the afternoon and drives her to the office at Savanna High School. The campus doesn't look much different than Ocean View, but she finds all the posters about grad night and senior prom depressing.

"You're going to have to walk to school," he says. "It's too much to ask Peggy to drive you. Once your mother gets her license back, we'll figure out some kind of transportation."

"You gave Peggy a car when she graduated high school."

"You haven't graduated, and you don't know how to drive."

"I also didn't get pregnant. Don't I get any credit for that? What about my birthday?"

His eyes are tired. "I'm paying for the attorney. That's more than enough."

KEVIN finally calls the next day and asks her to meet him on the corner of Brookhurst and La Palma because he doesn't want to chance running into her mother. Even when she tells him she's alone, that both Brenda and Peggy are working, he still doesn't want to come to the house, so she waits on the corner, sure everyone is staring at her. When he pulls up, her knees nearly buckle, she's so glad to see him.

He parks in front of the liquor store, opens the passenger door, and hands her a double bouquet of red roses.

"You didn't have to get me anything," she says. "All I want is to be with you."

"That's what I want too." He sits back and rakes his hair off his face.

"I have this," she says, handing him the ziplock bag of jewelry. "Maybe Connie could sell it." She doesn't expect him to look so immediately sad.

"No, babe. That won't work. Put it all back. I have another idea. I need you to do something else for us."

"Anything." *His eyes are such a beautiful color.*

"It's a lot to ask. But it's a way to get past all this crap."

"And we can take our trip?" *Why does he look so worried?*

"We can take our trip and get an apartment and be together, just like we always planned."

"Okay." Her stomach churns, probably because she hasn't eaten anything. She couldn't. She was too worried.

"Bledsoe wants to hang out with you." His smile is false.

She swallows a sudden sick taste in her mouth. "What do you mean hang out?"

"Make him feel good. Like you make me feel."

If he won't say it, she will. "You want me to fuck him."

He looks down at his hands. "I wouldn't ask you to do this if we had any other choice."

"No problem," she says before she can think about it too long. It's her body, like Peggy insisted that day at the clinic, and she can do whatever she wants with it. It's just a matter of letting something happen that has happened before. It doesn't have to mean anything. "We're in this together, babe."

BLEDSOE lives on Davenport Island in Huntington Harbour behind a guarded wrought iron gate. The road to his house is lined with neatly trimmed king palm trees. When they get out of the truck, the air smells like sulfur and gasoline. A half-dead sago palm, a jungle of overgrown birds of paradise, and an untrimmed banana tree cast Bledsoe's front door in dark green shadows.

"Dude!" Kevin says, when the front door opens. "You shaved!"

Bledsoe's face is reptilian without the mustache. "Red," he says, ignoring Kevin. "Go on outside. I'll grab us some drinks."

Bledsoe's furnishings are bland and beige, covered with a slight film of dust. An open spiral staircase splits the tiny living room in half. There's no view of the harbor and a lap pool takes up most of a tiny concrete yard. The hazy water reflects the gray skies. Kevin pulls the slider open, and Bledsoe follows with two bottles of Heineken and a glass of water.

He hesitates. "I wasn't sure if you drank beer or not."

"Water's fine. Thank you." She walks over to the pool and puts one foot in. It's not heated. Kevin and Bledsoe sit down at the table. A few faded pool toys are stacked on the side of the pump. There's a slight breeze. She goes back to the table.

"Why don't you go for a swim, babe?" Kevin says.

"I don't have my bathing suit."

"You don't need a suit. We're all friends here. Right, Bledsoe?"

Maybe this is all she'll have to do to be nice. "Can we smoke a little first?"

"Of course," Bledsoe says. "Whatever you want."

He pulls a pipe out of his pocket, lights it, takes a drag, and hands it to her. She takes a deep drag, then unzips her shorts and pulls them off, careful not to let her father's Swiss Army knife slip out of the front pocket. She'd taken it from her mother's purse and brought it with her today for reassurance more than protection, although the cold metal offers neither. Bledsoe sips his beer. Kevin plays with his keys and leaves his bottle unopened.

Underwear is just like bikini bottoms, she reasons. It isn't like she's naked or anything. She swims underwater toward the shallow end, the chlorine stinging her eyes. When she comes up for air, Bledsoe is alone, leaning forward in his chair, pressing his fingertips together, watching intently. She paddles to the edge and grabs the stair rails. Her tank top clings to her breasts as she steps onto the concrete. The breeze is cooler, and her heart is pounding. "Where's Kevin?"

"He'll be back." He hands her a towel.

Pretend you're fine, she tells herself, *and you will be.*

"Let's go inside. I have some coke too."

"I don't want any."

He looks surprised. "I heard different."

She picks up her shorts. "Why'd you shave your mustache?"

"I didn't think you liked it." He takes her hand and leads her up the stairs to the bedroom. "You can call me David."

"What did you hear about me?"

"That you got a little greedy with the product."

"Is that what Kevin told you?" She feels like she's standing at the top of a well, her words echoing below her. "I guess we both did."

In his bedroom, he lights the pipe again and they smoke for a while, and then he opens the drawer in a table next to his bed and takes out a condom. He undresses. He's fleshy, but not exactly fat, and covered with hair, which is not a big deal because this won't take long, and then Kevin will come back and they can leave. She strips off her wet tank top and underwear and hangs them on the back of a chair. He's stroking himself and pulling on a condom and she looks away.

"Please," he says, pulling back the bedspread. "Come here."

She lies down beside him. The sheets smell like bleach and lemon fabric softener, and his body—at least the parts she can bear to look at—is strangely formed. His torso belongs on a taller man; his legs are too short. She wills herself to float up out of her body toward the ceiling as he climbs on top of her, but she can't float anywhere; she's wedged under him, staring at the side of his reptile face and the cottage cheese ceiling above them. Her mother had that acoustic stuff scraped off years ago. There's a cobweb in one corner and a slight film of dust on the photograph on the side of the bed. A young boy, maybe eight or nine years old, holding a Star Wars saber. His son, she guesses, remembering the pool toys stacked on the patio.

He tells her to relax and she realizes she's crying. He even has hair on his back, prickly and rough against her hands. She thinks about Kevin's smooth skin and chokes back a sob. David is sweating now. He straightens his arms and pushes up from the bed, grunting and convulsing, his eyes thin slits, his teeth clinched. Kevin never takes this long. An eternity passes before he rolls off her, stands, and pulls on his shorts. She's stopped crying, but now she has the hiccups. "I knew this was a mistake." He pulls his shirt over his head, then combs his hair in the mirror above the dresser. "Take a shower if you want."

She doesn't want a shower. She wants to shed her skin.

Kevin is watching television in the living room when she comes down the stairs wearing her still-damp clothes. He jumps up immediately. "You okay?" he whispers.

"Let's just go."

David comes out of the kitchen and ignores Kevin's attempt at a fist bump.

"We cool?" Kevin asks.

"You're an asshole."

"Right," Kevin says. He looks at her, confused. "You ready?"

"Can you please turn on the heater?" she says when they are in his truck. Pearl Jam is on the radio, droning about some girl who can't find a better man. Kevin usually sings along to the chorus, but he is silent as he drives north on Beach Boulevard toward Anaheim.

"I still can't believe Bledsoe shaved his mustache," he says finally. "He looks like a different person."

She stares out the window, wishing she was someone else.

Chapter Thirteen

"WHAT KIND OF HUMMINGBIRD IS THAT?" BRENDA ASKS, TRAINING HER binoculars on a hibiscus bush in front of Connie's house.

"Anna's or Rufous," Tim says. "I can never remember which is which."

The poor bird must be exhausted. Female, judging from the drab feathers, using every beat of her tiny heart to feed her babies. Brenda hopes the nest is close by. At least her daughters are under the same roof now, although neither one is glad to be there.

"This is probably a waste of time," she tells Tim. "I just felt like I had to *do* something."

They're parked two doors down and across the street from Connie's house. Her idea, which seems foolish now, was to document what she'd assumed would be obvious drug trafficking, take photos, get license plate numbers, show them to the police, and have Kevin arrested. She has a notepad and pencil, and Tim has his camera. Tim also has questions she'd rather not answer.

"How are you feeling about the divorce?"

Like a failure, she wants to say. *Like I've given up. Because I have.* "I'll get alimony, not much, but at least I won't have to beg Frank for money. And I'll get part of his pension too when he retires."

"Well, that's something. Is Allison getting settled into Savanna okay? I wonder if any of my teachers are still there."

She doesn't want to talk about this either, but Tim will find out eventually. "Even with summer school she wouldn't have enough units to graduate. She's going to get her GED from the adult school instead. The program starts in July, which gives her enough time to finish her community service first."

Thanks to the attorney Frank hired, the charges for the Wal-Mart incident will eventually be dropped and Allison's record cleared once she picks up enough garbage on the side of the freeway. Allison apparently doesn't find the hard hat or the bright orange vest or the picking up of garbage at all humiliating, but Allison has no emotional reaction to anything these days, except open hostility toward her parents.

"I can't believe you painted this car pink, Tim. I'm sure all the neighbors have noticed us sitting here."

"The color is perfect for Vidavita, at least until I win the Cadillac. I'm really close, Bren. If you could make a few more sales, pick up a couple of distributors . . ."

"I don't have time for Vidavita anymore. I've got to find a real job. And I need to focus on Allison."

Tim tries for the third time to shake a few more drops from his empty Diet Coke. "Why would Allison steal from Wal-Mart anyway?"

"Why does Allison do anything?" She shouldn't snap at Tim when he's helping her, but she really doesn't want to tell him how Allison's always been something of—how to phrase it—a pickpocket? Kleptomaniac? Shoplifter? She should have done something a long time ago instead of assuming it was just a phase Allison would grow out of.

"I just meant, if Kevin's dealing, wouldn't he have a lot of money?"

"Drug dealers only have a lot of money in the movies, and then they go to prison and die horrible deaths. Which would be fine with me. Get down!" she adds as Kevin's white truck turns the corner. Tim lies sideways on the front seat and she bends forward, tucking her head in between her knees.

"He can't see us," Tim whispers. "We're too far away."

"Is he alone?"

Tim sits up slowly. "Allison's with him."

"You've got to be kidding! She's grounded and she's not allowed to see him." Brenda starts to open the passenger door when Tim says, "Hold on. There's another car."

A black Mercedes sedan parks in front of the house. Brenda slides down the seat and pulls down the visor of Frank's old Angels' baseball cap.

"Who's that?" Tim asks as an older man gets out of the Mercedes. He wears dark Ray-Ban sunglasses, a long-sleeved button-down shirt, and dark-washed jeans with cuffs.

"I have no idea."

There's something odd in Allison's posture as she walks slowly toward the Mercedes. She stops when she gets near the man and stares down at the street, strangely still, as if she's trying to make herself smaller. The man says something, and Allison nods her head slightly. "Take his picture." She glances over at Tim. "For heaven's sake. The lens cap is on."

Kevin's truck backs out of the driveway and drives off. The man reaches around Allison's waist and cups his hand over her ass. Allison visibly stiffens but doesn't stop him.

"Get your hands off her!" Brenda opens the passenger door as the man steps aside and Allison slides in the front seat. He glances over his shoulder and looks straight at her. He has the face of a lizard. "Dear God," Brenda says as he gets in next to Allison and slams the door. The car speeds away. "Follow him!"

Tim turns the ignition key, but the car stalls. "Shit. I'm in the wrong gear."

"He turned left," Brenda says when the VW finally lurches forward. "Can't you go any faster?"

"I'm doing the best I can."

"He must be going to Huntington Harbour," she says as a black Mercedes ahead of them makes a left turn on Algonquin, but when they finally pull into the Harbour entrance and stop at the gate, there is no sign of the Mercedes. A uniformed man with a clipboard and a walkie-talkie comes out of the guard shack, holding up a hand.

"Can I help you?"

Tim cranks down his window. "There was a black Mercedes that just pulled in. A man and a young girl?"

"There are a lot of black Mercedes. Who are you here to visit?"

"We don't know his name," Brenda says. "But my daughter is with him. Pretty young redhead?"

"This is a gated community. Unless a resident has put you on my list, I can't let you in."

Brenda takes off her sunglasses and removes the baseball cap. Her hand is trembling. She combs her fingers through her hair and leans forward. "We need your help. My daughter might be in trouble."

"What's the resident's name? I could call."

"I don't know."

"Do you have an address?" She shakes her head. "Sorry, ma'am." He goes back to his shack.

Tim backs up and makes a U-turn. "You want to go to the police station?"

"And tell them what? I don't know who that man is. I'm not sure we were even following the right car. Did you at least get a good photo?"

"It all happened too fast. Did you get the license plate?"

"How could I? You lost him."

"HE was a lot older and driving a black Mercedes," Brenda tells Connie when she finally gets her on the phone. "Do you have any idea who he is? Because Allison isn't home yet and it's almost eight o'clock."

"Eight thirty," Frank says, pacing back and forth in front of the window. "We should call the police."

"I have no idea who Allison's seeing," Connie says. "Kevin's moved on too. Did you hear he got into Cal State Northridge?"

"She was *with* Kevin," Brenda says. "She got out of his truck in front of your house."

"You're mistaken. They're not seeing each other anymore. What were you doing at my house?"

"Do you know who this man is or not?"

"It's not my responsibility anymore to keep track of who your daughter might be involved with. Kevin's off to football camp after graduation and then on to college in September. All his dreams are starting to come true."

"Cal State Northridge is not anyone's dream school. I have to go." She slams down the phone as Allison walks in the front door.

"Where the hell have you been?" Frank says. "You know you're grounded."

"Who was that awful man in the Mercedes?" Brenda asks.

Allison lifts her chin defiantly. "A friend, not that it's any of your business. Kevin's leaving anyway. Isn't that what you wanted?"

Her mouth quivers, which tells Brenda all she needs to know. "You're ruining your life."

Allison spits out a laugh. "You guys are the experts at ruining lives. Dad fucks anyone who smiles at him and you tried to fuck my boyfriend."

"That's not true."

"Don't be disrespectful to your mother." Brenda is momentarily grateful for Frank's support until he adds, "And don't you ever say anything like that about Linda again."

"Why is everyone yelling?" Peggy stands in the front doorway. "I could hear you all the way out in the street."

Peggy's skin is luminous in the porch light, her hair glossy. She holds a stack of textbooks in one hand, a lunch bag and her car keys in the other. She looks so incredibly beautiful, so very young, and so hugely pregnant. Brenda wants to weep.

"My class let out early." Peggy lumbers over to the couch. "My feet are killing me. I have to sit down."

Brenda glances at Frank. His eyes are wet too.

Peggy props her swollen ankles on the coffee table. "Is there anything to eat? I'm starving."

BRENDA closes her eyes and leans back in the lawn chair next to Tim, wondering if the color of her toenail polish, Flamingo Rose, is professional looking enough for her job interview tomorrow. She did a lousy job polishing them. She's too upset. Frank called this morning after doing some research. His health plan will pay for weekly visits to a therapist *if* they can convince Allison to go. She doesn't need therapy, Allison insisted, she needs Kevin. And then she put on her headphones, turned up that god-awful rap music, and slammed the bedroom door in her face.

"What did she say about that man?" Tim asks.

"That he's none of my business."

"J.C. Penney is hiring."

"How would she get there? Peggy's already complaining about me using her car."

"How much longer is Peggy going to work? She looks like she's ready to pop any minute."

Buddy Guy brags on the blues station playing on the small radio between them about the assets of some nineteen-year-old girl. Brenda peels the backs of her bare legs off the sun-warmed vinyl straps of the lawn chair and stands. She doesn't want to talk about Peggy's due date right now. Peggy has made zero effort to contact any of the adoption agencies on the Planned Parenthood lists Brenda compiled and left on the counter. "I'll get you another drink." She takes his tumbler and heads inside to check on dinner. Cooking is a welcome distraction. She's roasting a chicken and steaming some veggies later.

Peggy's sitting at the kitchen table behind her usual warren of books and papers, studying for the second part of the tax preparer's exam.

"You'll need to move all that when we eat," Brenda says. "Where's your sister?"

"In my room with the door closed. As usual."

One day at a time. She pours vodka over ice and fills Tim's tumbler with tonic and a slice of lime, imagining how impressed the group at the AA meeting would be that she can do this and not even be tempted. She's glad to be finished with AA. She has her driver's license in her purse. Now she just needs a car, a job, and a plan to convince Peggy it's not the right time for her to be a mother and to keep Allison away from Kevin and lizard man and on the path to her GED.

She watches Tim through the window as a pair of hummingbirds chase each other in and out of the hibiscus flowers. The birds click warning sounds and zoom straight toward Tim and then up over his head. He lurches up in his chair and swats at the air, a roll of fat doubling over the waistband of his shorts. He's gained back most of the weight he lost. He dropped by this afternoon to take the remaining Vidavita boxes, but she hopes he hasn't given up on the protein shakes. She's counting on him to win that Vidavita Cadillac and give her a deal on his VW bug. She's desperate enough to take it, too, even if it is a horrible color.

She pours herself a glass of water and carries both drinks outside, sliding the screen door open with her big toe, swearing as she chips the polish. She'll have to repaint it tonight.

AFTER Tim loads the last box of Vidavita into his tiny car, they watch the news recap the Simpson evidence presented so far. The television set is back in the living room. There are drapes on the front window courtesy of Tim's discount at J.C. Penney. Peggy even talked Tim into dragging Uncle Charles's ratty old recliner out of the garage. She likes sitting there with her feet up, her hands cupped across her belly.

"What a bonehead move by the prosecutors," Tim says, when Brenda tells them dinner will be ready soon. "Asking O. J. to try on those gloves."

"Those gloves are the saddest part of the whole murder," Peggy says. "Nicole bought them for O. J. and then he wore them to kill her."

"They never proved she actually bought them," Brenda says. "And they didn't fit him because they aren't his gloves. They were planted by Mark Fuhrman."

"No one believes that except you, Mom. The gloves probably shrank from the blood drying on them. O. J.'s gained weight. He works out all the time in his cell."

It's pointless to argue with Peggy. "Allison," she calls out. "Come set the table."

"Guess what I found in your garage," Tim says. "Your Barbie dolls! When I was a kid, I was so jealous of your mom, Peggy. She had everything. Barbie car. Barbie house. Barbie airplane."

She's forgotten about the Barbies. Her collection moved

with her out of her parents' house when she married Frank, and now it's ended up in her uncle's garage with all the cockroaches. "Frank used to give me a Holiday Barbie every year." She thought it was sweet then, but now it seems weird, a husband buying dolls for his wife.

"Holiday Barbies are collector's items," Tim says. "You could sell them for a ton of money. Depending on what kind of condition they're in, of course."

"Perfect, of course," Brenda says.

"Perfect condition means the boxes have never been opened, Mom."

"I'm aware of that, *Peggy*. I've always taken care of my things."

Peggy starts to say something else because Peggy always has to have the last word when Allison opens the bedroom door and comes out wearing cutoff shorts, a skimpy tank top, and no bra, her beautiful green eyes lined in thick black kohl and hideous purple shadow. Peggy snickers and Tim looks horrified, but Brenda tells herself not to react. This is one of those things she should wisely accept and not try to change. Or know the difference. Or something like that.

"Can you please set the table, Allison? Use the good china."

Allison shrugs. Her eyes look miserable under the makeup, but they still remind Brenda of Frank's eyes, and she has to look away. *Live In The Now.*

"I brought some wine," Tim says. "But if no one else wants any . . ."

"Go ahead," Brenda says. "Use the good crystal." She takes a Tiffany glass from the kitchen cabinet.

They sit down at the table together. Tim opens his wine. Brenda carves the chicken. It's a simple recipe, lemon, garlic, and lots of salt and pepper, but the meat is plump and savory and so full of flavor that she nearly inhales an entire breast, chewing the bone to its marrow. Everything is delicious. They have ice cream and cookies for dessert, and she hopes she'll fit in her skirt in the morning. She has a keyboard test tomorrow and she's worried. She's been practicing on Peggy's computer all week, but she can either be accurate or fast, not both, not at the same time.

Peggy makes them laugh when she tells them she's too big to use the copy machine in her office now. "I can't reach the control buttons because my belly gets in the way. My arms are too short. I'm like a tyrannosaurus rex." She waves her arms up and down and even Allison smiles.

"I think you're due before September," Brenda says.

Tim pushes back from the table and belches, which makes them all laugh again. "That was delicious. Thank you so much. I should get going. I'll check the garage again and make sure I got everything."

"I'll clear the table," Peggy says.

"I'll wash the dishes," Allison says.

It's like the old days, Brenda thinks, her girls getting along, a nice meal before the week starts. Except Frank isn't here, Allison looks like a prostitute, and they're living in a house in a destruction zone where Peggy's ready to pop out a baby any second. This version of "Living-In-The-Now" sucks. She follows Tim to the garage. The Vidavita boxes are gone, but there's still a bunch of crap everywhere. Tim stands next to the boxes of dolls, rocking forward on his toes and then back again.

"Take the Barbies, Tim." She opens the washer and puts the wet clothes into the dryer.

"You should save them for the girls."

"They don't care about them. See what you can get for them at the swap meet."

"I'll split whatever I clear with you."

"Don't worry about it. I still owe you some money."

"Well," Tim says, taking a crumpled piece of paper out of his shirt pocket and squinting at the numbers. "I need my glasses. You used a lot more protein powder than you sold. I'm not even sure what I can get for the dolls."

Brenda pulls the lint out of the dryer screen and slams the door shut. "Take them before I change my mind." He might not like it, but she's calling them even.

He puts the piece of paper back in his pocket and carefully stacks the boxes in the front seat. "See you next Sunday," he says, backing the overloaded bug down the driveway.

She watches a thin line of protein powder trail behind the taillights until the little pink car makes the turn at the end of her street. The moon is as full and as bright as the streetlamp on the corner and the night air has turned cool. She smells Laura's tomato plants and catches an undertone of lawn clippings and garbage from her neighbors' trash cans waiting on the curbs up and down the street, reminding her that tomorrow is trash day. Her trash cans are full and grate against the driveway as she drags them to the street.

"Let me help you," Peggy says, coming outside.

"You need to be careful about lifting things."

"I'm just pregnant. I'm not an invalid."

They both look up as a car turns at the opposite end of the street. The headlights catch the metallic shine of the sign on the front lawn. ASK ME THE WAY TO LOSE WEIGHT TODAY.

"That stupid sign," Brenda says, as a black Mercedes pulls into the driveway and Allison flies out of the front door.

"Where do you think you're going?" She tries to block her, but Allison darts around her and jumps in the passenger seat, slamming the door shut. The Mercedes screeches out of the driveway and races off.

"Did she tell you she was going out tonight?"

"She doesn't tell me anything, Mom. She was on the phone with someone, but I assumed it was Kevin. Was that the same man from before?"

"When did she get this call?"

"*She* made the call. Like I said, I thought she was talking to Kevin."

"She called that awful man? That doesn't make sense."

"Should we call the police?"

"And say what? I don't know his name. He didn't force her to go with him. This is so goddamned frustrating."

She stomps across the damp grass, yanks the sign out of the ground, takes it out to the curb, and jams it into the trash can. When she turns, Peggy has gone back in the house. She thinks about the half bottle of wine Tim left. She could call Karla, she supposes, and have her talk her through not drinking it, but she already knows wine will only make her headache worse and Karla will just spout another stupid saying.

She goes inside the house to look for Advil and finds Peggy sitting on the floor in the kitchen, in a puddle of water, sobbing. Surely her water hasn't already broken. The baby's not due this soon.

"I broke your glass." Peggy sobs. "I'm so sorry."

"Oh honey, it's okay. It's just a glass." She gets a broom and dustpan.

"It was so pretty. It just slipped out of my hands."

"I broke one a few months ago. And those idiots your father got to help us move broke one too. It's no big deal. I still have one left. Allison was supposed to wash the dishes." She dumps the broken glass in the trash can and gets a towel to wipe the floor. "You look exhausted. Go to bed."

"I can't even take care of myself. I obviously can't take care of a kid."

She sits down on the floor next to Peggy. "You don't have to keep this baby if you don't want to. We can find a family . . ."

Peggy blows her nose on the dirty dish towel. "Because that's what you wish you'd done."

"No, it's not! I love being your mom. I can't imagine raising you two without your father, though. He loves both of you so much."

"What if you had been on your own like me?"

"I would have muddled through and made a zillion mistakes like I did anyway. But you're stronger and smarter than I ever was. I am sure whatever you decide will be the right thing. It won't be easy though." She stands and offers her hand. Peggy lumbers to her feet. "We should both go to bed."

She leaves the front door unlocked and lies in bed listening to a mockingbird perched high in the sycamore tree in the front yard warbling mating songs, to the steady flow of cars coming and going across the street at Laura's house, to the wail of an ambulance in the distance, to a truck horn bleating on the freeway. If Peggy keeps the baby, she's going to have a tough time with motherhood as stubborn as she is, so convinced she has all the answers, so determined to be right all the time. She smiles. She can't wait to meet this child.

It's two in the morning when she finally hears a car door slam. She gets out of bed and opens the front door.

Allison walks past her into the house. "You didn't need to wait up for me. I'm all right."

"You are not all right." She locks the two deadbolts. "You need to apologize to your sister. We're all worried about you, honey."

"Worry about Peggy. Worry about yourself."

If she had money, she could fix this. Take Allison on a long trip somewhere, just the two of them, or send her off to a school where she could find something to be thrilled about. All she can do is put her arms around Allison and hug her in tight, remembering how sweet the crown of her head smelled when she was a baby. Allison was an easy child, much calmer than Peggy. She slept all night, only cried when she was wet or hungry, loved any toy you handed her. Tonight, her hair reeks of marijuana and her makeup is smeared from crying. She tries not to think about whatever it was Allison was doing with that man.

"You're shaking." Allison pulls away. "Don't try to understand me, Mom. You can't."

"We'll figure out what to do. I promise."

Chapter Fourteen

PEGGY BLASTS THE HORN WHEN SHE SEES KEVIN'S LITTLE WHITE TRUCK BLOCKING the driveway, but no one comes out, so she's forced to make a U-turn and park her car two blocks away. *I don't have time for this,* she fumes as she hikes up the street with her big belly and swollen ankles, lunch bag and purse over one shoulder, backpack full of books from her summer school classes over the other.

A fleet of Caltrans heavy equipment lines the streets—yellow bulldozers fitted with huge front blades and backed with prehistoric claws that can rip into the sides of houses and scrape roofs, walls, and plumbing fixtures down to the foundation and enormous dump trucks ready to haul away the rubble. The neighborhood is a nightmare with constant jackhammering, beeping trucks, and foremen in yellow vests and hard hats whipping from street to street in small forklifts.

She needs to pee and leave again in a few minutes to go pick up her mother from the job the temp agency found her, answering phones at a realtor's office. She has class tonight until ten o'clock, a paper to turn in tomorrow. She's sick of being her mother's chauffeur and sick of her sister spending her days with Kevin and lying about it.

Allison and Kevin come out of the house now and stand next to his truck. A decent sister would be considerate enough to tell the boyfriend she's not even allowed to see not to park in her pregnant sister's spot. Allison's wearing the skanky tank top and cutoff shorts she's worn for weeks. Kevin looks angry. Peggy plans on not speaking to either one of them. When she gets closer, though, she can tell Allison's been crying.

"I did everything you asked."

Kevin grabs Allison's arm and yanks her closer. "I didn't make you do anything you didn't want to do. Bledsoe says you like it."

"Hey!" Peggy yells, but her heart has moved up to her throat, and her voice isn't loud enough for them to hear.

"You promised I could go with you once we paid him back. You're hurting me." Allison pulls away from him.

"I'm sharing a dorm room with three dudes. How would that work?"

"You don't seem to have a problem sharing me with Bledsoe."

"What did you say?" Kevin pushes Allison up against the truck door, his forearm on her neck. Allison's eyes widen, and she starts to choke.

Peggy drops her bags and tries to run, which feels more like a slow-motion waddle. "Stop that!" Kevin turns and glares at her, his face blotched, his eyes wild. "Let her go!" she yells. He drops his arms and Allison sinks down to the driveway, gasping for air.

"Are you all right?" Peggy asks when she finally reaches her sister. "Can you breathe?"

Allison nods, wheezing. "I'm fine."

"I forget how strong I am." Kevin paces back and forth in the driveway, punching his fist in his palm. "You make me crazy."

"I'm sorry. I shouldn't have said that."

"Why are you apologizing? He was trying to kill you."

"Don't be so dramatic." Allison staggers to her feet. "It was my fault."

"I have to go," Kevin says. "I need to get on the 405 before the traffic gets worse." He turns and looks at Allison as he backs his truck out of the driveway, mouthing the words "I love you," then guns the engine and speeds out of the tract.

"Who's Bledsoe?" Peggy asks. "That guy in the Mercedes? Do you owe him money?"

Allison shakes her head. "Aren't you supposed to go pick up Mom from work? I'll get your stuff."

She watches Allison's long bare legs stride across the grass and wonders what the neighbors saw. There are always cars coming and going across the street at Laura's house except for right now. More than likely no one saw anything. Except her. The useless sister who really has to pee now.

"These are heavy," Allison says, coming back with her bags, trying to smile even though her face is streaked with tears. "What do you have in here, rocks?"

"You're going to have a bruise on your neck."

"Please don't tell Mom. She'll just make everything worse. Kevin's going to football camp. We're taking a break for a while."

"I wish I could believe you."

ANOTHER sleepless night. Every time she starts to doze off, she hears her sister's voice, "It was my fault," and then the baby kicks her ribs. She's a zombie the next morning. She drives to work on autopilot, not remembering how she got there when she pulls in the parking lot. She'd give anything for a cup of coffee, but caffeine isn't good for the baby.

"Did the rest of the paychecks come in?" she asks when she walks in the office.

"No," Phyllis says. "Still missing the last bundle."

"I'll go look for them." She puts her purse down and walks out to the workroom floor. Tomorrow's payday and people go crazy when the checks are late, and if she can't find them, she'll have to do salary advances all day, which is a huge pain in the ass. She hopes to God no one is watching her own humongous ass sticking up in the air over the dirty Express Mail hamper. There are a lot of envelopes to dig through, and when she finally spots the paycheck-size package at the bottom of the hamper, she can barely reach it.

She fishes out another thick flat envelope to use for leverage and recognizes a familiar name and address. Nelson's Jewels in Huntington Beach. Kevin's mother's store. The return address is Laie, Oahu, and there are more envelopes just like it in the hamper. All thick and flat and all from Hawaii. She drops the envelope back in the hamper and takes the package with the paychecks to her office.

The envelopes bug her all day. What kind of jewelry comes from Hawaii? Puka shells, she supposes, but why so many? She tells Phyllis she needs to leave early for a doctor's appointment and drives down to Connie's jewelry store, parks in a space on the opposite side of the lot, and watches in her rearview mirror, no idea what she's doing. The mailman rings the buzzer a few minutes later, his arms full of thick, flat Express Mail envelopes. Peggy ducks down when Connie opens the door, signs the receipts, and takes the stack of envelopes back inside. Fifteen minutes later she comes out again, keys in one hand, black attaché case in the other, gets in her Buick, and drives away.

It's not long before a black Mercedes parks in front of the store. A man with slicked-back hair wearing Ray-Bans gets out of the driver's seat. Peggy's heart crashes against her belly when she sees her sister follow him into the store. Peggy gets out of her car and walks toward the Mercedes. There must be cameras inside because suddenly the door flings wide open.

Allison, wild eyed. "What are you doing here?"

"Is that Bledsoe? How does he know Kevin's mom?"

"That's none of your business." Allison glances over her shoulder at the door.

"Do you need money? I still have the five hundred dollars Glenn gave me."

"Five hundred dollars is nothing."

"Would five thousand be enough?"

"Where would you get five thousand?"

The man comes outside, carrying the same black case as Connie's. "You must be Allison's sister." She can't see his eyes behind his sunglasses. "You look a lot like your mother."

"Are you Mr. Bledsoe?"

"Stay out of this, Peggy," Allison says.

"That's good advice." His thin lips tighten. "Take care of your baby, Peggy. And tell your pretty mother hello for me." He gives her a steady look that makes her skin go cold and gets in the Mercedes. She watches it back out and pull away, repeating the license plate number over and over until she's back in her car and can write the numbers down in her Business Law notebook. She tears the page out, locks it in her glove box, and watches her rearview mirror all the way home.

"DON'T you look comfortable today?" Phyllis says, as they walk through the workroom floor toward the stamp destruction cage. *I look fat*, Peggy thinks but doesn't say because Phyllis really is fat, and she is simply having this baby sooner than everyone predicted. She feels clown-like in the elastic-waist pants and loose tunic, newly purchased at South Coast Plaza this weekend with her thrilled-to-be-out-shopping mother, but it's a relief not to have the zipper of her jeans cut into her belly.

Phyllis has never mentioned her pregnancy or her dad leaving her mom to be with Linda. Phyllis doesn't gossip. She may not have much imagination, but she's a kind woman. Twice a week she brings green-shelled eggs with bright orange yolks, laid fresh from her hens.

"Such good protein for your baby," Brenda says every morning when she slides two sunny-side up eggs on Peggy's plate and goes back to her bedroom to meditate. She's bought a patchouli candle and a pink leotard and sits cross-legged on the floor twice a day for five minutes. "You should join me," Brenda keeps saying, but Peggy is sure she'd fall asleep if she closed her eyes for five minutes, and she's not sure she could get back up off the floor. She's exhausted from work and school and driving Brenda to and from whatever job she's working and listening to her complain about how boring her job is and how she's missing the defense portion of the trial.

She should have already told her parents about meeting Bledsoe, but Frank's still angry at her because of Glenn and getting Brenda involved never helps any situation. Lately she can't stand being in the same room as her patchouli-scented mother anyway. It could have something to do with the start of her third trimester, but whatever the reason, she can smell everything and everyone.

Phyllis is wearing strawberry lotion and chewing peppermint gum as they make their way across the workroom floor to the stamp destruction cage. The custodian is mopping the floor with dirty water and Pine-Sol. The tires on the truck that just pulled up outside reek of burning rubber. A technician blows a cloud of dust out of the flat sorter and she smells charcoal ash. The two truck drivers getting Cokes out of the machine in the break room need a more effective deodorant.

"What do you know about Juice Plus?" Phyllis asks. "That product O. J. is endorsing?"

"I wouldn't take his recommendation on anything. That juice sounds like another scam. I'm glad my mother finally quit selling Vidavita."

"Juice Plus is supposed to be good for arthritis. I was thinking about trying it."

"You can't be serious." When she notices the disappointment cut across Phyllis's face, she feels guilty. She should stop buying her all those peanut butter cookies. "I didn't know you had arthritis."

"In my knees. I guess the extra weight doesn't help."

"You could try the juice, I guess. Couldn't hurt."

"No. You're right. It's a scam. There's no such thing as a magic pill."

The cage with obsolete stamp stock is stacked floor to ceiling with boxes and envelopes returned by the twenty-six postmasters in the Santa Ana District. There's a lock on the cage and a spiral notebook to sign every time anyone goes in or out. Phyllis's plan is for the two of them to organize it enough to make it easier for the destruction committee to count. They add their signatures to the notebook. Peggy has stopped commenting on the way the post office mis-manages its finances. Phyllis gets defensive when she mentions the internal controls she's studying in her classes. Risk assessments. Segregation of duties. Adequate safeguards over access to assets. "We've always done it this way," Phyllis keeps telling her.

"This is a disaster," Phyllis says now as she locks the door behind them.

"We could start by counting all the full boxes."

"Good idea. You count and I'll make a list."

There is no place for either of them to sit and hardly enough room to work. Phyllis lasts a half hour and then says she needs to go finish the payroll adjustments.

"You okay by yourself? I'll be back if I get some time later."

Phyllis doesn't sign out when she leaves, and it isn't likely she'll return once she gets settled into her office chair and pulls out the box of chocolate-covered peanuts she keeps in her bottom desk drawer. The payroll adjustments take Phyllis at least two hours to finish; Peggy has timed her.

The boxes create a wall of cardboard, blocking all sides of the cage. She pushes both hands in the deep pockets of her pants to test how much room there is. She can still wiggle all her fingers. She stretches out her tunic and stares at her round lump. The baby is no longer an It. He's a boy. A new nurse at the clinic assumed Peggy already knew. Not that it matters. He'll be someone else's boy soon.

She counts the full boxes, adds them to Phyllis's list, and then starts on the envelopes. Half of them aren't sealed and the paperwork she finds inside is a mess. The handwriting is impossible to read and most of the multiplication is wrong. Phyllis is constantly complaining about how the postmasters can't do basic math or keep anything organized.

For example, Janet Chang is an infamous scatterbrain who forgets most of her daily receipts and messes up her bank deposit on a regular basis. Peggy removes five rolls of flag stamps from Ms. Chang's envelope and slides them into the deep pocket of her baggy pants. Everyone knows Peter Castle is a raging alcoholic who barely makes it to work in the morning and disappears after lunch most days. No one will be surprised he can't multiply. Everyone says Harvey Morales should have retired years ago. Counting stamps is a tedious task. Apparently, the old man wrote the numbers down wrong. She can easily fit five rolls in each pocket, which only adds up to a couple hundred dollars but isn't noticeable under her tunic. She takes her backpack to the ladies' room when she clocks out for lunch break later and hides the stamps under her Accounting Principles textbook.

The window clerks all smile when she waddles into the lobby with the stack of the monthly Express Mail refunds. Her hard, round belly has become fair game for everyone's wandering hands. She's sick of all the touching and at the same time she craves it. Julie is happy to give her whatever money orders she needs. "As long as you tell me which account to use. As long as I balance out tonight."

She's included paperwork for one refund for services not rendered to a made-up company with a made-up name, and signed it with an elaborate signature. She talks for a while to Julie about the O. J. trial. They agree the jurors must be exhausted. They both will be glad when the trial is finally over. She promises she'll tell her mother hello. When she goes back to the office, she waits for Phyllis to go to the restroom, and then she slips the blank money order in her backpack.

Four hundred twenty-five dollars. Just like that.

That night, she goes outside to the garage where Allison is taking wet clothes out of the washing machine. "Here." She holds out the rolls of stamps and the money order.

Allison opens the dryer. "What am I supposed to do with that?"

"Sell the stamps and cash the money order. I can get more."

"You'll get fired." Allison shoves her clothes in the dryer.

"I'm trying to help you." She'd like to slap her. "You take things all the time."

"And I got caught." She slams the dryer door. "I didn't ask you for help, Peggy. Stop trying to save me."

"Fine. It's your funeral."

Peggy hides the stamps and the money order in a box in the back of her closet with the high school yearbook no one ever signed because she's not the kind of person who has friends. She's not the kind of woman who should raise a child either, and she's definitely not the kind of sister who can save anyone.

"GET your space in if you're working out with the wife," O. J. says to the camera, still punching at the air with his thick, muscled arms. Then he chuckles and adds, "If you know what I mean, you can always blame it on working out."

"What is he talking about?" Peggy hands Brenda a bowl of ice cream as the news reporter explains they're watching footage from O. J.'s exercise video for men. Even though it means spending the evening with her mother, she's taking a night off from school. She's just too exhausted to drive there and sit in class for three hours under the horrible fluorescent lights. Between her widening ass and ballooning belly, she barely fits in any of the student desks.

"He was just kidding," Brenda says.

"It's not funny. What does that mean anyway, blame it on working out? Blame what? Beating up your wife?" She still hasn't told anyone about Kevin's forearm pressing against Allison's neck. There's a point where it's too late to say anything, a point when you have to stop caring, especially when the person you care about won't listen.

"His video isn't much of a workout anyway," Brenda says. "I can't wait until I can afford a gym again. The temp agency barely pays anything. It's almost not worth the gas it takes to get there."

My gas, Peggy thinks, *that I pay for and put in my car.* She's too tired to argue.

"You need more maternity clothes."

Shopping is a safe topic. What flavor of ice cream is another. They both love Ben and Jerry's, although Peggy says it's too expensive and Brenda says, "Live a little." They agree on what to watch on television. She would never admit it to anyone, especially her mother, but she looks forward every night to hearing all the details about what happened in Judge Ito's courtroom that day.

"Let's go to South Coast Plaza tomorrow," Brenda says.

"I have enough clothes, Mom. I'd rather save the money for after." She saw a stroller at Target when she stopped there to walk around in the air-conditioning for a minute, on her way to school after work last week. It costs $395 plus tax, is ergonomically sound, and converts to a car seat and a bassinet. She could use the stolen money order to buy it for the baby in case his new parents don't have one.

"You're right," Brenda says. "It won't be much longer until you have your body back."

She still has the $500 Glenn gave her. She could sell the stamps she took to someone (she has no idea who) and take a vacation after it (the baby, the boy) is born and given away to someone with a real life and a backyard and a swing set.

"Maybe I should join a gym too."

"We could go together," Brenda says. "Wouldn't that be fun?"

She nods. She's a horrible person, but she can't stand her mother's patchouli scent any longer and has to go finish her ice cream in the kitchen. She puts on her pajamas and washes her face, but she's too tired to sleep.

When she hears Brenda turn off the television and go to bed, Peggy tiptoes out of the house and gets in her car. She heads east on the Riverside Freeway, watching the moon rise over Santiago Peak. The sky's an inky black, the traffic's light. She takes the Lincoln exit, makes a left turn and then two rights, and parks in front of Glenn's house. She hasn't planned to end up here, but she isn't surprised either.

Jill's Honda is parked at the curb, but Glenn's truck isn't in the driveway. They are still at work, ready to clock out soon, unless there's overtime. They'll put their gloves and aprons away in their lockers, wash the grime off their fingers, then walk together out to his truck in the employee parking lot. They'll stop at some bar for a beer, the Fling or the Hunt Room or wherever they all go now. When the bar closes, they'll head over to Chico's house to shoot pool and smoke pot or maybe to Tessa's apartment to use the Jacuzzi and listen to music until the neighbors complain.

She gets out of the car and breathes in the sickly-sweet night blooming jasmine. The garage door is unlocked. She's heard Glenn complain about Jill's carelessness. Her breasts ache as she pushes the creaky garage door up over her head. She waits for lights to go on next door and someone to come out and ask why she's there, in her pajamas, but the neighborhood remains silent. The garage is swept and tidy. Glenn's toolboxes are locked up tight, but the door leading into the house is open. Inside, the only light on is a green one over an aquarium. A prehistoric-looking fish swims back and forth over the remnants of a dead goldfish. The light flickers over the rippled water, the undulations lapping up the walls and over the ceiling into the kitchen. There are dishes in the sink. The garbage in the trash can reeks.

She goes farther down the hall into his bedroom, their bedroom, their rumpled sheets, their clothes tossed carelessly on the floor. She opens the bureau and lifts out a baseball-style jersey from a Santana concert, pulls it over her head, and picks up a lacy thong from the floor. She takes it into the bathroom, drops it in the toilet, sits down, and empties her bladder and doesn't flush. Jill's makeup is spread all over the counter next to the sink. Foundation and highlighter, blush and mascara, an ugly mauve eyeshadow. Jill should put her things away.

She takes the makeup into the kitchen and adds it to the carrot peelings, empty yogurt containers, and coffee grounds in the smelly trash can. Glenn is drinking real coffee these days instead of instant. She opens the fridge. A piece of cake sits uncovered on a paper plate. She scrapes the icing off the top of the cake with her fingertip and licks it. Too sweet. She spits it out into an open carton of two-percent milk and watches it dissolve in an unappetizing swirl.

There is one Diet Coke. Her mouth waters. She hasn't had caffeine or soda since she figured out she was pregnant. She takes the Coke and leaves the refrigerator door wide open. It's barely eleven according to the clock over the stove. She closes the garage door and locks it. She starts the ignition, opens the soda, admiring the quick release of carbonation, the icy trickle down her throat, the caffeine coming alive in her bloodstream.

Glenn will notice the open refrigerator, the lacy thong in the toilet. He'll either look for his Santana shirt or forget he's ever had one. She'll make sure to wear it next time she sees him. He might even wonder if they'd gone to the concert together. None of it makes any difference and still she finds herself singing to the radio all the way home so the boy inside her can learn the words.

Her son.

She knows how she is. She can never let things be. She worries the details to death. If she gives her son up, she'll never be able to stop thinking about him. She'll look for his face on every kid on every bicycle, in every park, on every school ground. She'll always know exactly how old he is.

THE next day at work, Peggy buys a book of stamps on her lunch break. When Phyllis goes to lunch, Peggy writes a letter to the Huntington Beach Police Department: Attention Narcotics Division. She describes Kevin, Connie, and Bledsoe, includes the address of Nelson's Jewels and the license plate number of the black Mercedes. She doesn't sign the letter. She makes a photocopy, marks the envelope as "confidential, incriminating evidence," and uses three times the normal postage and no return address. She drops it in the mailbox in front of the post office.

That night after her mother's asleep, she burns the stamps and the money order in an old Marie Callender's pie tin. The smell from the adhesive is awful, and she's careful not to breathe in. The fumes won't be good for her boy.

CHAPTER FIFTEEN

THE ADULT SCHOOL IS AN EASY WALK OVER THE FREEWAY HILL, EVERYONE points out, as if Allison is supposed to be grateful. "Three hours a day, five days a week," the counselor says. "Take the GED test when you're ready. Depending on how committed you are, you could be finished by the end of September."

She intends to be committed, as she dresses in her uniform of cutoff shorts and tank top. She grabs Peggy's plaid flannel shirt as she walks out the door, just in case the classroom is overly air-conditioned. She lasts all three hours the first day. As she walks home, she notices a bus marked "Huntington Beach" pull up at a stop.

The next morning, she gets on the bus. The overcast brightens into blue skies, and the bus deposits her at Pacific Coast Highway. It's a long walk to the pier, but the sun feels good on her back, Peggy's flannel tied around her waist. She sits under the pier pilings for a long time, watching the kids, the lifeguards, the sun move across the sand. She can bring her nephew down here when he's older, show him around.

Peggy plans to do everything different from the way they were raised. She'll breastfeed. No formula. No packaged baby food. No sugar. No television. There will be rules and consequences. *It's up to me to be the bad influence*, she thinks, as she admires the breeze rustling through the king palm trees.

She smokes a joint at the end of the pier where the fishermen cut bait and ignore her. She watches the water change colors from gray to turqouise to an emerald green. She knows some of the surfers, but either they don't see her or don't recognize her without Kevin. She gazes out toward Catalina Island and then down the coast of Orange County. It's clear enough now to see the Edison power plant to the south, the Charter Center Building as she looks east, and in the distance, Saddleback Mountain. This is the way life is supposed to be lived, in the moment, the world spread out around her. There's no place she has to be. She is simply present, in this light.

HER mother and sister are eating bowls of cookie dough ice cream when she comes home. They've exchanged roles. Now Peggy watches the trial from the recliner with her hands spread wide over her belly and Brenda sits on the couch, wearing reading glasses and frowning over books on Word and Excel. Peggy's started her maternity leave and Brenda drives off in Peggy's car every morning to whatever crappy, minimum-wage job the agency offers.

"We already ate dinner," Brenda says. "This isn't a restaurant. You can make yourself a sandwich if you're hungry."

Allison sits down on the couch. "I stayed late at school."

Peggy snorts. "You're sunburned and there's sand on your feet. You went to the beach with Kevin."

"I haven't talked to him since he started camp."

Football camp is brutal, he'd explained, and he wants to give it his best shot. He thinks it would be good for them to take a break. Not good for me, she'd said, but he wasn't listening. She's called his dorm, but he's never there. She's written letters, but she's not sure she has the right address. She's even called Connie's house a few times, but no one ever answers.

"You'd better not be talking to him," Brenda says. "You need to focus on getting your GED."

"Is that my shirt?" Peggy asks.

"It's too small for you now. What are you guys watching?"

"Someone leaked the transcripts from the Mark Fuhrman tapes to the press," Peggy says. "Fuhrman used to work for Judge Ito's wife. He said some pretty horrible things about her."

The bleached-blond newscaster on the screen looks disgusted. "Mark Fuhrman described Peggy York as a woman with a stomach like a kangaroo pouch, big enough to hide two cats."

"How gross," Allison says.

"I feel sorry for Judge Ito," Brenda says. "His wife should take better care of herself."

"Give her a break, Mom," Peggy says. "Peggy York's the first female police chief in LA and she's had three kids. I'll probably look like her after this baby is born."

"No, you won't," Brenda says. "We'll start doing those Jane Fonda videos. You'll be back in shape in no time."

"Is there any more ice cream?" Allison says.

"Sorry," Brenda says. "We just finished the carton."

ALLISON sticks with the GED classes for another week and then calls David and asks him to come get her. She waits for him in the parking lot and wonders how much she and Kevin still owe. She doesn't want to ask, because where will the answer leave her? Paid or not, Kevin might never want to see her again.

She's never been good at math. She doesn't even know how much they owed to begin with or how much whatever she's worth divided into whatever the amount due was will equal David being satisfied. She should have asked Peggy to draw up one of her spreadsheets. Maybe she's actually paying off future debt now, which might mean a future with Kevin. A ruined future, more than likely, but still something, still more than she has now.

When the black Mercedes pulls into the parking lot, David asks if she minds making a few deliveries with him. "Pretty girl in the front seat never hurts. Plus, we can use the carpool lane."

A new routine. She walks over the hill to the adult school where David is waiting in the Mercedes, and they fly up the 57 Freeway to Brea, cut across Imperial Highway to the hills around La Mirada, and then drive down Whittier Boulevard to a dingy apartment building. Or they take the 405 South to El Toro Road and head out into a green canyon, toward an anonymous tract home. Or they speed out the 91 Freeway to the 10 and drive toward the desert and a mansion behind locked gates on a hill dotted with oil pumpjacks. She learns a new language of freeway interchanges. She either waits in the car or goes inside when he asks her to. She smokes whatever he offers, but when she refuses cocaine, he always looks slightly amused.

He drives the 605 Freeway south to the Garden Grove east and exits on Bolsa Chica, toward his house in Huntington Harbour. He takes money out of the pocket of his jeans and puts it in the drawer next to the bed where he keeps the condoms. He never complains about her rushing him or wanting more. "Greedy," he says, as if he is pleased, and then he moves her into another surprisingly satisfying position—satisfying that is, as long as she doesn't look at herself in the mirrored closet doors. David likes to watch, but she closes her eyes. Afterward, she lies naked in his bed waiting for him to get out of the shower, using the hem of the sheet to wipe the dust off the silver-framed photo of the boy with the Star Wars saber. David drives her back to the adult school and drops her off. She walks back over the freeway hill and into her house where Brenda and Peggy are drinking herbal tea, talking about an aerobics class at the adult school.

"They might let me teach," Brenda says, her eyes shining with pride. "Of course, I won't get paid, but it'll still be fun."

"It could lead to something," Peggy says. "You never know."

"Are you quitting the temp agency already?" Allison asks.

"Of course not," Brenda says. "This is just something extra I want to try. Don't worry. The classes are at night. You'll never see me. I won't embarrass you or anything."

"You don't embarrass me." Her mom looks so young and vibrant these days. It's impressive, how she's transformed herself. There are no beers in the fridge, no vodka in the freezer, no open wine bottles on the counter. Her skin is plump and firm. She drinks eight glasses of water a day as if it's a new religion.

"How's that GED coming along?" Peggy asks, her voice full of sarcasm.

"Fine." She knows she smells like weed, but they either don't notice or pretend not to. She could tell them she's been driving around Orange County with David Bledsoe, learning the freeway systems, visiting neighborhoods they've never heard of, selling cocaine and weed, going back to his condo to try out different sexual positions, all of it her idea. She imagines the horror on their faces, the questions that would follow. *I'm investing in my future,* she might explain, but they'd never understand.

Brenda asks Peggy's opinion about how to dress for work, how much makeup is too much, and how does she get people to take her seriously. Peggy rolls her eyes and pretends to be annoyed, but Allison knows she loves it. All those years of being treated like an ugly duckling and now she's the one with the secrets to the universe.

Allison picks up the newspaper thinking maybe she'll talk them into going to a movie. There's a cartoon on the last page of the front section showing a child watching the O. J. Simpson trial. "What's the forbidden N-word, Mommy?" the little girl asks. "Nicole," the mother answers.

"Did you see this?" Allison asks, but they're not listening.

They're talking about when Peggy might take the next IRS test and whether Brenda can claim her workout clothes as an expense.

"Not until they start paying you," Peggy says.

It's like standing in the ocean with her feet stuck in cold sand, feeling the tide pull against her legs, defeating any purpose or direction. The murdered blond wife forgotten in the media circus. Her unborn nephew with no father. Her husbandless mother, excited about not getting paid to teach old people to sweat. Her pregnant sister dreaming of tax write-offs. The boy in the silver-framed photo in David's dusty house. Meanwhile, Kevin is up in Northridge, flirting with sorority girls and going to keggers or whatever it is people do at college.

At eleven thirty-five, just as David Letterman starts his monologue, Peggy's water breaks, and Brenda drives the three of them to the hospital in Peggy's car. Her dad shows up too, but it gets later and later and there is still no baby, so he takes Allison home. Everyone keeps pretending she has the GED program to go to in the morning. She's happy to pretend too.

"THERE'S still no baby," Brenda calls to report the next day. Since she's home alone, Allison calls David and tells him it's okay if he picks her up at the house.

"I was wondering," she says after he's been driving for a while, "if maybe I could move in with you. I wouldn't be any trouble."

He laughs. "Yes, you would. And I'm not looking for a roommate."

"You know anyone who is?"

"How would you pay rent?"

"I can get a job. I can cook."

A few minutes later he pulls up in front of a ranch house in Costa Mesa. He lets the song on the radio finish before he turns off the ignition, checks his teeth in the visor-flap mirror, pulls a handkerchief out of his pocket, and cleans his glasses.

"Come inside if you want," he says finally. "They might want a roommate."

"Are they your customers?"

"They have their own thing going on."

The house looks normal enough from the outside. Tall pine trees in the front yard, grass slightly brown, three older sedans in the driveway. She follows David to the front door. A young man wearing a stained T-shirt over boxer shorts lets them in. His eyes scan her body, his grin is more of a leer, and he's missing a front tooth. Allison fingers her dad's knife in her front pocket, wondering if David is planning on leaving her here.

Inside, the house is dimly lit, unair-conditioned, windows closed, curtains drawn. It smells musty. The man goes back to the couch and sits down next to another man drinking a beer. They are watching an interview with Judge Ito on television.

"Come meet Cliff," David says. They walk down the hall to a small bedroom where an old man waits in a wheelchair, wearing a knitted skull cap over his bald head. His gray beard is braided and tied at the end with a rubber band.

"Did you bring us a present?" he says.

"This is Allison," David says.

Cliff reaches out a gnarled hand and motions her closer. He grabs her arm. "Pretty," he says. His voice trembles.

"Cliff and I have some things to discuss," David says. "Go talk to the boys. Check out their kitchen."

She walks past the open bathroom door and glances in. The toilet seat is up and there is urine splashed around the outside of the bowl. *That just needs a good scrubbing and some bleach*, she thinks, and then she notices that the tub is ringed in rust and a mushroom is growing up between the cracked tiles.

The men in the living room are focused on the television screen. "I love my wife dearly," Judge Ito is saying. He looks like he's going to cry. "And I am wounded by criticism of her."

"What a pussy," one of the men says.

Allison feels a flea jump on her calf from the carpet. She leans over and pinches it between her fingers. "His wife's a cop," she says. They turn and look at her.

"Oh, hey, sweetie. Where did you come from?"

"Bledsoe brought her," the man in the boxer shorts says.

"Judge Ito's wife is actually a boss of cops," Allison says.

"Women have no business doing police work," the man drinking beer says. "They don't have the right disposition."

"Unless they're ugly or lesbos," boxer shorts man says. He stands and walks over to Allison, cups her face in his palm, and turns her head from side to side. "Nice."

He smells. She pulls away from him. David is behind her now. "Did you take a look at the kitchen?"

"I don't need to. I'm ready to go."

"You just got here," the man on the couch says. "Why don't you stay awhile, sweetie?"

David looks at her. "Up to you, Red."

Allison swats another flea off her leg. "I don't think so."

"Seriously?" she asks when they are back in the car.

"Free rent." David is laughing. "That place could use a woman's touch."

"That's not funny," she says.

"What's wrong with living with your mother? Seems to me you have a pretty sweet deal there. And it sounds like your sister could use some help."

She sighs. He's probably right, and at least he didn't leave her there. She turns up the radio. The earnest singer is explaining all the reasons he really has to move. He sounds very convincing. "Who is this?"

"Grateful Dead. Jerry Garcia just died. All the stations are playing his music."

"Oh, yeah. My dad's a big fan."

"There you go, making me feel like an old man again."

"You are an old man."

"Getting too old for this business."

"What would you do instead?"

"Go back to Hawaii and make surfboards."

"What would Connie say about that?"

"Connie's not my boss."

"Who is then? You? Are you the head of The Family?"

David spits out a laugh. "No. Not at all."

"Who are they anyway? This Family. How does it work?"

"You don't want to know."

"You don't know what I want."

He laughs again. "I don't think you do either, Red. But you surprise me. Connie said you were a thief, but you haven't taken anything from me."

"Does she know I drive around with you?"

"Connie doesn't miss much. Kevin snorted all that coke, didn't he? It was never you."

"We were both responsible."

His laugh is bitter as he pulls into the adult school parking lot to let her out. "Such devotion. I don't see how he's worth it."

WHEN she walks up the driveway, her father's truck is parked in front of the house, and her mom and Peggy are getting out of Peggy's car with a crying baby wrapped in a blue blanket.

"This is Nick," Peggy says. Her hair is oily and stuck to her head, her eyes are rimmed with dark shadows, and she looks triumphant.

"He's so tiny," Allison says.

"Your father came by to put the crib together and you weren't here," Brenda says as they follow Peggy inside.

"I was at school."

"The office told me you haven't been there in weeks. I called."

"They don't always take roll."

"I can't deal with your lies right now."

The baby starts wailing and Peggy turns around, her eyes wide with panic.

"He just needs changing," Brenda says. "I'll help you."

Frank comes out of Peggy's room. "The crib's all set up. Look at this boy!" He holds out his arms and hugs Peggy and Nick. "I'm so proud of you, Peg-a-Leg!"

"Hey, Dad," Allison says.

He looks at her and turns away.

"You're lucky I don't kick you out," Brenda says.

"Can I hold him?"

"Maybe later," Peggy says.

THE third time David glances in the rearview mirror a few days later, Allison asks if something is wrong. He abruptly changes lanes and then gets off the Santa Ana Freeway at Euclid.

"I thought we were being followed. But it looks like I lost them." He pulls into the Target parking lot. "Stay in the store for twenty minutes and then go out through the garden shop."

"You'll be waiting for me?"

He shakes his head. "It's not that far of a walk back to the school."

She opens the car door. "See you tomorrow?"

He shakes his head. "I'm leaving town for a while." He reaches into his shirt pocket and hands her a rubber-banded roll of cash. "You're worth a lot more than you think, Red. I hope you realize that someday."

She waits until she gets home to count the money. A thousand dollars. Something, anyway.

NICK cries constantly. Peggy's frantic and exhausted. Brenda gives up the aerobics class and refuses every job the agency offers. They all sit in front of the television, watching the newscasters count how many times Mark Fuhrman used the N-word in the transcripts of an interview he did with some screenwriter. Brenda hasn't spoken to her for a week, but now at the commercial break she says, "Either go to school or get a job, Allison. And don't bother calling your father to complain. For once, he and I are on the same page."

"You've missed too many classes," the adult school director tells her the next day. "You'll have to start over next semester."

She takes the bus down to the beach and uses one of David's twenties to buy Nick a blue onesie that reads "Surf City, U.S.A." No one's home when she returns, and she remembers something about Nick having a checkup. She decides to surprise them and clean house. She takes everything off the coffee table and polishes it with Lemon Pledge, glancing through the open drapes in the front window. Kevin's truck is in the driveway.

She opens the front door and he's there, smiling that sweet crooked smile, just like in her dreams these past long weeks. He's shaved his head; his shoulders are huge. When he hugs her, though, she smells something sour and metallic, and even when he says, "You look good, babe. It's been too long," she feels the disappointment in his eyes.

He knows about the money David gave me, she thinks immediately, irrationally, because how would he know? She wishes she was wearing something other than the tank top and shorts, something pretty, something a college girl might wear.

"Let's drive down to the beach," he says. "I miss the ocean. I hate Northridge."

"Sure," she says, hurrying to find her sandals and purse, wishing he'd said that he's missed her. She follows him out to his truck and gets in. "How was the camp?"

"Over, finally."

"You look really strong."

"Coach has me on a program. Vitamins and shit. It's expensive."

"I could help you with that."

His smile is suddenly more of a sneer, and now he's driving too fast, swerving between lanes, swearing every time he has to stop at a red light.

"We're not in a hurry," she says, trying to keep her voice calm. "In fact, if you want to get a motel room, I have some money."

"Oh, really?" His laugh is sarcastic. "Why am I not surprised?" He tightens his grip on the steering wheel and the sour, metallic smell increases.

She tells him how the GED program is really lame, and Peggy's baby is really cute but cries all the time. She lists all the jobs her mother has had and tells him about the racist cop on the LAPD. She's talking so much she doesn't notice where they are until he turns left on Warner.

"I thought we were going to the beach."

"All your yapping is giving me a headache."

"I'm sorry. I guess I'm nervous."

He pulls into Mile Square Park, parks under a stand of eucalyptus trees near the golf course, and turns off the ignition. "Why don't you do something useful with that mouth of yours?" He unzips his shorts and pulls her head down into his lap.

If this is what he wants, she decides, *I'll make it my best performance ever.* But she tries for so long that her mouth gets dry and he still doesn't get hard. When she lifts her head and glances at his face, he's scowling.

"Is this what Bledsoe likes?" He pushes her away and she bumps her chin on the gear shift.

"Ow!" The taste of him in her mouth is nauseating. She reaches for her purse, hoping to find some gum or a mint. In the distance she sees a rabbit streak across the greens in front of a golf cart. Two women get out, wearing pastel shorts and matching visors, laughing about something, too far away to hear.

"I know you're still seeing him." Kevin zips his shorts up. "I heard he took you to that meth house in Costa Mesa."

She remembers the ranch house with the disgusting bathroom, the man with the missing tooth. "I didn't know it was a meth house and I was only there one time for a minute."

"How much cash did he give you anyway?" Before she can stop him, he rips her purse out of her hands and digs through it, taking out the Swiss Army knife and her wallet.

"I don't care about the money, Kevin, but that knife belongs to my dad."

"It's mine now." He slides the knife in the back pocket of his jeans and counts the twenties. "Connie had a good idea, using you to pay off the money we owed him."

No, she thinks. *I haven't heard him right.* "What are you talking about?"

"It was her idea. She knew you'd go for it too. She was right about you. I mean, she liked you at first. She thought you were good for me. But once she found out you were a thief, that was it. She said you'd do anything for a line and a joint and she was right."

Her heart stalls and then sputters into overdrive. "That's not true. We both made that decision about David. It was for us."

"Then why are you still seeing him? Why would you want to be with an ugly old man like him?"

"Because we owe him money."

His laugh is bitter. "You're not that stupid, Allison. That debt's been paid. You *want* to be with him. You always have. Does he like that noise you make when you come?"

I am stupid. I've been stupid all along. "I'm not seeing him anymore."

He slams both hands on the steering wheel. "Stop lying to me."

"He left, Kevin. He's gone."

"Gone where?"

"I don't know. He thought someone was following us a few days ago. He said he was leaving town for a while."

Kevin's eyes go wide. "Your dad probably said something to those inspectors. You're poison, you know that? I never should have gotten involved with you. Get out of my truck."

He jumps out, strides around the truck, opens her door, and yanks her out of her seat. She stumbles and scrapes her knee and scrambles back to her feet.

"You can't just leave me here."

"Take your shit too." He reaches in the truck and grabs her wallet and her purse, and throws them both in the oleander bushes lining the back of the parking lot.

"You know what?" she says. "David may be old and ugly, but at least he can get hard."

He lunges for her and she trips over a crack in the asphalt. Before she can catch her balance, his fist comes up below her chin, brutal and determined. She hears more than feels the bones of his knuckles connect with her jaw, and then she falls backward, stiff legged, too shocked to brace for the impact of her skull against the concrete.

"Get up," Kevin says. He kicks her in the ribs, and she moans. She tries to roll over to protect herself, but she can't move. He kicks her again and then she hears nothing.

WHEN she opens her eyes, there's an old man with milky blue eyes and a speckled forehead staring down at her, a blazing sun behind him. "A lady went to call an ambulance," he says. It's too hot for an old person like him to be outside without a hat. He sits down on the curb and puts his hand over hers. "They'll be here as quick as they can. Don't you worry about a thing." He holds up her purse. "I found this in the bushes."

"Thank you," she tries to say, but her jaw seems to have come unattached.

"Sssh," he says. "Don't try to talk."

The pain is a loud locomotive ripping through her skull. The faces above her are so silent and serious she can hear every heartbeat. She needs to vomit. "She's choking," someone says. There are strobing white lights and people rushing around her, shoes squeaking on linoleum floors. Her father's voice. "Was there brain injury?" He sounds like he's crying. "She'll need surgery," a deeper voice says. "Her jaw's broken in three places." A keening wail, like a seagull over the lunch tables at Ocean View, and then her mother's face, desperate, crazy-eyed. The other voice again, practical and calm. "She has a concussion, two cracked ribs, and a punctured lung. No sign of sexual assault."

Is it still the same day? A round-faced woman in a Fountain Valley police uniform stands next to the bed with a clipboard and a pen and a list of questions. What happened? Who was it? More than one person? Can she identify them? Were there any witnesses? The woman doesn't ask the most important question.

Why?

The voices of her family surround her hospital bed. "Tell her who did this, honey." Her mother squeezes her hand.

Her sister's anguished voice. *Who is watching Nick?* "Kevin's hit her before."

Her father punches his hand on the wall. "You should have told me, Peggy!"

"Let's all stay calm," the policewoman says. "Kevin is her boyfriend?"

"Ex-boyfriend," Brenda says. "She hasn't seen him in weeks. He's going to school up in Northridge."

"What about that man in the Mercedes?" Frank asks.

Allison tries to shake her head no, but her neck won't cooperate.

"His last name is Bledsoe." Peggy's voice is a choked whisper. "He's Kevin's mother's partner. At the jewelry store."

Allison moans.

"He's what?" Brenda asks. "How do you know that?"

"Let her finish," Frank says.

"I have his license plate number." Peggy hesitates and goes on. "I'm fairly sure he's dealing drugs. I even sent a letter to the Huntington Beach Police Department."

David thought someone was following us.

"When did you do all that?" Brenda asks.

"It was a waste of time. I never heard anything back."

"You should have said something, Peggy." Frank sounds angry. "The Inspection Service was asking questions about Kevin."

"The Postal Inspection Service?" the policewoman asks.

"It's confidential," Frank says, "but they're looking at drug trafficking at the post office where I work."

"Was it that awful man, honey?"

"Mom! She can't talk. She can't even move her head."

"She can blink," Brenda says. "Was it him?"

Allison closes her eyes and remembers the sound of Kevin's knuckle on her jaw, how he'd kicked her, and what he'd said.

"Or was it Kevin?" Peggy asks.

"Blink, honey," Brenda says. "Blink if it was Kevin."

Connie was right about you. She knew you'd go for it. Allison opens her eyes. The light hurts, but she blinks once and then again and again.

CHAPTER SIXTEEN

"YOU LOOK BEAUTIFUL," BRENDA SAYS AS SHE STANDS IN THE DOORWAY TO Peggy's room, watching her try to nurse Nick.

"I look horrible," Peggy says.

"You could try formula." She never breastfed either of her girls, but she supposes that's the point of all this anguish. Peggy doesn't want to do anything the way she did. "I'll hold him when you're finished, so you can go take a shower."

"He's never finished." Nick pulls away from chewing on Peggy's nipple and stares up at her. "He hates me."

"Don't be silly," Brenda says. "He loves you. You're just tired." Between Nick's squalls and Allison's nightmares, none of them has slept more than two consecutive hours the last few weeks. She's exhausted too, and worried and still completely thrilled to be Nick's grandmother. She had no idea she'd love this baby so much. "Look at those beautiful eyes."

"They're Glenn's eyes. Nick doesn't even look like me. I wish I could stop crying."

"It's just the hormones. Try to burp him so he doesn't get gas."

"That never works. Why's his face so crooked?"

"It's not crooked, honey." She tries not to think about Allison's broken face. "Give him to me."

"I have to learn how to do this myself."

"You need to rest. He's taking all your nutrients."

"I need to lose weight, so I can fit into my clothes and go back to work. I shouldn't have used so much leave before he was born. I'm going to run out of money."

"We'll figure it out. Go take a shower."

"Your mother's wrong," she whispers to Nick when Peggy hands him over and heads to the bathroom. "Your face is perfect."

Laura's at the door now, holding a plate of enchiladas. She's brought something delicious every day since Allison came home from the hospital. "Alejandro's recipe," she says proudly. "They might be soft enough for Allison to eat."

"She's still on liquid foods," Brenda says. "But thank you. Peggy and I will enjoy them." She hesitates. Laura has already done so much for them. "The agency found me something at an insurance company, but they want me there tomorrow. I don't know if it's the right time."

"Go," Laura says. "I'll keep an eye on your family. I'm glad to do it."

"I'll bring the plate back later. Thank you."

"MARK Fuhrman's pleading the fifth on everything," Brenda says when Peggy comes back from her shower wearing a clean pair of sweats.

"Did you want to sit here?" Allison asks through clenched teeth, a grating sound that makes Brenda's heart ache every time she hears it. Allison's taken over Peggy's usual spot in the hideous recliner. It's the only place other than the bed she seems comfortable.

"I'm okay on the couch." Peggy sounds like she's making a huge sacrifice.

"I'll get up," Allison says. "I don't mind."

"Stay where you are. It's fine."

The two of them are anything but fine. Allison is fragile and probably should have stayed in the hospital longer. Peggy is sleep-deprived and guilt-ridden, somehow convinced the assault was her fault and still furious with Allison for getting in Kevin's truck that day. She's afraid to leave the two of them alone, but she really hopes the insurance company turns into a real job.

"He has to keep pleading the fifth," Peggy says, still standing. "Once you take it, you can't answer any questions."

"Detective Fuhrman," the defense attorney asks, "did you plant or manufacture any evidence in this case?"

"I assert my Fifth Amendment privilege," Mark Fuhrman says.

"Which makes it sound like he *did* plant the glove. Mark Fuhrman will be the reason O. J. gets off," Brenda says.

"That's what you're hoping for," Peggy says. "Isn't it?"

Brenda glances at Allison. Her face is still bruised and swollen from the surgery. Her teeth will be wired shut for who knows how long in an orthodontic device reminiscent of medieval torture. Her beautiful child, beaten by a monster.

She has a sudden and vivid image of the terror on Nicole Simpson's face that night, when she'd opened her front door and found O. J. standing there, wearing those gloves, holding a knife. "I was wrong about O. J. He's the killer." She sees her girls exchange looks. "I wish I hadn't wasted so much time watching this."

"The problem is we're addicted to it too," Allison says.

"Let's watch something else then." She digs through the stack of videos and pulls out *The Big Easy*, one of the many reasons she's always dreamed of New Orleans. When the Cajun fiddle starts, Peggy sits down on the couch next to her. Brenda turns up the sound. The movie's even better than she remembered. The mouthwatering food, the romantic moss dripping from old oaks next to a dark bayou, a Cajun band, and most especially the infectious dancing. She'd love to be able to dance like that, especially with someone as charming as Dennis Quaid. His sex scenes with Ellen Barkin are delicious.

"I get why you want to go there," Peggy says.

The movie's nearly over when there's a knock on the front door. "Probably Laura with more food," Brenda says. "I'm going to get fat if she doesn't stop feeding us."

"Brenda?" It's not Laura's voice. "Can we talk?"

Peggy peeks out the window. "It's Connie and Sal," she whispers.

"What are they doing here?" Brenda stops the movie and the dreamy seduction of New Orleans evaporates.

Another knock, more insistent. "Please," Sal says. "It's important."

Brenda turns to Allison. "If you can stand it, I'd like them to see what he did to you."

"What difference will that make?" Allison says.

"They need to know."

Allison shrugs, Peggy opens the door, and Sal and Connie nervously inch their way inside. There's no place for them to sit and Brenda doesn't offer.

Sal's eyes flood with tears when he sees Allison's face. "Dear God. You poor child."

Connie keeps her eyes on the floor. "We found Kevin a really good rehab facility. He's trying to get healthy. He's doing his best to make all of this right."

"He's so sorry about what happened," Sal says.

"Sorry!" Brenda says. "He almost killed her. You're the ones who'll be sorry. We're suing you. Your son committed a felony."

Connie takes a deep breath and turns to Allison. "We're hoping you might be convinced to drop the charges, honey. You know he didn't mean to hurt you."

"It was the cocaine," Sal says. "That stuff is pure evil."

"It was those steroids and vitamins the coach put him on," Connie says. "We can give you some cash. Two hundred thousand.

Drop the charges and take the money. Let's all put this behind us."

"Put this behind us!" Brenda is so angry she has to stand. "What about her face?"

"Two hundred thousand would pay for a lot of plastic surgery," Sal says. "You could all start a new life."

"It's too late to drop the charges," Peggy says. "The Inspection Service is involved."

"They won't find anything." Connie's voice breaks. "Please. Don't ruin Kevin's life."

"Court cases take forever," Sal says, "and you never know what a jury will do."

"Are you kidding?" Brenda says. "A jury would lock up your son. Look at her."

Connie swallows hard. "The problem is I don't think Kevin could last through a trial much less do jail time. They have him on suicide watch. I'm really afraid he's going to hurt himself."

"Good. I hope he does." She sees Allison grip the edges of the couch. "This isn't fair to upset her like this. You need to leave."

"I was wrong about you, Allison," Connie says. "Kevin loves you. I'm so sorry. Let's make it two hundred fifty thousand."

Allison closes her eyes.

"Honey," Brenda says, "I shouldn't have let them in."

"At least think about it," Sal says.

"Kevin made a horrible mistake," Connie says.

They all look at Allison. She's going to agree, Brenda is sure. She's tried to be a different woman, a better mother, but she hasn't changed a damn thing. Allison will take the money, and Kevin will get away with everything, then beat her again, and eventually kill her.

"It wasn't a mistake," Allison says. "I'm not dropping the charges."

"What did she say?" Sal asks. "I can't understand her."

"Get the hell out of my house." Brenda opens the front door. "We'll see you in court."

"I'm proud of you," she tells Allison, after Sal and Connie leave. "You did the right thing."

"I hope you meant it," Peggy says.

"I'll still have to testify against him," Allison says. "I'm not sure I can."

"One day at a time," Brenda says.

SHE parks Peggy's car behind Countywide Title Insurance Company and hurries across the parking lot, already regretting the open-toed pumps crimping her toes into a painful origami. Her original blouse matched her skirt, but she had to change when Nick threw up on her, which is one reason why she's late. Allison had a meltdown about something Peggy said this morning, and both girls were screaming at each other when she left. The amount of traffic was shocking. Tomorrow she'll need to leave even earlier.

Despite everything, she feels optimistic. Countywide Title pays twice as much as the other jobs the temp agency offered. This could be the day her new life begins. She hums Aretha Franklin's song "Chain of Fools," which just played on the car radio, as she walks through the parking lot. The woman waiting by the employee entrance is obviously not happy.

"I'm Darlene."

"I'm so sorry to be late." Brenda tries her best smile. "Traffic was terrible." She almost adds she was delayed by her new grandson at home, but that will make her sound old. If she mentions her daughter with the busted jaw, cracked ribs, and ex-boyfriend in rehab, she will sound like a negligent mother. Which she has been. Until now.

Darlene shows her where to clock in and then offers "the grand tour," putting air quotes around the words. "Front office, copy room, the coffeepot, and the restroom. And this is our production pool." There is nothing pool-like about the rectangular open space lined with identical desks made of thin veneer over pressed wood. Brenda smiles at the women who glance up quickly at her and Darlene, but they all immediately look back down at their keyboards.

"Half hour for lunch. Picnic tables outside. A lot of the girls eat in their cars."

She'd envisioned a window with a view and restaurant lunches with new friends. The air in the office smells like vinyl. Everything is colored a dirty beige.

"This is you," Darlene says, pointing to the one empty desk at the edge of the pool. The chair seat is stained with coffee and sweat. Brenda sits down and tries to maintain an enthusiastic expression as Darlene stacks forms in a beige plastic inbox.

"These need to be keyed into our database. The most important thing is to keep the forms in the exact same order. Once you have them all entered, you generate the affidavit forms, make four copies of each packet, and restack them in the same exact order in your outbox. You know Microsoft Access, right?"

She has absolutely no idea what Darlene is talking about. "I'm a quick learner."

"Unbelievable," Darlene says. "I specifically asked for someone who knows databases."

By the end of the first hour, the spring in Brenda's chair cushion has worked its way up into her left sciatic nerve, but by the end of the day, she thinks she might be getting the hang of things, although Darlene doesn't look happy.

"You're going to have to pick up the pace."

"WHAT do you know about databases?" she asks Peggy that night. "Something called Access?"

"I have a book somewhere. Hold Nick and I'll see if I can find it."

"Has he been crying all day?"

"I finally got him down for his nap and then Allison cranked up her CD player."

"He wasn't sleeping. I thought music might help."

"Whatever you were listening to wasn't music."

"It wasn't the music anyway. It was the goddamned bulldozers. I'm sick of living in a war zone." Allison stomps off to Brenda's bedroom and slams the door.

"She's still in a lot of pain," Brenda says. "That's why she's so irritable."

"I know, Mom. But she's got to be quiet when Nick's sleeping. His routine's important. That's what all the books say."

"I'll talk to her. Did you take a shower today?"

"What do you think? I'm going to put him down and then I'm going to bed."

Brenda sits at the kitchen table and flips through Peggy's Microsoft manual while her Weight Watcher's lasagna warms in the microwave, listening to the replay of O. J. on television saying "did not, could not, and would not have committed this crime."

"Bullshit," Brenda tells the screen. "You did it."

Nick has the hiccups but is starting to calm down. She smiles when she hears Peggy singing to him. She takes a smoothie to Allison and watches her finish it before she gives her another pain pill. When the lasagna is cool enough, she sets it on the kitchen table, fills her Tiffany glass with water, and opens the Microsoft manual to Chapter One.

ON Wednesday, she assumes a Diet Coke out of the fridge doesn't belong to anyone. "I'm sorry," she says when Darlene confronts her. "I'll replace it tomorrow."

"That doesn't do me one bit of good today," Darlene says.

When she comes home with groceries and a six-pack of Diet Cokes, Peggy has company. Brenda assumes the tall long-haired man on the couch is Glenn and the scrawny woman sitting next to him, wide-eyed and nervous, the new girlfriend. They've brought gifts for Nick. A Raiders' onesie that is already too small for him and a huge leather football. "What do you expect him to do with that?" she asks. Peggy looks miserable and Allison must be hiding behind the firmly closed bedroom door. At least Glenn has the decency to help her carry the groceries in from the car.

"We've never officially met," he says as he sets the groceries on the counter. He flashes a dimple and holds out his hand. He does have nice eyes, but his grin is too practiced.

"I know who you are." She puts the milk in the fridge.

"I hope you don't mind us stopping by. We wanted to meet the baby."

"You mean your son? Nick's going to be awfully expensive."

"We could babysit," the skinny girlfriend is telling Peggy as Glenn follows Brenda back to the living room. "Whenever you're ready to go back to work."

"I'm not driving all the way out to Norco every morning," Peggy says. "And I can't picture either one of you changing diapers."

"My sister uses cloth diapers," Jill says. "She has a service and everything."

"Does she really?" Brenda says. "And does the service change the diapers for her?"

Jill gets even smaller on the couch, and her eyes dart from the clock to the front door.

"My cousin's getting rid of her minivan," Glenn says. "You need a bigger car."

"I have a car already," Peggy says.

"You need something safer."

"I can't afford payments."

"It's paid for," Glenn says.

Please take the van, Brenda thinks. Glenn is right. The stroller barely fits in the trunk and Nick's car seat is almost impossible to get in and out of the back seat. And then she could drive Peggy's Ford. This would solve a lot of problems.

"I want to help," Glenn says. "You don't have to do everything on your own, you know."

Peggy looks as if she might burst into tears.

Jill jumps up. "We're starting a bowling league September twenty-first. You should come, Peggy."

"Do you have some kind of a mental deficiency?" Brenda asks.

"I'll wait in the car," Jill says.

"Nice to meet you," Glenn says.

"Was it?" Brenda slams the door while he's still standing on the porch. "Bowling? What is wrong with that girl?"

Peggy wipes her eyes and laughs. "The expression on her face."

Nick makes a spit bubble and grabs his toes.

"You can come out from hiding, Allison," Brenda says. "They're gone."

Allison opens the door. "I wasn't hiding. I just didn't see the point of talking to them."

"The van's a nice gesture."

"You don't have to pretend you like him, Mom."

"He's Nick's father. We're stuck with him."

ON Thursday afternoon, Brenda doesn't realize she's forgotten to select "collate" from the copy machine menu until she's finished stapling all her packets together. She digs the staples out with her fingernails, re-sorts the forms on the floor in the copy room where she is in everyone's way, and then re-staples the packets back together again. By Friday, she's sure they'll send her back to the agency.

"I could come in tomorrow and catch up," she tells Darlene.

"We don't pay overtime," Darlene says. "But that might be a good idea."

Saturday morning, Brenda backs Peggy's car out of the driveway, praying there is enough gas to make it to the office and back. The employee entrance is unlocked, there are lights on in the front office, and she can hear the coffeepot sputtering in the copy room. She hopes Darlene didn't make the pot. She needs a Darlene-free day. It's easier to concentrate without her office mates clacking away on their keyboards. She makes fewer mistakes, gets into a rhythm, and finally has enough of a stack of completed forms to justify a trip to the copy room and a quick cup of coffee. Copies first, she decides. She loads the duplicating tray and pushes the start button. The first sheet of paper goes through fine, but the second one jams in a sickening crunch. Red lights flash.

"Fuck," she says, kneeling on the hard linoleum floor, trying to remember what Darlene had told her about clearing jams. "Follow the instructions exactly," Darlene had said in her snippy little voice. The instructions are inside the machine door. She studies the chart and tries to match the flashing red lights to the source of the problem. "Open Door B3 and then clear C1." To reach Door B3, she practically has to stand on her head. She opens B3 and clears C1. Twice. Nothing. She slams the door hard. "Damn it!" She suddenly feels someone standing behind her, probably staring at her ass. She smooths her skirt down over her hips as gracefully as possible and stands, praying it isn't Darlene.

"Need help?" The man's smile is so immediately sympathetic she regrets slamming the door and swearing. She's seen his picture in the front lobby over a plaque reading, Richard Cavanaugh, General Manager. It's a good likeness, although instead of the gray wool suit and blue striped tie in the photo, he's wearing a teal blue golf shirt that matches his eyes. Up close he seems too young to be so bald, maybe even younger than she is, and judging from his trim torso, he spends time in the gym.

"That machine's kind of tricky. You have to sweet talk it a little." He opens a small door and pulls out a crumpled piece of paper. She can smell his cologne, bergamot with musky undertones, as he flips a lever and steps back. The lights on the copier turn green and the copies pile up in the tray in tidy collated stacks. "There you go." He holds out his hand. "I'm Richard. I don't believe I've had the pleasure."

His nails are clean and trimmed. His empty coffee cup reads "Kiss My Putt." He likes her, she knows immediately by the way his gaze doesn't break, as if he finds it impossible to look away from her. She's finding it hard to look away as well. She's never seen eyes quite that color.

"I'm Brenda. I just started this week." Which is a dumb thing to say since he must already know who she is, the new temp who doesn't understand databases and steals Darlene's Diet Cokes. She wonders if he's really bald or if he shaves his head every day and if he uses an electric razor. Would his hair feel like beard stubble if he let it grow out or would it be as soft as baby fuzz? It's hot in the copy room and his cologne might have a little too much musk because she's suddenly imagining his bald head between her thighs. He smiles as if he can read her mind.

"It's nice to find someone else in the office on a Saturday. I usually stop in for a few hours before my golf game."

"I should get back to work." She gestures in the direction of the pool room. "Thanks for sweet-talking the machine. You saved the day."

"Why don't you come up to my office and have some coffee with me?" He walks out into the hallway, motioning with his head for her to follow. "I've got creamer and sugar if you need it."

"I like it black," she says, following him.

"I knew we had something in common."

In his office, Richard leans back in his chair and sips his coffee. She crosses her legs and watches his eyes follow the line of her skirt. She notes an expensive-looking watch, but she doesn't see a wedding band. She takes a discreet look around the office, checking for signs of wife or family. Not that it matters. He really isn't her type, although maybe she needs a new type. The desk and bookshelves in his office are almost as cheap as the furniture in the production pool, and the only pictures on the walls and desk are of Richard at various golf courses. The dusty vertical blinds behind his desk don't quite meet in the middle and shiver together periodically between rotations of the floor fan ruffling the papers on Richard's desk. Outside the window, she sees a cream-colored Lexus parked in the manager's space.

"Tell me about yourself," he says. "Are you married?"

"Divorced. Well, almost."

"Me too. See, I knew we had things in common."

She wonders how long it would take to either get used to his aftershave or convince him to wear something else, while a little voice in her head wants to know what he means by *almost* divorced.

"How's your commute? I drive in from Modjeska Canyon. Saturday's the only day I can make it in less than an hour."

"Modjeska Canyon. How nice. Do you have a view?" He smiles. Of course, he doesn't have a view if he lives in a canyon. "I bet there's lots of trees."

"Oaks and a few olive trees. And I do have a view of Santiago Peak."

"That sounds lovely."

He finishes his coffee and says he needs to get to the golf course, but he's enjoyed talking to her and is so glad she's joined their insurance family. He follows her to the copy room where she retrieves her packets and then back to the production pool.

"This is me," she says when they get to her desk.

"Would you like to have dinner with me tomorrow night?"

She shouldn't say yes on such short notice. She has plans anyway. She needs to do laundry, go grocery shopping, run the vacuum cleaner, and swab down the bathroom. She would like to give Nick a bath and put him to bed. She should study the book on Microsoft. And then it will be Monday and Darlene will put another stack of forms in her inbox.

"I'm sorry. I'm busy all weekend."

"Maybe some other time then."

After he leaves, she puts the packets in order in her outbox, washes her coffee cup out in the sink in the break room, and dries the cup with a paper towel. It felt right to turn Richard down. He'll ask her out again—if Darlene doesn't fire her before he gets another chance—but she'll tell him no again. He's obviously still married and he's also her boss. She's not going to screw this up.

When she opens the door of the cabinet to put her cup away, she finds an open box of See's Candy. She picks out a walnut chew, letting the dark chocolate dissolve slowly in her mouth.

It's delicious and utterly satisfying until it occurs to her the candy probably belongs to Darlene, who most assuredly will take inventory Monday morning. She hides the wrapper in her skirt pocket, closes the box, and puts it back on the shelf where she found it.

CHAPTER SEVENTEEN

October 3, 1995

PEGGY HOLDS NICK'S WARM LITTLE BODY TIGHT AGAINST HER CHEST. "MAYBE I should stay home today," she tells Allison, glancing at the television screen. A huge crowd has gathered in front of the Los Angeles courthouse. It's a warm October morning and the jury is back, the verdict imminent. "It looks like they're expecting a riot. They've already notified the feds they might need help."

It's her first week back in the accounting office, and even though it's only part-time, she hates every minute. She misses Nick fiercely, her clothes don't fit, and her breasts leak. But she's run out of leave and there's not much money left in her checking account.

"No one riots in Orange County," Allison says. The wires are finally off, but she still talks as if her jaw is sealed shut.

"There's not going to be a riot anywhere," Brenda says, coming into the living room with her briefcase. "Because the jury is not going to convict him."

"I hope you're wrong," Allison says. "Is there a TV set at your office?"

"Of course not," Brenda says, "and I really don't care. I'll be in an Excel class this morning anyway."

Somehow, Brenda has convinced her boss to send her to computer classes twice a week. He's finally stopped asking her to go out with him, so that's not the reason. Whatever it is, Peggy's never seen her mother this determined to learn something new.

"I'll be home by one o'clock," she tells Allison, reluctantly relinquishing Nick to her sister's arms. "He's got three bottles in the fridge, there's a new box of diapers, and Laura's across the street if you need anything."

Allison sways Nick back and forth, and he giggles. "Go to work. Nick and I are fine. Aren't we, Mr. Handsome?"

Nick looks happy in her sister's arms, which is both reassuring and annoying. Peggy follows her mother outside. Brenda puts her briefcase in the tiny Ford and gets in the driver's seat as Laura comes down her driveway and hands Peggy a package.

"Would you mail this for me?" she asks.

"What did you make this time?"

"Tamales. Alejandro can't get good masa in New Orleans."

Peggy puts the package in the back seat of Glenn's van. She can't call it anything else even though the title is in her name now. They both wave at Brenda as she makes a U-turn and beeps the horn.

"I was sure your mom would call in sick and stay home to watch the verdict."

"She's sure he's going to get off."

Laura shakes her head. "I hope she's wrong." They watch as three Caltrans trucks park down the street. "Looks like another noisy day."

"It won't be long before we all have to move." Half the neighborhood's been demolished. She'd really like to get her own place, but what can she afford? Besides, she needs someone to watch Nick. Thank God for Laura. And for Allison and her mom. They both have more patience with Nick than she would have ever expected. More patience than she does, most of the time.

"The city will change their mind," Laura says. "I bet we never have to move. Don't worry about Nick or Allison. I'll check on them."

"Thank you," Peggy says.

THE long-legged man sitting in the chair next to Phyllis's desk stands immediately when Peggy comes in the office. "This is Jeff Robinson," Phyllis says. "He's a postal inspector." Peggy sets her purse on her desk. The inspector has a short crew cut and even more freckles than Allison. He's not nearly as intimidating as she'd expect a law enforcement official to look. Hopefully, he finally has news about Kevin and David Bledsoe. It would make more sense for him to talk to her father, but Frank must be out in the field.

"I'm auditing the stamp destruction committee," Jeff says.

"Oh." Peggy glances out of the dirty office window. The electrical lines between the telephone poles across the street sag and the carpet feels unsteady under her feet. *A small earthquake,* she thinks, although Phyllis and Jeff don't seem to notice.

"The count was short," Phyllis says. "Again."

"There's a real problem with controls over inventory," Jeff says. "The postmasters aren't sending the stock by registered mail for one thing. That leaves all kinds of potential for theft."

"Peggy's always talking about internal controls," Phyllis says. "She's studying accounting at college."

"It's just Golden West." If only she'd kept her big mouth shut. She can't even give back what she took because she's destroyed it.

"The postmasters aren't documenting the stock accurately either," Jeff says.

"What do you expect?" Phyllis asks. "Half of them couldn't balance a checkbook if you held a gun to their heads. None of them have any financial background. Most of them used to be truck drivers."

Peggy exhales slightly. If Phyllis starts preaching about the poor decisions the district manager makes on his postmaster selections, she might be able to make some excuse and leave the room. Go find her father. Maybe he can hire an attorney. Or maybe she can pretend to be sick, go home, and never come back. It was only a couple of rolls of stamps and one money order, but they'll still fire her.

"The good news is the shortage wasn't as much as last quarter's difference," Jeff is saying.

"Thanks to Peggy," Phyllis says.

"Excuse me?" She wonders if postal inspectors are required to read the Miranda Act. Do they carry handcuffs? Glenn will get custody and Jill will be the one to raise Nick.

"Phyllis tells me you've been a tremendous help organizing the stock," Jeff says. "Maybe you could put together a list of weaknesses you've noticed and ideas for improvements."

"Peggy has all kinds of great ideas," Phyllis says. "I'm lucky to have her working with me."

"Make a few notes and I'll give you a call later this week," Jeff says. "You ever think about the inspection service?" She stares at him, uncomprehending. "You might want to apply once you get your degree. The service is always looking for people with accounting backgrounds."

She breathes. "That'll be a while."

"Think about it," Jeff says.

"I'd better get to work." She backs toward her desk. *Focus*, she tells herself as she sits down. The fluorescent light blinks and hums. Someone has already burned popcorn down the hall. She gets the letter opener from her top desk drawer and starts opening envelopes. Jeff talks to Phyllis for what seems like an hour but is only five minutes according to the clock on the wall. Which may have stopped, she isn't sure.

"Nice to meet you, Peggy," he says, before he leaves.

"I think Jeff likes you," Phyllis says. "He's cute, isn't he?"

"I didn't notice."

"If I were twenty pounds lighter and ten years younger, I'd ditch my husband and go after Jeff myself."

Her mother would say twenty pounds wouldn't make much difference. Peggy starts to feel normal again. If the count was short once, maybe it's not that big of a deal for it to be short again. Maybe no one has connected her with what's missing. Maybe she's in the clear. Maybe this is the calm before all hell breaks loose.

AT nine thirty, the woman from the budget office sticks her head in the door and says the verdict's in. Peggy and Phyllis go to the lunchroom where there's already a crowd around the television. Linda motions for them to join her.

"Your dad had to go out to the canyon this morning," Linda says. "Harvey Morales gave his notice."

"That old man's finally retiring?" Phyllis says. "Hallelujah."

"I have a new outfit for Nick," Linda says. "Stop by my office later."

"You don't have to keep buying him things." Peggy's cracked nipples itch and her breast pump's in her purse, but she'd like to hear the verdict, although she's fairly sure the jury is going to let O. J. off. She hates to admit it, but her mother is probably right.

"I love buying him things," Linda says. "Are we still on for babysitting this weekend?"

"If you really want to. It would be a big help. I have a review class."

"Your dad and I can't wait to see Nick again. He grows so fast."

"Just two more tests to go," Phyllis says. "And Peggy will have her certificate."

"Are you going to work for the IRS when you pass?" Linda asks.

"I still need to pass those tests. And get a degree. And eventually go for the CPA. By then, I'll be a hundred years old."

"You'll do it," Linda says. "Your dad is so proud of you."

"I'm exhausted."

"It'll get easier," Phyllis says. "Nick won't be a baby forever."

The TV cameras scan over the crowds standing outside the Los Angeles County courthouse, watching the outdoor television screens.

"Look at all those people," Linda says. "Don't they have jobs?"

"Look around you," Phyllis says. "The world's come to a standstill."

The supervisors in their white shirts and ties sit at one table; the truck drivers in sweat-stained uniforms with keys hanging low off their belts take up two tables in the back. The custodians stand near the door, eyeballing the supervisors, expecting to be told to go back to work. Julie tells the other window clerks in a voice loud enough for the supervisors to hear that there aren't any customers in the lobby; everyone's home watching the verdict.

Peggy smiles when the microwave dings. Someone is heating up their lunch. Someone's life is going on.

"I can't believe the jury made a decision already," Linda says.

"Nine months of testimony," Peggy says, "Forty-five thousand pages of evidence and eleven hundred exhibits. There is no way the jury could have made a decent decision in four hours."

Linda laughs. "How do you know all that? I thought your mother was the expert."

"Osmosis. Plus, I watched TV a lot while I was home with Nick."

"Sssh," Julie says. "Something's happening."

The jury forewoman hands a sealed envelope to Judge Ito. Flanked by Johnnie Cochran and Robert Kardashian, Simpson stands and faces the jury. He swallows a few times and then settles on a forced, pained grin. "We the jury find the defendant Orenthal"—the clerk trips over his name but then continues in a clear and firm voice—"James Simpson, not guilty."

"You've got to be shitting me," one of the truck drivers says.

Relief floods Simpson's face as he mouths the words "Thank you" after each additional verdict of not guilty.

"Of course, they can't convict one of their own," Julie says.

"Never should have married that woman in the first place," the woman from the budget office mutters under her breath. "But he shouldn't have killed her either."

The lunchroom quickly empties. "I'll meet you back in the office," Peggy tells Phyllis and heads to the ladies' room. When she finishes pumping in the cramped stall and opens the door, the two young Black women from the Personnel office are standing by the sink, hugging each other. "He's free!" one of them says, but they move away from each other when they see her, which is confusing. She assumes they're celebrating the verdict, but why stop because of her?

She doesn't really know them, she realizes, as she walks back to her desk. She's never even tried to get to know anyone in the offices. She's back to having no friends again. She never sees Tessa anymore. She barely talks to her own sister.

She's not sure why she's still furious at Allison. Pre-Nick, she would have examined her feelings, drawn a pie chart, divided her anger into slices of jealousy, revulsion, and betrayal. Her parents have always cared more about Allison, even now when she's the one who gave them a grandson, but sometimes *she's* jealous of how natural Allison is with Nick. The idea of her sister having sex with David Bledsoe is nauseating, and her telling their parents about Glenn is unforgivable. But she misses how it used to be with her sister. They were friends.

Her mom calls a few minutes later.

"Congratulations," Peggy says. "You were right about the verdict."

"I feel awful. Like it's my fault."

"That's ridiculous, Mom."

"I sat there and watched the whole thing. I even defended him. I've been sick to my stomach all morning. I'm going home at lunch."

"I'll see you soon, then. I hope you feel better."

It's a strange morning and she's glad when her four hours are over, and she can go home and hold her son.

"There's a call for you," Phyllis says as she heads out the door.

"Is it my mom again? Tell her I'll talk to her at home."

"It's a man," Phyllis mouths.

Please not the inspector, Peggy prays. Surely, Phyllis would have said if it was.

"Hey," Glenn says. "How's it going? How's Nick?"

"He's fine," Peggy says. "I was just leaving."

"You sure you should be back at work already?"

"I need the money. I'm out of leave." *And you don't get to have an opinion.*

"Can you believe they let O. J. go?"

"I'm not surprised. What did you want?"

"Just to check in. How's the van? Is it running okay? It's going to need new tires soon."

He wants to be thanked, again, and she doesn't mind. The minivan's a huge help. His kindness still amazes her. "It's fine. I really do appreciate it. How's Jill?" Saying Jill's name is like pinching herself to make sure she's awake.

"Jill's Jill. She's talking about getting married."

"To you?" She's trying to be funny, but he doesn't laugh.

"It's her idea, not mine."

It's so typically Glenn to expect her to believe he has no say in whether he's getting married or not. "Good luck with all that," she says.

ALLISON meets her at the front door when she comes home, her hair in wet ringlets on her shoulder, smelling like coconut shampoo. "Let's go to South Coast Plaza. I need some new clothes." Allison hasn't gone anywhere since the wires came off her jaw, won't even walk outside to pick up the newspaper because someone might see her. But now her green eyes are lively, and she's put on lipstick.

"What's got into you?" Peggy asks. She'd give anything to lie down on the couch and sleep. The house is quiet. Nick must be napping. There is no rap music blaring from Allison's speakers and the television set is off. The bulldozer drivers are probably still at lunch.

"I'm going stir crazy. Come on. Nick will love the carousel."

"Nick's too little for the carousel. I'm tired. Mom will be home early today. She'll be glad to go shopping with you."

"I'd rather go with you. Please? It'll be fun."

She's trying, Peggy thinks. *I should try too.* "If you steal anything, I'll leave you there."

Allison pretends to be shocked. "I have no idea what you mean."

"We can't leave until Nick wakes up from his nap."

"Are you kidding? I'm sure he woke up as soon as he heard your voice."

Peggy smiles as Nick raises his tiny arms and giggles when she walks into the bedroom. It's the best part of her life, how delighted he is when he sees her. "Hey, pumpkin. You ready for an adventure with your klepto aunt?" She starts a list in her head. He'll need a change of clothes, extra diapers, and baby wipes, which means the bigger diaper bag. And the stroller. And some toys because he'll probably get bored. And a bottle if she can't find a place to nurse.

Nothing in the tiny house is ever where it's supposed to be. She finds the diaper bag in the kitchen and decides she'll change Nick first and then strap him in his car seat. It's easier to carry him out to the car that way, but after she buckles him in, she realizes she has to pee. "Can you watch Nick for a second?"

"I'll be right there," Allison says from the backyard. "I'm looking for the stroller."

"Stay where you are," she tells Nick. He looks up at her and they both laugh. "I know. It's not like you have much choice." She hurries to the bathroom and pees as quickly as she can, then she washes her hands. She looks in the mirror and wonders why she never remembers to wear lipstick. She could use some new clothes too. She hurries back to the living room.

The car seat is empty. A muscular man with a shaved head is sitting in the recliner holding Nick in his huge left arm. Nick stares up with wide trusting eyes at the open knife in the man's right hand. Both the knife and the man look familiar for some awful reason. She smells beer, adrenaline, sweat, and something confusingly floral. *Grab Nick and run*, she tells herself, but she can't move her legs or speak or breathe. She's not even sure her heart is still beating.

"Found it!" Allison rolls the stroller in from the patio. "Mom must have left it outside when she pruned the lemon tree yesterday." She sees the man, then, and all the color drains from her face, her freckles dark stars against her skin. "What are you doing here?"

It's Kevin, of course, giving her sister that stupid crooked smile he's used all his life to get away with everything.

"I thought you were in rehab," Allison says.

"I'm done. Turns out rehab's not for me. You all right, babe? You look a little pale."

Allison's hands go to her face. "The doctor says the swelling will go down eventually."

She still cares what this monster thinks! Peggy finds her voice. "Give him to me."

"I brought some flowers." Kevin points to a bouquet lying on the coffee table, red roses, pink lilies, and lavender mums. "Cute kid." He makes figure eights with the blade, so it catches the light. Nick reaches up as if it's a game. "What's his name?"

"Nick. Is that Dad's knife?"

"He took it from me, that day." Allison's eyes well with phony tears. "Kevin, please don't hurt him."

"Little Nicky's going to get nicked if he's not careful."

Nick swats at the blade with his chubby hands, turns to Peggy, and grins. Her boy. She moves closer, holding out her arms. "Please, Kevin."

"You have to drop the charges, Allison," Kevin says. "I can't do jail time."

There is too much white around his blue eyes. He's high on something. He holds the knife over the crown of Nick's head, as if he's going to scrape off the tiny blond fuzz.

"Put down the knife," Allison pleads, "and give Peggy the baby. I'll do whatever you want."

Of course, you will, Peggy thinks. Nothing's changed. Nothing will ever change.

Kevin's laugh is loud and bitter, and Nick gapes up at him, bewildered. "You're coming with me. We'll go tell my lawyer you lied about everything."

Nick squirms in Kevin's arms.

"Give him to me," Peggy says.

"Relax. The little bastard is fine if you both do what I say."

Nick looks at Kevin, scrunches up his face, and farts. It sounds like an explosion, but it smells like sweet yogurt, to Peggy's nose anyway. Like her milk.

"He took a dump!" Kevin holds Nick out at arm's length, with both hands now, still holding the knife, perilously close to the baby's tiny ear. "I'm going to hurl."

"I'll change him." She moves closer to Kevin. "It won't take a minute."

"Give her the baby," Allison says. "I'll get my purse and we can go."

Nick whimpers as Kevin stands and moves toward her. She holds out her hands. He's going to give her Nick, and this will be over. Her sister can do whatever she wants. But now Kevin is glancing out the window, frowning. She turns. Brenda's car is in the middle of the street, the driver's door wide open, and Brenda is sprinting up the driveway.

Allison races to the front door, holding up both hands. "Don't come inside. Please, Mom. We're okay."

"Why's Kevin's truck parked in my driveway?"

Nick is bleating now, and Brenda pushes Allison out of the way. "What's wrong with the baby?" She jerks to a full stop when she sees Kevin. "Oh, my God! Put that knife down!"

"Allison and I were just leaving."

"You're not going anywhere with him."

"Let her go," Peggy says. "It's what she wants."

"Your choice," Kevin says. "Allison or the bastard." He tucks Nick under his arm, gripping the back of his neck like a football, and kicks the sliding screen door to the side patio open.

"No!" Peggy rushes after him and Brenda follows, but Allison's uselessly rooted in place. "At least hold him with both hands," Peggy says and Kevin spins around. His elbow around Nick's tummy is the only thing stopping her baby from diving headfirst to the concrete. "You're going to choke him!" she yells. Kevin slides his other hand under the baby's back. Nick looks at her, his eyes round circles, the open knife terrifyingly close to his ear, but at least he can breathe. He sucks air in and out and lets out a furious wail.

"He's just a baby," Brenda says. "Don't do this."

"He stinks. I've changed my mind. I don't want him in my truck."

Kevin's eyes are frantic. Peggy wonders what he's looking for, and then she sees the metal trash can at the end of the concrete slab. Brenda trimmed the lemon tree yesterday when she got home from work. The metal can is surely full of thorny stems and rotting fruit, and she screams as Kevin lifts the lid.

Allison's on the patio finally, sobbing hard. "Please, babe. I'll go with you."

"No one's leaving," Brenda says. "Let's all go back inside and talk."

"Okay." Kevin drops Nick in the trash can, replaces the lid, and sits down. "I'm listening."

Nick is silent for a millisecond, then howls in outrage. Peggy lunges at Kevin with both hands. He pulls his feet in and kicks her hard in the chest. The knife clatters out of his hand down to the concrete as she falls backward and lands on her tailbone, her shirt instantly soaked with breast milk. Brenda pounces on him, fingers splayed like cat claws, and knocks him to the ground. He lands on his side, three stripes of blood on his cheek. Brenda flops down on his calves. Peggy races to the trash can and pulls Nick out. He slaps his arms furiously, but there's no sign of injury. When she looks down at the can, it's miraculously empty.

"Is he okay?" Allison asks.

"No thanks to you."

"Get off me!" Kevin thrashes his feet and Brenda struggles to hold down his legs.

There's a fast knock on the front door, then Laura's voice. "You girls okay?"

"Who the hell's that?" Kevin tries to reach for the knife. Peggy kicks it out of his grasp. Laura's in the living room now, staring openmouthed at all of them through the sliding glass.

"Laura," Allison yells. "Call 911."

Laura whips around and runs toward the phone in the kitchen.

"Fuck you, Allison." Kevin kicks hard and Brenda falls away from his legs. "Fuck all of you!" He jumps to his feet and charges toward the wooden side gate, yanking it open.

Allison stands stock-still for a moment and then chases after him.

Brenda staggers up from the ground. "We have to stop her."

Peggy pulls Nick in tighter. "Let her go."

"You don't mean that." Brenda races through the gate after Allison.

"I called the cops," Laura says. "Is Nick okay?"

Peggy nods, watching the tug-of-war in the driveway. Kevin tries to get in his truck while Allison pounds on his back with her fists. Brenda puts her arms around Allison's waist and tries to pull her away.

"Dios Madre," Laura says. "Is your sister trying to kill him or go with him?"

"I don't really care. This is all her fault."

"Get away from me," Kevin yells as he slams the door.

Allison steps back in Brenda's arms and Kevin starts the engine. Brenda murmurs something Peggy can't hear. Allison sobs and Laura mutters a prayer. Peggy pulls Nick in tighter and he starts to squirm.

"You're okay," she says, and he is, and it's a miracle.

Kevin slams the truck into reverse, backs out of the driveway, and tears off down the street. They all hear the bulldozer come alive around the corner, the huge metal plate in front catching the sunlight as the bulldozer slowly makes the turn, but Kevin's driving too fast, his brakes squeal too late, and the back wheels of his truck shimmy uncontrollably as he slams head-on into the dozer's claw.

Peggy covers Nick's ears at the screech of metal on metal and her sister's screams. She turns away as Laura makes the sign of the cross and Allison takes off running, Brenda right behind her. A Caltrans pickup truck speeds around the corner. Men in yellow vests and hardhats get out and sprint toward Kevin's truck. The neighbors are coming out of their houses now.

"The paramedics are on their way," someone yells.

"I'll move your mom's car," Laura says. "The ambulance will need to get through."

"I hope the keys are in it," Peggy says over her shoulder.

She walks up the driveway through the patio and sees her father's Swiss Army knife lying on the concrete next to the metal can. She bends down carefully to retrieve it and closes the blade, takes it with her into the house, and sets it on the dresser next to Nick's changing table. She can hear the sirens coming over the freeway hill. Nick's not trembling anymore and she's starting to calm down too, although she's too jittery to nurse him right now.

"It's all right," she whispers, kissing the top of his head. "We'll get you into some clean clothes, then you can have a bottle and take a long nap." After she changes him, she wraps his dirty diaper around the knife and throws it away in the diaper pail.

THE morning of Kevin's memorial service is cool and drizzly. Brenda links her arm through Allison's as they walk out on the pier and down past the surf break. Connie and Sal are ahead of them, holding each other up. Frank's out in the water with the surfers on a rented board. "I'm doing this for Allison," he'd explained. Nick's wearing his warmest clothes and is wrapped in three blankets. He's fussy and Peggy's ready to take him back to the car.

Everyone seems to have forgotten about the assault charges. Connie and Sal are supposed to cover Allison's medical expenses, but no one's mentioned that he'd be in jail today, if he wasn't dead. Kevin's still their hero, somehow, and still entitled to a hero's funeral. Peggy hasn't forgotten or forgiven anything. She didn't want to come today, but Allison begged her and both parents insisted. There's a huge crowd of people, but she doesn't recognize anyone.

"Cute kid," one girl says, kneeling to pick up the beanie Nick has just pulled off his head. Brenda asks how she knows Kevin and the girl smiles, as if she's embarrassed. "I saw a flyer. There's a party afterward."

They watch from the pier as surfers wade into the ocean and slide onto their boards.

"I should be out in the water too." Allison is thin and pale in a white dress, her hair in loose ringlets on her shoulders, a lei of white plumerias around her neck.

"That's Kevin's girlfriend," someone whispers, and Allison lifts her chin slightly as if this is something to be proud of. Allison hasn't cried at all today, probably because of the sedative the doctor gave her.

The surfers paddle out past the surf break. Peggy counts twenty boards. Connie nudges Sal. "Look at all the friends he had! He was so popular."

"These people weren't his friends." Allison grabs Peggy's hand. "Come stand next to me."

The surfers form a circle and one of them hands her father the urn. When he twists off the cap, he wobbles slightly, nearly toppling over as the ashes spill out. What looks like chunks of gritty sand float briefly on the surface and then dissolve immediately into the murky seawater.

Peggy smiles, unexpectedly glad she's come to witness this after all. She vows to never go in the water in Huntington Beach again. Allison takes off her lei and tosses it over the railing, then stares expectantly at the horizon. Someone mentioned earlier that sometimes during paddle-outs, single waves spring up, or a lone dolphin will suddenly appear, or even a rainbow might form. The sea remains flat and gray though, and the sky is the same color.

Down in the water, her father has an arm around one of the younger surfers who is crying. People around her are sobbing. Connie has crumpled into Sal's arms. Sal's face is streaked with tears. Even her mother is wiping her eyes. She looks embarrassed when she sees Peggy watching. "He was so young," she says.

There might be something wrong with me, Peggy thinks, *but I'm glad he's dead.*

Allison shakes her head as if she's trying to wake up. "I guess that's it."

Peggy looks away. "Nick's hungry. I'm going home."

CHAPTER EIGHTEEN

January, 1997

ON NEW YEAR'S DAY, ALLISON GETS OFF THE PLANE AND FOLLOWS THE SIGNS to baggage claim. Laura said her son would meet her at the airport, but she's not sure where. Somehow, she's never met Alejandro, although she's heard enough about him. Her mother and Laura cooked up this scheme, sending her halfway across the country to work as a waitress in New Orleans, as if there aren't plenty of qualified waitresses there already. New Orleans is her mother's dream, never hers, but she didn't have any better ideas when Laura asked Alejandro to pull some strings and get her a job at the restaurant where he's executive chef. He's even found her a room to rent with one of the waitresses.

It's more than a year since Kevin died, enough time for her family to decide she needs to move on. Connie and Sal moved and left no forwarding address. Her dad married Linda. Her mom loves her job and being a grandmother. Peggy's going to Cal State Fullerton and dating some postal inspector. Meanwhile she's tried three different therapists and a variety of medications, and earned her GED and a certificate in hospitality management, which qualifies her for exactly nothing. Her sister doesn't even trust her to babysit Nick. It won't take long for Alejandro to realize he's made a mistake.

She passes a group of young men sitting in the airport bar and is so sure Kevin is one of them that she has to stop in the ladies' room and splash cold water on her face before she can go on. She saw him on the plane too, sitting a few rows back. He's always somewhere. She no longer tells anyone she sees him. It only makes them worry. She can't figure out what else he wants from her. She's never once called David Bledsoe, never even thinks about him, never collected one penny from Connie or Sal.

Kevin was at fault in the accident, everyone agreed, especially when the autopsy and toxicology results came back showing a cocktail of drugs in his system: steroids, alcohol, cocaine, and methamphetamine. That was the real shock. She hadn't known about the meth.

A jazz band is playing in the baggage area when her mother's red Samsonite comes rolling around the conveyor belt and then Alejandro is suddenly there. His eyes are a deep brown and he keeps them focused on her, as if she is some exotic, fragile creature who might perish if left unattended. She can guess how Laura has described her, pathetically incapable, unprepared for any kind of practical life.

He immediately takes charge of her bag, puts his arm gently on her back, and guides her outside where the atmosphere swamps over her like a steamy blanket. It was cold when she'd left John Wayne Airport. Now, her jeans stick to her legs. They get into a tiny red Fiat that smells like ground cloves and chocolate and travel east on the 10 Freeway, following the signs toward New Orleans. Alejandro talks excitedly about music, travel, and art galleries as if he's trying to impress her, which makes no sense at all.

"Why is it we've never met?" he says.

"Your mother says you don't come home enough."

He laughs. "She tells me that all the time."

Allison stares out of the passenger window at the crowded freeway and dirty concrete and wonders how much a return ticket would cost. She shakes her head when he exits at Tchoupitoulas Street. "How do you even pronounce that?"

He laughs again. "I never get any of the names right the first time. They have their own way of talking down here."

He turns into a neighborhood of long skinny houses. She's never seen so many Black people in her life, crowded together on front porches, clustered in miniscule front yards, leaning up against parked cars. Alejandro pulls into the driveway of one of the skinny houses, the exact width of one room. She wonders if Carol, her roommate-to-be, is Black too and wishes she wasn't the kind of person who wondered things like that.

A busty white woman wearing shorts and an LSU T-shirt opens the turquoise front door. She looks tired and unfriendly. Allison and Alejandro follow her past a green leather couch in front of a television set, past a table and chairs, through what must be Carol's bedroom, and on into the kitchen. There is no hallway. There are no doors.

"The bathroom's there," Carol says, pointing to the opposite wall of the kitchen.

"Well, at least *that* has a door." Allison hopes she sounds like she's joking. She feels like crying, which is stupid. She's only tired and probably getting her period.

"It's called a shotgun house," Alejandro says. "The design's perfect for heat and humidity. Before air-conditioning they'd open the front door and let the breeze run through the back."

"This is you," Carol says, pulling a curtain aside to a small space that was evidently once a porch and is now almost big enough for the twin-sized bed and chest of drawers. Alejandro sets her suitcase in a corner.

"The other reason they call it a shotgun," Carol says, "is because if you fire a gun through the front door, the bullet will pass straight on through."

"Is there a lot of gunfire?" Allison asks and immediately regrets. She sounds scared and judgmental, like someone who's never been anywhere.

"It's a safe neighborhood," Alejandro says. "I live a few blocks away. You shouldn't walk alone at night though. There's a bus stop four blocks up across from the grocery store. The Quarter's only three miles from here."

The French Quarter, Allison thinks, where Venerable is, the restaurant where she starts work tomorrow.

"Are you hungry?" Alejandro asks. "Want to go get something to eat?"

She notices Carol's disapproving smirk. "Maybe I should unpack."

"You're right," he says. "I'll see you tomorrow. I'm really glad you're here."

"What's the deal with you and Chef?" Carol asks as soon as he leaves.

"I just met him today. My mom is friends with his mom."

Carol says it must be nice to have connections like that since lots of people want to work at Venerable, but when Allison hands her the cash for her rent, she halfway smiles. "There's some pasta in the fridge if you're hungry."

THE next morning, she dresses in the black slacks, white shirt, and black loafers she'd been told to bring with her, feeling like a Mormon missionary. At least Carol is dressed the same. They walk up to Magazine Street and catch the bus. Allison sits by the window and stares up at Mardi Gras beads hanging in oak trees and wrought iron balconies on old brick buildings.

Oh, she thinks. *This is really pretty.* Maybe she hasn't made a mistake after all.

"Sorry if I was rude yesterday," Carol says, when they get off the bus at Canal Street and start walking. "I was kind of hungover."

Allison nods, realizing they now are on Bourbon Street in

the French Quarter. The swarms of people and the musicians on the corners remind her of the French Quarter at Disneyland, but the heat, humidity, and conflicting smells of garlic sauce and raw sewage are overwhelming. She follows Carol through packs of young men who remind her of Kevin, their necks looped with stacks of beads, carrying large cups of beer and lime-green daiquiris. She dodges conventioneers streaming out of hotels with lanyards and go-cups, dentists, accountants, and engineers who look like older versions of what Kevin might have looked like if he hadn't smashed his truck into a bulldozer.

She's dizzy by the time they get to the restaurant, which feels like an oasis, blessedly air-conditioned with lots of dark wood, white linens, a saxophone playing softly on the sound system. Alejandro is embarrassingly glad to see her but too busy to talk long. "I'll come find you later," he says.

It's a long day. Everyone is frustrated with her. "We know how *she* got the job," she overhears one of the busboys tell a cook.

"I owe you dinner and a tour of the city," Alejandro says when her shift is finally over. She reads the expressions on the kitchen staff's faces.

"You don't have to do that, Chef," she says, because she's already figured out it's not a good idea to call him Alejandro in front of her coworkers.

SHE and Carol sit on the green couch one night after their shifts are over, passing a joint back and forth. Carol sips a beer. Allison holds an ice pack on her knee from where she rammed it into the side of a table before she spilled an entire tray of drinks.

"I don't know why Chef doesn't fire me."

"Oh, give me a break!" Carol says. "He's obviously into you.

You might as well sleep with him. Everyone thinks you are anyway."

The next time Alejandro asks her to have lunch with him on a Monday, when Venerable is closed, Allison says yes. He meets her at Carol's shotgun house and calls a taxi, then points out Lafayette Cemetery on their way to the Quarter. She's never been in a taxi before, and never realized graveyards could be above the ground. When they turn right on St. Charles, she's sure she sees Kevin standing on the corner, narrowing his blue eyes as he blows cigarette smoke out of the corner of his mouth. He never smoked cigarettes, but he could have changed.

She's changing too. Despite the banged-up knees and long hours on her feet, she likes waitressing. The tips are decent. She concentrates on getting the orders right, ignoring the open handbags, unattended wallets, and forgotten sunglasses. Last week she found a red leather jacket, which would have fit her perfectly, hanging on the back of an empty chair. She took it up to the hostess. "Someone will be back for this."

They get out of the cab and Alejandro leads her into Café du Monde. "It's touristy," he says. "But you have to do it once." She knows the Mississippi is close; she can smell the water and sees the tops of steam pipes moving above the levee. "We're below sea level," Alejandro says, which only reinforces the feeling she's fallen off the map.

They finish their beignets and chicory coffee and walk up Dumaine Street. Just as they pass a Voodoo Museum, it starts to rain. "Come on," he says, taking her hand, and then the skies rip wide open, releasing a deluge of water. The streets flood quickly; her feet are wet inside her sandals and Alejandro's silk shirt is soaked. They run and she's laughing so hard she can't catch her breath. The rain is weirdly warm, the city is wildly beautiful, and when Alejandro pulls her close to him under an awning to get out of the rain, she feels his heartbeat. His skin smells like cilantro and lemon.

"They have good oysters in the restaurant upstairs," he says. The tables are empty and the television behind the bar is on.

"Looks like you two got drenched," the bartender says, handing them a stack of paper napkins. "What can I get you?"

"A dozen charbroiled oysters and a couple of Miller Lights," Alejandro says.

"Sure. Sit anywhere you like."

"She didn't ask for my ID," Allison says when they sit down at a table. She mops her hair with the napkins.

"You're tall enough. That's all that matters." Alejandro wipes his arms and pulls his wet shirt away from his chest, laughing. "I don't think these napkins are going to help much."

The man on the TV is talking about five inches of rain and then switches to national news. The guilty verdict from O. J.'s civil trial has just been announced. Allison leans forward to listen.

"Simpson wasn't even in the courtroom," the newscaster says. "He was out playing golf. He'll have to pay the families thirty-three million dollars."

"My mom is into this O. J. stuff big time," Alejandro says. "I never had time to follow any of it."

"My mom was convinced he was innocent for a long time." *Until Kevin broke my jaw*, she almost adds, when a busboy with hair as long as Kevin's once was, crosses the room with a tray full of glasses. She shivers as the air-conditioning cuts on. The bartender mutes the sound on the television and a soulful voice croons "Tell It Like It Is" on the speaker above their table.

"So, what do you think?" Alejandro says.

"About O. J.? Definitely guilty."

He has the easiest smile she's ever seen. "That's not what I meant. How do you like New Orleans?"

"I like it so far. It's really different from home though."

"I miss California too. But I love living here."

"I really appreciate everything you've done for me, Chef. The job. The roommate. You didn't even know me. And I'm a terrible waitress."

He laughs. "I can tell you're trying. And please call me Alejandro."

"Seriously, though, I don't understand why you agreed to any of this."

"My mom has never asked me to do anything for her. I couldn't say no."

"I hope you aren't sorry." She should call her mother. She keeps meaning to, but the time difference confuses her.

"I'm not sorry at all." There's the easy smile again. "And my mother has nothing to do with me asking you out today. I wanted to spend time alone with you."

A crack of lightning streaks the sky behind the shutters, and the overhead lights flicker off and on again.

"Holy shit." She reaches for his hands across the table. Thunder echoes a few seconds later and the wooden shutters tremble. "That was awesome. Can we go outside and watch?"

"You'd better stay put," the bartender says, setting down the tray of oysters. "Unless you're trying to get yourself electrocuted. You don't know about lightning?"

"I'm from California," Allison says.

"California! You couldn't pay me enough to live there. All those earthquakes? You want another beer?"

"Sure," Alejandro says. "One more and then we'll go find some dinner. What would you like to eat tonight? Jambalaya? Cochon de lait? Crawfish étouffée?"

His words sound like poetry and his dark eyes are beautiful, the way they spark gold. He is still holding her hands. A drop of rainwater trickles down her neck. "We can't go anywhere like this. We're both a mess."

"Are you cold? I'm sorry. I should have realized."

"How about if we just go to your house?"

THE week after her first Mardi Gras, her mother calls. "What's going on with you and Laura's son? She says he's in love with you."

Of course, Alejandro's already told his mother. He's told everyone else. He tells her twice a day and insists she doesn't have to be in love with him right now.

"He makes me happy, Mom." Which is true, although Kevin hasn't gone away. Last night he sat at the end of the bar at Venerable, raking his hair out of his eyes, giving her that crooked smile.

"You barely know this person," Brenda is saying. "I can't even pronounce his name."

"Alejandro. He's your best friend's son."

"Laura's a good friend, but their family situation is . . . different than ours."

"Different as in Mexican?"

"You know that's not what I mean."

It's exactly what she means, but it doesn't matter. "He's a gentle and generous man, Mom, and he listens to me. He cares what I think. And maybe different is what I need. This feels right, living here, being with him."

For once her mother has nothing to say.

ON St. Patrick's Day, Allison stops in Jackson Square on her way to the courthouse across the Mississippi River in Algiers. It would make more sense to drive over with the others, but she'd told Alejandro it was bad luck for him to see her dress before the wedding, not wanting to explain this last-minute errand. She smooths the skirt of the dress now, cream-colored silk with a lacy collar, and surveys the fortune-tellers. Their folding tables are draped in scarves and accessorized with crystal balls and tarot cards, but the only one who doesn't have a customer is more of a girl than a woman, young and athletic, dressed for a soccer game, not the gypsy-type she'd expected. The ferry leaves in twenty minutes. She doesn't have time to wait for someone else.

"What a pretty dress," the girl says. Her face has never taken any beatings. Allison can recognize the signs now. This girl doesn't flinch, for example, when a trombone in the middle of the square bleats out a minor chord.

Allison hands over two twenty-dollar bills and offers a three-sentence summary of her busted-up jaw, Kevin's smashed-in truck, and how she still sees his face everywhere, twisting the dolphin ring on her little finger as she tells the story.

"I'm getting married today," she adds. "I need him to go away."

The girl shuffles a deck of ragged tarot cards and asks Allison to cut them twice. The girl turns up the top three cards, studies them for a while, and then says, "Kevin needs to tell you he's sorry."

"I was partly to blame."

The girl reaches out for her hand and Allison turns it flat, thinking she wants to read her palm. Instead, the girl grasps her fingers and squeezes softly, her expression so earnest it's embarrassing. "It wasn't your fault. He knows he's guilty. He's trying to make amends."

"Well, it's too late." Allison pulls her hand free. "Since he's dead."

"Tell him how much he hurt you. Tell him what he did was wrong."

"You mean right now?" She looks around her. A brass band is setting up in front of the church and a crowd is forming, tourists in green T-shirts and shorts, conventioneers with go-cups, homeless people with their homeless dogs. "I've kind of already forgiven him. Isn't that enough?"

"You can't forgive him if you don't think he's guilty. Your sister won't forgive you either, until you do this."

Allison feels the hairs rise on the back of her neck and tells herself not to fall for this girl's bullshit. Lots of people have sisters. "Fine. He's guilty. He hurt me. The end."

"Tell him, not me."

She feels ridiculous. "Kevin. You ruined my face."

"Louder. And be more specific."

Her voice rises. "You and Connie used me and then threw me away."

"Good," the girl says. "Go on."

"My teeth don't line up straight in my jaw anymore. And I can't afford a fucking dentist." One of the conventioneers (an orthodontist, she guesses) glances over his shoulder. "I loved you, Kevin," she yells. "But now I need you to leave me alone!"

A pigeon flutters purple wings and hops up on the wrought iron fence. Glasses clink in a bar on the corner. The orthodontist turns back to the brass band. The tuba player blows through his mouthpiece, making a farting noise. Two little boys laugh.

"That was perfect," the girl says. "Don't you feel better?"

"How is this supposed to fix things with my sister?"

"That would be another twenty-five dollars."

"I have to go," she says, standing. She has a ferry to catch.

THE Mississippi is choppy, and the wind makes a mess of her hair. She stands by the railing, gripping the hem of her dress with one hand to keep it from flying up around her. The dress was slinky enough to tuck in her purse in the Macy's dressing room at South Coast Plaza where she'd bought her waitress uniform just before she'd left for New Orleans. She'd like to tell Peggy she hasn't stolen anything since. Her eyes fill with tears. She wishes her family were here even though they'd try to talk her out of it. She knows she's doing the right thing. Alejandro wants her on his insurance plan, and it's not a bad idea to change her name. It will make her harder to find in case anyone is looking.

There's no one on the deck. She slides the dolphin ring off her finger and lets it drop down into the muddy water just before the ferry docks. The Algiers Courthouse at the top of the hill is both Victorian and rustic. She admires the old archways and the beautiful dark wood as she heads inside to the restroom to repair her hair and fix her makeup.

"Sorry," she says, when she notices the uniformed woman standing behind her with a bucket and mop. "You need me to move?"

"Take your time," the woman says.

"I don't know why I'm so nervous."

"Nervous is normal." Her dark eyes are kind and Allison feels the tears start again. The woman pulls a Kleenex from a box by the sink. "Don't ruin your mascara. You look really pretty."

"Thank you." Allison pats her eyes dry and goes out to the lobby.

Alejandro, in a dark suit, stands with his back to her, silhouetted in light from the high, arched windows, talking to Carol, in a short green dress, and Raul, one of the line cooks, also in suit and tie, holding a bottle of champagne.

Carol notices her now and touches Alejandro's arm. He turns and smiles when he sees her, delighted and loving and so very handsome.

"You look amazing," he says, walking toward her with open arms. "Want to get married?"

She grins. "I do."

Chapter Nineteen

October 4, 2008

THE PARKING LOT BEHIND HOLY FAMILY CATHEDRAL IS ALMOST FULL WHEN Brenda pulls her white BMW into an empty space. She wasn't expecting such a large crowd, but since she's never been to a Catholic baptism, she really didn't know what to expect or what to wear. Her simplest blue dress and lowest heels seemed the best choice. She listens to the news on the radio while she waits for Peggy and Nick. O. J.'s attorneys are already planning to appeal his thirty-three-year sentence for armed robbery. It's unfair, they claim, the sentence is too harsh.

It's karma, Brenda thinks. What an idiot O. J. turned out to be, bumbling the robbery of his own memorabilia, waving guns in his former friends' faces, trying to steal back his own belongings. His wife's wedding ring, for God's sake.

She'd googled Nicole Simpson this morning after the verdict was announced, remembering how people used to say they looked alike. There was a resemblance, she decided, but it was a mistake to scroll through the pictures. She'd seen a few crime scene photos years ago, but Nicole's face had always been blacked out. Now all the evidence was splayed out in graphic detail on her computer screen: Nicole's throat ripped open; her head nearly decapitated; gobs of blood, thick and crimson, on the bricked front patio; the soft curve of her calves jutting from under the wrought iron gate. Brenda shut off her computer, nauseated. She still can't get the images out of her head.

The news commentator says O. J. delivered a five-minute apology, his wrists shackled, his husky voice cracking. He is so sorry. She's sorry too, for those wasted months she spent in front of the television, bearing witness to what she's no longer sure. Wearing her ratty nightgown, drinking too much wine, and wondering why everything had gone so wrong. She got through it, somehow, although it would have been easier if she'd known that was the beginning of the rest of her life and not the end of the world.

Peggy's new Honda Accord finally pulls into the last open parking space, and Nick gets out of the passenger seat, handsome in a white shirt and jeans, taller every time she sees him, her favorite human being in the world.

"Hey, Grandma. Sorry we're late."

"Allison texted me," Peggy says. "They're already inside."

Peggy's wearing what she wears to her office every day, black slacks, a blue cashmere twin set, a single strand of pearls. No makeup of course, but her hair is freshly cut in a short glossy bob with beautifully done highlights.

Brenda hooks arms with Peggy and Nick. "I'm glad I have you two to walk in with. I'm nervous, for some reason. Is the service going to be in Spanish?"

"I have no idea," Peggy says. "I don't know anything about baptizing kids."

Inside the church, Allison is already standing in front of an octagon-shaped font next to a double stroller, tall, slim, and sophisticated in a pink pleated skirt and matching silk sweater, talking to Alejandro and some of his relatives. She waves when she sees them as an organ begins playing from somewhere above.

"We'll talk to her afterward," Peggy says. "They're getting ready to start."

"I don't understand why you aren't a godparent," Brenda whispers as they slide into an empty pew.

Peggy grins. "You have to be Catholic for one thing. And you have to promise you'll make sure the kids are raised Catholic. No thanks."

Brenda smiles in agreement as a priest, decked out in a long robe and some kind of a stole, comes down the aisle toward the babies. Alejandro and Allison lift Molly and Emily out of the double stroller. Her exotic granddaughters (redheaded, brown-eyed, olive-skinned with fiery dispositions) both wear ornate white gowns, another sensitive subject. She'd offered to buy them brand-new dresses, but Laura wanted them to wear the family heirlooms, handed down from generation to generation. The gowns are lovely, but she's sure the old lace is scratchy against their tender skin.

The priest asks what names have been chosen, makes the sign of the cross, then sprinkles water and oil on each girl's tiny head, and what looks like salt on each tiny tongue. Emily swats his hand away and giggles. Molly bursts into tears.

There are more prayers, renouncing of the devil, and forgiveness for original sin. (*What sin?* Brenda wonders. *They're not even a year old yet.*) But when the priest reminds everyone of "the joy with which Allison and Alejandro have welcomed Emily and Molly as gifts from God," Brenda smiles. Peggy and Nick are smiling too. She doesn't know about the God part, but she definitely feels the joy.

Thankfully, there's no required audience participation other than shaking hands with everyone around her when the service is finally over and saying, "Peace be with you," which is awkward but nice. Alejandro invites them all over to Laura's house for carnitas and margaritas, and the service is over. Molly is still crying by the time the three of them make their way through the crowd to Allison and Alejandro.

"Mom!" he says, as Emily squirms in his arms. "You look

incredible as always." She'll never get used to a grown man calling her Mom. Alejandro always tries to say the right thing. She wishes he felt more comfortable around her. She wishes she could let him. "I brought you some boudin sausage," he says. "It's out in the rental car in a cooler."

"You remembered!"

"You can't make good jambalaya without it."

"I'll take her," Brenda says, holding out her hands, but now Emily bursts into tears. Brenda turns to Allison and tries to kiss the top of Molly's head. Molly pushes her tiny fists into her eyes and snuggles in closer to Allison's neck.

Allison laughs. "They're both exhausted. I'm going to take them to Laura's and put them down for a nap. You are coming to the house, aren't you? Laura made a ton of food."

"I don't know." She was hoping they would all stop by her condo for a real visit, but this is Laura's day, not hers.

"Laura will be disappointed if you don't, Mom," Peggy says.

"I suppose you're both right."

"Write that down," Peggy tells Nick. "Your grandmother actually admitted we were right about something."

"How's life, Peggy?" Allison asks. "Seeing anyone new these days?"

"No," Peggy says. "Which is fine because I'm really too busy. But Mom thinks I should sign up for one of those online dating services."

"Talk her into it," Brenda says. "She won't take advice from me about her love life."

"Well," Peggy says.

Both girls look at each other and laugh. Brenda watches their faces, trying to convince herself the two have reconciled.

"How's work, Mom?" Allison asks.

"Crazy busy. Richard just had a new computer system installed. Of course, I'm the one who has to fix all the problems."

"And Sam?" Allison asks.

"Sam's a saint," Peggy says. "Everyone knows that."

Brenda ignores Peggy's sarcasm. "He's really sorry he couldn't be here. He's showing a house this afternoon."

"How's his mother?"

Allison's voice doesn't sound critical. Peggy's smile remains cynical, but she's blessedly silent. "The doctors are hopeful."

"Well, that's good news! As long as you're happy, Mom. As long as he's good to you."

"He is. And I am happy. I assume you're staying with Laura?"

"You know we'd rather stay with you, but she has more room. She's already giving us grief about not coming back for Christmas. I hope you understand."

They're not coming for Christmas! She thinks about the presents she's already bought and sighs. Soft stuffed animals. Green plaid flounced dresses. Tiny diamond earrings for their already-pierced ears.

"Why don't you come visit *us* for Christmas this year? New Orleans is beautiful in winter. They light bonfires on the levees and carol in Jackson Square. You'd love it."

"Maybe I will."

She's visited Allison a few times, most recently right after her granddaughters were born, but always on her own since Sam can never get away. He'd promised to try when they first met years ago, at the real estate office next door to the salon where she gets her hair cut and colored. Frank had just married Linda and she was depressed. Sam found her a small condo she could almost afford and put a smile back on her face. He comes over for dinner three times a week and was in her bed until eleven o'clock last night.

He can't travel though, not all the way to New Orleans. His

mother needs him to drive her to doctor's appointments, sit with her during chemo, and make sure she takes her meds. She won't live forever, which Brenda is honestly starting to worry about. She never thought she'd like living alone so much.

She'd hoped Allison would come home to California after Katrina, but she and Alejandro relocated to Houston for a few months and then went straight back to New Orleans, opened their own restaurant, and bought one of those ridiculous shotgun houses. New Orleans is no longer Brenda's dream city. The streets feel treacherous, not only because of the crime. The potholes have potholes, the sidewalks are fractured, the mosquitos vindictive, the humidity oppressive.

She feels an immediate and all too familiar heat rise from the center of her chest and flash through her entire body. She's immediately sweating. *This will pass,* she tells herself. She hopes her face isn't glistening. "Maybe Peggy and Nick can come with me," she says. "He'll have two weeks off from school for Christmas break."

"That would be terrific." Allison's smile is so eager, Brenda wishes she hadn't said anything, especially when she notices Peggy's irritated expression.

"I'm trying to make partner, Mom. I can't take time off right now."

Brenda sees the disappointment flood Allison's face. Although the scars are invisible under her makeup, she remembers exactly where they are. She has a sudden vision of Nicole Simpson's slim calves under the wrought iron gate and shivers. Her hot flash is over. "Don't take it personally," she tells Allison. "Peggy works all the time."

Allison shrugs. "One of these days I'll talk her into it."

At least Allison is still willing to try, she tells herself. *Peggy will come around, eventually. Savor the moment. All of us together, my girls and my grandchildren.*

THERE'S no traffic on the freeway when she drives home from the party at Laura's house. She didn't stay long. There were too many people and no place to sit, and it was too noisy to talk once the mariachis started. She'd kissed Allison and the grand-babies goodbye, thanked Laura, and slipped out the patio door.

"In tonight's news," the jazz deejay says, his voice tempered and low. "O. J. Simpson will spend the first three weeks of his thirty-three-year sentence in an eight-by-ten cell at High Desert State Prison in Nevada. Simpson is planning an appeal, of course. He'll be eligible for parole in nine years."

In nine years, she'll be closing in on sixty and her grandchil-dren will have lives of their own, turning into capable human beings just like her amazing daughters, who will surely be better friends by then. She's a lucky woman and she will try to remem-ber this more often.

She's a hungry woman too. She'll make jambalaya for dinner tonight, she decides, and use Alejandro's boudin. Her mouth waters, thinking of the flavors. Sam will open a beer and tell her the latest bad news about the real estate market. He'll want to see the pictures on her phone of her granddaughters and ask if she remembered to invite Nick to the Ducks' game. They'll make love while the rice cooks, eat dinner in front of the televi-sion, and go back to bed.

"It's the end of a saga the nation watched for years," the dee-jay says.

Brenda steps on the gas and accelerates into the open lane ahead. She can't wait to get home.

ACKNOWLEDGMENTS

Thank you, Eduardo Santiago, for believing in this story from the beginning. Thank you, Diana Wagman, for your wonderful insights and ideas. Thank you, Lisa Alvarez, for constant creative inspiration. Thank you, Virginia Shank, for publishing a version of the second chapter as a short story called "Promises" in Volume 22 of *The Ear*. Thank you, Richard Bausch, for reminding me to work every day and for including me in your wonderfully generous community workshop.

Thank you to all the writers, teachers, and friends who read early versions of this story and offered encouragement and advice—Dina Andre, Tom Barbash, Barbara Demarco Barrett, Roxanne Barrish, Dawn Bonker, Christina Brubaker, Lan Samantha Chang, Mark Childress, Samantha Dunn, Peter Gerrard, Erica Lansdown, Nanaz Kashefi, Martin Mitchell, Sheila Nassabi, Valerie Orleans, Gwendolyn Oxenham, Katy Parker, Linda Tacy, Andrew Tonkovitch, and Alice Toth. Thank you to all of those readers I've forgotten to mention.

Thank you to the workshops and classes that helped me figure out how to tell this story—Community of Writers, IVC Community College, Napa Valley Writer's Workshop, Stanford Continuing Education, UCLA Writers Workshop, and Writing Workshops Los Angeles.

Major obligations are due Shelley Blanton Stroud for her constant cheerleading and support. Thanks to Brooke Warner, Julie Metz, Windy Waite, Stacey Aaronson, Pamela Long, Samantha Strom, Crystal Patriarche, Taylor Brightwell, and Paige Herbert for getting my novel out into the world and to the power of sisterhood at She Writes Press.

I relied on many sources to refresh my memory about the Simpson case—Vincent Bugliosi's *Outrage*, Marcia Clark's *Without a Doubt*, Christopher Darden's *In Contempt*, and Jeffrey Toobin's *The Run of His Life*. I especially appreciated the archives of the *Los Angeles Times* daily newspapers for this time period. Any errors concerning the murders, the trials, or the media coverage are my own.

Thank you, Alma and Lewis Parker, for raising me to be a reader.

Thank you, Riley, for listening to me read out loud.

All my love to Steve for everything.

ABOUT THE AUTHOR

Credit: Brooklyn Hargroves Photography

Mary Camarillo lives in Huntington Beach, California, with her husband, Steve, who plays ukulele, and their terrorist cat, Riley, who has his own Instagram page. This is her first novel. Her short stories and poems have appeared in publications such as *166 Palms*, the *Sonora Review*, *Lunch Ticket*, and *The Ear*. To learn more, visit her website at https://www.MaryCamarillo.com.

SELECTED TITLES FROM SHE WRITES PRESS

She Writes Press is an independent publishing company
founded to serve women writers everywhere.
Visit us at www.shewritespress.com.

Center Ring by Nicole Waggoner. $17.95, 978-1-63152-034-1. When a
startling confession rattles a group of tightly knit women to its core,
the friends are left analyzing their own roads not taken and the vastly
different choices they've made in life and love.

As Long As It's Perfect by Lisa Tognola. $16.95, 978-1-63152-624-4.
What happens when you ignore the signs that you're living beyond
your means? When married mother of three Janie Margolis's house
lust gets the best of her, she is catapulted into a years-long quest for
domicile perfection—one that nearly ruins her marriage.

Shelter Us by Laura Diamond. $16.95, 978-1-63152-970-2. Lawyer-
turned-stay-at-home-mom Sarah Shaw is still struggling to find a
steady happiness after the death of her infant daughter when she
meets a young homeless mother and toddler she can't get out of her
mind—and becomes determined to rescue them.

Stella Rose by Tammy Flanders Hetrick. $16.95, 978-1-63152-921-4.
When her dying best friend asks her to take care of her sixteen-year-
old daughter, Abby says yes—but as she grapples with raising a grieving teenager, she realizes she didn't know her best friend as well as
she thought she did.

The Trumpet Lesson by Dianne Romain. $16.95, 978-1-63152-598-8.
Fascinated by a young woman's performance of "The Lost Child" in
Guanajuato's central plaza, painfully shy expat Callie Quinn asks the
woman for a trumpet lesson—and ends up confronting her longing
to know her own lost child, the biracial daughter she gave up for
adoption more than thirty years ago.